PRIVATE LIES

BOOKS BY WARREN ADLER

Novels

Private Lies
Madeline's Miracles
We Are Holding the President Hostage
Twilight Child
Random Hearts
The War of the Roses
Blood Ties
Natural Enemies
The Casanova Embrace
Trans-Siberian Express
The Henderson Equation
Banquet Before Dawn
Options

Mysteries

Immaculate Deception
American Sextet
American Quartet

Short Stories

The Sunset Gang

PRIVATE LIES

Warren Adler

WILLIAM MORROW AND COMPANY, INC.
New York

Epigraph from *The Snows of Kilimanjaro* by Ernest Hemingway. Reprinted with permission of the Hemingway Foreign Rights Trust and Charles Scribner's Sons, an imprint of Macmillan Publishing Company. Copyright © 1936 by Ernest Hemingway, renewed 1964 by Mary Hemingway.

Recognizing the importance of preserving what has been written, it is the policy of William Morrow and Company, Inc., and its imprints and affiliates to have the books it publishes printed on acid-free paper, and we exert our best efforts to that end.

Library of Congress Cataloging-in-Publication Data

Adler, Warren.
    Private lies / by Warren Adler.
       p.   cm.
    ISBN 0-688-10120-8
    I. Title.
    PS3551.D64P75   1990
    813'.54—dc20
                                         90-46874
                                             CIP

Printed in the United States of America

First Edition

1 2 3 4 5 6 7 8 9 10

BOOK DESIGN BY PAUL CHEVANNES

To HK and SL

"Kilimanjaro is a snow covered mountain 19,710 feet high and is said to be the highest mountain in Africa. Its western summit is called the Masai 'Ngaje Ngbi', the House of God. Close to its summit there is the dried and frozen carcass of a leopard. No one has explained what the leopard was seeking at that altitude."

—ERNEST HEMINGWAY,
The Snows of Kilimanjaro

PRIVATE LIES

1

I T ALL began, as Ken perceived it, with a sudden fit of precognition, and he knew instantly that the mooring lines that stabilized his life were about to show the first signs of major slippage.

He had been observing this couple just coming out of the slanting April rain all aflutter and out of breath as they shook off drops from their raincoats before handing them over to the hatcheck girl at Pumpkins, the pricey restaurant on Second Avenue, Maggie's choice, where the cooking was West Coast eclectic and the atmosphere luxury-liner Art Deco.

Ken, who was sitting facing the restaurant's entrance, saw her first in profile as she patted her cheeks dry with a tissue. Couldn't be, he decided at first, realizing suddenly that he had actually searched for her face in crowds for more than two decades.

Of course, he tried denying it, knowing it was the trigger to this precognition. No way. This could not be Carol Stein. The process of aging cannot stand still. Yet he could not tear his gaze away. There was that same easy grace of the floating swan, the same question-mark dancer's posture, the same high-cheekboned cat's face, the same angled head, emphasizing the sharp line of tilted chin overhanging the long, thin, white neck.

Aside from the emotional power of this hard punch to the solar plexus of his psyche, his physical reactions, too, took him by surprise. His heart seemed to skip a beat, many beats. His back broke out into a cold sweat and his throat ran dry.

Then his wife, Maggie, waved and the tall man in the blue double-breasted wide pinstripe and elegant gold-and-blue-striped tie beside this replica of Carol Stein acknowledged the gesture with a movement of his own, tapping the shoulder of the woman who could not be Carol Stein.

He watched her move toward him with a ballerina's dainty precision, her body gliding in step with some inner rhythm that made her long challis skirt seem driven by a gentle breeze over soft kid boots. The movement seemed to have a remembered signature, vibrating an old erotic chord within him.

Was this Carol Stein walking into his life after twenty-three years? He felt a blast of heat from that old furnace, firing up the passion and possession that had inflamed his youthful soul.

As she came closer, denial faltered and he felt trapped with all exits closed off. He would be an exhibit for her to observe and gloat over. Another tide of anxiety washed over him as he imagined the bloated remains of his former being lying on a cold slab awaiting Carol Stein's coroner's knife. Who could hide one's failure from that kind of scrutiny? He felt ashamed, the bitter bile of his lost dreams on the verge of exposure. Suddenly there was no place to hide.

Ironically, Ken had resisted this dinner. Earlier, he had been overflowing with self-satisfaction and self-esteem. A top client of the agency had approved his campaign. His butt was bruised with kisses. He had been showered with praise, accolades, the usual exaggeration that was the idiom of the advertising business. They had, in fact, used the familiar buzzwords: *creative genius, a gargantuan talent, awesome brilliance.*

Of course, he understood the hyperbole. It was all part of the self-congratulatory culture of the advertising game. And the truth of it was that he had actually exhausted himself by feigning humility. An advertising copywriter could feign that often. It was expected. It telescoped to others that he knew he was good.

For this present exercise in painful knife-in-the-flesh truth, he had had to turn down his colleagues' celebration dinner in which he would be the trophy guest, able to bask all evening in the warm syrup of their admiration. This getting-to-know-you appointment with Maggie's client, the formidable Eliot Butterfield, would be strictly Maggie's show.

And here was the sight of this facsimile of Carol Stein, steering his thoughts into these dark cobwebbed corners, and forcing a confrontation with the dead past. Except that it wasn't dead, could never be dead. It flushed out reminders of the glory days of possibility and promise, and directed his attention to the reality of his defeat.

It had been the moment he had feared for more than two decades.

How old had he been in the season of Carol Stein? Twenty-one, was it? It was still a time when he had been dead certain of his talent and his future. Hadn't his teachers, his friends, his mother especially, through elementary school, high school, and college, assured him that he had the literary right stuff?

He had thought of himself as Hemingway incarnate. Hemingway in those years was his literary god, and the imitative rhythms of his prose reflected it. Ken had a way with words, they all said, stretching his confidence, feeding his ambition and all those secret fantasies of fame and celebrity.

If encouragement was judgment, he was destined, according to them, to walk in his master's footsteps. Of course, he believed it. Doubt is not a serious issue at sixteen. Even at twenty-one, in the season of Carol Stein, the dream was reasonably intact, although hard reality, the so-called real world, had already begun to rattle the foundations of certainty.

Had she made it, scaled the heights, become the prima ballerina of her young obsession? Had the sacrifice of their love been worth the candle? For her? For him? Actually, he could not remember a time when he was so acutely embarrassed by his failure. Especially since, in the narrow world of advertising, most people considered him a success. It had been a comfortable illusion.

God, he hadn't felt such obvious regret for what might have been for years. Perhaps this was not *the* Carol Stein, he thought hopefully, but an apparition. Go away, he begged it. Only it still kept coming, challenging his vanity, his sense of himself, his essence.

He dared not face her, dared not allow himself even to consider jogging her recollection. He could not bear the idea of showing her his failed self, especially if she had been successful, was successful. Worse for him, on the arm of this solid-looking, confident fellow, she looked successful.

Twenty-three years ago, still at least five years too late to be trendy, he wore the Jesus look, a beard, long hair, and little round glasses. Now he was slightly balding in front, the jet black was flecked with peppery gray, and he had shaved the beard. Now he wore contacts, the extended-wear kind. He wished he were wearing sunglasses to further hide his eyes from her. The eyes, he asked himself, the good old windows on the soul, would they be the dead giveaway?

She was coming closer now, moving in tandem with this tall, elegant man who had acknowledged Maggie. He felt himself flush, the heat dampening the thinning wisps on his forehead.

Would she recognize him? Him? At twenty-one, America's greatest unknown writer. First would come the novels, the prose sharp and clean. True sentences marching like determined battalions across the page as true as "Up in Michigan," as true as "The Snows of Kilimanjaro," truer maybe than "The Short Happy Life of Francis Macomber." He had pretensions then. True, indeed.

As for Carol Stein, she was to be a prima ballerina, the heiress to the mantle of Margot Fonteyn, Moira Shearer, Maria Tallchief. It was she, Carol Stein, who would be the half-bird, half-woman of Stravinsky's *Firebird*, the equal of Markova's Giselle, the Sugar Plum Fairy of *The Nutcracker*. Not maybe. Assuredly. Talk about dreams that burn, Carol Stein's was as hot and focused as nuclear fusion. Like his.

Put on this the added burden of addictive love, consuming passion, red-hot lust, Kismet, or however one describes unquenchable hormonic eruption, and you get a flame too greedy to compete with other obsessions. Like ballet. Like literary achievement. Discipline demanded they end it. Didn't it? He tried his best to ridicule the idea in the light of later events. What, after all, had all that burning ambition achieved?

But then, twenty-three years ago, to part seemed the only

logical alternative, the only cure, which resulted in a necessary, cruel, wrenching but brave and courageous act. Cold-turkey amputation. How else to describe it? Try as he might to drive the memory away with ridicule and sarcasm, it was just too powerful to fully obliterate.

The parting was bad enough. Worse, he recalled the promise. In keeping with the passion of their relationship, they took solemn oaths to pick up the reins when they had "become," made it. In two, three years, maybe five, bemedaled and enshrined, they swore reunion, fealty, and faithfulness. Even in the recollection, the melodrama of it was beyond excess.

From the beginning it was all excess, magnified and multiplied. Everything was ritual and ceremony. Sex was holy. Their lovemaking had the fury of exorcism.

"You must," she had cried that first time, urging him to thrust forward past the pain of what they then called that tight, unopened palace of her womanhood. Oh, God. To suffer that purple image now was a mortification.

But still she came forward and he remained frozen and fearful, unable to take his eyes off that smooth, chiseled, almost ageless alabaster face, probing his memory for clues. Is she or isn't she? Since he was not going to melt or disappear, he girded himself for this surreal reunion.

"The cab service was a half hour late," Eliot said, offering a smooth apology in an accent that resonated with upper-crust schooling, making it clear by implication that he was not one to chase cabs on rain-swept New York streets. Certainly not like Ken had done.

Eliot took Maggie's hand, Maggie looking up at Eliot's craggy features, all ruddy with charm and good cheer. He was extraordinarily tall, with steel-blue eyes and a sweeping ski-run nose. His forehead was high and shiny, crowned by a full head of dark wavy hair with distinguished gray sideburns. Thin lips tightened over large teeth in what passed for a smile but seemed suspiciously insincere. Ken, perhaps in order to avoid facing the real or ersatz Carol, was actually studying him comparatively, which embarrassed him. He was older than Ken, perhaps by a decade, big-boned, his hands large and hard, not fleshy.

"My husband, Ken," Maggie said as the men's hands joined.

Eliot's glance lingered for a proper moment until his hand disengaged and touched Carol's shoulder.

"And this is Carol," Eliot said with a lilting air of pride and possession, as if he were showing off a prized greyhound. Not *the* Carol. Surely not.

"So nice to meet you at last," Carol said to Maggie.

She was never a broad smiler with her mouth. It was her eyes that always danced a greeting, hazel eyes that often picked up any green within sight. As they did now. She wore an emerald pin on a cream-colored jewel-necked cashmere sweater. Her black hair, parted in the center, ballerina-style, was slicked back severely, emphasizing her sculpted features.

After acknowledging Maggie, the woman's eyes shifted toward him and he braced himself. There was no question in his mind now. Here she was. Carol Stein, reborn. His stomach lurched as his eyes, after the briefest flicker, evaded hers. In that split second he knew that he had not the courage to make the first move of recognition. Perhaps he would escape, he told himself, vowing to let her make the first move.

"My husband, Ken," Maggie said. Ken forced himself to lock into her gaze. Here's your chance, he told himself. She offered not the barest hint, not an iota of recognition.

"Pleased to meet you," Carol said.

He had taken her hand, feeling for signals. None came, although for him the touch had had the impact of a lightning bolt.

Despite his desire not to be recognized, he was crushed by the lack of it. How was it possible? Perhaps it merely mirrored his self-image, made even more self-critical by this event—that of the failed man whose only attainment had been anonymity.

Then, suddenly, as quickly as it had come, the idea of his failure slithered like a snake back to its dry and rocky den. He was reclaiming his courage. His coping mechanism was activated. He assured himself that in his universe, the advertising world, he was looked up to, considered enormously creative, an appellation of great prestige value. There were times when he had loved it, believed it, had gamboled in the swill of its cachet and status. All right, against the old dream, the dream of becoming the great writer, the "creative" label was, in a sense, a debasement of the term, not to be confused with the real thing. He had always known it was bullshit. But in the increasingly junky

American culture it had its place. Who could tell a great writer from a hack these days? And in terms of labels such as "creative," a "best" seller was rarely really best and half of them were skewered to pander to fantasies of suburban females. Weren't they?

"A Stoly Gibson on the rocks with three onions," Ken told the waiter, feeling the salutary effects of his venting. Eliot ordered a bottle of French red, fussing over the wine list with half-glasses, showing serious interest, as he probed the waiter for explanations about the year and the vineyard.

Maggie listened raptly, her long blond hair rustling as her head moved between Eliot and the waiter. Ken was suddenly aware of the contrast between the women. The one delicate, black-haired, swanlike; the other large-boned, yellow blond, blue-eyed, sculpted out of northern-clime Norwegian stock.

"Suit everyone?" Eliot asked, choosing the wine finally. Carol nodded.

"Sounds great," Maggie said. "But Ken isn't much for wine."

"Make mine a double," Ken called to the waiter as he moved away. Maggie cut him a glance of disapproval, then turned back to Eliot.

Maggie, no question about it, was impressed with Eliot Butterfield. She was a software consultant, installing and creating computer programs for various clients on a free-lance basis. Eliot Butterfield was a client. Maggie, wearing her midwestern openness on her sleeve, was often an enthusiast about people, and when she was impressed with one or another of her clients, the invariable game plan was to drag Ken out to dinner as a first step to greater intimacy.

Unfortunately, Ken was rarely cooperative and the follow-through usually fizzled after a few encounters. The objective for Maggie was always to have "couple" friends, so far a fruitless endeavor. Ken was not a natural friend-maker, although he was forced by circumstances to allow a truncated form of friendship with some of his co-workers at the agency.

Carol, in keeping with a genuine memory lapse, sincere non-recognition, or an obvious determination not to acknowledge her past, barely looked toward Ken during the aperitif session. Mostly, this was filled with the small-talk and information ex-

change of new acquaintanceship. Ken, as if he were consciously
exercising some form of spite, maintained a deliberate silence
while Maggie and Eliot carried the main dialogue and Carol answered only questions put to her by each of them.

But while Ken's façade might have seemed to register a shy
reticence, inner turmoil persisted and he listened carefully to the
exchange. The Butterfields lived in an apartment on Fifth Avenue
in the Seventies facing the park, which usually meant old money
and big bucks. Wasps, of course, never ever acknowledged such
crass numerical facts.

Maggie, on the other hand, always volunteered their own
circumstances, which were hardly lavish but seemed so in the
recounting. The fact was that they had been living above their
means for years and, after deducting private-school tuition for
their daughters, their high co-op fees, designer clothes, entertainment expenses, and other "necessities" of the New York life-style,
they were forever in debt.

"Mother's place in Maine suits us fine when the thirst for
change of place seizes us," Eliot pointed out with a nod toward
Carol.

"Wonderful," Maggie volunteered in response. "We seem to
be running counter to the second-house trend. We don't have a
Connecticut house or a place at the beach."

She hadn't said it in a resentful or whiny way, but Ken, nevertheless, felt a twinge of shame, as if somehow it characterized
other shortcomings as well. He offered no response, suffering
through the revelations, knowing he was helpless to offer any re-
futation. Any comment of his would be a surrender to recognition.

He simply had to live with the fact that Maggie and Eliot
had undoubtedly exchanged such surfacy social information during breaks from their computer consultations. Again his stomach
churned with the realization that Eliot, on the basis of Maggie's
information, would simply have dismissed him as hardly worthy
of any real interest. Was it possible that he had conveyed this to
Carol?

Maggie had told Ken what Eliot "did."

"He researches, offers papers, is active in organizations that
promote his wide-ranging interests. Mostly he is a thinker."

"Nice work if you can get it," Ken had said sarcastically.
Her enthusiasm over Eliot had rankled him.

"Eliot doesn't work, not for money," Maggie had explained. "He is an independent. As I told you, he thinks."

"Profound thoughts, no doubt?"

"Quite profound," Maggie had countered patiently. "Alternatives to war. Disintegrating ecological systems. The preservation of wildlife. This is his most pressing and fervent cause."

"Man included?" Ken had asked, not without a twinge of intimidation. The man, after all, was independently wealthy.

"He has a very brilliant mind. The breadth of it is extraordinary. That's why the computerization process is essential. We are creating a vast data bank."

"Of thoughts?" Ken had responded, snickering over the idea that a man could have the bent, leisure, and gall to label his occupation "thinker." Later Ken had suspected that the source of his irritation was his jealousy over the man's ability to do this. If he had the wherewithal, not forced by circumstances to pump water uphill like oxen on the Nile, he could use that leisure to truly create, articulate the great stories lying just beneath the surface of his mind, like mining some valuable mineral deposit.

"As long as he pays you on time," Ken had muttered.

Maggie, wisely, avoided any response to his sarcasm. Evasion was her weapon of choice. Actually, Ken preferred confrontation, but he rarely got that kind of a reaction out of Maggie. Just evasion. But from Maggie's description of Eliot he had concluded that the man was both an intellectual snob and a prig. Then he had been guessing, and yet now, studying Eliot across the table, he was certain he had been on target. But to Ken the real mystery of the man was how in the world he had landed Carol Stein.

The waiter came with the wine and poured it into Eliot's glass. He picked it up, whirling the liquid around the glass with a flick of his wrist. Then he sniffed it, sipped, and seemed to gargle with it. Ken thought for a moment that he was about to spit it out, as he had observed connoisseurs do at various wine-tasting events. The only receptacle for such an act was the centerpiece of flowers on the white tablecloth. He was relieved when Eliot, after a long gargle, swallowed finally. Then he nodded his approval to the waiter who then poured. Ken covered his empty glass with his palm. He would stick to his double Gibsons.

So Carol had married a man with a lot of money who had pretentious tastes, thought profound thoughts, and wanted to save wild beasts and mankind, Ken reflected as he fished with his

fingers among the slippery ice cubes of his drink for the last
onion. Snaring it, he popped it in his mouth, then washed it down
with the liquid dregs. He caught the waiter's eye and signaled for
another one. He'd need the extra jolt to get him through this
dinner.

"So it's advertising, is it? I suppose it's a necessary evil,"
Eliot said, chomping a breadstick. Ken had dreaded the revelation, although the quick rush of the vodka was already working
its dulling magic.

"Ken contends that it gives people choices," Maggie said, a
bit too quick to defend him.

"We could argue the merits of the choices," Eliot said. Was
it his imagination or did Ken note a slight twitch of the nostrils
as if a distasteful odor had been detected.

"Ken practically invented Slender Benders," Maggie volunteered. "You know, 'the splendor of slender benders.' You've seen
the commercials where the candy does these complicated acrobatics. Probably win an award. Actually, it's a whole new way to
market low-cal licorice."

"Christ, Maggie," Ken sighed, sipping his drink. Again he
resisted looking directly at Carol. An advertising man? You've
sold out for *that*, he imagined her saying to herself. He had
decided, halfway through his first drink, that she had indeed
recognized him but was faking it for her own secret reasons. But
why? Had he changed that much? Or was she being kind? Sparing him?

"Always hides his light under a bushel," Maggie said, shaking her head. Ever-nurturing Maggie. Was she really as proud of
his career as she made out? Admittedly, her unflagging support of
him had made it easier to rationalize his predicament, but was it
real, or, like her lovemaking, merely practical and efficient, but
undeniably nurturing. It was as if she had been built for that,
with high, large, billowing breasts that hadn't drooped, the kind
that could envelop and soothe a man.

Her belly had stayed flat and her buttocks full, flaring out
from solid hips down to legs that were sturdy and well turned. To
lie between them also offered a comforting quality. Yes, Maggie's
body and emotions had a compatible Earth Mother quality.
Often, he thought of her as a place of refuge. Freud, he knew,
could do wonders with these secret images, especially considering

that he had lost his beloved mother early, before he was out of his teens.

Seventeen years before, he had crawled into Maggie's warm cocoon and had learned how to preserve hope. Now that the vodka had partially restored his courage, he had the urge to explain this to Carol, to say that he had, indeed, kept his dream alive and that someday, when all this prologue is over, he would become the great writer of his earlier aspirations and his mother's unshakable prediction. He had merely postponed. Not failed. He held his tongue, having at least the insight to understand that the drinks had given him only Dutch courage, not real courage.

"Advertising has its place, of course," Eliot said. "In the system as it is now constituted, consuming goods and services keeps our society afloat."

"Like Slender Benders," Ken said, his hand reaching out to grasp the drink the waiter had just delivered. "Makes their teeth rot." He felt a ball of irritation begin to form deep inside himself, expanding painfully in his gut. "Then we sell them toothbrushes, pastes, powders, mouthwash. Good for dentists, too. Dental equipment . . ."

"And gold," Eliot interjected with a soothing smile, as if he had picked up on the sarcasm and was determined to avoid any alarming response that would create a distasteful scene. "Remember gold."

"And mines."

"Exactly," Eliot said. "Which nature created and is also finite." He was unstoppable in his pedantry, Ken decided, determined to attempt some repression of darker feelings. The fact was that what he had finally determined was that Carol's deliberate snub was making him angry.

"The unfortunate part," Eliot went on, "is that the entire process is based on perpetual motion. A never-ending spin. At some point it will run down. The environment simply won't support it."

"And we'll all be charcoal when the ozone layer goes kaput," Ken muttered.

"Exactly," Eliot agreed. "The tragedy of it is not that it's inevitable if we follow our present course. We all know that. The tragedy is that we're not going fast enough to replenish ourselves before Armageddon arrives."

"That bad?" Ken said.

"Problem is we're all connected. All life interacts on all life." Eliot whirled the wine again, sniffed, sipped carefully, then swallowed. "Environment deteriorates," he went on, looking into his glass. "No grapes, no more wine."

"Heavy stuff," Ken said, feeling somewhat belittled by the man's smooth sense of confidence and annoyed at his own resort to sarcasm. Rather than risk offending, he resorted to silence.

"And you, Carol?" Maggie asked, filling in the gap. "Eliot tells me you're a dancer." Eliot had undoubtedly informed her of that and it provided the kind of status worth repeating.

Had it happened? Had she become a prima ballerina? Ken wondered, remembering Carol in her leotards and warm-up stockings practicing at the bar for hours on end. Loveliness and grace in human form. God, there was beauty there. And obsession. Like his. No room for love and loving getting in the way of that avalanche of intensity. After all, a writer wrote and a dancer danced. Everything else was extraneous to that, trivial. Loving, too.

Not once during the conversation with Eliot had Carol turned his way. His reaction was to respond in kind, relying on his peripheral vision to study her.

"Were you with a ballet company?" Maggie asked, not one to leave a loose end.

"Principal ballerina, the Ballet Company of Sydney, Australia," Eliot volunteered.

"For a bit. A few seasons only," Carol added quickly. "I had this injury."

At first Ken decided she was merely being considerate, self-effacing, sensitive to his own predicament. Hadn't she really danced longer than a few seasons? He was suddenly ashamed, searching himself for its source. Actually, he was happy for her, felt good for her. So she had made it and this, he decided, might be at the heart of her not acknowledging him. She had seen into his heart and was sparing him. Only a caring person could do that.

"A tough business, ballet," Eliot said. "She's still at it. Practicing for hours. We've got a studio in the apartment where she gives lessons."

There had been a time when he had pored over names whenever a ballet was reviewed and had failed to see hers, leading him to believe that she might have changed her name or gone abroad, which apparently was the case. Why hadn't he tried to find her? He did not have to dig too deeply for the answer. Simply put, he felt diminished by his defeat and too devastated to reveal his surrender. That was it. Or was it because he feared that she had been successful? He a failure; she a success. Could he have coped with that?

Well, now he knew. His reaction surprised him. He hadn't expected himself to have such generosity of heart. Good for her, he thought. He picked up his drink and silently toasted her.

Maybe such generosity was stirred by her self-effacing comment "for a bit." All right, it wasn't worldwide celebrity. But it was a victory of sorts, a vindication of one's talents and hard work. Better than he had done. What had come of his efforts? A few hundred pages worth of manuscript and an outline that went nowhere. His solace was to convince himself that he was a talent unrecognized. He had even devised a litany of logic to explain it: bad timing, changing tastes, American culture's downhill slide, and the usual cast of knaves, fools, and idiots who couldn't tell a diamond from a zircon but had the power to bar the door. But he also knew, emptying his glass again, that those excuses had worn thin over the past two decades.

The waiter, a slim actor type, appeared with the inevitable catalog of specials, spoken with serious and well-trained intensity. Ken barely listened. He detested this ritual of the specials, a process that Maggie adored. There was something promotional about it, manipulative. Like advertising. It was a firm policy of his, whenever possible, to avoid buying anything that was advertised.

Carol kept her eyes hidden behind the menu. Ken noted that she had barely sipped her wine. Years of bodily discipline had apparently become second nature. Time, too, had been especially kind. She would be exactly forty now, four years younger than he was. She looked ten years younger, perhaps more.

". . . sautéed shrimp cakes with lime herb butter and rocket salad," the waiter chanted. "Another appetizer is home-smoked salmon with dill cream on toasted brioche."

Eliot and Maggie listened as if the young man's rendition were a holy chant.

"And the pasta special is duck-filled herb raviolis with zinfandel rosemary butter."

"Not doughy raviolis?" Eliot asked.

"I've had them," Maggie said. "Light as feathers."

"For pizzas," the waiter continued, "the chef suggests a pizza with artichokes, shiitake mushrooms, eggplant, and caramelized garlic."

"As long as the chef is not too light-handed on the garlic," Eliot said seriously.

"Eliot is a gourmet," Maggie said.

"Obviously," Ken offered, unable to control his sarcasm. Then he said, "I'm more of a gourmand."

"There is a difference," Eliot said. His amused tone struck Ken as nasal, as if the tip of his nose were angled slightly upward.

"For a main dish," the waiter continued, "we have farm-raised chicken with Italian parsley and double-blanched garlic. We also have the sautéed sweetbreads with arugula salad and sherry wine vinegar butter."

Ken felt a tickle of nausea and he washed it away with the melted ice of his drink.

"How is that prepared?" Eliot asked. "Too much oil would be fatal."

The waiter went into elaborate details, with both Maggie and Eliot offering various comments. Odd, Ken mused, how the subject of food reveals character. It struck Ken that Maggie's interest in it had an intensity he hadn't quite noticed before.

"I'm inclined toward the sweetbreads," Eliot announced. "And I'll start with the salmon."

"And I'll do the other, the chicken and begin with the duck-filled raviolis."

"And your pleasure, darling?" Eliot said, addressing Carol.

"A little green salad, dressing on the side, and angel hair with garlic and basil."

"Boring but effective," Eliot sighed.

Carol ignored his comment. Still, she did not look toward Ken.

"I'll have the same as this lady," Ken said, pointing to Carol. He also pointed into his glass. "And another of these."

He caught Eliot's sudden raised eyebrow and blink of disapproval.

"Calls for white," Eliot said, with a barely perceptible flutter of disdain.

The booze was giving Ken an edge, exaggerating his sensitivity. Something was beginning to trouble him and he began to feel a subtle shiver of irritation. Why was she deliberately not recognizing him? Soon his mind was racing for reasons. Perhaps he had misread her. Maybe her success "for a bit" was really an embarrassment to her. Maybe the injury that apparently had cut short her career was merely an excuse for failure. Maybe she genuinely had not recognized him. But if she did know who he was, well, then, her failure to acknowledge him could only be interpreted as an insult. Now that she was married to this super–tight-assed employer of his wife, why dredge up the banal acquaintances of her lower-class origins? Booze could also induce a mild paranoia, he decided, groping his way back to balance.

The waiter came with the white wine and Eliot tasted it, making odd expressions as he sloshed the liquid around in his mouth.

"Too much acid," he said.

"Perhaps I should have recommended the Ggrich," the waiter said.

"I wish you would have earlier," Eliot replied with flouncy superiority. They agreed on Ggrich and the waiter scurried off. "Probably getting a commission on the other," Eliot sneered.

"The American way," Ken chuckled sarcastically, wondering if his words were beginning to slur. He picked up his fresh drink and sipped. Maggie's eyes flickered a sharp warning. With good reason. A snootful, a rarity for him, could make him caustic, his words barbed and insulting.

I'll be fine, his eye reply to Maggie said as he aborted a deeper sip on his drink, fishing with his fingers for the onions instead. He had tried to catch Carol's expression from the corner of his eye, to see if she had observed the caretaking exchange with his wife. No sign. He was relieved by that. It wouldn't do at all for her to see how mother-smothered he had become, not he, her manly deflowerer.

"So how long have you guys been married?" Maggie asked as the waiter peppered her duck raviolis.

"Ten years," Carol said, chewing daintily on a lettuce leaf.

Ken calculated that that would have put her at thirty, a

chronological watershed for most dancers who weren't established by that age.

"Are you a New Yorker?" Maggie asked. Off and running now, she had a passion for personal history. Another mark of their social inferiority, Ken supposed. He had married a busybody. Once he had thought this quality attractive, a characteristic of her open and giving nature.

"I was born in Frankfurt," Carol replied. "My father was an American army officer stationed there."

"French ancestors. Titled. Le Roc was her maiden name. Great-grandfather was a marquis," Eliot said.

Ken felt an odd rearing sensation. Le Roc. American army officer. Great-grandfather a marquis. What elaborate, unmitigated bullshit. Carol was from Forest Hills. Born and bred. When he suddenly looked at her full face she did not stir, her gaze still hidden. What's going on here? Ken thought, glancing at the others, who ignored him. Eliot was intently sampling Maggie's raviolis, nodding approval.

"Where did you study?" Maggie asked sweetly without looking up.

"Paris, actually," Carol said. "My mother insisted. Then I studied in San Francisco. I didn't get to Sydney until I was twenty-three."

"Twenty-three? You don't look much more than that now," Maggie said with obvious sincerity.

"Fact is, I'm thirty-one."

Jesus, Ken thought. She's lopped off nine years. The alcohol buzz receded. Perhaps his own powers of recognition had been faulty.

"Robbed the cradle," Eliot said. "She's a few years older than my son."

Ken reached for his glass and observed her over the rim. Was this really Carol Stein? Or an alcoholic fantasy? The old Carol, the one engraved in his memory, was not a dissembler. If this was the real Carol, she was lying through her teeth.

"Carol's father was killed in Vietnam," Eliot interjected casually.

The declaration caught Ken in mid-swallow, although he prevented himself from coughing. Mr. Stein, Carol's father, was an accountant, an older man with thick glasses and badly fitted false teeth, hardly a warrior and very overage for Vietnam.

"Tough break," Ken heard himself say.

"You poor girl," Maggie said with her Earth Mother sincerity.

Ken felt absolutely compelled to join the investigation, if only to validate his own sanity. He studied Carol's face. She still kept her eyes hidden, but her hands, which had been transparent with blue veins showing, were still transparent with blue veins showing, without a hint of the spots of age that were beginning to sprout on the backs of his own hands. And when she talked he saw that one crooked eyetooth which she thought flawed her smile, but didn't as far as he was concerned.

For further identification there was a circle of brown frecklelike beauty marks just above the areola of her perfectly shaped right breast. This was hardly the place to go searching for that. There was also a tiny half-moon scar at the upper end of her inner thigh just at the spot where her pubic hair began. How's that for details, he thought, taking another sip of his drink in self-congratulation. And there was more. He felt his skin temperature rise as his mind began to search for some clever question that might explode this preposterous myth. Then it came.

"Been to the Washington wall, Carol?"

She showed no reaction, nor did she raise her eyes to acknowledge the question, concentrating instead on the lettuce in her barely touched salad. When she didn't answer after an appropriate interval, he pressed the point.

"You know the one. The Vietnam Memorial wall. All those engraved names."

"Too painful, I'm afraid," she whispered.

"I might be going next week. I could make a rubbing of your father's name." An inspired idea, he decided. He took out a ballpoint from an inner pocket. Gotcha, he told her silently.

"To Washington, Ken?" Maggie asked. "You never mentioned it."

"Research," Ken shrugged, his mind turning over, alert, shocked to sobriety. Not once had Carol's eyes met his. "New candy product. Minty marzipan. They want to make it look like real silver dollars. Get the mint angle."

"And they pay you for this," Eliot said sardonically, sipping his wine.

"Really," Ken pressed, ignoring Eliot's comment, addressing Carol. "What was your father's name? Le Roc, was it?"

Only then did she look up at him, her eyes flashing a brief, unmistakable warning to cease and desist. Whatever her reasons, this particular subterfuge had been a mistake. Now he was dead certain. She hadn't forgotten him at all. No way. She was hiding, all right. For reasons known only to her, she had reinvented herself. A wry chuckle escaped his throat.

"I really would prefer you didn't," she said.

"Sure," he shrugged, retreating quickly, putting the ballpoint back in his inside pocket. It was over. He had gotten what he needed.

The waiter came with their main dishes.

"Marvelous," Maggie said, looking at the concoction on her plate.

"You must try some," Eliot said, spearing a sweetbread and popping it into Maggie's mouth. She did the same with her chicken. They offered a chorus of appreciative oohs and ahs over the food.

Both Ken and Carol picked at their pasta, growing silent, leaving the conversational field to Maggie and Eliot, who started on computers, then turned to wildlife. Carol listened with rapt attention as Eliot's intensity grew. No question about it, Ken could tell. The man was a fanatic about his causes.

"Greed is endemic. Whole herds of elephants are being massacred for their ivory. The rhinoceros is almost beyond saving. The leopard is having lots of trouble coming back." He had adopted a slightly pompous, pedagogic tone, lecturing in his superior, nasal voice. Maggie, Ken could tell, was enthralled and Eliot was encouraged by her interest.

"Africa," Eliot continued, "is the standard by which we must be judged. It's our most vulnerable continent. If our greed destroys Africa, then we are all doomed. Not only is African wildlife threatened, Africa itself is an endangered species."

"Africa is Eliot's particular interest," Maggie said, turning to Ken, as if this lecture were for his benefit alone, which was apparently true. He was the only real outsider in this group. "They've been three times."

"Carol loves it as well," Eliot said, glancing toward his wife. Then he launched into a long diatribe against man's methodical destruction of Africa, "the planet's most important asset."

Maggie listened with rapt attention.

"He is inspiring when he gets going," she said to Ken.

Not like me, Ken supposed she meant. By comparison, he felt bested by Eliot's cool eloquence, his touted wisdom, his sense of purpose and personal fulfillment. He was certain that Carol thought that as well. It was obvious that Maggie did. On a scratch sheet Ken Kramer would show a lot longer odds than Eliot Butterfield.

But on reflection, Ken decided that Eliot couldn't be all that smart to fall prey to Carol's reconstituted history. Too much into yourself to see the truth, eh tight-ass, Ken thought, feeling the bile of his nastiness building again.

He was, in fact, puzzled by Carol's lies. They were public lies, checkable lies. The business of the birth date alone. And the elaborate convoluted personal history. Never mind the Le Roc on the wall memorial. Where and how had Carol journeyed for two decades to bring her to this?

"We're off to Kenya again in few months," Eliot said. "Another safari. I try to go every two years. Draws me like a magnet. Makes me sad, too, watching it go downhill." He turned to Maggie. "Ever been?"

"No. But I'd love to," Maggie said, looking toward Ken.

"We tent," Eliot said. "Not exactly the Ritz, but remarkably comfortable. And I've got this fabulous guide. Former white hunter until they banned it in 1977. Nobody like Jack Meade. Right, Carol?"

"The best there is. It's a bit Spartan, very nineteenth-century, but that's part of the charm."

"Ken's not much of a rough rider," Maggie laughed. "He likes his creature comforts."

Must you. Now she was making him out to be a self-indulgent weakling.

"Did the primitiveness bother you, Carol?" Maggie asked.

"It took some getting used to," Carol said. There, for a fleeting moment, was the old Carol, the one that didn't dissemble.

"Going downhill in a hand basket," Eliot said. "Unless we do something drastic."

"We'd better hurry over, then," Ken said, unable to hide the pique that had been building inside him. Don't, he warned himself, rolling the pasta on his fork, stuffing his mouth to shut it up.

"We share our planet with lots of competing forms of life,"

Eliot said. "We need a plan to balance it all, but first we need to decide that we must have a plan. You see . . ." He was plunging into it now, offering all that his thinking had wrought on this subject.

While Eliot spoke, barely pausing between bites and sips, Ken's thoughts raced along another path.

Down memory lane.

2

THIS LOCAL girl had won a prize, coming in first in a ballet competition sponsored by the New York Ballet Company. The prize was five hundred dollars toward tuition at the ballet school run by the company. There had been a brief piece in *The New York Times* announcing the prizes, and Jack Holmes, the editor of the *Mid-Queens Post,* had sent Ken to interview her. Local Forest Hills girl wins ballet prize. Two cents a word and a byline.

Holmes liked Ken's stuff. It was a beginning, after all. He was a senior at City College then, full of himself, borderline arrogant, cocksure of his talent. Hadn't he mesmerized his fellow student writers when he read his short story "The Other People" before the creative-writing class just two days prior to that fateful interview?

Funny how that juxtaposition of detail had hung on, appended itself to the recollection as if it were essential to his state of mind at the time. Stunning, the teacher had said about his story. It had the rhythm of a clear stream rolling down a mountain in springtime. Even that hyperbolic image had stuck in his mind. He had his own private analysis, redolent of Hemingway.

31

It was about a man in crisis alone, not up in Hem's Michigan, but here in the wilderness of New York. He had sent it off to a prestigious literary magazine and was certain of its acceptance.

He had been extremely lucky to get these assignments. Hell, journalism was writing, albeit a notch down on the literary scale, but it had an element of craft and he was good at it. And the bylines gave him a sense of authorship and would look impressive in a portfolio.

Despite literary pretensions, Ken could not escape his failed father's admonition that one was compelled to scheme toward one's practical economic future. Of course, he was absolutely certain that he was programmed for early literary discovery, which didn't mean that he couldn't hedge his bets.

"Won't do to get left behind," his father had warned. "Like me."

His mother of blessed memory, his most avid reader, had never faltered in her belief that he could be anything he wished. An amateur genealogist, she had tracked a literary bent back four generations to a great-uncle from Kozin, a shtetl not far from Kiev where amusing stories had appeared in the local paper, scrupulously preserved in cellophane and carried across in steerage on the U.S.S. *St. Louis* by Ken's great-grandmother. He had read them in translation from the Yiddish. They had struck him as extremely clever, and his mother had impressed upon him that such tendencies and talent could come down through the blood.

He took that as one more clue to a growing conviction that he was being urged on by some inner force, some mysterious and compelling need to become a writer, a teller of stories.

"He always loved to make up stories," his mother had told anyone within earshot, as if, for her, his writing career had always been a foregone conclusion. From earliest childhood the use of words had fascinated him. He had also been an early talker, reader, and compulsive frequenter of the public library.

As early as elementary school he had shown signs of literary talent, winning a poetry prize in the seventh grade. Later he became editor of the high school paper and literary magazine. And it was always Ken Kramer who was called upon to write the class satire or a speech for his favored candidate running for the student council. Weren't these activities the foreshadowing of his future?

"This is a very talented boy," his mother had been told again and again when she appeared on open-school days.

The writing gift also had a profoundly positive effect on his popularity with his classmates and friends, especially when puberty arrived and he could write good rhyming love poetry to the girls. His friends had concluded that this was the true reason why he was the first of their crowd to go all the way sexually with a female. He had just turned fifteen.

Such early successes had made the idea of a brilliant literary career a natural progression and, therefore, prophetic. From that conviction flowed the decision to major in English at City College, much to the chagrin of his unemployed and expendable bookkeeper father, who, by then, was plagued by a certain fear that his son would emulate his own failure.

On the other hand, although she had never gone to college, his mother had always read voraciously and encouraged him in his pursuit. His father, true to his fears, would have preferred that his son, at the minimum, become a CPA like his sister's husband.

"Writing is not a career that you pick," his mother had repeatedly explained to his father. "It picks you." The explanation invariably confused the poor, beaten man, whose experience had convinced him that becoming a professional man was the ultimate ticket to financial security. Logic, after all, was on his side.

But Ken reveled in his mother's explanation and agreed with it. How else to explain the thrill of being transported beyond himself when he read the stories of Ernest Hemingway, John Dos Passos, William Faulkner, F. Scott Fitzgerald, and others? It was as if these writers were pulling him into their circle.

Yet even then, he recognized a dark side to his mother's militant support of his grandiose ambitions. His father, although a sweet, gentle man, had no obvious creative impulses, no compelling drives. It showed, of course, in the modesty of his income and in the simple adequacy of creature comforts in the household.

The background music of Ken's early life was his mother's perpetual drumbeat of disappointment over the man's failure. There was no other word for it.

"How can you be satisfied with being nobody, taking

crumbs," his mother would rant. "Where is your pride? Is this kind of failure a good example for your children?"

"I do my best," his father would say, or some variation of the same theme. "I didn't have the opportunities."

"You didn't take them," his mother would counter.

"He gets a free education," his father would reason. "He could be a professional man. Look at me. I'm an example of what happens when you're not a professional man."

"A writer is a professional man," his mother would point out.

"No. A writer is a gambler. He could do it on the side. First he should be a breadwinner."

"Like you, I suppose."

"That's the whole point."

"You don't understand. You're born an artist. You have no choice. He's not like you. You have to be dedicated. You can't do it on the side. It takes every ounce of his being."

Every ounce of his being. Of course. She had it right as far as it went. But experience would teach him that even dedication and obsession were not enough. And yet, not once did he ever inject himself into his parents' psychological Ping-Pong, which seemed to permeate their lives when he was in his late teens. He told himself that he had too much love for them and too much delicacy to be involved in their marriage wars. Yet, in a profound way, their words seemed to define himself to himself.

To have this fierce maternal support that brooked no doubt was an enormous motivating factor. Her early death from cancer had robbed him of her supportive presence, but spared her from the ultimate realization of his failure, although she might not have defined it that way. It could be argued that he had made it as a writer. Couldn't it?

There was guilt in it, of course. But it was always mitigated in his own mind by the way he had said his farewells, hoping to fulfill her most fervent wish by reading the entire seven volumes of *Remembrance of Things Past* by Marcel Proust to her as she lay dying.

"Thank God my Ken doesn't do anything halfway," she told him, drifting away with a smile, her hand in his. He had barely finished *Swann's Way*, the first volume in the series.

It was that kind of emotional baggage that Ken Kramer carried into Carol Stein's home on that fateful day in early July.

*   *   *

He had entered her family's modest red-brick row house on 108th Street in Forest Hills. Carol's mother ushered him into the living room where Carol sat, her legs tucked under her, in the center of an overstuffed couch.

Her mother had pointed him to an upholstered chair, one of two beside the cocktail table in front of the couch where Carol sat. Carol's mother took the other chair.

Observing the room, Ken was struck by one central fact. This family's life and fortunes were totally tied to Carol Stein's aspirations. There were pictures in silver frames almost exclusively of Carol. Carol on a pony. Carol in a tutu as a tot. A spindly Carol, all legs, dancing on her toes. The exception was a wedding picture of two people who obviously were her parents. Her father, with his thick glasses and doughy features, her mother, all smiles and dimply in the picture. In real life the woman seemed far more intense, extremely earnest. There was no doubt about it, his insight told him. Her daughter's career was the only real spark in an otherwise colorless life.

"We're very proud that she won," Mrs. Stein had said, looking at Carol.

There were lots of plants in the house, and spears of sunlight coming through the window made Carol's eyes glow green. There was not a spare ripple of flesh on her delicate kittenlike face, framed by black hair parted in the middle. She was wearing a gray skirt that fringed perfect, smooth kneecaps, and a white silk shirtwaist with a bow that flowed down to her chest.

She struck him as a kind of living Dresden doll with creamy skin and a shy smile and eyes that were alert and curious, not at all shy. He remembered being drawn to them. From that first moment she had stirred something in him.

"Isn't she just a perfect Cinderella. That's the piece she used from the second act when they're at the ball and . . ."

"I'm sure Mr. Kramer knows the story of Cinderella, Mama."

"Well, it was hard work, you know," Mrs. Stein said. "This is an art that requires absolute discipline and focus."

"No artist can succeed without that," Ken said, still locked into Carol's gaze. She seemed to offer her silent consent. He wondered what impression he was making on her, knowing such a thought was a distinctly unjournalistic response. He was, after all, the observer. What should it matter how he was observed by his subject?

"And how do you feel about winning first prize, Miss Stein?" Ken asked, an open pad resting on his thigh, his ballpoint at the ready.

Carol hesitated, losing eye contact, observing her fingers, looking uncomfortable as she groped for the right words.

"She's still quite excited," Mrs. Stein said, coming to her rescue as she nervously fingered a string of pearls.

"I never thought I'd win," Carol said modestly in a soft voice.

"She's very determined, Mr. Kramer," Mrs. Stein said.

"That's what it takes," Ken said knowingly. "Nothing less."

"Night and day she worked," Mrs. Stein said. "She barely eats. She's at the bar first thing in the morning."

"Just a bar fly," Carol said, offering a smile. "Mother, shouldn't we offer Mr. Kramer some tea?"

"Of course."

Mrs. Stein struggled out of the deep chair and went off into the kitchen, leaving Ken alone with Carol.

"My family's very supportive," Carol sighed. "Maybe overly so. Considering what I have to go through, it's practically a requirement."

"It means a great deal to you, doesn't it? A career in ballet?" Ken asked.

"Everything, I'm afraid. It's my life."

Her eyes had again locked into his and he felt her commitment and sincerity. Her intensity filled the room, although he seemed even then to detect something beyond that in her eyes, something indecipherable but compelling. Suddenly she uncurled her legs and stood up, walking about the room.

He was surprised at her height, which was much greater than had appeared when she'd been sitting on the couch, and when she walked she reminded him of a reed being swayed by a gentle breeze. He noted that her legs, displayed under her short skirt, were perfectly proportioned and lightly muscled. Her walk seemed like a glide, her buttocks' movement rhythmical. Without warning, the sight stirred an erotic thrill in Ken.

"This scholarship will at least take the financial pressure off

my parents," Carol said, as if to herself. She might have said
more, but he hadn't caught it.

At that moment, Mrs. Stein came in with a tray that held
tea, cups, and chocolate chip cookies.

"No sacrifice is too much," Mrs. Stein said. "Ours is nothing
compared to hers. A career in ballet requires a hundred percent.
Right, Carol? No. A hundred and ten percent. Believe me, if she
was not giving that, we would have to think twice."

"I wish there was a shortcut," Carol said, moving back to
the couch. She sat down and again tucked her legs under her. He
caught a brief glimpse of white panty, which embarrassed him,
as if he had been watching for it, which he was. He felt his face
flush and he turned away.

"I started her at three," Mrs. Stein said. "This scholarship
could put her in the New York City Ballet Corps de Ballet before
she's eighteen." Mrs. Stein looked at her daughter pointedly. "I
know she will do it."

"It's no big deal, Mama. Baronova, Riabouchinska, and
Toumanova were all under fifteen when they became famous."

"She gets paranoid sometimes about time. Remember,
Pavlova never retired, danced right up until she died at fifty."

Mrs. Stein poured the tea, handed Ken a cup, and offered
him a chocolate chip cookie, which he took. She poured out a cup
for Carol, then herself. Then she settled back into the chair and
put the cookie dish on her lap.

"This is my very first interview," Carol said, her voice modulated and mellow. She sipped the tea, but did not reach for a
cookie.

"I'm sure there'll be many more," Mrs. Stein responded.

"So you were turned on to ballet at an early age," Ken said,
his eyes shifting to the picture on an end table.

"Before that," Mrs. Stein said. "You should have seen her.
I think she danced when she was still in my womb. I swear I
felt it."

"Mama," Carol snapped, looking at Ken for sympathy.

"I'm embarrassing her, I guess." Mrs. Stein said.

"It's my interview, Mama, please." Then, more gently, Carol
added, "She's not really a stage mother."

"Actually, I spend more time telling her to stop. Believe me, she doesn't need pushing. You should see her, Mr. Kramer. A dream. An absolute dream."

"I'd love to," Ken said.

The story was coming together now. The obsessed daughter and the sacrificing family. He was getting a handle on it, writing the lead in his head. He needed some facts to flesh things out and pressed Carol for more background. Years of lessons, constant effort, perpetual coaching. He wrote it all down.

"Where do you think it comes from?"

Carol seemed to worry over the question for a long time. Then her mother spoke.

"I took her to see Tchaikovsky's *Swan Lake* when she was three. She sat there hypnotized. I'll never forget . . ."

"That was part of it," Carol interrupted. "The exposure. Something happened." She shook her head. "It's hard to explain it. But that's all I ever wanted. It's my fantasy."

"So where do you go from here?" he asked.

"Manhattan. The New York City Ballet School. As Mama says, hopefully the Corps."

"Not hopefully," her mother interjected. "Definitely."

"That's obvious. You want to be a professional ballerina," Ken said.

"A prima ballerina, Mr. Kramer," Mrs. Stein said, exchanging glances with her daughter. "Nothing less."

"Mama, please," Carol said, blushing. "I don't want to even think about that. Just to do my best. That's all I want to focus on." She turned toward Ken. "The title 'ballerina' isn't to be taken lightly, Mr. Kramer. Not many really earn the title until they're in their late twenties, and then they have to work to keep it. As for 'prima ballerina,' that's like a dream."

"I suppose it's enormously competitive. Girls coming from everywhere with the same burning ambition."

Carol shrugged, then said, "That's why you can't be unrealistic about your expectations."

The sudden flash of doubt seemed jarring.

"She's superstitious," Mrs. Stein said. "She thinks that if she's too confident and optimistic it would be a jinx."

"Well, it must work. She did win a first prize," Ken reflected. The idea of all that competition struck home. Wasn't he faced with the same situation? Working toward the same level of expectation?

"Fact is she wants to be the best in the world," Mrs. Stein said. Carol shot her mother a rebuking glance and frowned.

"A champion," Ken said, thinking, God, for your sake I hope so. He felt it emanate from the girl's aura, from every symbolic pore, this drive to be the best. And the doubts.

"I plan to work very hard, which is no guarantee of success," Carol said. "I'll give it my best."

"Tell Mr. Kramer what that means, darling," Mrs. Stein said. Then she filled the pause with her own explanation. "Eight to ten hours of practice a day. Practice and discipline. The body is the instrument. A careful diet. Early to bed. No social life. It's not a hobby. It's a life."

"You find it hard?" Ken asked Carol.

"Hard?" Mrs. Stein began.

"I need the quote from Carol, Mrs. Stein," Ken said, throwing a wink at Carol, who flashed approval with her eyes. Ken waited through the long silence.

"A dancer dances," Carol said serenely. "I've made this my priority. It's everything to me. I hope I have a good career. That's what I'm shooting for."

"I like that," Ken said.

"Is that a special person?" Mrs. Stein interjected. He ignored her.

"So your life is your dancing?" Ken asked, as if her mother no longer existed. "To the exclusion of everything else?"

"Yes, it is." Carol said firmly.

"Not even boyfriends?" he asked. Despite the ulterior motive, it was a good journalistic question.

"No," Carol said. He looked into her eyes for something tentative about the answer, and found none. He hid his disappointment.

"There's no time for boys," the mother said.

Carol's eyes smiled.

"You don't think that will make you . . . well . . . socially backward," Ken asked slyly.

"We'll see. It's just not important at the moment," Carol said. Her mother nodded approval.

"So art is all," Ken said.

"In a way, I suppose. But I don't think about it," Carol said, her eyes greener now as the lowering sun threw more light into the room. "My plan is to take it one day at a time. And give it every ounce I have."

There it was. Well, he knew what that was all about.

Ken wrote what he thought was a good story. Holmes, who edited it, agreed.

"Think she'll make it?" he asked.

"Well, I'm rooting for her," Ken said.

"That sure comes through, kiddo."

The girl had made an impression on him. The story ran, complete with picture, with a headline that read: LOCAL GIRL PIR-OUETTES TO PRIZE. There was a shot of Carol in a frilly tutu in mid-spin.

The day the story ran, Ken brought the paper over to her house, then watched her as she read it. Thankfully, her mother was out. She had been practicing at the bar and her face was moist with perspiration. He noted how perfect her body looked in a leotard. Nor could he deny to himself the erotic pull of her.

"I'm embarrassed," she said after she had read his story.

"I told the truth," he told her.

"You seem so sure I'll make it."

"I have no doubts at all."

"Well, I do. Lots of them."

"I can tell a winner when I see one," he said.

Then he asked her out for a cup of coffee, asking in such a businesslike way that she would not think of it as a kind of date. What he feared most now was that she was deadly serious about having no distractions in her life. The fact was that he wanted to distract her, wanted to be with her. And more.

There was a coffee shop a couple of blocks away, and when they had settled in and the waiter had taken their order, Ken spoke:

"I feel slightly guilty, taking you away from your work."

"Don't be silly. I have to take a break sometime."

"We all do," he said, laughing. "And that's kind of you to say after all that talk of focus."

He noted that her fingers were thin and delicate and that her neck was long and graceful. Yet for all her attractiveness, there was something so obviously natural, even naïve, about her. He sensed a vulnerability, which somehow made his own thoughts predatory. It was clear that she had no experience with the opposite sex. Not that he was an expert on the subject, but he had acquired a lot more knowledge in that department than she had. He wondered if she had the slightest inkling that this coffee klatch was really an exercise in flirtation. Even in his thoughts, he dared not use the word *seduction*, but the fact was that he did want to interest her in himself. It was more daunting than he had expected.

"Well, you've told me your story. Now, if you're interested, I'll tell you mine."

She nodded. "Yes, I'm interested."

She had ordered coffee and was sipping it lightly, but mostly her fingertips played with the rim of her cup. Despite her politeness, he had the sense that the time she had allowed him was limited.

"I . . . I understood what you meant about, you know, making it. You see, I want to be a writer . . ."

"You are a writer."

"I mean a creative writer. In a way it's like dancing. A dancer dances. A writer writes."

"Absolutely," she said, nodding to emphasize her understanding.

"'Up in Michigan' was my *Swan Lake*," he said. She looked puzzled and he explained. "You saw *Swan Lake* and knew you wanted to be a ballet dancer. I read Ernest Hemingway's 'Up in Michigan' and knew I wanted to be a writer. People like us are the luckiest people alive," he added. "We know what we want."

Then he laid out his own goals as if she were the journalist and he the subject of the interview.

"To be published by twenty-five. That's my goal," he told her. "I feel the pull of it, that I have things to express, that there is an important voice in me."

"Yes, I see," Carol said.

She didn't ask what exactly it was he was being urged to express, but he was certain she understood it.

"Like ballet, also a form of expression."

"Except that you're especially lucky," she told him. "A writer has got longer possibilities, an extended career life. Not like a dancer. You don't have to depend on the body as much as I do." He looked at her thin, delicate wrists, the narrow watch strapped around the small bones. And yet she did not seem frail at all.

"Your mother called you paranoid about time," he said, as if seeing the watch on her wrist had reminded him.

"It's an occupational hazard," she said. "A dancer is always racing with time."

"At seventeen?"

"I've been racing with it since I was three," she said.

"You're so intense," he said.

"You have to be."

He looked at her for a long moment, studying her face, but mostly stalling to find some way into her confidence. Above all, he knew what he was seeking. A relationship with her. Perhaps, intimacy. Flirt back, he begged her in his heart.

"I . . . I have to say this. I really think you're . . . well, beautiful. Very beautiful."

"You do?" She seemed surprised. "Then I thank you very much."

"Kind sir."

"What?" She seemed confused.

"I thought you might say, 'Thank you very much, kind sir.' The 'kind sir' would be like . . . well, a saucy response, a flirty thing to say."

"I guess I don't know too much about those things," she said, blushing. Her eyelids fluttered with a brief nervousness.

He was suddenly tempted to reach out and touch her hand. He didn't. Instead, he shook his head.

"Do you ever think about anything else but ballet?"

She paused and smiled. "Everything relates to ballet," she said.

"Never about boys."

"Not usually," she said, giving him a tiny opening.

"So we must seek the unusual," he said boldly.

She laughed, but she offered no repartee.

"So what happens next?" Ken asked.

She had an answer, one not quite expected.

What happened next, she told him, was that she would begin studying in Manhattan next month. Because of the transportation time factor she had taken a tiny apartment in the Village.

"I just found you and off you go," he said. He meant it literally. Her impact on him had inspired yearning. Perhaps pain. Is this what was meant by falling in love?

"I'm sure we'll meet again," she said politely, but without conviction, deepening his disappointment.

He groped for something more to say. Something that would stimulate a reaction. Did she feel anything, any reaction at all to him? He doubted it and it was discouraging.

"Does your mother object?" he asked instead, deliberately choosing the banal. "To your being in Manhattan."

"Object? Not at all. Anything that makes it easier for me is okay with them. This will cut out the commute, give me more time for work and study. My parents subsidize everything. Of course, the scholarship helps immensely."

"Can I see you dance someday?" he asked.

"I hope so." She paused. "And you'll give me things of yours to read. You know . . . the real stuff."

A tiny something, he thought. She had struck a personal note. Not quite a breakthrough. Was he making headway? He looked up at her and she lowered her eyes.

"Can we keep in touch?" Ken asked. "I really would like to know you better."

"That would be nice."

"Will I be able to get your number?"

"My mother will have it."

"And will she give it to me?" He stumbled for a moment, trying to come up with the right tone. "I mean, I don't want her to think I mean to be a boyfriend. More like a friend friend."

Carol smiled. "I'll tell her."

Did she mean it? He wished he could convince himself that despite all the caveats, the discipline, the avoidance, a powerful inexorable force was working its will between them. It was, of course, but he didn't know it then.

"Until next time," she told him as they parted, shaking his hand, showing strength in the grip. Nothing frail in that package, he thought then as he watched her walk away.

Next time? He doubted there would be a next time.

*　　*　　*

Not long after that meeting with Carol, he caught the first icy breeze of literary rejection. The story he had sent off to the magazine, "The Other People," had come back refused, but with a scribbled comment on the printed rejection slip: "Find your own voice, Kramer. Hemingway hated poor imitators."

Rejection, Ken told himself, was the fate of all great writers until their moment came. His would come.

After graduation from City College he took a job as a copy boy at the *Daily News*, the four-to-midnight shift, which gave him hours in the daytime to write, and he would not be damaging his style by writing free-lance drivel for two cents a word.

He lived in a studio apartment on Houston Street in Greenwich Village, one square room really, with a tiny fridge and gas stove on a shelf in one corner of the room and a bed in another. Against one wall was a table, which served also as Ken's writing desk, and a single wooden chair. It was a dark basement apartment with wrought-iron bars on the window. The atmosphere was damp and dingy but all he could afford. Nevertheless, he had his electric Smith-Corona and sheaves of stolen copy paper from the *News*. What more did he need to create immortal prose?

Some months had passed since he had met Carol. He had managed, by wheedling charm, to get her number from Mrs. Stein, and discovered that Carol lived on Prince Street, just a few blocks from his Houston Street apartment.

Carol seemed happy to hear from him, although he couldn't be sure. As before, she was polite, noncommittal, and vaguely interested. To him, she seemed always on the cusp of indifference, which disturbed him. Since meeting her, he had found it impossible to get her out of his mind.

"I'm writing now," he told her with all the solemnity of someone taking holy orders.

"That's wonderful," she replied, inquiring no further.

"It's a novel," he volunteered. "A story about a family that lives in Brooklyn. Not the usual cliché of the first novelist discovering himself and the evil that men do. It's about how the death of the mother disintegrates the family." All right, he told himself, it had elements of autobiography, but all novels did. He wished she would probe further. She didn't.

He told her that he was working for the *Daily News*, that he lived just a few blocks from her on Houston Street. After a while, he discovered that she was not really responding. He was merely providing data.

"But enough about me. What about you?"

"A dancer dances," she sighed, but he detected a lack of effervescence.

"You sound tired."

"It's tough, Ken, really tough. There's lots of competition."

"But you are holding your own?"

"Yes. I think so."

"You think you'll make it into the Corps?"

"I've got a chance," she said.

"Maybe I can come over, share some laughs and a pizza. That is, if you're eating these days."

"I'm not laughing much either."

There were long, unfilled pauses that troubled him, but he did not push it.

"So, when can I see you?"

Another long pause, then a sigh.

"I'm not sure, Ken. I'm really busy around the clock. When I get home all I do is fall into bed exhausted."

"Can we set a date? You name the year."

"I'm sorry, Ken."

"How about calling? Dialogue is one of my strong points."

No reaction.

"It would be nice. Yes, let's stay in touch."

It was not a very encouraging prospect.

He thought of her often. In fact, he was thinking about her more than he was thinking about his novel, which seemed to be going in an endless circle. Sometimes, when he got back from work after midnight, he would walk the streets, invariably ending up in front of her apartment house, staring up at what he assumed was her darkened window.

He pictured her sleeping curled in the fetal position, her mind spinning with endless ballet routines, dreaming of herself soaring through the air without the restraints of gravity and the limitations of the body.

To become more knowledgeable about her art, he read a secondhand book about ballet. He learned the difference between an arabesque and a developpé, between an entrechat and a pirouette. And he secretly wished that he could do a tour en l'air to truly impress her.

He listened to records of ballet music, to *Swan Lake, Afternoon of a Faun, Giselle, Pillar of Fire, The Nutcracker*. Although he had a tin ear, repetition allowed some musical memory and he longed for the day when he could impress her with it.

He wished he could inject something of himself into her dreams, something to make her notice him. Pay attention to me, he begged in his heart.

Then he took to walking the city during the day, when he should have been writing. Again and again, he would find himself in front of her apartment. Once he rang her bell, but no one answered. Of course not. She would be at the ballet school. Invariably he would call, but she was rarely at home to answer. When she was, she always seemed rushed, yet was always polite and apologetic.

"Sorry, Ken. But let's stay in touch."

"In touch, yes," he agreed. How he longed for that.

"I passed your apartment today," he told her when she found the time to listen. And the day before and the day before that and so on.

"Did you?"

"I wanted to ring your bell."

"You should have."

"It was noon."

"Oh, then I would be at the school."

"When aren't you?" he asked.

"I'm afraid that's where I spend most of my time."

"Is it going well?" he asked.

"As well as to be expected."

"Sounds ominous."

"No. Very well," she told him, a bit too hurriedly. He was certain that was the way she explained it to her mother.

"Keeps you on your toes," he said, offering a chuckle.

She didn't laugh.

Days crowded into each other. More and more Ken was having difficulty with his novel. He was becoming moody and withdrawn even at work. For the first time in his life, doubt began and took hold. He could not shake it away and it panicked him. Once on his night off, unable to sleep, he called her. But when he heard her muffled sleepy voice, he lost his courage and hung up. He did not want to show her his weakness. Certainly not his doubt.

Then something odd happened. She called him. At first he couldn't believe his ears.

"I've been temporarily shut down," she said.

"I've been shut down for days," he replied.

"Just a sprain. A tough one, though. Usually I can work through them. But this one is a doozy. I'm lying here with my feet up, waiting."

"You're waiting for me, that's what you're waiting for." It was, for him, an act of desperate boldness and he paused for her response.

"Maybe so. I'm starving."

"Well, then, I'd better get you some birdseed."

"Maybe that would be fine. All I can do is hop like a bird. But I sure can use a sandwich." She told him what kind.

He wondered why she hadn't called her mother, then he realized that she wouldn't do that, that, considering her parents' sacrifices to her dream, she wouldn't want to disappoint or frighten them. Their loss was his gain, he supposed.

He filled the order he had been given. Cottage cheese sandwich on whole wheat bread, iced tea, an orange.

The door to Carol's apartment was open. It was small and she had done it up cutesy, with funky pillows and Degas prints of ballet dancers and a poster of Nureyev. There was also a mirror on one side of the living room and the inevitable practice bar.

Carol lay on the couch, reminding him of a broken porcelain doll. Her wrapped ankle was raised on a bolster. As he came in she struggled up on one elbow.

"Look at me. Am I a mess?"

"Not to me."

"Well, I am. I'm out of the student show because of this. I had a pas de deux, too. Dammit."

Her upper lip trembled and she seemed to be struggling to repress a good cry. On his shoulder, he hoped, because when he had seen her as he walked into the room, so sweetly vulnerable and actually spangled by the mirror's reflection, which hyped the sunlight in the room, his heart had jumped clear into his throat.

She was wearing a white leotard, and her legs stretched out along the sofa seemed lathe-shaped to perfection, the good leg

moving in emphasis instead of her hands as she spoke. Occasionally, she would lift it perpendicular, bend it at the knee and
sometimes bring it up to her chest.

"Nature's way of saying slow down. I actually felt it coming," she said, nibbling on her sandwich.

"I'm flattered that you called me," he said sincerely.

"You were available," she responded mischievously, her eyes
teasing. Under all the intensity and dedication, he finally saw a
playful streak. "But I've interrupted your writing."

"For you, always," he joked. But the fact was that Ken
was still bumping into obstacles. Not faced with the blank paper
of his Smith-Corona but only the fluid wonders of his mind, his
story soared, characters infused with insight moved through
miraculous complications. They laughed and cried and loved
and suffered. But the soaring ceased after a half page's typing.
It wasn't writer's block exactly, more like a fear of flying.
Carol's call came as sweet balm. Seeing her, he truly believed,
would replenish him, set the fictional world in his head going
again.

"If I called, would you have stopped in the middle of a pirouette?" he asked.

"What? And sprain my other ankle?"

She lifted her leg again as if that were the way she expressed
real laughter, stretched it out, and touched his shoulder. He lifted
his hand and touched her ankle. It was his first caress. Let us
keep in touch, he told himself, hoping she might hear.

They talked through the afternoon. Mostly he remembered
how the light had changed on her face, which went from ivory to
pink alabaster in the lowering winter sun. By the time he left, he
had surrendered to the certainty of knowing he loved her, had
always loved her, would always love her.

At that point the memory compressed, abiding by the
mind's real time, which was not chronological. She had vowed
"no dating" and they hadn't, but they managed to "see each
other." She was, of course, less a master of her time than he.

Nonetheless, after that first reunion when he sat with her
beside the couch, he felt himself back on track again. His characters resurrected themselves. His imagination resumed its acro-
batic intensity, his story moved forward, and the stack of neatly

typed, completed pages mounted. He could barely remember the story now, although then it was biblical in importance, especially the great death scene, the mother's dying. The son was reading Proust to her.

Carol was on her back for a week, and he took full advantage of the opportunity. He made himself indispensable, bringing her meals, cleaning the apartment, offering conversation, and generally keeping her from boredom.

"You've been great, Ken," she told him. "I don't know what I would have done without you."

She hadn't told her parents about her injury, explaining that it would have panicked them.

"Everything's going great guns, Mother," she told Mrs. Stein, sometimes in his presence. Invariably when she hung up, she felt guilty.

"It's just a temporary thing. You haven't let them down," Ken admonished her. "You couldn't help yourself."

"Any letup, whether it's my fault or not, lets them down."

"Why do you flog yourself over it?"

Slowly, he sensed that their intimacy had grown, not that it was obvious. He scrupulously eschewed any hint that there was more here than friendship, certainly not at first. Then, suddenly, he got a reaction.

She had been lying in bed, her foot on the bolster, watching her image on the mirrored wall. He was sitting on a chair near the bed. Outside it was raining.

"You still think I'm beautiful, Ken?" she had asked.

"You remembered."

"Of course I remembered. I'm a performer. You can't accuse me of having no vanity."

"No," he replied. "I won't accuse you of that. But I can make quite a case for indifference."

She thought about that for a while.

"I'm afraid you can," she agreed. "It's not really indifference. It's a matter of focus. I wear blinders."

"Always?"

"I'm not sure."

"Would it be imposing if I asked you take them off around me?" It seemed as if he had been waiting for this moment since he had first laid eyes on her. "I want you to see me."

"I see you." She seemed puzzled.

"I mean really see me," he told her, moving toward the bed. He sat beside her and looked deeply into her eyes. "Like I see you."

"I do see you."

"Do you see what I feel?"

"Maybe," she said.

He bent closer to her, pressed his lips on hers, held them there for a long moment, and then increased the pressure. Her lips parted and he prolonged the kiss. He felt his heart pounding against his chest.

"I adore you," he said. He had wanted to say "love," but held back. What he wanted most was her to feel the same way about him. Was it possible to will her to feel that? Love me, he begged. Love me.

Then he kissed her again. And again. After a while she turned her head away and a tear crept out of her eye and flowed down her cheek.

"What's that for?" he asked.

"I'm afraid," she said.

He didn't pursue it, since he suspected what she feared most. Instead he said, "What's wrong with being human?"

"More than you think," she said. He puzzled over that answer for days.

So they had kissed and he did not press her further. Understanding her fear, he did not want to panic her.

After a week she was reasonably recovered and returned to her classes. Then began another round of unavailability, although he had grown bolder about calling her late in the evening. It was, he knew, cruel work. At that hour of the day she was at low ebb, on the cusp of exhaustion.

"It's tough going, Ken," she told him. "I'm having trouble catching up."

"You will."

"I'm trying as hard as I can."

"I know."

She was totally self-absorbed. Not selfish, exactly, but completely directed. There was nothing to be done but to encourage her, show support, cheer her on.

"And you?"

It always surprised him to hear her concern and he always wondered if she was sincere.

"I think about you all the time, Carol."

"I mean your work."

For some reason it had turned around. Things were moving again. Perhaps her sense of focus and commitment had inspired him. Of course, he wanted more. He wanted Carol, yearned for her. Make her love me, he cried, invoking unseen forces. Is there a limit to longing? he wondered.

At some point, always after a frenzy of writing activity, Ken took to hanging out around the ballet school, peering through a window in the studio door, watching Carol at the bar or being instructed on the floor with the others, delicate dancing-girl dolls and sinewy boy dolls made of rip cord. She wore those mid-calf warm-up stockings on her precious legs and he was certain she was the standout. On her toes she seemed the tallest of the group.

One night, he admitted to her his clandestine spying.

"That's awful," she said.

"Awful?"

"You're seeing me klutzy, with all those imperfections. Now you'll only make me more nervous and unsure."

"Imperfections? That's not what I saw."

"Besides, I'm the tallest and it's not an advantage. On pointe we can't look taller than our partners."

"I did notice that. The men looked small."

"Too small," she muttered. "That can hurt."

"Well, I thought you were great."

"You don't understand. You only see form and style. Whipping and willing the body to move against nature is a terrible struggle. That's the battle a ballet dancer must win to be truly great. The teacher sees the tiniest imperfection as a defeat."

"Well, I don't see that," he protested.

"You wouldn't. You're not a dancer."

Of course he saw it, saw it then, saw it now. The artist's struggle was universal. But so was the struggle of the lover for the loved one. Not that he had gone from the future immortal of the pen to a smitten Romeo. His creative zeal was still furious, more furious than ever now that he was resisting the distraction of her. He pounded away at his story, the novel that would launch him to the world.

Yet this obsession for Carol was a test of his capacity for accepting anxiety. Unrequited love enabled him but did not empower him. Inspiration came in fits and starts. Sometimes it did not come at all. When that happened, he tried to empty his mind of her, force forgetfulness, obliterate all images of her likeness, her sounds, the erotic pull of her. His entire being yearned for her. Desire plagued him, mocked him. It was like he was a swimmer fighting against a powerful riptide.

He knew exactly what she felt, this need to protect her single-mindedness, to husband her obsession. Of course he worried that sooner or later these powerful feelings would completely inhibit his concentration, torpedo his creativity, dampen his imagination. At times it became, in his overheated and youthful mind, a matter of life or death.

At the same time, he was besieged by the idea that Carol could never love him, certainly never love him more than ballet, more than her ambition to excel, more than her thirst for immortality or notoriety or celebrity, all those secret compulsions that he, too, knew so well.

None of this stopped him from pursuing her. Others had both love and fulfillment. Why not he? She would enhance his creativity, wouldn't she? Wasn't there stability in satisfying desire?

Yet he still feared pressing her, appearing on her doorstep without notice. His pursuit could not be without calculation. Most of all, he feared that heavy-handedness would turn her off completely. Above all, he told himself, he must keep hope alive. At times, when it was impossible to write his novel, he would write to her instead, long agonizing letters of longing, pouring out his love, his needs, his fears, the terrible pain of separation. Of course, he never mailed them. She'd think he had gone mad.

But there was still the telephone. He called it his weapon of necessity. It was the era before answering machines and it was frustrating to hear its ring without a response. Sometimes he would spend ten minutes just listening to it ring. When she did answer, the conversation was always polite, predictable, and noncommittal. He had the impression that even his phone calls were an intrusion on her time.

"Let me come up," he would say.

"No. Please."

"You've got to rest, Carol, stand back, contemplate."

"I'm not improving, Ken," she admitted.

"You're trying too hard."

"There's no other way."

More and more she seemed anguished, depressed. He, too, had come to a crossroads. New snags had developed. The burst of inspiration had faltered. The muse was being stubborn. His characters were exhibiting a crisis of nonaction, were bored with interacting. He knew why. She was dominating his life.

"Let me comfort you, Carol. Please." And myself, he thought.

"It won't help."

"Yes, it will."

She seemed overwrought and fearful. By then he had learned that nervous breakdowns were common to ballet dancers.

One night she called him. "Come quick, Ken. Please."

He was surprised by her appearance. Her complexion was ashen, and her eyes seemed to have sunken behind her cheeks. She looked unhealthy. When she saw him, she burst into tears. Was it for love or solace? At twenty-one the distinctions were blurry. It was enough that she was in his arms.

"I wasn't picked," she sobbed, blurting out the travails of her rejection. For her it was a catastrophe. And yet, when she finally explained it, it seemed only a small setback. One out of a dozen in the student ballet corps had been picked for a solo.

"There's always a next time," he said, hoping to be comforting.

"Don't you understand, Ken? I can't catch up."

He saw in this sudden revelation a glimpse of her vulnerability. He felt her pain and disappointment but also saw it as an opening for him, a way into her heart. She needed his love, he decided. His love would comfort her, inspire her. It was time to act.

Up to then, out of fear, he had hidden his true feelings. Hadn't she made it clear that there was no room in her life for anything but dance? Such a position had its logic and its truth. But so did love.

She was in his arms and he was caressing her, brotherly at first. And then he kissed her deeply and she responded.

"Let me love you," he whispered.

"Love me?"

She had stiffened for a moment, then continued to cling to him.

"You need me to love you," he said. "Let me love you."

They kissed again, deeper than before. Her body seemed to melt against him.

"Everything will happen the way you want it," he told her. "I promise you."

She sighed but said nothing. His body's reaction was unmistakable and he felt her hips rotating against his erection. It surprised him and he began to caress her tight buttocks. Then she stopped suddenly and tried to sit up. He continued to hold her.

"Be human, Carol," he whispered. "We're not machines. You can't just live in one dimension."

"I'm afraid," she told him, yielding again, bringing her body beside him. He brought her hand to his lips, kissed her fingers.

"Of me?" he asked.

"Of me," she whispered. But her response seemed to trigger something inside her. She became more ardent, more aggressive, reaching for him, exploring. Her breath came in tiny gasps.

"Maybe I need to know I'm a woman, Ken," she said.

He remembered his surprise. And elation. He had carried the details of that moment for more than twenty years, the sights and sounds, the emotion. In his memory, it had always defined the meaning of joy.

She wanted to see and be seen, insisting on light. To reach her apartment, he had run through rain. It had stopped and an orange setting sun had appeared like a giant pumpkin peeking over the skyscrapers. Walking to the windows, slowly removing her clothes as she moved, she had raised the shades to ceiling height and a golden glow had filled the room.

Her tight dancer's body approached him, her skin like burnished velvet. Getting off the bed, he stepped toward her, exhibiting himself. Her eyes lingered, studying him. They circled each other before touching again and she stood on her toes when they embraced. It seemed like a ritual, a dance.

"We mustn't forget this," she told him.

"Never."

She was made unlike any woman he had seen before or since. That spot was like a pink tea rose embedded in the center of her. Around it was the same smooth marble of her flesh. Yet the petals opened to moisture like rain on the flesh of any blooming flower.

Even the difficulty of penetration did not destroy the poetry. At first he had thought that the fit was not possible, but she had urged him on as if it were absolutely necessary. Fitting, she had said, half-joking. It was fitting.

"I'll hurt you," he protested, holding back.

"Of course you will," she told him, grasping him, guiding him, bringing herself forward to the force of her upward thrust.

Miraculously, the petals had opened and he had entered her. He supposed she had experienced pain, but she did not cry out. He remembered that their eyes had met and hers had filled with tears and he had licked them off her cheeks.

"Am I a woman now?" she had asked.

"The woman I love."

"Is it lovely, really lovely?"

"It is now."

It was odd to this day, how preserved in his mind was this romantic intensity, the melding of body and soul. What surprised him most was the way she took pleasure in it. He had fantasized about this moment for months, and having achieved it had surpassed his wildest expectations.

What he had not expected was its ferocity.

Their world became totally circumscribed. Had it been gradual, a slow peeling away of other interests, other obsessions? Or had it come about like an instant explosion, an all-enveloping eruption, obliterating everything, destroying all extraneous distractions except themselves?

Things outside their orbit became blurred, incomprehensible details. It was bottomless between them, insatiable, an onslaught of nature.

Everything surrendered to its power. In his memory, he could not find a single detail during that period of the banality of survival. Did they shop for food, cook, clean? Did they wash their clothes? Did they perform even the most routine ablutions? Did they shower or brush their teeth? There was simply no record of any of that in his brain.

In memory, they made love. Made love around the clock, against every available surface of his basement room or her apartment, or anyplace else that was convenient, and in every configuration capable by the limited bendings and foldings of the human body. It was an endless orgasm, a continuous shudder of ecstasy, an eruption of limitless desire.

And yet, they rationalized this fury by referring to it as "a time out." Perhaps he had tried to go back to his novel. He couldn't remember. Did she return to her ballet classes?

He recalled walks down city streets, lying in the sun in Washington Square Park, trips to the zoo, lazy meanderings on sunny spring days. In his memory it was merely background, props. The real interaction was between them.

The bar in her room would have been a constant reminder of her neglected responsibilities. His typewriter, too, would provide physical evidence of his own banishment of ambition.

Naturally, there were flurries of guilt, triggering an attempt to get back on the old track. Once he awoke to find her working out on the bar. His reaction was surprising. He felt jealousy.

"I've got to get back to it," she told him when she realized he was watching.

"You will," he muttered.

She had stopped suddenly and turned toward him.

"And your writing."

"First things first," he said, getting out of bed, moving toward her. They had learned how to deflect obsessions.

Her mother's calls, sporadic at first, grew more intense and pleading. So far, she had placated her mother with a battery of evasions and outright lies.

"She's called the school," Carol told him one day.

"It was bound to come."

"I feel awful about it. Like I've betrayed them."

"It's a matter of priorities," he had told her, trying to appear reasonable, knowing there was no reason in it at all.

They did make attempts at rationality.

"All right, we love each other," she would tell him on occasion. "But does that mean that everything has to stop?"

"Of course not," he agreed.

"Not everything is the present. There has got to be a future."

"I agree."

But rational attempts went nowhere. No sooner had they talked reason than they were rutting again, making love always, everywhere, all motivation concentrated on themselves.

Weeks went by. Joyous weeks. Time had lost all meaning. He gave up his job, which forced him into another reality. He had saved some money, but not much, and when that ran out he'd have to find a job out of necessity. Carol was still able to rely on her parents' monthly check to supplement her scholarship. There was guilt over that as well. More and more she would burst into tears without warning.

They both seemed to be waiting for reality to assert itself. They began to argue.

"I thought you said we could have both," Carol told him. "Why must I give up my dreams?"

"Who told you to do that?"

"Well, I have. So have you."

"We'll both get back to it."

"When?"

"Soon."

"It's not fair. Not fair to my folks. Not fair to me."

"Have I stopped you?"

"Yes."

Reality exploded one day. Carol's mother showed up at her apartment, her finger on the buzzer, insistent. Perhaps it was her timing. They were, as they say, in flagrante delicto, at the very height of passion on the far edge of orgasm.

"I know you're there, Carol," she cried. "Don't try to fool me."

They were beyond stopping, letting it happen as her mother's voice offered a grating background of unwanted noise.

"And I know what you're doing in there," Mrs. Stein cried.

"She does?" Ken said, trying to force humor. It didn't fly. Carol was panicked. The blood drained from her face. She cowered naked in a corner of the bed, unable to act.

"Open up this minute," the woman screamed.

"What shall I do?" Carol pleaded.

"Open the door," Ken advised. "Tell her the truth."

"I can't."

She started to cry.

"I know you're there, darling. Please. If you're in some kind of trouble, I'm here for you."

"She's fine, Mrs. Stein," Ken said suddenly. He helped Carol get into her robe and quickly put on his shirt and jeans. "Tell her you're fine."

"I'm fine, Mama," Carol said.

Mrs. Stein's response was to bang on the door. After a while Ken opened it. Mrs. Stein's face was livid with rage, but then Carol ran into her arms and both women began to sob.

Of course, he felt bad for both of them. Also useless, a third wheel. He excused himself and went out for a walk. He must have walked for hours contemplating what was going to happen, what had to happen. Their lives were obviously out of balance. He went back to his apartment and spent the next few hours reading his novel, trying to stoke the fires of his imagination. The characters had become strangers. The story seemed juvenile, the dialogue trite. It was then that he knew it had to end. For both their sakes.

That night, when he returned to her apartment, they both knew it.

"We can't do anything halfway, Ken," she explained. "That's the problem. Everything has to be full throttle, all out."

"Maybe after we've made it . . ." he began.

"When the pressure is off."

Is it ever off? he wondered, thinking suddenly of the struggle that lay ahead. It was his first realization that success was not assured, that the dream was, at best, a mighty gamble with the odds stacked against you. The old obsession came flooding back into his sinews. A writer writes. A dancer dances.

"I wish it didn't make so much sense."

"Would we want to look back and one day say to each other: 'We threw it away because we loved each other too much'?"

"And after," he told her, "I'm coming back to claim my prize."

"You'd better," she laughed.

"I'll be your permanent stage-door Johnny."

"And I'll be your severest critic."

How long had this addiction persisted? He would never be able to fix it exactly. Two months. Maybe three. Years later it had lost all context, like an aberration, an episode of madness, a fire-cracker that had disappeared as quickly as it flamed.

They parted after a week or so of monumental intensity, sex prodded by the impending loss of one's love object. There was nothing for it except to empty themselves, to reach the outer lim-its of their physical and emotional resources. They made love as before, around the clock, excited by tears and vows, determined to leave nothing for anyone who might come after, no experience that could be superceded by what they did together.

Such energy had to be redirected. They would put their love-making into their art, reach heights beyond imagination, then re-turn to the source of it all, to each other, the one true love for each.

Well, he sighed now, staring laconically at the sticky-looking lukewarm pasta, they had had the absolute peak experience, the highest of highs. Good sense had prevailed, he supposed. In his memory the ending was abrupt, like taking a single step off a sheer cliff.

The dessert routine snapped him into present tense and he listened and watched Eliot and Carol interrogate the waiter on his various offerings, displayed on a cart. The waiter offered a running commentary as he pointed to each concoction.

"Majolalaine with raspberry sauce; walnut cranberry tart with orange caramel sauce; the crème brûlée." On and on. Ken could barely look at them.

"Oh, the crème brûlée," Eliot said. "Can't be too sweet. Are you sure it's not?"

"Some palates are different," the waiter said.

"And the tart?" Maggie said. "Looks scrumptious. We could share," she said coquettishly. She looked toward Ken. "My hus-band hasn't got much of a sweet tooth."

"Not Carol's cup of tea either," Eliot said.

"Ken likes berries, though," Maggie said, pointing to the raspberries.

"Not tonight, Maggie," Ken said. He had hardly touched his pasta. There was more discussion and the dessert was finally or-dered, with Maggie and Eliot opting for café au lait and he and Carol ordering ordinary decaf coffee.

By then, panic had mellowed to reflection. He had passed

through the one moment that he had dreaded for more than two decades. In an odd way it was a miracle. Sometimes people who had grown up together in New York and stayed to live there could go their entire lives without ever seeing each other again.

Ken looked at his watch. The meal was drawing to a close and still she had not acknowledged him. Nor had he acknowledged her. Because it was deliberate on his part, he assumed it was deliberate on hers. Nor did he wish to blow her cover. For whatever reasons she had chosen to lie to her husband, he had respected them, had allied himself with her in her subterfuge. Surely, she would appreciate that.

And yet, why had he suddenly groped in his rear pocket and extracted a card from his card case, palming it in his left hand? A harmless reflex, he decided. Perhaps, if he gave it to her, it would be a reminder, a symbolic gesture of their conspiratorial collaboration. Or, if she hadn't remembered, it might jog her recollection.

He would not call her, he promised himself. He hadn't tried in twenty years. Not that he hadn't wanted to. It was no small feat to suppress his urge for her, but time had repressed it finally, then he had met Maggie. For a long time he had believed that the past could be buried.

Until now.

After dinner, they wrapped themselves in rain gear against the storm which had diminished to a light drizzling dampness. Under umbrellas in front of the restaurant they said a final goodbye. Only it wasn't really final.

"We'll do this again, Eliot and Carol," Maggie chirped. Eliot kissed her cheek; she held out her hand to Carol.

"It was lovely," Carol said.

"See you in the morning, Maggie," Eliot reminded her. "Promptly at nine."

"The man's a slave driver," Maggie laughed. She looked toward Carol. "We must do this again."

"Absolutely," Eliot said, obviously speaking for both of them.

This was not the end of anything, Ken observed, gripping Eliot's hand in farewell. Then he turned toward Carol. Nothing. Not the tiniest hint that she had ever known him.

Two can play that game, he decided, but he did not turn

away. Not yet. He had moved the card into his right palm, then, reaching out, their hands joined.

"So very nice to meet you," he said. She squeezed his hand lightly and the card passed, but her face revealed nothing. She had turned away quickly. He watched Eliot and Carol dash into the street to flag a passing cab. Then they were gone.

"Weren't they wonderful?" Maggie said. "I told you the evening would be interesting." Ken turned to look at her. Everyone to their own truth.

"Very," he said.

3

THEY WEREN'T big lies, Carol thought, merely a series of little ones. So she had pared her age by nine years. What did it matter? She could have passed for an even younger age. Why not? It had taken hard work to maintain such an illusion. As for her other vital statistics, she had embellished her past achievements to give Eliot the satisfaction of having married a woman of some accomplishment, a traveled, broadened woman. Where was the harm in that?

Of course, Ken knew that she was lying. But she had every right, she told herself. He had no business disturbing her tranquillity, no business appearing from nowhere like a burglar. The fates had conspired against her. How was she to know that this woman, this Maggie whatever, was the wife of Ken Kramer.

Surely he understood, had sized things up, gone along with this re-creation of herself. She supposed she owed him her gratitude for remaining silent, perhaps even an explanation. Dare she open that compartment of her life again?

Why all this turmoil about self-justification? False pretenses were, after all, a strategy for . . . if not survival . . . upward mobility. Economics! It had all come down to economics.

To snare Eliot, the Yalie blue blood whose father was a member of the Society of Cincinnatians, descendants of officers in George Washington's army, whose mother was an active committed member of the DAR, had required a pedigree of achievement, if only to catch his initial attention.

She hadn't realized that such a contrived cultural lineage could be so smoothly institutionalized into a system of beliefs. Eliot doted on her "accomplishments." Nor had he required press clippings. To inquire would have been, in his view, slightly vulgar.

Ballet, from the time of the Medicis, was an amusement of aristocrats, a refinement of the culturally sophisticated with great snob appeal for the rich. Her contrivance was right on target and he was quick to accept it hook, line, and sinker. It validated his choice of her as his wife, made her a kind of trophy.

She could even delude herself into believing that she had been, really, a ballet star in Sydney, Australia. With that background, teaching had status. She was the ballet master imparting the wisdom of her acclaimed experience. And how far was Le Roc from Stein, which meant *stone* in German? And the little royal prefix had its own cachet in Eliot's world, with its clear implication of royal ancestry. Life had taught her the value of such a provenance.

One might say that her meeting Eliot was more coincidence than calculation, although when the opportunity had arisen to embroider the truth she had certainly been quick to respond. She had met him in the most prosaic way—in the City Center watching a performance of the Ballet Russe de Monte Carlo.

Until that moment ballet had not been overly kind to her. Considering her early dedication to it and the years of her life thrown away on its behalf, it had been, well, a catastrophe.

Until Eliot.

She had come up from Philadelphia for the performance, the single ticket being a "gift" from Miss Perkins, who ran the Ardmore School of Dance on the Philadelphia Main Line. Carol knew it would hardly qualify as a gift, since the frugal Miss Perkins was sure to include it in lieu of cash as part of her two weeks' severance.

Not that Carol was being fired. It was early May and the end of the school year was fast approaching. By then Carol had experienced eight years of ending dance-school years. What, after all, was a failed ballet dancer qualified to do? Or, for that matter, even a successful ballet dancer?

In August she would once again send out résumés to dance schools everywhere. If anything, she had mastered the art of the résumé and her credentials were quite impressive, including one year at the Paris School of Ballet where she had been, her résumé validated, a teacher. In fact, she had been only an assistant, but the tiny white lie had carried her halfway around the world, to Australia, Japan, and Guam, of all places, where she had actually been in charge for two years.

She no longer brooded over her lost career. The truth of it was that she had never really had one. Economics was her priority now. How to survive on an itinerant dancing teacher's wages had been the mission of her last eight years.

Yet she had made do with ambition and aspiration. Her mother, to the day she died, had blamed it all on that writer fellow. Poor dear woman. Carol's failure had been her ruination, yet nothing could convince her that Ken Kramer hadn't ruined her daughter's career. If she had lived she might have spread the blame around.

There had been other men. Not many. But enough to have provided her with the possibilities of marriage, although she never gave herself the chance to explore them beyond a certain point. After Ken, she had deliberately hidden behind a psychological armor plate of her own invention. Discovering her vulnerability had frightened her, and the habit of discipline had protected her from herself, from unproductive distractions. That was before the dawning of greater truths, that there was life after failure and that not all relationships with men required emotional upheaval or sexual frenzy.

One could find lots of excuses for her failed career, she supposed. That was the year the men were too short and she was too tall. Or she was too eager, which had caused her to suffer injuries. She had had to dance through pain frequently. That was it. Her technique was superb, but her body not quite up to par.

Carol blamed no one but herself. She wasn't good enough. Oh, she was dedicated, single-minded, focused. Just not as good as the others who were picked. That was the only way to live with it, face up to it. It was pointless to flog yourself forever.

She had tried her hand at the musical stage, and for a year or two had made it into a number of road shows. She had actually toured in *Fiddler on the Roof* for six months and did play in *A Chorus Line* in Atlanta, Georgia. Not as a regular. She had been called in when other dancers suffered injuries.

The strange fact was that she had never lost her drive or her ambition. Even when she had failed at ballet and was teaching, she was pursuing dancing auditions as if her life depended on it, saving all her energy for the possibilities of her career. Unfortunately, by twenty-five she knew it was over. Her parents had died, which may have had something to do with it. She hadn't married and she was broke.

But she could count at least one blessing. She had acquired the habit of bodily discipline. Not a day went by when she didn't work out, keeping her body youthful and tight. It was the habit of years. A Spartan diet and plenty of exercise. Whenever she could, she exercised at the bar. Her legs were still good, her figure shapely and firm. She had been thirty when she had met Eliot. Even then she looked at least ten years younger.

They had been watching *Orpheus*, Stravinsky's ballet about Orpheus charming the god of the Dead to let him into Hades in order to bring back to Earth his beloved wife, Eurydice. Orpheus had promised not to look at her until they had reached Earth again, then broke the promise, thereby sending Eurydice back to Hades.

"Quite good, don't you think?" Eliot had said when the performance was over. They were, after all, strangers sitting together by the accident of seating. His words, spoken more to himself than to her, could hardly be construed as a flirtation. She had noted that he was well groomed and distinguished-looking, with gray sideburns, craggy features, and steel-blue eyes. Her response seemed at the time merely a reflex. Later she would recognize it as the fateful moment that changed the course of her life.

"I've seen better," she had replied, adding quickly, "but I did like the vision of Hades. All that lashing and forced labor."

They were moving out of the seating row. He did not speak until they had reached the exit aisle.

"Yes. Hades. If it was my wife I would have left her in Hades where she belonged." He turned to look at her suddenly. "My ex-wife, that is."

She absorbed the information with an odd sense of inner goading, as if an antenna in her head had picked up distant signals.

"I prefer his *Firebird*. I'm a sucker for happy endings."

"My God, was that wonderful," Eliot said as they trooped up the aisle to the lobby. "I saw Tallchief do it. Chagall did the scenery and costumes. Balanchine choreographed. Stravinsky used the old Russian legend about a stupid prince who triumphs over more clever foes." He continued as they drifted together out of the hall, telling her the full story of that particular performance. Francisco Moncion as Prince Ivan, "dashing and wonderfully stupid," Tallchief was "in her zenith."

She was, of course, impressed by his knowledge, but was unprepared for his verbosity. He seemed to revel in providing her with everything down to the last detail without seeming to draw a breath. Finally, as they walked down the block, he stopped and looked at her pointedly. "I'm talking of the early sixties. But, then, you're much too young to have seen that particular performance."

Young? It was a feedback of his impression of her. Yes, young, she thought. She certainly would not deprive him of that illusion.

"You have a remarkable memory," she told him, certainly honest and well-placed flattery.

"A curse and a blessing," he replied with a kind of charming arrogance, as if the compliment were an obvious tribute. She could see he was pleased.

"Is ballet a hobby?" she asked.

"One of many, I'm afraid. I'm a practicing generalist."

She wasn't quite certain what that meant, and didn't respond. He seemed to take it as a signal to continue to explain himself.

"Although I do have some specialties. Like the planet and its preservation." This set him off on a compressed dissertation on the warming of the planet and the ecological disaster ahead.

An intellectual, she decided. A bit talky, but entertainingly so. Concentrating on her attitude, she hoped she looked responsive, searching herself for some operative mode of behavior, deciding finally on deference. She listened, and the more carefully she appeared to be listening, the more expansive he became.

It was a pleasant spring evening, and when they approached Fifth, they headed toward the Sixties.

"We seem to be going in the same direction," he said with an air of Old World gallantry. "Do you live on Fifth?" he asked.

"Madison," she said quickly. It would be the first of many tangible lies employed in the reinvention of herself. A test, really. She had wondered how far she should go. Thankfully, he didn't ask for a specific address on Madison. Actually, she had booked a room at the Twenty-third Street YWCA.

"And you?" she had asked.

"Would you believe I've lived on Fifth all my life, in the very same apartment in which I grew up. With Mother and Father gone now, alas, it's become a family heirloom."

She supposed it was the way he had said "Mother and Father," the intonation and the nasality of it, redolent of a certain way of life and station. Old money! Her nostrils twitched as if she were sniffing it.

Later she would determine that she must have been laying down a scent. They had stopped at the Sherry-Netherland's bar. Why not, she remembered thinking when he had invited her in.

Deference had turned out to be a lucky call. Apparently, he needed an audience, needed a good listener. For her part, she sifted through his words for information. In her former incarnation, her life up until then, she had not been exposed to such a type. Moneyed. Upper crust. With the economic freedom to pursue his inclinations and intellectual hobbies. Clearly this was an opportunity.

He did not turn the floodlight on her until the end of the evening. By then she had decided on her role, had toted up her assets and liabilities and rearranged the balance sheet in her mind.

Dance the ballet in your head, she urged herself. Show him the illusion. She was twenty-one, she volunteered with subtlety. Ten years lopped off. Ballet had been her life and her living. The Ballet Company of Sydney. The star, of course. She cut short her fictional career with an injury. A tradition in the family. She invoked a long line of Le Rocs. Her father was a viscount, but never could bring himself to use the title. Not America. A branch line used it in Paris.

She could see the equivalent of a standing ovation flashing

in his eyes. He was buying it, mesmerized. And all the time she
was dishing it out, she was thinking: Enough of being alone,
enough of a third-rate life, of furnished rooms, fast-food dinners,
balcony seats, secondhand cars, recycled clothing, bus and sub-
way travel. Enough of dead dreams. This was one dance in which
she would defy gravity.

All right, so she had pushed fate a bit. Because it was there,
the mountain climber would say to explain his passion to ascend.
Eliot was there, a goal and a challenge.

Analyzing it later, after she had brought Eliot to bay, wore
his marriage ring, and shared, as they say, his bed and board, she
attributed this achievement to the lessons learned from her
failure. She had molded herself, like Eve, from Adam's rib, to become what he desired, what he expected.

Not once had she wavered from her original purpose, which
was essentially financial security and creature comforts. She approached it as a role in a ballet, in full costume, listening carefully to the music until it became second nature. Deference was
the theme. Devotion the subtext. She was the good and faithful
wife of his imagination.

Eliot's first wife had been the traditional choice, a product
of matched breeding with little interest in anything but horse-
manship, yachting, tennis, and cocktails. And no interest in
Eliot's intellectual passions and causes, none whatsoever. Nor, in
the end, did she have any interest in the two children they had
bred.

Whatever had to be done, Carol did. She was the avid listener, the charming companion, the passionate lover, the giving
friend. For her, it would always be "On with the show." Catering
to his contentment was not without effort. Eliot Butterfield, notwithstanding his efforts to "make the world a better place," was
a committed snob. And yet there were moments of wilting beneath the makeup.

The strain of deception was sometimes exhausting. The pattern of lies had to be preserved. He was forty-two when he married her and assumed he was twenty years older than she. "My
child-bride," he often told others. This meant elaborate subterfuge, falsifying documents, monitoring the mail, managing her
past.

There was physical subterfuge as well, feigning sexual passion, showing interest as basic as faking her climaxes. She had, after all, the memory of her experiences with Ken Kramer to draw from. That had been the zenith of her sex life. After him her body had gone into a kind of sexual paralysis. Not that Eliot was an unattractive man. It helped, but never to the point of pleasure for her.

The old habit of discipline served her well. Perhaps, one day in the future, she might be secure enough to tell him the truth, that she had invented herself for his pleasure and comfort. And her own. She hoped he would pat her on the cheek and laugh and they would go on to live happily ever after.

She had made it her business to learn Eliot's moods, his needs, his eccentricities, and she tried to do her job accordingly. Just another discipline, she assured herself. Maybe it was against nature, like ballet, but as long as she showed the ease of grace and balance, how could he suspect? She was, after all, giving him good value.

She had also succeeded in making a good impression on his children, who, thankfully, would spend most of their time at schools in Switzerland or with their mother.

There were, of course, revelations and disappointments. The rich, she had discovered, were very adept at preserving their fortunes. Eliot Butterfield was no exception. Accountants and lawyers were good buffers and could fashion hundreds of ways to prevent a fortune hunter from taking advantage of a situation.

She had been baffled by the prenuptial agreement put in front of her in his lawyer's office on the eve of their wedding.

"It protects everyone," Eliot's lawyer had explained. Reading it, she had been surprised at the language and had difficulty pretending indifference.

The document indicated that in the event of Eliot's death she would inherit everything that was acquired in her name exclusively, such as gifts, artwork, antiques, and real estate, during the lifetime of the marriage. The rest was tied up in family trusts for the benefit of Eliot's children. But if the marriage ended because of her adultery, she would get nothing.

"My adultery!" she cried. She had turned toward Eliot. "Really, Eliot." He shrugged and made no comment.

"A standard protective device," the lawyer told her. "We have to cover every contingency." He was a small man with tiny hands and wore rimless glasses and a pin-striped suit with a polka-dot bow tie on a white shirt. "Especially in the light of Mr. Butterfield's first divorce."

"It's unthinkable," she said indignantly. "That I would ever . . ."

"I know, darling. It's all pro forma nonsense."

"But it also holds true if Mr. Butterfield ends the marriage on the grounds of his adultery," the lawyer pointed out. "In that case, it would be he who forfeits any rights to any property you had acquired during the life of the marriage."

"I insisted on that. It's only fair." Eliot laughed, squeezed her hand, and kissed her cheek. "A completely farfetched premise. This marriage is for keeps."

"And if the marriage ends on other grounds?" she asked the lawyer, trying to make the question sound facetious.

"At your instigation?" the lawyer asked seriously.

She nodded.

"You would get five thousand dollars a year for five years," the lawyer said, pointing out the language in the document. "And, of course, give up all rights to the articles."

The lawyer paused and looked at Eliot, then continued.

"And if Mr. Butterfield instigates the divorce, you would still get the stipend . . . and"—he cleared his throat—"the inheritance right to the articles providing you do not marry before Mr. Butterfield's demise."

"It's all so complicated," she had sighed.

"We don't intend it to end on any grounds," Eliot said. "Do we, darling?"

But the lawyer was still in the middle of his explanation.

"Mr. Butterfield has chosen"—again the lawyer cleared his throat, and it was clear that he was about to say something that he disagreed with—"to provide you with this inheritance even if he remarries. Indeed, he has the use of these articles, but cannot dispose of them in any way."

It struck her as oddly generous, though in a backhanded way, and she did not dispute it. There would be no point. She hoped none of these eventualities ever came to pass. But she did understand the reasoning behind the agreement. The rich knew how to hold on to their money and their possessions. They were simply closing any loopholes for transferring assets with sinister intent.

"One would think I'm a fortune hunter," Carol had commented, turning indignantly to the lawyer. "Haven't you ever heard of a love match?"

"Many times."

"Don't expect a lawyer to understand feelings," Eliot sighed.

"Of course Mr. Butterfield can choose to change the rules as time goes on, and with your consent," the lawyer said. Carol was growing impatient with the discussion, but the lawyer droned on.

"There is one other item to be considered," the lawyer said with a cryptic glance toward Eliot, who, Carol noted, had nodded for him to continue. He cleared his throat. "The issue of children."

"Children?" It puzzled her. She had already met Eliot's two children by his first marriage. "You mean about their trusts. Eliot has informed me about that. Of course, they should be adequately provided for."

"He means our children," Eliot said, avoiding her eyes.

It had been the one overriding fear of her deception. She was on the cusp of child-bearing age, but she had no desire for them, not only on the grounds of personal danger and the possible ruination of her figure. She had absolutely no wish to be a mother. Nor had the issue ever come up in their discussions, largely, she thought, due to her deliberate evasions.

Her reaction was to scan the agreement to determine whether she had missed something.

"It's not in the document," the lawyer said.

"I've had a vasectomy, Carol," Eliot said. He was obviously apologetic. Her first reaction was enormous relief, which she hid under a façade of contrived regret. "I was still married to Helen," he explained. "It wouldn't do to have more children."

It surprised her that he would have chosen this moment and, of all places, his lawyer's office for his confession. It had been entirely unexpected, which both disturbed and alerted her. So Eliot, too, had his little deceptions and agendas.

"We already have two children, Eliot," Carol said solemnly, certain that she had struck exactly the right note.

She had, of course, signed the agreement. What did it matter? She had no intentions of ever walking away from this marriage. And the issue of adultery was hardly worthy of consideration. Protection and liberation from economic stress

had compensations after long years of struggle. She intended to
keep this marriage intact at all costs. And since she had taught
herself discipline, she had no trouble teaching herself obedience
and sublimation. So what if it flew in the face of modern trends of
female behavior? Consciousness-raising does not put bread on the
table.

Nor was it penal servitude. Eliot, who spent most of his time
in his office on Lexington Avenue, a few blocks from their apartment, was, basically, a loner, a thinker, and an intellectual.
Thankfully, she did not share this life with him. Nevertheless, she
was always on tap when he emerged for his forays into the "real"
world of sophisticated pleasures.

She wasn't called upon often to act the hostess, but when
she was, her performance was smoothly elegant. She could run
their ten-room apartment on Fifth Avenue with efficiency, could
pack his clothes with dispatch, and arrange for tickets for his
various conferences. Most of all, she had learned to perform
cleverly all acts of availability—availability for meals, for conversations that were mostly listening, for adornment, and for what
passed for companionship. She had learned to be available for
availability.

Eliot's sense of the aesthetic extended to food, wine, art,
classical music, opera, and, of course, ballet, all the highly
rarefied cultural refinements. She was really knowledgeable only
about music and dance, but that gave her enough of a cachet so
that she could fake the rest.

Eliot had wide-ranging scientific interests as well, appropriate to his professed idea of himself as a Renaissance man. This
gave rise to certain enthusiasms, such as an overwhelming concern for ecology and wildlife preservation. She had accompanied
him on a number of safaris in Africa, grueling treks to an increasingly disappearing world. On these occasions, too, she had
learned to be a good soldier, feigning intense interest. She was
always feigning something or other.

She did not view her life in terms of happiness or unhap-
piness. If Eliot, to her, was sometimes dull and self-absorbed,
moody, cranky, distracted, withdrawn, demanding, so be it. Her
compensations by comparison with her earlier life were considerable. If there was hypocrisy in it, there was no unkindness on her
part, no meanness, no cruelty, no indecency or disloyalty. She

gave him no cause for dissatisfaction. From his perspective, she hoped he saw her as dutifully admiring, caring, loving, and concerned.

She was not, of course, without guile. She was certainly entitled to it, especially when it came to accumulating possessions in her own name. Under cover of aesthetic compulsion, she had piled works of art and antiques into their apartment, carefully procured with expert advice, often by perfectly legal sleight of hand. Not being privy to Eliot's total financial picture, she assumed that, since he did not protest, there were ample funds available for this purpose. He seemed proud of her taste and what he thought was her canny eye for beauty. Considering the huge rise in the art and antique market, she had accumulated quite a tidy personal nest egg. She thought of it as security for her old age, since it was both chronologically and biologically possible that she would outlive him.

So far she had been extraordinarily lucky in keeping the real truth of her economic success hidden from Eliot. It could be said that ever since she married Eliot, she had learned to walk through life defensively. If she sensed danger ahead, she always took evasive action.

This was her recourse at Pumpkins. At first, she had been stunned to see Ken Kramer. The parts of her body seemed to have rearranged themselves. Her heart had jumped to her throat. Her knees had barely carried her to the table.

She might not have made it through the evening if he had acknowledged her. Throughout the meal, she had tried to will him out of her presence. She hoped no one had noticed her agitation. She had been very careful about using her hands, which had shaken briefly when she had tried to lift a water glass. It was warning enough to keep her hands hidden. Then she had had to control the tremor in her voice. The best way to do that was to keep her talk to a minimum.

Hiding behind this hastily constructed façade was difficult enough, until Eliot began to sketch in her ersatz past. She had kept her eyes from Ken's face, despite the tremendous temptation to see his reaction. When he embarked on that challenge to her authenticity, that attempt to get a rubbing of her fictional father, Le Roc, at the Washington Vietnam War Memorial, she had very nearly given the game away. Then he had graciously surrendered.

Or had he actually forgotten her? Perhaps, along with the radical change in her life, her entire persona had changed, become unrecognizable?

Or he might have, as she had done for years, blocked out the memory of her. For her, apparently, it had been an imperfect process. Recall had hit her suddenly with the full force of an ice shower. She felt panicked, vulnerable. Her body's reaction confused and embarrassed her, but she could not bring herself to leave the table, fearful that she would faint if she stood up.

Thankfully, neither Eliot nor that woman, Ken's wife, had noticed. They were so busy impressing each other. As with everything in her marriage, Carol had forced herself to tolerate Eliot's gourmet grandstanding and wine snobbery. She had learned to participate occasionally in the pompous dialogue with waiters, wine stewards, and food mavens. But seeing it done in tandem with this woman seemed ludicrous. She had been instantly offended by Maggie's perky manner, her huge breasts, her long, soft blond hair, her saccharine enthusiasms, her shared interests in Eliot's gourmet tastes. How was she to know that her married name was Kramer?

Had she sensed that something like this might occur? Ironically, she had attributed her silent reluctance to attend this dinner to snobbery. Maggie was, after all, not a social acquaintance of Eliot's, but a hired hand, though well paid for her services. Eliot had praised her skill as a computer programmer. They had spent hours closeted together in his office. The job she was doing, according to Eliot, would take months, perhaps a year. What more was required of an employer? It was a poor excuse to put her through this hell, this confrontation with Ken Kramer.

The source of her irritation was terror, the terror of discovery. But there was also the terror of an inner, very physical disturbance. Images, erotically stimulating images, long repressed, had jumped into her head. Worse, she couldn't control it, resenting this sudden waver of her discipline.

Was that really her in this mad movie of memory unreeling in her head? She saw his nude body, fully aroused, saw herself reaching out, touching, caressing, accepting, inserting. The movie advanced wildly, in slow motion, in fast forward, in fast backward. Jesus. Inside herself, she felt the sexual tension accelerate. Of course she resented this Maggie Kramer. Didn't she have good reason? It had taken the entire dinner to get herself under control. By meal's end, she was able to feel gratitude for Ken's keeping her secret.

"Her husband seemed rather quiet," Eliot had said that night after they had gone home. "He didn't reveal much about himself."

"Still waters and all that," she had replied with studied indifference as she prepared for bed. "Apparently his wife spoke for him."

"I somehow feel I might have been too harsh on his profession," Eliot said. "There's probably a lot more to him than meets the eye."

"Maybe," she said, then remembered how his very presence had disrupted her. "He created Slender Benders." She was instantly sorry for her attitude. At least he hadn't given her away. He surely deserved her understanding. "You can never tell about spouses. It's always a surprise. I thought he was rather a good sport."

"I suppose he was," Eliot agreed. "Perhaps in the future we can draw him out. I rather liked their company."

"Perhaps we can see them again," she said, surprised at her acquiescence.

"Yes," Eliot said. "I think that would be nice."

"Whatever you say, Eliot. You have a much better sense of people than I have," she replied, fingering Ken's crumpled card.

After overcoming some initial trepidation, Carol called Ken at his office a week later. It had taken her the week to find the courage. A matter of simple self-interest, she told herself. There was every indication that Eliot's growing business relationship and friendship with Maggie would bring Carol and Ken together again. Some ground rules would have to be established between them, she told herself, wondering if she was really telling herself the unvarnished truth.

"Yes, Mrs. Butterfield," Ken said. She detected a touch of sarcasm.

"Please, Ken," she said.

"Carol," he replied, his voice lowering to a whisper.

"Ken. I . . . I don't know exactly how to put this," she began.

What kind of response should she have expected? Less intimate? "Am I connecting?"

She had to wait several seconds. She could hear his breathing, perhaps the sound of his thoughts.

"Yes," he said.

"We have to talk," she said. Had she meant on the telephone? She wasn't certain. There were dangers here, she warned herself, although avoiding any further analysis. She definitely sensed certain reactions inside her, emotional and physical. Was that the danger she had meant? Or the other? The danger of Ken raising questions in Eliot's mind, the danger of being unmasked, of her carefully constructed house of cards collapsing? Ken made the decision for her.

"Name the place."

Pals suggested itself—a coffee shop on Second Avenue. She had noted his office was on the East Side. An hour? He agreed, but when she hung up, the idea of urgency was repellent. She felt uncomfortable and was tempted to call him back, call it off. And why was she calling from the lobby of the Pierre as if this were meant to be clandestine, an intrigue? And why in her mind did she think of Pals? Because it was not a small, dark, romantic place off the beaten track, not intimate, not an environment for secret trysts? Now, how had such an idea insinuated itself?

The hour seemed an eternity. It was late afternoon, a cool day. A breeze had suddenly come up, sweeping in from the East River, bringing a slight chill. Or was it her, trembling from other causes?

When Carol came into the coffee shop she rejected a booth and chose a visible table in the center of the room instead. Ken was a few minutes late and she studied him as he came forward, compared him to the twenty-one-year-old boy she had known, as if she had not seen him just last week. She noted that the mysterious long-haired Jesus look had disappeared along with the little round specs. How old would he be? Mid-forties? He had not fleshed out, his walk was loose and rangy. His jacket was open and she could see the rhythmic movement of his hips, remembering that he had always worn his pants tight and low. Her eyes drifted toward the pouch of his crotch and she blushed.

"And the verdict?" he asked as he reached her, sitting down in the chair across from her, his eyes assessing her shamelessly.

"Guilty as charged," she said. She knew it was not the answer to the question he had posed. That answer, the real answer, was that she was quickly discovering that it was possible to resurrect emotion. The discovery frightened her. But she dared not get into that. Never again. Never that.

He rubbed his chin.

"Beard came in gray. My business is a youth cult. I thought it was the lack of beard that threw you."

"No way," she said, studying him. "You look great." His eyes focused on her face, then found her eyes. They engaged for a long moment.

"Time stopped for you, Carol," he said.

"I work at it," she replied.

"You had me spooked. I thought I was in a kind of time warp." She felt the inspection of his eyes, probing deeply now.

"I'll explain all that," she said. A waitress came by and they ordered cups of coffee. It was a large place, but it was, as far as she knew, off the beaten track for Eliot. She could not shake off the idea that she was betraying him in some way, endangering her position, her security.

"You had me going," Ken said. "I figured you had your reasons and I went along with them. I felt I owed you my silence."

"No reminiscences," she said. "I called merely to explain. It looks as if we're going to find ourselves together at times. I wanted to clear the air."

"Your husband and my wife seem to be becoming real buddies. She's been raving about his brainpower." He shrugged. "I found him a little too encyclopedic."

She ignored the reference. Eliot's superior airs could be grating.

"He's quite taken with your wife's skills. That's a compliment. He is quite a taskmaster," Carol said.

"From the time she spends with him, it would seem so. At her hourly rate that's okay with me," Ken said.

"Apparently it will be a long project," Carol said. "With Eliot, work doesn't stop at the office door. There's also this social component. And since we might be seeing more of each other . . . as couples . . . I wanted to be sure that you understood, well . . . why all those strange historical facts."

"I know why," Ken said. "You made them up."

"Embellished. I embellished."

The waitress brought their coffee, giving them a chance to assess each other further. His good looks had matured well. His hair, speckled lightly with gray, was thinning in front. His eyes seemed set deeper into his face than she had remembered. And the eyes themselves? She recognized the young man in them, the eyes of the man that had for one brief, glorious moment turned her inside out. The memory brought a charge down the center of her.

"I was afraid you might give it away," she admitted.

"Descendant of a French marquis, your father killed in Vietnam. You put a lot of imagination into that one."

"And you certainly did find a way to expose me. The wall idea was very creative."

"It was nasty and I apologize."

"It frightened me. But you saw that."

"And retreated. I guess I was just resentful. You not even acknowledging me, as if I had never existed."

"I guess I sensed that, hence this explanation."

Ken sipped his coffee.

"Does Eliot believe all that?"

"Implicitly."

"Your age?"

She nodded.

"I'd believe that," Ken said, studying her. "Is the other true? About being . . . in that Australian ballet company?"

"No. More little make-believe. I'm afraid I bombed out as a dancer."

"I'm sorry," he said, his eyes evading hers.

"It was once everything. My whole world. God, I tried. After my scholarship was over, I was simply dropped. Oh, I tried other schools, other companies. I think my lack of success after all those sacrifices broke my parents." She shrugged and stamped down a welling of tears. "I did do six months with a musical theater road company." She forced a smile. "Mostly I taught. Remember the old saying 'If you can't do it, teach it'?"

"Well, you look none the worse for wear," Ken muttered. "You seem to be doing quite well with Mr. Butterfield."

"Proves there's life after failure, Ken. I found a way to get through the long night in a very comfortable, tranquil way. I just got tired of being poor. You probably think it's a kind of exile and it is, a golden exile, and I don't want anything to screw it up."

"It certainly is a lot clearer than it was the other night."

"In some ways I had to re-create myself. Make me marketable for Eliot to have wanted me. Sure, it's a pack of lies, Ken. All of it. Harmless lies. Although I do teach kids ballet. I'm everything he expects and I'm true to that creation. Too late now to confess all. Eliot thinks of me as that person I concocted out of whole cloth."

She hadn't meant to bare her soul, only explain. But she felt better for the telling.

"We do what we have to," Ken said. "Maggie tells me Eliot's loaded, that you live in this big place on Fifth Avenue. All looks great from here."

"It's a lot more comfortable life than I had," she whispered. "Following a dying dream without money is not very edifying."

"Well, I guess, then, you have cleared the air," Ken said. Then, suddenly, he reached out and covered her hand with his. It surprised her that she did not remove it. "Believe me, I appreciate it. Once we never did have any secrets from each other."

Their eyes locked. This is crazy, she told herself. She slid her hand out from under his.

"Think we made the right decision?" he asked.

"What decision was that?"

"Us," he said.

"Come on, Ken. This is ridiculous. I only wanted to be sure . . ."

"I understand," he said, putting up the palms of his hands. "Just being near you makes me feel . . . strange."

She shook her head. "Please, Ken . . ." She averted her eyes and her words seemed to drift away.

"Never again or before was it ever like that," Ken said, once again stimulating the old images in her mind. She beat them back.

"That's gone. What you're talking about happened to other people. This is more than twenty years later. We're different people in different circumstances. I have a husband, stepchildren. You have a wife, a family." She paused for a moment. "A career."

"You gulped on that one," Ken said. "The career part."

"I watched for your books," Carol said. She saw her comment's effect on him and was sorry she had said it.

"A bust," he sighed. "Whatever I had I must have lost somewhere. It was there once. I was so damned sure of it."

"Maybe you'll find it again," she told him.

"Maybe I have already," he said pointedly.

She ignored his comment. He was moving again into dangerous territory. She felt him study her face. "But I did have one true thing in my life. One great true thing." His eyes again locked into hers. "We, you and I, were as good as it gets."

"Sometimes good things in the past get exaggerated," she said.

"Depends on how good it was."

"And how young we were," she said, hoping to stem the tide of feeling that was obviously opening between them. She paused to grope for the words to prevent it going any further. "And foolish."

"Yeah, foolish," he muttered, offering a thin smile. "Anyway, life went on. In fact, some people think I'm a great success. Very creative guy, old Kramer. I do things like Slender Benders. I could do it in my sleep and it keeps the wolf from the door." He was silent for a while. "It's shit, Carol," he said finally.

"Come on, Ken, you're much too hard on yourself," Carol said.

"Maybe," he answered broodingly. "We're on this truth kick so why not put it all in the right perspective? Fact is I'm very, very disappointed in myself, Carol."

"It's not over yet for you, Ken. You're not a dancer where age is the mortal enemy. I can always say I was forced to surrender. At least as a writer you can still harbor hopes."

"That's me, the lighthouse at Hope Harbor. Maybe the old light can lure back the lost inspiration." He looked at her intensely, forcing her to avert her eyes.

"You seem to be doing quite well," Carol said. "You have a wife, two daughters. Apparently your marriage has lasted."

"We've learned to avoid the marriage minefields, I guess. I suppose you might say we've got this habit going. There is also a comfort level in it. Maggie, as you might have gathered, is a born nurturer."

"You didn't tell her about us?"

"I told you. We avoid minefields," Ken said, reaching for her hand again. "That's private domain. As it turned out, our noble parting wasn't worth the candle. We never did get the brass ring, Carol. Not you or I. We should have stayed on that merry-go-round forever."

"Nothing's forever, Ken."

"That's for sure. But did you ever think about it, have any regret?"

"I pushed it out of my mind."

"And it never came back, not even in dreams?"

"I don't dream much anymore," she said, wondering if it was true.

"I do. Certain things never go away." He tapped the side of his head. "As Maggie would say: 'It's in the RAM.'"

Carol tapped her head to mimic him. "And that's where it must stay."

"We had a high tide in our lives. Too short. But it sure had power. How many people have that?"

"In a lifetime it was nothing more than a wink," she said.

"Maybe one wink like that in a lifetime makes it all worthwhile."

Was it really that good, that special? Would she be here if it wasn't? She felt some distant disturbance, like a brewing storm. The old images flooded back again, vivid, all-encompassing.

He took her hand and brought it to his heart. "Feel that. The old pump is raging."

Their eyes met and he brought her hand to his lips, kissing her palm.

"My God, Ken." She pulled her hand away. But the simple act had sent shockwaves through her, triggering conflicting emotions. She felt herself trying to assemble an expression of indignance, but without success. Being here was a mistake, she decided.

"I'm sorry, Carol," he said. He shook his head. "You can't go home again. Everybody knows that. And the fact is, that I've been a good and faithful husband. It was very stupid of me."

Her coffee had gotten cold and she had covered her cup when the waitress came to refill it.

"I just thought it was important for you to know all this, Ken." She hoped it would sound a concluding note.

"And I appreciate it. Now the four of us can be friends." She caught the sarcasm in his tone.

She looked at her watch. Eliot would expect her to be home. A brief tremor of resentment washed over her. But she knew the meeting could not end, not yet. There was still something left unsaid. She hesitated, gathering her thoughts.

"What is it, Carol?"

"I'm not sure I can ask this of you," she said. "And of myself."

"Ask away."

"I would like this to end it."

"End it? We did that more than twenty years ago."

"I mean all references, all talk, all acknowledgment of our previous life. I know that the four of us will be together again and I would like your promise."

"To block out the past. Pretend we never met . . . never . . ." His voice trailed off into a chuckle.

"Like we met the first time last week at Pumpkins."

He was silent for a long moment.

"I promise," Ken said, lifting his right hand.

"I'm serious, Ken." She felt his eyes studying her.

"I never saw you before in my life," he whispered.

She inspected his face, searching for sincerity. Yes, she thought. He will not betray me.

"Well, then. I appreciate our chat. And I feel better for it."

She stood up. He did as well, then stepped forward as if to offer a farewell kiss, but she moved away and put out her hand instead. He took it, pressed it.

"You have nothing to fear from me, Carol," Ken said.

"I know that now," she said.

What did one more lie matter?

4

"I 'M so glad we're all getting along so splendidly," Maggie said, applying makeup remover as she sat at the dressing table in the bedroom of their Park Slope row house in Brooklyn.

Ken lay in bed, fatigued by his four-month effort of dissimulation, wondering why he was putting himself through this torture of denial and proximity. But Carol's presence in his life was pervasive, crowding out all other thoughts and ideas, exaggerating the trivial aspects of his work, and emphasizing the shame of his surrender.

They had come back from yet another evening together. They had seen *Phantom of the Opera*. He had sat next to Carol throughout the performance, fighting the urge to place his leg next to hers, to kiss the beauty mark on her white swan's neck, to smother her with his embrace. The fantasies were becoming too vivid to tolerate and it took all his energy to exercise self-control.

They were, as always, appropriately polite. An observer might say they were actually visibly disinterested in each other. That had been the agreed-upon conduct. But it was getting increasingly difficult for Ken to abide by the game plan.

Worse, Eliot appeared to him to be even more pompous and authoritarian every time they met, although, considering Ken's growing but secret animosity toward the man, he suspected he might be reacting unfairly. He even admitted to himself a slight tinge of jealousy, an embarrassing misapplication of emotion since its root was not Maggie's interest in Eliot but Eliot's interest in Carol.

Maggie and Eliot always enjoyed these evenings. They seemed to be tapping into an endless well of interests and enthusiasms, especially baffling since they were spending a great deal of time together during the day working on Eliot's ever-growing data base.

"No more hopping and churning with Eliot's data," Maggie told him. "We're integrating everything. And it's one helluva job. This fellow has a claptrap mind and a mountain of interests."

"And he pays on time."

"Yes, he does," Maggie agreed. "But he's getting value received, state-of-the-art computerization. Well worth it from his point of view."

The financial aspects of the relationship were not to be ignored. Nor was the cost of these evenings. Ken insisted on paying his and Maggie's share of all checks, which usually meant sharing costs down the middle, submitting two credit cards for the proprietors to split between them.

At first, Eliot had tried to pay for everything, but Ken would have none of that. He was certain that passive acceptance of Eliot's largesse in any form would diminish him in Carol's eyes. To be fair, Maggie would never have allowed that either. But it was telling on the Kramer exchequer.

It never ceased to amaze Ken how what had once seemed like fairly high incomes still left them tight financially, with little left to put away for the proverbial rainy day. He supposed they could manage better if they tried, but that would only add parsimony to their already stretched lives. And, after all, weren't they the get-it-now-by-living-on-credit generation? It wasn't admirable, certainly not noble or practical, but it sure beat the shit out of penny-pinching.

They were, in fact, sitting on a pile of mounting debt, and the truth of it was that it could only get worse. College was on the horizon for the girls, who were this summer on the obligatory chaperoned teenage tour of Europe.

"Every generation must boost the next," Maggie told him, "whatever the cost." When he offered her his occasional protests, especially on indulgences for the girls, she turned a deaf ear. Not that Maggie was blind to their financial realities. She was, after all, a practical midwestern girl. And she did represent more than a third of their earnings. But she believed, in apparently boundless optimism, that things could only get better.

"We're no longer Yuppies, we're Brokies," he told her often. Maggie did not dispute him, adopting the philosophy that their income must rise to meet the standard, not the other way around. Between them they were earning nearly $225,000 a year, and Ken was paying more taxes in one year than his bookkeeper father had earned in two decades.

They owned their own row house near Prospect Park and had borrowed against the equity. The girls' school tuition was costing more than twenty thousand a year and college tuition would be much higher.

They hadn't realized it at first, but the truth was that as the children grew older, their life-style was eroding. They were falling more and more behind. The old measures of financial success no longer applied.

Even the comfortable rationalization that Ken had applied to himself, the idea that he had somehow sold out his artistic ambitions for money and creature comforts, did not apply. He was, indeed, a failure on both counts. The brutal fact was that an after-tax income of approximately $150,000 a year no longer bought the quality life-style that such a number suggested. Unfortunately, the illusion persisted far beyond the reality.

His father, long gone, who had lived through the Great Depression, would have laughed at him for complaining. He had come through an era in which to earn ten thousand a year was Valhalla, and when his son was earning three times that much, he assumed that his greatest hopes for his son's success had been fulfilled. What a laugh.

It was as much of a disappointment to Maggie as it was to Ken, to be earning what had once seemed like big money only to discover that it was like a price tag before the markdown at a fire sale, a label that did not represent the real cost.

Still, they had both agreed not to take the children out of their schools, not to be deterred by tuition costs at the better colleges, not to cut down on the other amenities that city life had to offer, such as the theater, concerts, restaurants. After all, they had to live up to their upwardly mobile status. The important thing, they had concluded early on in their marriage, was to understand the ideals of an ethical life. Such ideals protected you from those other values, the empty ones you lived by, the hollow little hypocrisies.

It was true, he told himself, that Carol had failed in her bid to be a prima ballerina, but at least her failure had ended in a soft financial landing. That was something, not much in the context of artistic idealism, but something, or, more to the point, better than nothing.

Carol's pep talk about it never being too late for a writer had briefly sparked him into channeling his thoughts into more than bravado and fantasy. He began to think again about stories, characters interacting, plots, ironies. To further inspire him he had returned to reading Hemingway. But the physical act and the financial reality of starting to write again was daunting. His life was bogged down with responsibilities. And there was the drain of his job at the agency, his ersatz "creative" life. Carol's presence had simply added more weight to his many burdens.

"Frankly, I was worried that Carol and you would have little to say to each other," Maggie said, obviously to deflect the attention from the cost of the evening.

"She's okay," Ken murmured. Oh, God, deliver me from such faint praise, he cried in his heart.

"At first you seemed absolutely antagonistic toward her. You actually ignored her. But I'm glad you're giving her a chance. She's really a lovely person."

"Why concern yourself? Eliot is obviously the star of that relationship," Ken said cautiously, showing his loyalty to Carol's wishes.

"He's a very intriguing man, don't you think?"

"Yes, he is," Ken lied. It was hard enough keeping his true feelings about Eliot repressed to himself in the man's presence. "And a good pay," he added. It was as far as he dared go with Maggie. His opinion of Eliot as a tight-assed boring snob would have raised her hackles, set off Maggie's silent antagonisms. No upside in stepping on that mine, he decided.

"Carol seems to have an interesting background. A prima ballerina," Maggie said. "That's quite an achievement. If only she wasn't so withdrawn."

"I guess we should try harder to get her out of her shell," Ken said, in a saccharine tone of concealed insincerity.

"Eliot truly wants us to have a long couples relationship." She looked at him and smiled benignly. "So do we. We owe ourselves a couples relationship."

"What does he think of me?" Ken asked, ignoring her enthusiasm. Did he care, he wondered, what the pompous prick thought of him?

"He finds you very interesting," Maggie said without conviction. "I told him about your wanting to write novels."

So now she was selling him as something more than the creator of Slender Benders. Suddenly he regretted the lip service he had given to his writing ambition, although it had gained him some credibility with Maggie, especially in the early days of their marriage.

"I wish you wouldn't," he protested.

"He was very impressed," Maggie said, putting the finishing touches to her pre-sleep ablutions. "Might be of some help getting you published someday. Eliot has connections."

Ken felt his stomach flop over. He would rather be tortured on the rack in Macy's window than use that man's connections.

"It's you and he that are the real soul mates," Ken said, instantly sorry for the statement, which might be interpreted by her as a husband's indignation.

"In a way, I suppose," she said, studying herself in the mirror, oblivious to his indignation. Then she turned to him and smiled gently. "You can't be jealous?"

"I'm not," he told her truthfully.

"He's a close colleague and, as you can see, very much married to a lovely girl."

"I think they're a great couple," Ken muttered.

"It's nice to have couple friends."

"Especially rich ones."

"That's unfair. They're substantial in other ways as well."

"Of course they are," Ken backtracked, fearful that any further antagonism on his part might inhibit their social relationship with the Butterfields. To be deprived of being with Carol, however painful, was better than never seeing her again. Above all, he didn't want that to happen.

There was a practical consideration as well. Eliot was also Maggie's client, a dispenser of dollars for their family coffers. Ordinarily, Ken would have consented to the obligatory friendly get-together with the man's spouse. But a superior self-righteous prig like Eliot would have been tolerated for one time only, and despite all pleadings, Ken would have rejected any second meeting out of hand.

Maggie also rejected any corporate-wife bullshit with Ken's co-workers, except for the occasional command performance with the powers-that-be. But, then, Ken avoided all corporate political entanglements, relying on his so-called "creativity" to generate enough mystique to make him a neutral asset in this small-time corporate game.

Aside from their client relationship, Maggie and Eliot did have common links. They were both wide-ranging intellectual generalists with gourmet tastes and sentimental attachments to causes and movements. Ken was actually proud of Maggie's interests, her deep-thinking quick mind, and, despite her less than efficient command of their financial matters, her marvelous stewardship of their daughters' education and emotional well-being.

Maggie was, above all, an organizer. She had forced an outward organization of Ken's life, leaving him to the sometimes dubious luxury of a messy, fantasy-ridden, and secret interior life. Sometimes he felt claustrophobic, in tow. She chose his clothes, his food and entertainment, planned their vacations, and looked out for his health concerns, his exercise routines, and what she believed were his sexual and romantic needs, most of which could be defined as unlimited access to her big, beautiful breasts.

Maggie, he was certain, could never jump off the cliff of emotional stability into the whirlpool of sexual obsession and romantic excess that had characterized his episode with Carol. As for Maggie's physical needs, they were, he suspected, somewhat less than what she revealed. Her programmed sexual enthusiasms were always suspect, however energetic his technique and vocal her exclamations of pleasure. She had, he suspected, developed a repertoire of mechanical bedroom moves that, combined with his active imagination and her well-cared-for body, was enough to carry the moment. It wasn't exactly passion, but it wasn't masturbation either.

Marrying her was one of Ken's more rational acts. He had once included his breakup with Carol in that category. An artist, he had consciously decided, needed a stable outer life to counter the turmoil of his self-absorbed creative inner life. Excess, as he had learned, was dangerous and destructive. And his relationship with Carol had been both.

Maggie, on the other hand, was "state of the art." From the beginning it seemed the operative description, from the moment she walked into BBD&O's copy-writing bullpen, where he was a fledgling "sell-out," which was the way they referred to themselves in those days.

"This is Maggie Nielsen," a BBD&O vice-president, nameless and faceless in his memory, had announced. "She's going to computerize us."

What struck Ken most about her was the air of openness and good humor she exhibited even when subjected to the smart-alecky comments of his brash co-workers, who, like himself, were determined to resist the computer and all it portended as the enemy of creativity.

"I am going to give you state-of-the-art support," she had pledged, offering her big-toothed smile. There was something unflappable about her with her long blond hair and concentrated energy. There was also something unexpected about her. From afar her clean, blond Scandinavian good looks indicated that she was sure to have blue eyes. They were gray.

Nor did she look anything like an expert at computers. In those days there was a nerd quality to people who were into computers. There wasn't a trace of nerd in either her delivery or her appearance. She was a tall woman with high large breasts that seemed larger in relation to her flat stomach and small waist. Yet, once she began her teaching chores, one forgot about her appearance and listened with rapt attention to her explanation of the mysteries of binary bytes and rams.

He had been a rotten student, the worst of the group, and, although it embarrassed him, he was able to mask his inability to understand the material by noisy sneering protestations about trying to make robots out of creative people.

This attitude singled him out for Maggie's special consideration.

"Think of it as a tool, like a fork or knife," she assured him in her midwestern twang. "It has no effect on the substance of the object, not on its taste nor caloric content. It will affect the product of your mind only by increasing the speed and ease by which it transfers the creative material to market."

He had felt like a dumb kid forced to accept tutoring after school and had obediently consented to "stay after class."

"You realize that I have no desire to learn this," he told her. "I'm probably wasting my time."

"It's my time," she told him. "Besides, I like a challenge."

The more she tried, the more stubborn became his resistance. It didn't faze her. She pressed on. He had, of course, accepted the idea of her as a teacher, which somehow inhibited his seeing her in another dimension, as a woman.

"You're continuing to resist me," she told him after a week of persistent after-hours' tutoring. It was Friday night and the weekend stretched before them. She had suggested that they have dinner together to discuss the problem.

"I guess it's a hang-up," he confessed.

"You mustn't let yourself be left out. Computers will be everywhere. Not to know how the system works will hurt you."

She was sincerely concerned.

"Why all this attention? Why not write me off? Give me up. I'm hopeless."

"No!"

She was emphatic. They drifted into a restaurant and ordered a few drinks. There wasn't, he remembered, much conversation, but he was conscious of her watching him, as if she were evaluating him, sizing him up.

Up to then, his social life had been a disaster, as if his experience with Carol had left him sexually paralyzed. His mind-set at that moment in time was that he had given up everything for nothing. He knew by then that his writing ambition was a pipe dream. Earlier, the advertising agency, like his newspaper experience, had been a stopgap. It was now a career. He thought of himself as injured.

"It's not the computer," she told him for the first time that evening.

"What, then?" he had asked.

"I'll tell you when I know."

Odd, he thought later, how people took different paths to the same destination. He hadn't remembered Maggie triggering his desire. Certainly there was no emotional pull on his part.

It was she who was the aggressor and it startled him.

"Take me home with you," she had asked. It was a straight-forward request, more in the nature of a suggestion than a command. They had just gotten up from their booth at the restaurant. She had insisted on paying her half of the bill.

"Why?" he had asked stupidly.

"Because you need someone like me."

Later, cuddled together like spoons in his bed, his hands cupping her lovely large breasts, he knew she was right. He hadn't realized the extent of his injuries.

After that night, he had no trouble learning to use the computer.

He and Maggie had lived together for a year before their marriage, enough time for both of them to make a sensible decision. She was a warm and giving woman, and with her gift for organization and detail, she would protect him from the more mundane aspects of daily life, leaving him time for the far more important struggle with the artistic muse.

The struggle, he allowed himself to believe, was merely temporarily suspended. Babies had come. A steady stream of income was needed to maintain a certain standard of living. He provided that or thought he had. At times, his mind drifted back to the possibility of again trying his hand at serious writing. Sometimes an idea would surface, but somehow he would reject it as off the mark, out of fashion, unsalable.

Yet, never once had Maggie berated him for his failure or offered any ego-dampening conclusions. One day "the book" would come, she always assured him. In the meantime, he was putting his creativity to work in the service of commerce. She offered solace for him in that as well. To her his jingles were cantos; his headlines, sculpted bits of poetry; his copy, masterpieces of minimalist art. Her encouragement was not without its rewards. It bolstered his confidence, made him think he was good at the game. His colleagues apparently agreed. He began to develop a reputation as a "brilliant wordsmith." He liked the sobriquet, but wasn't thrilled with the implication.

"What does Ken think?" clients often asked the account people. There was currency in that to get him through the day. Wasn't there?

For his part, he barely tolerated her cerebral, mostly computer-obsessed companions, both male and female, while she diligently sought the perfect couple friends, admittedly a tough chore, even for an ordinary couple. He knew that a disgruntled frustrated closet loner like himself was a hard case to match up, but since he kept that part of himself mostly hidden, he let her continue her search. As he had told Carol, his marriage was now based on an avoidance of the minefields.

Meeting Carol again was forcing a reappraisal of his marriage, of his life. It was a subject he had, up to then, preferred to avoid.

"And you?" Ken asked Maggie cautiously. "How do you find Carol?"

She had come into bed and now lay stretched out beside him reading a book. She stopped reading and grew thoughtful.

"Quite beautiful," she paused. "Mysterious, too. Probably a lot more to her than is apparent."

"Yes, I think that's true," he agreed, knowing how close to the mark her comment had come.

"It's an odd match," she said. "But no odder than most."

Did she mean ours? Ken wondered, observing his wife through slits in half-closed eyes as she continued her reading. He debated reaching out his hand, caressing her thigh, starting the process. Maggie would, as always, oblige. Never once had she rejected an advance. But, as always, he would sense that her performance was in another place than her body. His, too.

He turned away from her instead, his thoughts racing back to these new events in his life.

Above all, he wanted to continue to be in Carol's presence. Perhaps that was the real reason that he was less than honest about what he really felt about Eliot. It took all his restraint to keep from making contact with Carol outside their couples evenings. Was it, as he hoped, a deliberate postponement of their inevitable "reunion"? Or was it a conscious effort to prevent a conflagration in their lives, an eruption with potentially dangerous results?

It was sufficiently obvious to him that Carol was protecting her security, certainly the financial as well as the emotional. What was he protecting? The status quo? The responsible life? His children's material and emotional future? What? At least in the past he had known that he was rejecting blind passion for an ideal. Thinking about it in that way left him annoyed and embarrassed. But it did not stop him from letting Maggie nudge him further forward on the road to what she falsely perceived as an intimate couples relationship.

By the beginning of August they were seeing Eliot and Carol once a week on average. Sometimes it was dinner in a restaurant, sometimes a show with supper afterward, or a Sunday art opening. Once in July they had rented bicycles and gone to the New York Philharmonic park concerts. Maggie had packed a picnic dinner.

There was a certain similarity to each event. Maggie and Eliot would chirp away on a variety of topics with occasional comments by Carol and Ken, benign comments designed mostly to simulate their camaraderie with the others. Even when they were out of earshot of the others, they maintained the agreed-upon distance.

"Above all I keep my word," he whispered to Carol on one occasion.

"Now, that's a paradox," Carol said. "By saying that, you're breaking it." Her eyes smiled to show him her forgiveness. "Nevertheless, I'm very grateful."

"Are you really?"

"There is no other choice," she said firmly.

"Isn't there?"

He thought he had caught a flicker of hesitation in her eyes. But she had left the question hanging in the air.

In early August, they had planned to meet at Eliot and Carol's apartment, then have brunch at Tavern on the Green, followed by a performance of *Anything Goes* at Lincoln Center. Midsummer weekends, despite the heat, were special times for New Yorkers who chose to stay in town rather than brave the crowds that hovered like flocks of sandpipers along the shore.

Eliot, apparently, had to beg off. It had never happened before. An emergency meeting somewhere out of town, he explained to Maggie.

But there was no need to disappoint Carol, and Maggie had assured Eliot that they would, under no circumstances, cancel the date. But on Sunday morning, Maggie developed stomach cramps and couldn't get out of bed.

"Let's just cancel," Ken said for form's sake, although he was having difficulty hiding his elation.

"Don't be silly," Maggie said, propped on pillows and holding a hot-water bottle on her stomach.

"Shouldn't we call a doctor?" Ken asked.

"If it gets any worse I will," she promised. "A day's rest ought to do it. Feels like a stomach virus to me."

"It's only brunch and a show," Ken said, searching for the correct balance of protest.

"We mustn't disappoint Carol," Maggie said. "Eliot would be very appreciative."

"Maybe we could skip the meal and just do the show?" Ken suggested. For some reason, he felt that it would be important to show reluctance, although he worried that too much reluctance might prompt Maggie to call and leave the decision up to Carol, who would probably insist upon canceling.

"Don't be silly. You two just have a great time. I'll be fine and I have the Sunday papers. Besides, you know how I hate to be hovered over when I'm ill."

"If you say so," Ken said, feeling he had been sufficiently concerned for appearance's sake, yet knowing that his promise to Carol was in serious jeopardy.

5

"THERE WAS no way out," Ken said as he followed Carol into the cool apartment filled with artworks and antiques. He watched her glide forward in her dancer's walk in high heels, swan neck high, buttocks swathed in form-fitting white slacks. Sunlight filtered into the large living room through a line of plants hung artfully from the terrace roof.

From their twentieth-floor apartment on Fifth Avenue, one could see across the green Central Park meadows and the lake to the line of apartment houses on Central Park West and the tall narrow buildings that anchored the park's southern end.

"Maggie insisted," he shrugged, taking a fluted glass filled with champagne and orange juice, a mimosa, from the silver tray that she had placed on the large antique cocktail table that formed a conversational setting in front of the fireplace.

"Eliot was also insistent," Carol said, sitting down opposite him.

"Why not?" Ken said. "We've given them no cause for alarm."

"None at all," she said, sipping her mimosa and gazing out the window. It struck him that she was deliberately avoiding his eyes, which gave him a chance to admire her. There was no denying his yearning for her. It was there. Strong as ever, fully resurrected now, smoldering-hot embers ready to burst into flame.

"Nevertheless," he said cautiously, watching for her reaction, "it does seem like a test of some sort." He finished his mimosa. Then he reached across for the bottle in the ice bucket.

"May I?"

She nodded and he poured champagne into his glass.

"I expect we'll both pass with flying colors," she said, showing him a twinge of belligerence.

"You don't think this was a good idea?"

She shook her head.

"Why not?" he pressed. "We're perfectly proper. We have the consent of our spouses. More than that. We have their blessings."

"I just feel funny about it," she shrugged.

"Why?"

"Well . . . because." She looked at him briefly and turned away. "I can't explain it."

"Yes, you can," Ken said, surprised at his sudden surge of aggression. He moved forward in his chair, studying her intently. She sipped her mimosa, holding the glass near her lips, avoiding his gaze.

"Really, Ken. It was long, long ago," Carol said, continuing to avoid his eyes, looking through the terrace windows. "I'm a totally different person."

"Are you really?"

"I had different priorities then." She paused and whispered: "Different priorities."

"Oh, yes, quite different. But what happened between us? Can that be forgotten completely?"

"That was an aberration, Ken. We were young and vulnerable." She paused, her eyes flashing a brief connection with his. "My God. It was more than twenty years ago."

Again she lapsed into silence and looked toward the terrace. He sipped his champagne, studying her.

"Then why didn't you acknowledge me that first night?"

"I told you why, Ken."

"Do you really believe I would have given you away?" He paused. "Or was it something more?" He sucked in a deep breath. "What were you really frightened of, Carol?"

She shot him an angry glance. "Are you trying to put an idea into my head?"

He hesitated for a moment, continuing to observe her. Perhaps he was letting his desire rule his better judgment. She might, after all, be totally indifferent to his advances, totally empty of any reciprocal feeling. And yet, he did sense something more. Didn't he?

"Does it show?"

"Yes, it does. And I don't appreciate it."

"Maybe I'm reading things into this that aren't there," he confessed. His eyes drifted around the room. "There is a lot at risk here. I'll grant you that." The apartment was, indeed, a cornucopia of valuable possessions.

"I'm glad you see the point," she said, sipping again.

It was odd, a discordant note in his memory. Economics, money, possessions. They would have been the furthest things from her mind in those days. His, too. Did it come down to that?

Don't feel so superior, he told himself. He, too, was tied into an economic yoke, an ordinary ox walking around in circles, pumping the water to high ground.

"So now you have everything you want," he said. "Too much at risk."

"As I've tried to tell you, Ken, I've made my peace," she murmured. She turned to glance at him. "And my choice. It's over."

"Certainly the dancing part."

"Mediocrity took care of that, I'm afraid," she sighed. "And time."

Ken emptied his champagne, felt his face flush.

"Forgive the flashbacks, then," he said.

"Flashbacks?"

"Like I'm in the same place that I was twenty-odd years ago. In my head. In my heart. I apologize for feeling the way I once felt, Carol." He was throwing caution to the winds, revealing himself, something he hadn't done in years. "It's still there. I guess it's always been."

"It's your imagination. You're fantasizing."

"Look who's talking. I didn't invent a past. French royalty, a father killed in Vietnam? A prima ballerina in Australia. Ten years off your age. Come on, Carol."

"That's different," she protested. "That's survival."

She fell into a brooding silence as she quietly sipped a swallow of her drink. The way she nursed it, it seemed to last forever.

"Just tell me the truth," he said.

"I've told you the truth," she said with some indignance. She got up and moved toward the terrace window, not facing him.

"Some things can't be erased."

"Others can," she said. "They have to be."

"No flashbacks?"

"None," she said, but it sounded tentative, less certain. And she had not turned to face him. A sign, he wondered, pressing her.

"Really? You never thought about it, what we had? The passion of it? The intensity?" It was an interrogation, but he couldn't stop himself. She did not turn.

"I have to know," he cried, then in a whisper: "I need to know."

She turned toward him.

"I remember that it was destructive." There was a slight tremor in her voice. "And we chose to give it up."

"We chose wrong, Carol."

"Why am I listening to this?" she said, turning away again.

"Because you're still part of it, still in it."

"This is crazy."

She walked across the full length of the room, put her half-finished drink on a table, and looked at her image in a smoky mirror on the wall. Again she turned to face him.

"I don't want this, Ken." She shook her head. "I don't need this. And I would prefer that you leave."

He finished his drink and stood up.

"You're right," he said. "I'm sorry. But I won't lie. I've thought about this moment, wished for it. I know I'm disturbing you. I know it's wrong and I apologize. You see, I haven't felt this way for twenty-three years. Not this alive."

"You have no right to do this. No right to say those things."

"I'm speaking from my heart, Carol. And I'm sorry. I really am."

"No, you're not. You're . . . you're trying to bring back something that's gone, that died years ago."

"It didn't die for me," he murmured.

She continued to stare at him and he did not avert his eyes.

"I've made a damned fool of myself," Ken said. "I'd better go."

He started across the room. As he began to move past her, she stepped forward, blocking his way.

"I'm afraid, Ken," she said.

"So am I."

He came toward her, stopping directly in front of her, not touching her, looking deep into her eyes, fearing to go further, his heart pounding, the entire center of him on fire. He was close enough to see the tiny yellow flecks in her green eyes.

"It's now," he whispered. "Not a flashback."

"No. Not a flashback."

He sensed that she was trying to say more, but he had already reached out and folded her into his arms.

Crushed against her he felt the pounding of their blood. His lips mashed against hers. It was as if they were in the grip of a powerful magnetic force drawing them together. They dropped to their knees, continuing their embrace. His hands caressed her hair as his lips traveled over her face, her forehead, her eyes, her cheeks.

Her response was equally as fervent, the attraction between them overwhelming. Her hips pressed against the middle of him, her hand caressing, reaching downward.

He unzipped her slacks and pulled them down below her knees and she kicked off her shoes and stepped out of them. And while he unbuttoned her blouse and unhooked her bra, she undid his pants, rolling down his jockey shorts, reaching for his hard, throbbing penis. She touched him, her hand exploring, gently squeezing his testicles as they kissed, their tongues caressing.

They made a trail of discarded clothes as they moved toward the couch. For a long moment, their eyes drank in the sight of their nudity.

"How lovely you are," Ken whispered, his hand reaching out to caress her shapely breasts, moving downward, tracing the length of her still youthful body. "I can't believe it," he said.

Her hand gripped his penis, bringing it into the furrow of her vagina, moist with excitement and need. She trembled in his arms, abandoning herself to their lovemaking. Then she moved over him with the strength and grace of years of ballet training, looking into his eyes as she rubbed the tip of his penis along the moist lips, guiding it deeply inside her, their eyes probing each other as her body gyrated in a circular motion, her thighs clamped against his hips as he cupped her buttocks.

Then he felt the pleasure begin as her motions became more concentrated, and he knew what was happening as her body seemed to merge further into his. Then the miracle began as they crested at the same time, exploding together with a shuddering force.

"It's more than memory now," he whispered as they lay cooling. She had put her head on his chest and he was caressing her hair. "Like we leapfrogged time. Were there years between?"

"Not for me," she replied.

"It was wonderful, as good as ever."

"Maybe better." She kissed his chest, traveling downward with her lips.

"I'm sorry," he said abruptly.

"For what?" She looked up at him.

"For complicating your life."

He hadn't yet confronted consequences. It was not time. Not now. He started to speak again, but she put a finger over his lips.

"Not now," she said.

Carol moved from the couch, gathered up their clothes, and went into the bedroom. Ken followed her. It was a large room, dominated by a huge four-poster bed complete with elaborate canopy. He lay down and she went into the bathroom, giving him time for reflection.

What they gave each other could not, not then or now, be explained in simple biological terms. It went beyond that, beyond sex in the clinical sense. Their orgasms had always been deep, erupting, multiple, mutual, rapturous.

She came out of the bathroom and lay down beside him.

"Some things are meant to be," Ken whispered.

"I suppose I can't deny that," she said. "Only . . ."

"Only what?"

"We mustn't be slaves to it. We're mature adults now, Ken. We have to find a way to handle this, a way that's right for all of us."

She grew silent, reflective.

"We'll think of something. I promise."

He got up, leaned on his elbow, and with his fingers traced her body, starting with her forehead, down to her face, to the beauty mark on her swan's neck, to her high upturned breasts, circling the areola with the crown of freckles on her right breast, then down over her flat stomach to her curling pubic bush, then to the lips of her vagina, exploring its tightness with his finger. Then he moved over her and kissed her lips there, his tongue circling her clitoris. He did this for a while, then looked up at her.

"Touching you, I have no sense of time having passed. Your body is like that of a young girl."

"And you, a young boy. A big beautiful young boy." She reversed herself and kissed his penis.

He pinched the flesh of his belly, softer now than then. "Some things have changed," he said.

"It's an illusion."

She continued to kiss him there and his erection surged.

Then she sat up suddenly and smiled, inspecting his face, his body.

"What is it?" he asked.

"I just want to be sure it's you. Ken Kramer."

After watching him for a while, she closed her eyes and her hands moved over his face, across his chest, then downward.

"And?"

"Ken Kramer, all right. But different."

"Older and wiser?" he asked.

"In some departments," she sighed. "Fortunately not in others."

"First things first," he said, reaching out to her, bringing her closer. She lay beside him, arranging her body so that they could still see each other's faces. Then they moved together languorously.

"If only we could stay like we are, just like this," she said.

"A perfect fit. You and I."

"Perfect," she said. Then she was silent for a while. She had closed her eyes. "I can feel the pounding of your blood, the pulse of your body."

"And I feel your heat, the wonderful warmth of you."

They continued a slow movement together and then it started again and she began to tremble, triggering his own pleasure. They climaxed again, then held each other gently in a cocoon of themselves. Suddenly, Ken became conscious of time and looked at the digital clock beside the bed.

"We're missing the show," he said.

"No, we aren't," she laughed. "We're the show."

"Anything Goes."

"Starring us."

"They'll ask what we thought, whether or not we enjoyed it."

The idea injected a somber note into their mood. She grew silent, her expression vague, as if she were looking inward.

"Later," she said. "Let's not spoil the day."

She went into the bathroom and soon he heard the shower going. Again he grew reflective. There were issues to confront. Maggie and the children, the emotional baggage of his marriage. He was locked into responsibilities, expenses, obligations. It was a dilemma that he would have to face. Above all, he must resist any thought of relegating this new relationship with Carol into a sleazy back-alley affair. No way. Never.

Of one thing he was certain. Nothing would ever be the same again. How could it possibly be business as usual for either of them?

He rushed out of bed and into the bathroom, joining Carol in the shower. She giggled, taking the soap. She smiled up at him and held out her arms.

"We predate them. We were together first, before Eliot, before Maggie. They have no rights to us. None. Besides, we have twenty-odd years to make up."

They kissed again. He took her tongue in his mouth and sucked it.

"Well, then," she said, impaling herself on him. "Then we had better not waste any more time."

6

THEY CROSSED Fifth Avenue into the park. A refreshing breeze had rolled in, chasing the late-afternoon clouds, leaving the sun to throw a golden glow over the sky. He had reached out for her hand, but she had quickly withdrawn it.

"You're my girl. I want the world to know," he told her.

"To the world, Ken," she replied, "I'm Mrs. Eliot Butterfield."

"For the moment," Ken agreed. But it was a worrisome notion. And there was, after all, a Mrs. Kenneth Kramer.

"We mustn't be reckless," she said. They walked beside each other, not touching. It was a far cry from the intimacy of the afternoon in her apartment. She seemed to be brooding and it troubled him.

"You're not sorry?" he asked when she was silent for a long time. Her attitude puzzled him. For his part, he felt joyous, fulfilled, brimming with happiness. They continued to walk, but when she didn't answer the question after a long pause, he felt compelled to speak.

"I need to know what you're thinking, Carol. I need to know where we stand. I'm too old to set out on uncertain journeys."

She nodded. He could remember her being intense, but not moody, never despondent.

"So what happens now?" he asked.

"Nothing."

"But I thought . . ."

The Sunday crowd was thinning out. The golden light was turning a bright orange. They meandered along a path, crossing the major park arteries, dodging the few cyclists, roller skaters, and joggers still around. He didn't press her, choosing to walk beside her in silence.

Suddenly she looked at her watch. It was after five. The show would be breaking.

"You should call Maggie," she said suddenly. There was a phone booth up ahead.

"Why?"

"To reassure her," she said. "Besides, you said she wasn't feeling well. A devoted husband would call."

"Really, there's no need. But if you really think I should, I will."

"Please, Ken. Where's the harm?"

"You okay?" he asked when Maggie answered the ring.

"Better," she said, sounding as if she had just gotten up from a long nap. "How was the show?"

"Corny."

"Carol like it?"

"About like me."

He felt himself falling into a role, mouthing words that described someone else, telling lies. He was a man going into hiding to survive.

"You're being nice to her, I hope."

"Very," he said, crawling deeper into the emotional underbrush.

"Be sure to escort her home," Maggie said. "Eliot would expect you to do that."

"I will," he told her.

"No problems?" Carol asked when he returned. It seemed an odd question.

"Problems? How could there be? Isn't everything the same as it was when I left our apartment this morning?"

"That's the point," she whispered as she took his hand. "Everything must seem the same."

They came to the edge of one of the park meadows. There she sat down cross-legged under one of the old elms that formed a boundary of the green expanse. For a moment he stood over her, then she reached up and pulled him down.

"First I want to say this," she began, her eyes locking into his.

"Good news, bad news."

"In a way, yes. There is no question about the chemistry between us. I can't explain it. I won't even try. I don't think we should put a name to it, either. It's . . . it's beyond reason. Most people, I'm sure, don't have anything remotely like this in a life-time. I've also lied to you. I did have flashbacks. At times they have been . . . well . . . very vivid. I knew what we had years ago. I know it now."

"Let's not throw it away again," Ken said.

"No. Let's not." She hesitated, as if she were marshaling her inner resources. "But there is one thing I will never ever give up." Again she hesitated, her body stiffening. "Security and . . ." She seemed to struggle for the right phrase. "Peace of mind. I don't want to struggle again, Ken. Not for ambition. Not for an idea. Not for pleasure. Not for anything. And especially, not for love. That frightens me more than anything. I've gotten used to . . . a kind of freedom, Ken."

"You call what you have freedom?" he said. "What I hear is about money." As crass and unromantic as it sounded, it had the hard ring of truth. He waited for a tough reaction, perhaps a confrontation. None came.

"Not money as such," she said calmly, lowering her eyes as if there were a touch of shame in the idea. "It's what's called reality. I've thought about it ever since I saw you in that restau-rant, Ken. Romeo and Juliet were teenagers, dumb kids playing with fire. You and I both know what they felt."

"Christ, Carol. What are you talking about? I'm not ad-vocating a joint suicide."

"There's a modern form of slow suicide. It's called short of funds. I've been there and I don't like it one bit."

"How about greed?"

He was baiting her and he knew it. But she wasn't biting.

"Tell me, Ken. How free are you?"

He knew what she meant.

"Well I'm not poverty stricken," he said.

"I'll bet you're overloaded. Pressured. In today's world that's like a new kind of poverty. I'm finished with all that, Ken. Forever. And I'll never ever go back. Sounds awful, doesn't it? But you see, Eliot and I have this prenuptial agreement."

He started to speak, but she put her fingers on his lips.

"It's very simple, but legally binding, worked out by the best lawyers money can buy. Put simply it stipulates that everything I acquire in my name during the course of our marriage comes to me on Eliot's death, providing I am not unfaithful to him."

"And if you divorce, say, on other grounds?"

"It's quite foolproof, Ken. Hardly enough to live on. If I don't remarry, I might claim my possessions as an inheritance on Eliot's death." She shook her head and waved her hand as a gesture to put the subject aside.

"You agreed to this? What about the shoe being on the other foot. His . . ." He thought carefully about the word. "His behavior?"

"If he is the guilty party, the adulterer, an unlikely premise I might add, he forfeits his rights to anything I've acquired during our marriage."

"I agree," Ken said. "The odds on that happening seem impossible."

"So, you see," Carol said, "I've already put myself at risk."

"That's about the most awful agreement I ever heard of."

"At the time I would have agreed to almost anything," Carol said.

"And you did. Is that your idea of freedom?" he scowled. She ignored the remark and continued.

"To give Eliot his due, it was understandable for him. He had just come through an expensive divorce. The family money was hit pretty hard. He has children that must be protected as well."

"Doesn't seem fair somehow," Ken sighed.

"And not entirely unfair. You've seen our apartment. As you must have gathered, there's been enough acquired during our marriage to leave me very well provided for. The price of art and antiques have gone through the roof. I've got millions tied up in those possessions. Millions."

"Sounds like a business transaction, not a marriage. Whatever happened to love?"

"Love?" She chuckled wryly. "The energy of Eliot's passions are elsewhere, I'm afraid. Unfortunately for me, Eliot is the kind of man that works things out carefully before he acts." She paused and shrugged. "I suppose he loves me in his way."

"I wasn't talking about Eliot's love," Ken said angrily.

"What I feel for him is not a priority," Carol said.

"That's for sure," Ken muttered. "You've raised pragmatism to an art form. I was referring to us."

He wanted to argue the point openly, but he held back, mulling it instead. Love required proximity, access. Love was a basic need, like thirst and hunger. Life without love was barren, empty, ugly. Love was the essence of the life force. It was everything. The idea pushed back chronology and he was twenty-one again. Perhaps one day soon he would validate that truth in his own way, in his words, his own stories.

"The hell with the money. I earn enough." He paused and looked at his hands. "Shit." He was being a hypocrite now and his present circumstances came rolling back on the tide of inescapable reality.

"Ken, you have kids, too. You'll be plagued by tuition, child support, alimony. I'm talking serious wealth. I know this has to fly in the face of all those pretty stories of eternal love, all the romantic fantasies."

"I don't like people reading my mind," he said, deliberately trying to lighten the mood, fearful of frightening her with this sudden emotional pressure.

"Rational people have to compromise, Ken. There's also another consideration."

"The bad news goes on and on."

"If we were ever to have a life together, I think I would press you to go back to writing. At least to try. That would mean you'd have to give up everything to write. No more Slender Benders. Yes, I would insist on it. Think about it. Let your mind grasp what I'm saying. Carry the fantasy all the way. Maybe we'd go to Europe, places where you'd be inspired. Like Hemingway." She paused. "Consider all the ramifications and you'll see what I mean about freedom."

Her explanation, so clinical, so practical, both elated and depressed him, and he was certain it was at the root of her earlier moodiness. He had been stretched beside her, his head supported by his elbow, which now felt stiff and tingling. He sat up and looked out on the meadow, slowly emptying of people.

For the first time that day, he felt the weight of years, of experience, of the ineluctable ravages of fate. Once he had been a threat to her artistic endeavors. Now he was a threat to her financial security. It was a troubling irony.

And yet the nature of love hadn't changed, certainly not the mystery of attraction. And passion. Their desires, their hearts, perhaps their souls, had resisted time's decay. Love could endure, he had discovered. But nothing could untangle the complicated wiring of the past.

"So where does that leave us, Carol?" he asked.

"On the horns of a dilemma," she sighed.

He watched her, sitting, legs crossed, Indian style. She had barely moved. Taking her hand, he pulled her up, then guided her into the carefully landscaped stand of shade trees. It was getting darker, and where they stood was now in deep shadow.

Pressing her against a tree, his lips found hers.

"No matter what, I will never let you go again," he whispered after a long kiss.

"Then we must be very clever, very discreet. No risks. Absolutely no risks. You must promise me."

"Why am I always doing the promising?" he said.

He felt her warm tears on her cheeks.

"Because I believe your promises, Ken. I've put my life in your hands. There, you see. I've proved the way I feel. I've taken the ultimate risk. Made myself vulnerable."

"I'll keep all my promises. I promise."

She started to laugh and his embrace tightened and he kissed her wet cheeks, licking the salt tears.

"One promise especially, my love. I'm not going to throw away any more years. I'm going to find a way."

7

CAROL WAS surprised when Eliot asked her to go with him to the Wildlife Federation Convention in Washington, D.C.

It was late September. They were lying in bed. Eliot was reading a book and she was pretending to read. Instead, she was thinking of Ken, of this miracle that had occurred between them. Images of them together floated through her mind, like a continuous-reel motion picture that she never tired of watching. When Eliot spoke it was like shutting down the projector and turning on the houselights.

"Convention? I thought you were going yourself," she said, instantly alert. Normally, he would attend conventions only if he was giving a paper, which, she assumed, was the case. Also, he rarely invited her to go with him, since he was usually back the same day.

"We'll be there three days, Friday through Sunday," he told her.

Friday, she thought, her heart pounding. Not Friday.

"I thought you were just giving a paper," she said, determined to keep calm.

109

"I am. But I decided to stay on and attend some of the sessions."

"I thought they always bored you."

"They do." She had turned toward him. His head was still in his book, and his half-glasses had slipped to the tip of his nose. "But this time some of them sound quite interesting." He turned a page and continued to read.

"But my students," she said, hearing the waver in her voice. Mustn't, she warned herself.

"That's Mondays and Wednesdays," he said, unconcerned. "We'll leave Friday morning, be back Sunday night."

"This Friday?"

It was Tuesday. He nodded.

"Friday? Oh, no, Eliot, that's my workout day. You know how important that is to me."

"I'd like you to be there. I really would, Carol."

"It's not very fair of you, Eliot."

This appeal to fairness had proven currency with Eliot, who prided himself on making intellectually balanced decisions based upon, as he called it, candor, and fairness. Unfortunately, such decisions were always skewered in his direction. Fairness was what Eliot wanted.

"You could work out in Washington," he said. "It is, after all, despite its arcane political practices, a very modern city." He had turned toward her and inspected her face over his half-glasses. The injection of sarcasm was a sure sign that he meant business.

"What is so important about me coming?"

He appeared mildly surprised. "There are going to be social events." He had assumed a stern tone, as if he were talking to an adolescent. "Contacts to be made. It's awkward to be a single at these events."

"I hate those things, Eliot."

She felt as if she were testing parameters, stretching boundaries. This was definitely a new attitude for her.

"Carol, I'm insisting on this," he said, still watching her.

She knew this was unusual conduct for her. She had always acquiesced. It was, after all, a perfectly reasonable request on his part. Under normal conditions, a mere suggestion would suffice, or he would simply say, "We're going," and she would immediately begin to make a mental checklist of preparations.

"It's such short notice," she persisted, but her protest was running out of steam.

"Well, just rearrange your schedule," he muttered, turning back to his book.

"I don't know if I can," she said.

"Dammit, Carol," Eliot said, his face flushing. "Just do it."

She feared saying more, turning her back to him. Giving up her Friday afternoon was like withholding water from someone stumbling through a desert.

Friday afternoon was reserved for them, for her and Ken. Real-life time, they called it. This had been going on for the past two months. All energy, all passion, all joy, sexual and psychic, was focused on Friday. Their moment.

As she lay there, the projector in her mind started up again and she watched the flickering pictures.

Last Friday.

Ken was the creative one, creative and resourceful. He had found a little tourist hotel on the West Side. There was a charming room on the fifth floor with a bay window, a queen-sized bed, and Art Deco pictures on the walls, slim ladies with question-mark figures. The old-fashioned bathroom boasted a bathtub on porcelain lion's paws and a shower with a flat head as big as a sunhat. There was a toilet with a high flush box, pull chain, and oversized faucets.

Somehow the room had been remarkably preserved and had resisted modernization. Ken had told her that it was symbolic of them, their love, which had also resisted time.

"How did you find it?"

"Research," he said, and he had reserved it for three months of Fridays, subject to renewal, of course, giving the desk clerk a "sweetener" of a hundred-dollar bill.

By then they had established the ground rules: public caution, safety, discretion. In their room, however, their private sanctum, all rules were suspended, all inhibitions scuttled, and they indulged themselves in furious, frenzied lovemaking intense enough to carry them through the week.

The Butterfields and the Kramers also met as couples now on a regular basis, Saturday evenings for dinner and a show and during the week for dinner and conversation. On occasion they exchanged visits to their respective homes.

Throughout these events, Carol and Ken maintained an air of scrupulous indifference between them, an aloofness that would often prompt their spouses to remark on it.

"He's really a very pleasant fellow, Carol," Eliot would tell her. "But sometimes you treat him as if he wasn't there."

"Really, Eliot," she had told him, especially after their first "reunion" together. "I did spend an entire afternoon with him, remember."

"But you were watching a show," he had pointed out.

"We did talk," she had protested, injecting the kind of inflection that indicated that she had been less than enthusiastic.

"Give it a chance. I really think he's worth knowing . . . for both of us."

It seemed an oddly tolerant comment for Eliot.

"Oh, Ken's all right," she had concluded, not wishing to belabor the issue. "Really, it's great being with both of them."

Ken was reporting a similar response.

"Better this way," Carol had commented, "as long as we don't take unnecessary risks."

The projector hummed in her brain, throwing glorious images on the screen of her mind. Oh, God, she sighed, like a booming voice-over, as she tried to slow down the images of last Friday. They needed to make up in intensity what they lacked in time. Remembering, she pressed her legs together, feeling the wetness between them.

They were lying on opposite parts of the bed, she at the head and he at the foot, legs spread, observing each other in a similar pose.

"Make love to me with your mind and your eyes," he told her. "Let your brain snap photos to carry us through the week."

She giggled consent, delighted with the sense of abandonment, observing him, concentrating on the intimate details of his body, watching his penis harden as his eyes and mind reached across the bed.

"Imagine it," he told her.

"I am," she assured him, gyrating her hips, forming a picture of him inserting his hard penis, pumping. She could not resist moving her hand downward to her pubic hairs.

"No touching," he said.

"Not for you either?"

"Just picture it," he said. "Put out your tongue."

She did as he asked, rolling it around between her lips. He did the same.

"I'm kissing you everywhere now," he said. She began to accelerate the movement of her hips, lifting her pelvis, making humping motions. She watched his penis throb, moving like a jumping bean.

"Please, Ken. I want to take you in me."

"It is in you," he said. "Feel it. See how it goes in and out. I'm stroking your breasts now."

"Can I touch them?"

"No," he said as he watched his penis jump and his pelvis move up and down in time with hers. Then she saw the shiny moisture on its tip and his tongue licking his lips, and then she felt the first faraway waves begin, coming closer, closer.

"I love you, my sweet love, my sweet love," she heard him say as he came and she felt her own climactic contractions begin at the same time.

"And I love you. My man. My beautiful man."

When her body settled, he reached across the bed and enfolded her in his arms.

"You see," he whispered, "now we have pictures. We can be away from each other and still make love."

"I never believed it was possible," she said, kissing his chest.

"The human brain," he said, tapping his temple. "It has limitless powers."

The days were getting shorter and the afternoon sun quickly disappeared behind the taller buildings, darkening the room.

"Anything's possible," Ken said.

"Yes," she agreed. "Anything."

These cloistered moments together, when the fury of their passion had subsided, seemed to kindle a sense of renewal. Past regrets faded and their thoughts seemed to reflect a resurgence of optimism. Even the old ambitions, once so obsessive, seemed to reemerge in a mellowed, more mature state.

Last Friday she had told him about the way she had conducted her ballet classes. She had never before thought about it in these terms.

"I used to look at these kids with a cynical eye, especially the ones with the bit in their teeth, the obsessed ones, whose ambitions exceed their talent. I used to push them, too. As hard as I could, take them to the edge. There was something mean-spirited about it, as if my own failure was forcing a kind of revenge."

"Bitterness does strange things to people," he had responded, as if he, too, were discovering insights into his own past.

"But in the classes I conduct now," she confessed, "I don't feel that. Oh, I can sense the obsessed ones. Many times I can see it in their mothers. But my view and my methods seem more balanced, more understanding, more compassionate. I actually enjoy teaching now."

"That may have more to do with economics than understanding," he had commented wryly. "You don't have to teach to eat."

One of the joys of their relationship was the dissolution of boundaries. They had no secrets between them and could speak their minds and hearts.

"Maybe our sights were too high," he told her.

"Like Hemingway's leopard," she said.

Her reference startled him.

"You remembered," he said.

"Yes, Ken. Everything."

"Maybe, like that damned leopard, we sought to reach too damned high. Perhaps we could have been happier, stayed together, if we hadn't wanted so much so fast, if we hadn't been so focused and sweaty-palmed."

"How profound when you have twenty-twenty hindsight."

"Why the great American novel? Why a prima ballerina? Sometimes I have the urge to write just one good well-executed short story." He chuckled. "There it is. The urge returning, but on a more realistic note. I think maybe you had it right. I would like to go back to it."

He had paused, his expression growing darker, the optimism fading.

"But not without you," he said.

"Please, Ken."

"I mean it."

His determination showed in his expression.

"Remember Hemingway's leopard on Kilimanjaro. He aspired to reach the summit and froze to death for his trouble."

"Screw the leopard. It doesn't have to be impossible," he said firmly.

"What are you trying to say to me, Ken?"

"Well, it can't be just playtime on Friday afternoons and mind-fucking memories." She caught his flash of anger, sensed his frustration and, of course, her own.

"This is better than never at all," she told him, guiding his head toward her lips, kissing him deeply. At least they could express themselves through this sexual intimacy.

"It's ecstasy, my darling," he told her. "It's like feasting. The euphoria is fabulous, but I can't take the famine."

"Then settle for the euphoria."

He moved her body across the bed sideways so that her head rolled over the edge. He stood over her and put his penis on her face and she took it and kissed it. Then she put it in her mouth and reached over and grasped his buttocks as he pumped his penis in her mouth until he came, and then he bent over and kissed her lips.

The splays of late-afternoon sun playing across the room reminded them that she would soon have to go. To avoid suspicion she would be home at six, which was the normal time she would return from her workout.

As Carol dressed, Ken lay in bed, hands behind his head, looking up at the ceiling.

"I can feel there's something throttling through that mind of yours," she had chuckled, watching him in the mirror as she combed her hair. He didn't comment at first. Then, without looking at her, he spoke:

"Maggie and Eliot. What do you think they do up there in his office for hours on end?"

She turned to observe him, struck by the curiosity of his comment.

"Work, of course. They're creating this data bank, Ken. You know that." He had not alluded to it before.

"Alone?"

"I'm not sure. He has a part-time secretary."

"So, they do spend a great deal of time alone."

"Well, yes, I suppose," she said.

"You don't think . . ." He let the words hang in the air.

"You have to be kidding. Eliot and Maggie? No way. That's strictly business. All platonic."

"But look how they delight in each other's company."

"That's true. But you have to understand Eliot. His real passions are cerebral, not physical. Actually, he can go for weeks without . . ." It embarrassed her to talk about this. It was necessary to keep things in separate compartments. That was duty, she told herself. This was love.

"Even at the beginning?"

"Must we, Ken?"

"It's just an idea," he muttered. But she could see he was still concentrating on the subject.

"Believe me. It's ridiculous."

"Because he's, well, less than ardent?"

She started to laugh, then checked herself. Where was he heading, she wondered.

"Ken, really."

"And lately?"

"Let's not say it's one of his foremost priorities. Oh, he's human. Like any healthy man." She paused, remembering. "No," she said with an air of finality, assessing his original question. "I've detected no difference lately, if that's what you want to know. Neither more nor less."

"You don't think Maggie could turn him on?"

"You tell me, Ken."

He was silent again for a long time.

"There's a lot to say for big breasts. Any man could find comfort in them."

"And do they comfort you?"

"They did once. But that was before."

"And she?"

"Hard to tell." He shrugged. "She can take it or leave it."

"She doesn't notice?"

"Notice what?" he said coyly.

She had finished dressing and grooming herself. He still lay on the bed, naked, reflective. Bending over him, she patted his penis.

"Let's face it, Ken. I haven't left her much."

He sprang upright and gathered her in his arms.

"Ken, please," she squirmed coquettishly. "It's getting late." But he did not release her, holding her to him.

"Fact is," he said, "when it does happen, I feel like I'm betraying you, that I'm being unfaithful. Imagine that."

"I know the feeling," Carol confessed.

"Proves that it's not sex that holds marriages together. There are other considerations." He paused and studied her face. "Like prenuptial agreements."

She stiffened and insinuated herself out of his embrace.

"That's not fair. You have things that anchor you as well. Your children, the concept of family. And don't tell me you're without financial worries."

"Nothing that can't be handled. What's keeping us apart is that damned agreement of yours. Not to mention your idea of material security, of the good life."

"Unfortunately," she snapped, "they go hand in hand." She waited until the brief flash of anger dissipated. "Do I have to explain once again the debilitating effects of financial pressure?"

"Not to me, Carol," he sighed. "I'm sorry."

He got out of bed and went over to a chair where he had thrown his clothes. Then he stepped into his jockey shorts. She watched him. His attitude was puzzling. Suddenly, perhaps feeling her inspection, he looked up at her.

"But it has been percolating in my head," he said, putting on his socks.

"No one ever accused you of not being creative."

He chuckled, then seemed to slip into concentration as he paused in his dressing. She saw he was self-absorbed and remained silent.

"When we're all together," he said after his pause, "*they* look like the married ones. They're the ones with the most to say to each other. They're the ones with the most obvious compatibility."

"By design. We've agreed to show as little interest in each other as possible."

"More than design, Carol. They may actually have more in common with each other than with us."

He nodded as if to underscore the point. Then, rising, he stepped into his pants, zipped his fly, and tightened his belt.

"Kindling ready to be ignited." He stopped all movement suddenly and looked at her. "All we have to do is take it one step further."

"Ken, I'm not looking for something we can't handle."

"In a sense they're already together."

"Working together," she corrected. "It's inconceivable that it could be otherwise."

He shook his head as if he were questioning himself, waiting for an answer. "So far," he said, looking at her pointedly. "Our job will be to make something happen between them."

"Like what? An affair? Force them to fall in love?"

"Why not? It happens," Ken said, buttoning his shirt. "It happened to us."

"But you're talking about something else," she said. "Falling in love is like . . . like Kismet, mysterious, involuntary. You're talking about inducing them. How can you possibly do that?"

"Ideas can be planted in people's heads," Ken said, looping his tie quickly, then pulling it together in a Windsor knot. "Iago did it to Othello. And there are cults that do it to people all the time."

"Brainwash them into loving each other?" Carol asked nervously.

"In a manner of speaking. Why not? Look at the upside. We succeed in drawing them into an adulterous affair. Discovery would mean a divorce on your terms. If it works, it will solve everything."

"It's impossible," she said flatly, although the idea did intrigue her.

"We throw them together. Make ourselves less attractive to them. We suggest. Persuade. Insinuate. Seduce them into the idea. Play with their heads."

"Play with Eliot's head? He'd be way ahead of us."

"Not on that subject. I've seen it. When it comes to human behavior, he's a retard."

"And Maggie?"

"Despite her intellect, she has a certain naïveté."

"It sounds bizarre," Carol said, but her skepticism was wavering.

"I'm in the advertising business, remember. I have seen the power of persuasion. Especially when conditions are right," Ken said, warming to his own arguments. "Hell, Carol. Study them when they're together. They're like cream cheese and jelly. A computer dating service would spit them out in tandem. They're matchable. Compatible." He was growing increasingly excited. "There seems to be a propensity between them, a bent in the right direction. Barring your unwillingness to scuttle your nest egg on your own, admit it's worth trying."

In the abstract, she thought, it was, indeed, a solution. But there it hung, like some elusive apparition in a fevered dream, unreachable and transparent.

"Considering the human material," she asked with a clinician's intonation, "do you think they can be induced into actually being unfaithful?"

He took his wallet and keys from the dresser and put them in his pocket. Then he turned and looked at her archly, offering a thin smile of amusement.

"Why not? Why should we have all the fun?"

She laughed. "I have to confess," she said, cocking her head, "it would be like winning the lottery."

"Maybe for them, too," he muttered, injecting an odd, wishful note.

"You really think we can be that clever?"

"We are that clever," he said, reaching out, gathering her into his arms.

"At least on Fridays," she whispered.

"It will be like offering them medicine that, in the end, will be good for them. And everybody gets what they want. You get your divorce and the art and antiques. And me?" He paused, and cupping her buttocks, drew her close to him. "I get you every day of the week."

He kissed her deeply, then released her.

"It's so . . . so conspiratorial," Carol said. "Although I'm not quite certain how we do this."

"I'm not sure myself." Ken put on his jacket and studied himself in the mirror, patting his hair in place. "We'll observe them first. Study them carefully. Then we'll come up with a strategy." He tapped his teeth, obviously in deep thought. "Some variation of selling, making them picture themselves as a twosome. We reinforce the obvious. Keep nurturing the idea. Watch for the opportunities. Keep the pot boiling." He sucked in his breath. "Goddamn, I like this."

"And us?" she asked. "How must we appear?"

"Aloof, distant, disinterested in each other," he replied with some authority. "But ingratiating to them. Charming. Always appearing innocent, unobserving, without an iota of suspicion.

Make them feel secure enough to show warmth to each other in our presence."

"Very good, Ken." She smiled. "You should have been a writer."

"Maybe someday," he laughed. "Anyway, it's food for thought. Grist for next Friday's mill."

"Oh, God, Ken. A whole week. How will I bear it?" She looked at her watch. It was nearly six. "It's late," she said. "Mustn't give them the slightest cause for alarm. Not Eliot. Or Maggie."

She embraced him near the door, lingering over a long kiss. "We'll be very clever, won't we, Ken?" she said.

"Very," he said. "And we'll be doing them the greatest favor of their lives."

"Wonderful," she said. "And isn't it better to give than recieve?"

The next morning, Carol did not get out of bed at the usual hour.

"Are you all right?" Eliot asked when he came in later and she was still in bed. She shrugged and kept her eyes closed, mostly to avoid any discussion about going to the convention. She toyed with the idea of feigning sickness to get out of it.

"I'm a bit under the weather," she told him, closing her eyes.

"Then you should get your rest. We want you better for the weekend."

He didn't bother her after that. She heard him dress. Then later she heard the front door buzz. That would be the maid. After a while the maid knocked and asked if she wanted coffee and toast. She said yes, got up, and dressed.

Of all their Fridays together she wanted this one to happen because of what they had discussed. She had, as he had suggested, thought about it, observing Eliot during the week. They had gone out for dinner with Carol and Ken on Sunday. A reconnaissance mission, she had characterized it to herself. Was it possible? She avoided Ken's glance all through dinner. Or was he avoiding hers?

As usual the conversation was dominated by Eliot and Maggie, the main subject being a plan by officials in Nairobi to fence in the animal parks to stop the poachers. Maggie, Carol had noted, had begun to be quite passionate on the subject.

But mostly, she was observing them, contemplating the possibility that Ken had suggested. Their relationship seemed too cerebral and, when it came to computers, even esoteric. They talked about data banks and bytes and binary theory with an intensity that was passionate, but gave no indication of anything either physical or emotional beyond that. Theirs appeared to be an excitement of the mind only, not the stuff that could induce the kind of relationship that triggered sexual passion.

Nevertheless, occasionally she noted something between them that might be a starting point, an intimate look, a fatherly pat on the hand, a guiding arm on Maggie's back. Possibilities. She would discuss that with Ken next Friday. They would compare notes. In her mind, she had built it up as a most important Friday, a Friday among Fridays.

Now this thing with the convention had intruded. She would have to talk it over with Ken. She called him at the office, something she had previously forbidden herself. No point in exposing herself to a secretary's recognition. One never knew how these little innocent sorties could backfire. People observed other people more keenly than was suspected. But one little call might do no harm, she decided.

She called him from a street booth on Broadway.

"He wants me to go to this Wildlife convention," she told him.

Ken laughed.

"What's so funny?"

"Manna from heaven," Ken said. "Maggie is going as well. Seems that the Wildlife people are interacting to put together a massive data bank, countries, species, genetics, all very complicated, but Eliot wants Maggie to be there as well. And Maggie wants me to come. Says she doesn't want to be a third wheel."

"And are you?" Carol asked.

"I refused," Ken said, lowering his voice.

"You didn't," she said.

"Think of the time they'll spend together. It's an opportunity."

"Unfortunately, I have to go," she protested. "The three of us will be together."

There was a long silence on the phone. She heard him breathing.

"That dictates a change of plans," he muttered.

"They'll be attending meetings all day," she said slowly.

"That clinches that, Mrs. Butterfield. We have therefore to create our own agenda," Ken said, suddenly businesslike, as if someone might have just walked into his office. "Work on that plan we discussed. Yes. I've been giving it lots of thought. I've got some ideas."

"I'm developing some myself," Carol said.

She felt her heart lift. It was, indeed, manna from heaven.

"And in between we can take in the sights," Ken said with obvious elation.

"Absolutely," she said saucily. "And have I got some sights for you."

"Good. I could use another week's worth."

She giggled and hung up.

8

THE FOUR of them attended the opening cocktail party in the ballroom of the Mayflower Hotel. Eliot cut a dashing figure in the group, dressed in a dark pin-striped suit and silk striped tie. He wore a white carnation in his buttonhole, which designated him as an important official of the group.

"My friends, Mr. and Mrs. Kramer. Maggie and Ken. And, of course, you know my wife, Carol."

He made numerous introductions in this vein as they slowly circled the room, drinks in hand. Carol had stepped back a bit, deliberately putting Maggie by Eliot's side. Both Carol and Ken were supernumeraries here, which suited their motives perfectly. After a while, Eliot was squiring Maggie around, introducing her, showing her off.

"Maggie's a computer expert," they could hear him say above the din.

Seeing them both like this only reinforced the idea that they could be . . . Ken searched his mind for an appropriate word . . . mated. That was it. They had an obvious commonality. All that was needed was a little stimulation.

123

Both he and Carol, as if on command, faded into opposite corners of the room. Their eyes met. They nodded and circled. Ken observed Maggie and Eliot. Eliot's handsome face was flushed with the excitement of adulation. At times a circle gathered around them, men and women standing about, rocking on their heels, listening with rapt attention to Eliot, Maggie respectful, occasionally interjecting a comment. She looked happy, in her element, belonging.

Closely observed like this, they were a natural fit, the perfect couple. It struck Ken then that perhaps their logic, his and Carol's, was wrong, that the situation should be confronted head-on, the obvious articulated. Eliot and Maggie were a far better fit than their present mismatches.

The cocktail party droned on, the din rising, as more and more delegates piled into the room. Ken and Carol were traveling around the room in an opposite circumference, intersecting finally near the door. Motioning her with his eyes, Carol followed him out into the grand chandeliered hall, past smaller party rooms. Finding one that was empty, he ducked in and she followed.

The room was dark, lit only by the light of the corridor. Inside, he took her hand and led her into the darkest corner, where they embraced, kissing deeply.

"You saw them," he said. "Made for each other."

"No question in my mind," she said. He felt her breath tickling his ear.

"We encourage that idea. Put it in their heads. Be subtle, casual. How much they have in common. What an outstanding couple. Show pride. No jealousy."

"Make them compare, is that it?"

"I think so," he whispered. "It's not a science."

"And us? How do we act?"

"Like always. Friendly and tolerant. Cool and distant."

"Yes," she said, her breath coming in gasps as he stroked her hair with one hand, while the other came to rest on her buttocks.

"If only you could sit down with him. Have a civilized discussion on the merits."

"What merits? Not for Eliot," Carol said. "I'd be on the street in seconds. You don't know him."

"Surely, he wouldn't want to stay with someone who wants out."

"Oh, he'd let me out, all right." She shook her head. "I wouldn't want to risk it. Eliot can be devious and subtle. We get him suspicious and there's no telling how he'd react. He finds out about us, he could take it all away."

"Take it all away," Ken said. "There it is again."

There was no point in pursuing that argument. She had convinced herself that if she came away from her marriage with Eliot empty-handed, sooner or later it would have a corrosive effect on their relationship.

"That's settled, darling," she said sweetly. "Especially now that we've found a way out."

So she had bought the idea completely, he thought. He was elated. The plan, after all, needed two prongs.

"We have to make them see it," Ken said. "That's the objective."

"The spark is there between them, Ken. If only they can feel the way we do, the way we do now."

He sensed the rising need between them.

"Yes, now," he said.

"God, yes," she responded. "Besides, it's Friday."

She leaned against the wall and began to shimmy her long cocktail dress upward. He helped her when the hem had reached her thighs. She was wearing stockings alone, held up by a garter belt and no panties.

"As promised. Always ready for you, my love." With the wall as support, he lifted her and inserted himself. The room was dark and quiet, the only sound their gasping breath. It was uncommon and risky, which accelerated their excitement.

Just then the room burst into brightness.

"And this is one of our smaller rooms," a male voice said.

Alert to her condition, Carol moved away from Ken and hurriedly arranged her dress. None too soon. A moment later they stepped forward. Two men stood at the entrance, one with a clipboard. As expected, they were both surprised.

"We'll be needing a larger room," Ken said. "What's the capacity?"

"One hundred," the man with the clipboard said.

"That won't do," Carol said. "The wedding guests are up to two hundred."

They started to walk toward the entrance.

"I can show you a larger room if you wish," the man with the clipboard said.

"Maybe tomorrow," Ken said. He looked suddenly to the left of the entrance. "There it is."

"What?" the man with the clipboard asked.

"The light switch," Ken said. "We've been groping around."

They walked out of the room and headed back to the cocktail party.

"What a team we are," Ken said. "How can we miss?"

"We could have been caught," Carol murmured. "That's how."

They got back to the cocktail party and split up. At the far end of the room, Ken spotted Eliot and Maggie in the center of a group. He was certain they hadn't realized that they had been gone. He watched them for a long time. Made for each other, he thought. All we have to do is make them see it.

Later they had dinner at Duke's, a large restaurant with an old-fashioned steak house feeling. It smelled faintly of garlic from the pickles placed in a boat dish on each table.

The waiter was an older man who had obviously seen much service.

"Watch this," Ken said with a wink. It was, he realized, an act of ingratiation, despite the fact that this was not Eliot's kind of restaurant. He looked at Carol. See, I am beginning, his eyes told her. "What are the specials, my good man?"

"Specials?" the waiter sneered. "You want specials?"

"My friend here loves to hear about the specials," Ken said. "He greatly appreciates culinary artistry."

"So, you've noticed," Eliot replied, not quite getting it.

"He's teasing you," Maggie said.

"We got specials," the waiter said. "Fat frankfurters." He made a ring with his thumb and forefinger. "This big."

"Oh, those specials," Eliot said, forcing a tolerant laugh. The others joined in. Couple friends, Ken thought. How jolly we all are. How simpatico we must appear to observers.

"I've been here before," Ken said.

"Choose from the menu," the waiter harumphed. "Here we still got pickles on the table."

"Some things never change," Ken said.

Maggie ordered broiled chicken, Carol swordfish, and Ken and Eliot sirloin steaks, which prompted Eliot to plunge into the subject of the Masai, the African tribe in Kenya that literally lived with and measured their wealth in the numbers of cattle they owned.

"They recognize every cow and bull they have by their markings. They even name them. Their entire lives are built around them. They construct their houses with cattle dung, placing them in a circle in the center of which they keep the herd."

"Things must get pretty pungent around the village," Ken said, determined to be affable.

"The stink is rather gamey," Carol said.

"Shall I tell them what the staple of their diet is?" Eliot asked Carol. He was being playful, Ken observed, feeling good.

"I hope you all have strong stomachs," Carol said.

Eliot continued. "They cut a vein in the neck of the cow." He picked up a knife and demonstrated on his own neck. "They catch the blood in a gourd already filled with milk and this mixture is their staple."

"It must have nutritional value," Maggie said.

"They are tall, beautiful people. Quite striking in their orange robes. Quite distinctive." Eliot paused and elaborately broke a salt stick in two, on which he spread butter meticulously. "And do you know how they clean these gourds?" Eliot asked after he chewed a piece of the salt stick.

"How?" Maggie asked.

"You really want to know?" Carol said.

Maggie nodded and turned to Eliot.

"With cow urine. They wash the gourds out with cow urine. In fact, cow urine is considered a useful disinfectant for the body as well."

"Interesting," Maggie said.

"I told you," Carol said.

"That's Africa for you," Eliot said. "A continent of unbelievable customs, sights, sounds. Nature's last stand. An ecology system in its death throes. That's what all this wildlife preservation is about. Preventing a holocaust. That's why we keep going back time and again. Not only to revel in the glory of this vast wilderness. To bear witness and try to do something about it."

Eliot's eyes seemed to glow with religious fervor. He glanced toward Ken, then, as he spoke, toward Maggie.

"Purple sunsets, clear sweet air, the only place left in the world to contemplate one's personal value system, to confront the truth of oneself away from the pressures and distractions of the modern world."

Of course, Ken and Maggie knew that Eliot and Carol were going for three weeks in December. In July it had seemed such a long time away. Now it was October, just around the corner.

"Carol's been three times," Eliot said. "What did you think, Carol? Tell them."

"There's nothing quite like it."

She had talked about it with Ken from time to time, calling it "wonderful at first, but repetitious." Now she was suddenly describing it in more glowing terms. "It stays with you for a long time. Each time you go it becomes totally different, like entering other alien worlds. There are all these fantastic and amazingly diverse creatures living together on these vast plains, struggling to survive. It's incredibly gorgeous and inspiring."

She paused for a moment, then glanced first at Maggie, then at Ken, to whom the message was immediately telescoped.

"I wish you could both come with us," Carol said.

"What a wonderful idea," Eliot interjected.

Maggie and Ken exchanged glances.

"Sounds a bit out of our range," Maggie said cautiously.

"Well, at least it might be fun to think about," Ken said to Maggie.

"Tantalizing," Maggie sighed.

"Well worth the contemplation," Eliot said.

Then the subject was gone and they turned to more mundane matters. Throughout the meal, Ken remained alert to nuance and opportunity, awed by Carol's sudden stroke of brilliance. Africa! Of course. Toward the end of the meal, Eliot read from a printed program he took from an inside pocket.

"Tomorrow we have a breakfast meeting. Then I give my paper. A luncheon meeting. A bit of free time. Another meeting at four. Then, of course, at night the black-tie awards dinner."

"Sounds like a full plate," Ken said, his glance drifting to Maggie.

"They're welcome to join us," Maggie said. "Aren't they, Eliot?"

"Absolutely," Eliot said, turning to Ken. "Unless you'd rather sightsee."

"Good idea. I've only been to Washington on business," Ken said. "I thought I'd hire a car. Take in Mount Vernon." He was pleased with his fast thinking; the excursion to Washington's home suggested distance and, therefore, a longer time frame. Besides, their absence would provide an opportunity for Eliot to bask in Maggie's admiration, unfettered by their presence.

"And you, Carol?" Eliot said. "What's your pleasure?"

"I've read Eliot's paper," Carol said.

"You could sightsee with Ken," Maggie suggested.

"That would be wonderful. Mount Vernon is incredible. And it's filled with American antiques," Eliot said.

"I'm not much for sightseeing," Carol said, obviously cautious, feigning reluctance, playing it perfectly. "We'll see how I feel tomorrow," she added with indifference.

Bingo, Ken thought. They are playing into our hands.

But it was the idea of Africa that most intrigued Ken. It seemed the perfect venue for what they had in mind. Three weeks together. Opportunities for still greater intimacy between Eliot and Maggie in a place of beauty, mystery, and romance. Purple sunsets. Clear sweet air. His mind clung to those images. And others of his own creation. Days of exploration on the vast plains. Nights by the open fire.

Of course the money was an issue and Maggie would balk at the expense. Had Carol considered that aspect of it? Perhaps she had.

Going in style with Eliot would cost, Ken calculated, fifteen, maybe twenty thousand. But money, in this instance, wasn't the point. Carol had cleverly planted the idea in Eliot's and Maggie's minds. She had made it seem so perfectly natural, so seamless, so expertly manipulative, as if she were a veteran of the process, a skilled practitioner of the brainwasher's art.

Suddenly he felt a twinge of guilt. The method had the aura of a charade, but it was not harmless, not merely a game. His

thoughts were leading him down a forbidden path. He checked
himself quickly. The means, when the cause was worthy, justified
the ends. Didn't they?

Later, in their room, Ken contemplated his timing and tone.
It was important to have it just right. He waited until Maggie
came out of the bathroom dressed for bed, her skin moist with
cream. She wore a single plastic curler on top of her head. A nice
person, he told himself, observing her without guilt or desire. At
the beginning, there might have been something between them,
but that was long ago, far away, dead as cold ashes.

"Quite a brilliant fellow, Eliot," he said, sitting on the chair
as he took off his shoes. Maggie had settled herself in the bed,
propped the pillows, and put on her reading glasses. When he
mentioned Eliot she took them off again.

"I quite agree," she said. "A very unusual man."

"Inspiring, too."

"You noticed that?"

"Yes, I did. He's fun to be around. Deep. Interesting. The
way he described Africa."

"And Carol. She was equally as eloquent."

He ignored her comment and pressed on.

"Do you enjoy working with him?"

"Yes, I do," she said. "He's patient, analytical, and brilliant.
He has a mind that cuts to the quick."

"Yes, he does," Ken agreed.

"She, as well."

"They seem to live well," Ken said. "He's got lots of style,
don't you think?"

"Oh, yes. That he has."

Enough, he decided. When he didn't speak further she put
on her glasses and began to read. After a while, it was Maggie
who spoke.

"She's quite beautiful, isn't she?"

Ken turned to look at her. Her glasses were off again and she
was swinging them lazily.

"Pleasant," he said. "I find her pleasant."

"I think she's more than that, Ken. A woman that gets a
man like Eliot isn't just pleasant. There must be a lot more to
her."

"Yes. I suppose. If you put it in that context."

"She seems to worship the ground he walks on."

Ken paused, contemplating the opportunity, searching himself for exactly the right nuance.

"Wouldn't you?" he asked. "A man so accomplished." He hoped he had screened out rancor, envy, or jealousy.

"I'm proud he's my friend, not just my client," she said. Not "our" friend, he noted, wondering if he was finally making some headway.

Suddenly he remembered something he had written once when he was writing copy for a lawn-grass product. "Obey the soil's need. Never overseed." He remained silent as he undressed and got into his pajamas. Only then did he speak again, hoping to divert her attention from her book.

"I find the African thing very tempting," he said.

She looked up from her book and turned to him, her eyes brightening.

"God, yes."

"It would cost a bundle, I'll bet."

"I'm sure of that," she said.

"But it would be the experience of a lifetime."

"Yes, it would." He could tell that it was working on her, that a commitment was growing in her mind.

"We could borrow it maybe," Ken said casually.

"You think we could?" she asked.

He thought about that, how it could be accomplished. The idea was growing in his mind as well. Africa seemed the perfect atmosphere for matters to thrive between Eliot and Maggie. Maybe he could borrow the money from his company, against his pension plan. Call it an investment.

After a while, Maggie put out the light.

"Africa," she sighed. "How romantic. I'd love it."

Romantic, he thought. Exactly right. He lay beside her, not touching, not wishing to touch her. He thought of Carol lying beside Eliot in another part of the hotel. Had she done her job, he wondered, seeding Eliot's mind?

He dozed, then awoke with a start, trying to remember the dream that had disturbed him.

It was then that he got out of bed and sat in the chair, watching the sleeping Maggie, wondering if she could absorb ideas in her sleep, a method often suggested as a persuasive technique, but not proven scientifically.

"Love Eliot," he whispered. "Arouse him. Make him fall in love with you. Free Carol. Liberate us."

He whispered these words over and over again like some weird mantra. Then he tried others in the same vein. She did not stir. Finally, he felt silly, like an Indian medicine man offering meaningless incantations. He was allowing his hopes to dominate his logic, but somehow this method seemed less menacing, more honest.

Then he grew drowsy, crawled back into bed, and fell asleep.

9

T HEY DROVE in the rented Oldsmobile along the Potomac on the road to Mount Vernon, past trees painted in autumn colors. Ken drove, one hand on the wheel, one hand in Carol's. Occasionally he would lift her hand and brush it with his lips.

"A whole day together," she said.

"For them, too."

"Yes," she said. She felt good and her thoughts drifted back to the events of yesterday, her mind recycling last night's conversation with Eliot after they had returned to their room.

She had, following Ken's instructions, sung Maggie's praises.

"She's quite a lady," she told Eliot, eyes averted from his, pretending absorption in the chore of brushing her hair.

When she had come out of the shower, Eliot had been sitting at the desk making notes on a yellow pad. There was something about the way he was working, hunched over, crowded in, that suggested he was being overprotective about whatever he was doing. But, then, it could have been her imagination, another aspect of her paranoia.

When he did not turn around, she repeated the comment. Perhaps he had not heard.

"She's quite a lady."

"Who?" he said, continuing to make his notes, still hunched over like a schoolboy preventing someone from copying a test paper.

"Maggie," she said after a long pause.

At the mention of her name, he stopped writing. Then he tore off the page he had been working on and turned it over. There seemed an air of secrecy about the act, but Carol quickly dismissed it from her mind. She decided she was simply observing too hard, a consequence of her own deceptive conduct.

But when he swiveled to observe her, she was surprised at the intensity of his scrutiny. For the moment, she felt a stab of cold fear. Then she rebuked herself for reacting to her own guilt.

"She's a real professional asset," Carol said. Hearing her own words calmed her, so matter-of-fact and devoid of the slightest hint of emotion. Also, Eliot's imagined scrutiny seemed to soften and he smiled benignly.

"Yes, she is," he agreed.

"I'm sure she'll get a great deal out of this convention," Carol said.

"Yes," Eliot replied. "It should be quite productive for us."

"My impression is that she's a crackerjack at what she does."

"I agree," he said. "And she does know computers."

Eliot was wearing a robe over his naked body and when he stood up it opened, showing his genitals. For a moment, she thought he might be on the verge of reaching out for a rare embrace. He didn't, for which she was grateful. Instead, he turned, took the paper on which he had been writing, folded it casually, and stuffed it into the briefcase beside the desk. Then he moved into the bathroom and started to brush his teeth.

Carol got into bed and, with the remote, flipped on the television set, going through the various offered programs by rote, merely passing time. When he came back into the room, she clicked off the set and he got into the bed, opening a file on his lap.

"She's pretty, too. Don't you think?" Carol said, hoping he would see it as an extension of her earlier remarks.

"I suppose," he said abstractedly.

"Seems an odd match," she said after a while. "Maggie and Ken."

"Why odd?" he asked.

She did not look at him directly, but she could see him peripherally. He had closed the file and was looking at her, a puzzled look on his face. She did not turn to look at him.

"It just struck me," she said cautiously. "She seems more your type than his." There was a gamble in that, but she took it anyway, a deeper probe into the realm of suggestive persuasion.

"My type?"

"You seem to have lots in common."

He laughed and shrugged.

"Do you feel threatened by Maggie?"

"Don't be silly," she said, reaching out and patting his hand. Considering his vanity, it didn't seem much of a gamble after all. "I mean in a cerebral way."

Was she being too blatant? There was, of course, a strong current of logic in her remark. She was certainly less intellectual than Maggie, more of an ornament and admiring companion than a brainy equal. But that was the way they had defined their roles from the beginning. Eliot, at the time of their meeting and courtship, didn't seem interested in a professional helpmate, someone to assist him in his work. His wifely requirements were more old-fashioned and she accommodated herself to that idea. Besides, his work was far too esoteric to arouse her interest.

"Well, we do have many common interests and she does know her business," he said. "She's organized my work with great skill. I'm very pleased with what she's doing."

"I'm glad," Carol said. "I really like her."

From the corner of her eye she could still see him studying her. One thing was certain. She had captured his attention.

"You both seem so simpatico," she said, knowing instantly that she had gone too far.

"What are you trying to tell me, Carol?" he asked abruptly. "Maggie and Ken are our friends."

"Of course they are. I was only . . ."

"She's wonderful, I agree with you. As for Ken, he's smart and insightful." He paused. "Don't you think?"

"He's nice enough," she said, denuding her remark of any

conviction or enthusiasm. She decided that she had bungled this new effort.

"I'm not too familiar with men of his type, I'll admit," Eliot said. "He comes from a different world and plies a trade that could be considered slightly disreputable. But I find him very affable."

"I'll say this," Carol said, clearing her throat. "He is an acquired taste."

"Maggie says he's deep and introspective. And much misunderstood."

"Creative people generally are," she said, realizing that her knee-jerk defense was the wrong tack. And yet his sudden interest in Ken made her uncomfortable. When the four of them were together, Ken hardly revealed himself, and Eliot's attitude seemed patronizing.

"I suppose," he commented, showing little interest.

She heard him prop the pillows and open the file again.

"He's very lucky to have a warm and open girl like Maggie for a wife," Carol said after a long pause. She hoped this remark might refocus the conversation.

"If you draw him out," Eliot said, "I think he'll be a lot more interesting. Sometimes these relationships have to be worked on."

That remark also seemed out of kilter. Eliot rarely worked on relationships. She remained silent while he continued to read, unable to come up with anything imaginative.

"Anyway, tomorrow you and Ken will get a chance to know each other better," he said. "I'm sure you'll find him fine company."

Wrong direction, she thought. She was really bad at this, she decided. But even if she were better, more subtle, more devious, more suggestive, Eliot was essentially too tepid, too controlled, to be a fertile target for this process. And if he didn't catch the scent, how was he supposed to be enticed by its lure? Had he sincerely seconded her suggestion about Africa? Or had she read more into it than was apparent?

Her own experience should have warned her, she rebuked herself. To persuade Eliot of anything required massive effort, not just words. In Carol's case, she had transformed herself by checklist, becoming what she imagined he wanted in a wife—to be docile, available, amiable, and to gratify his vanity, a showpiece, cool, elegant, obedient.

She wished Ken were here, not to be seen or heard, of course, but to tell her what to say and how to say it. She was already running out of words and ideas. She was on the verge of turning her back on Eliot in frustration and going to sleep when she heard him drop the file on the floor.

"You wouldn't mind them with us on safari, would you, Carol?"

She held her breath, desperately trying to hide her excitement. There it was. Had it worked? Her suggestion at dinner had had a delayed fuse, but it had exploded at last. The idea had come to her out of the blue. Of course, Africa. It was the perfect place. She checked her elation. It was too early to declare victory.

"It certainly might enhance Maggie's value to your work," she said cautiously.

"Yes, it would," he agreed.

"You think she'd leave Ken for that long a stretch?" Carol asked.

"I wouldn't think of it," Eliot said. "I would expect he'd go as well."

"Might be fun seeing other people's reactions," she said.

It had always been his preference to go with her alone, the two of them and Jack Meade, their longtime guide, and his staff.

Meade, a mercurial character, was the best guide in Africa, when he wasn't on the bottle. He had taken them on their rounds of the wilderness parks in Kenya, Zambia, and Tanzania.

After the second trip, Carol was bored with Africa, although, as always, she maintained an enthusiastic façade. How many lions, gazelles, elephants, cheetahs, wildebeests, giraffes, buffaloes, and an endless list of other species was it possible to observe with fresh eyes? Eliot never tired of it, treating it as if it were his sacred duty to monitor the situation periodically and report on it to organizations with which he was affiliated.

As with most of the other tagalong chores of their marriage, Carol faked her responses. Availability was everything.

The savannas of Africa offered a cornucopia of suggestive sensations for what she and Ken had in mind for Eliot and Maggie. Turn any corner and there it was—a happy humping ground. The sights were pervasive. Even Eliot had reacted, making love to her, abandoning all restraint, after seeing a lion mounting a lioness every ten minutes for hours.

At the same time, she forced herself to close her mind to any projection of how she and Ken would behave in Africa. For them abstinence would have to be the order of the day. It would be foolhardy to risk their future together.

"Maggie's eyewitness experience might be very helpful to our project," Eliot said. "I think I'd benefit from her seeing first-hand what wildlife preservation is all about. You know we are computerizing my photographs."

"But can they afford it?" Carol asked casually.

"Of course. It would be a business trip. I wouldn't expect them to pay their way. Yes. A business trip for her."

"A perk for him," she said, yawning deliberately. She wanted to scream with delight. Instead she closed her eyes and said nothing, concentrating on controlling her happiness.

Maybe, just maybe, this might work after all.

There were few cars on the road, and once they had passed the outskirts of Alexandria the road curved gently in such a way as to create the illusion that theirs was the only car on the road traveling through one of those enchanted forests depicted in English nursery-rhyme books. As Ken drove on Carol nestled herself in his shoulder and he caressed her hair.

"We could just keep going, never come back, never look back, start over," he said suddenly.

"We might just have that chance," she mused.

"I mean right now. Before things get more involved."

His comment surprised her and she thought it odd since she had just finished telling him about her success and how Eliot was going to pay for their safari. Reflecting over Ken's reaction, she had expected more enthusiasm.

"It was your idea, Ken. I was the doubting Thomas, remember."

He was silent for a while, watching the road and continuing to caress her. She sensed that something was awry.

"What is it?" she asked.

His response was to turn the car into a recess in the parkway that led to a parking lot, obviously created for strollers who wished to follow the footpaths beside the Potomac. They got out of the car and, holding hands, walked in silence through stands of evergreens and came out on a promontory that opened to a view of the river and the capital city beyond.

A cool breeze caught a pile of dead leaves and moved them in odd patterns toward the water's edge. After a while, he stopped and, holding her in the crook of his arm, looked across the river.

"You're having second thoughts, right?" she asked, searching his eyes for the answer.

"Not second thoughts, exactly. Qualms," he said.

"That it won't work?" she asked.

"That it will," he replied.

"I don't understand."

He kissed her cheek and held her close, pressing her to him.

"I want you more than anything in the world. Full time. Every day. Night and day. Until time ends. And I know we owe ourselves that."

"Yes, we do," she agreed. "We've got years to make up." She poked him playfully with her elbow. "And it can't all be made up on Fridays."

Ken chuckled and pressed Carol closer. But when she looked up at his face, she saw a trepidation that she had never seen before.

"It's the idea of it, the sheer ruthlessness of it." He shook his head and sucked in a deep breath. "Even though I see it as a way out for us, even though I'm the fellow that thought of it, I don't feel comfortable about it. The whole idea of manipulating other people just sticks in my craw. That's what's so offensive to me about my work, this business of creating needs in people's minds. I don't feel right about it."

"But it works. I saw it happen. And, as you said, it will be great all around. Nobody will get hurt and everybody will get what they want."

He turned her head with his hand and kissed her deeply on the mouth, their tongues intertwining.

"It would make things a lot simpler if we just told them," he said when they had disengaged. "Let the chips fall where they may."

She stepped back from him, putting his face in focus, then caressed his cheek.

"That again," she sighed, then looked into his eyes. "You

think I'm terrible, squirreling away my nest egg, wanting to protect it at all costs."

Ken shook his head. "Not terrible. Practical. Maybe if we explained it properly and sincerely, Eliot would consent. Is he that much of a monster?"

"Funny," she said. "He said you were a different kind, not like him. He was right. You don't understand his mentality. How do you think these people have preserved their fortunes over generations? By sentimentality? Eliot is not a monster, but he will do what he has to do if he feels betrayed or if his fortune is threatened. I'm sure of it. Believe me."

She paused, feeling the eruption of anger inside her. Instead of raising her voice, she clamped her teeth together and spoke in a whisper, her tone emphatic:

"I will not leave Eliot Butterfield without my possessions. If that makes me a greedy, covetous woman, so be it. I've earned them and I intend to keep them."

Her sudden eruption seem to shock him. His face became ashen, his expression troubled. An angry burst of regret had exploded inside her. How dare Ken come back into her life, disrupting her peace, challenging her comfort, making her feel again? Just when she had learned to live without feeling, without love, without passion.

Suddenly she broke away and ran along the footpath, heading back to the car. She heard him moving swiftly behind her, catching up just as she opened the car door.

"It needed to be said," he told her as he slid in beside her.

"No, it didn't," she protested, concerned suddenly about this strange reversal in their roles. "You pushed it, remember. Now that you see it can work, you get cold feet."

"I was simply exploring other alternatives," he muttered, still obviously shaken by her response.

"You sound as if you'd like to keep things as they are. And it makes me worry now that you'll want Eliot to catch us, force the issue."

"And what would we gain by that? A lifetime of resentment."

They were silent for a long time. Finally, he turned the ignition and started the motor.

"Maybe it was cold feet," he said.

"Why now?"

He looked troubled, vague, as if his mind were searching for an explanation.

"Maybe the power of it frightened me. Seeing it happen. How simple it was." He was silent, his gaze drifting toward the Potomac.

His words had frightened her as well. She could not deny it. Nor could she deny the shame that her practicality engendered in herself. It stunk of greed. It wasn't heroic, wasn't noble, wasn't loving. Stop that, she screamed inside herself. She had been a victim for too long. Ken had given her the means to fight back and she had no intention of surrendering now. Hadn't Eliot manipulated her into signing that horrible prenuptial agreement? It was time to undo that travesty.

"What's wrong with wanting to take charge of our own lives?" she asked. "Do it our way for a change?"

"Not a damned thing," Ken replied. He seemed to have conquered his private war with doubt.

"We mustn't turn back now," she told him firmly.

"No way," he agreed.

Her iron resolve surprised her. It was a far cry from the young girl who had given up love for ambition. Never again, she vowed. She would give up nothing. She moved toward him again and they embraced, lingering together in a long, loving kiss.

Ken drove the car in silence. He had turned off the Washington Memorial Parkway and was heading south. After a while the roads became two-lane and threaded through the browning hedgerows and horse meadows of the Virginia countryside. Again Carol lay in the crook of his arm as he drove.

"I'm pinning my hopes on Africa," Carol said suddenly.

"You and Francis Macomber," Ken said.

"Macomber?"

"A Hemingway character. He went to Africa with his wife to reclaim his manhood."

"And did he?"

Ken nodded and smiled.

Suddenly he stopped the car in front of a colonial structure. A sign outside read STONEWALL INN.

"Eliot wanted you to see American antiques," he said. "The reservations clerk told me they're loaded with them."

Carol followed Ken into the reception area. He signed the register while she looked over the posted menu at the entrance to the restaurant.

"First things first," he said as they followed the clerk to their room. He gave the young man a five-dollar tip, then looked up and winked at her. "That was for not noticing we had no suitcases."

In the room was a bottle of champagne and an opened can of beluga caviar over ice with pieces of toast and a variety of condiments.

"You're an incurable romantic," she said.

"Not really," he said, kissing her ear. "I'm trying to manipulate you into making love to me."

"I'm easy," she laughed.

The makings of a fire had been prepared and Ken lit it while they both watched it burst into flame. Then he uncorked the champagne, poured it into glasses, and spread caviar and all the makings on a piece of toast for her. He popped it into her mouth.

"Hmmmm," she said, delighted with both the wonderful taste and the idea. "You see," she said.

"See what?"

"Not all the good things in life are free."

"Not all," he said, taking her in his arms, kissing her deeply. Then he began to undress her.

Later, after they had made love, she grew thoughtful. Something he had said nagged at her.

"What is it?" he asked. She was suddenly aware that he had been studying her face. Then she remembered.

"This Macomber, the man who found his manhood in Africa." She turned to look at him. "What did his wife find there?"

"Her freedom," he said, reaching out to caress her hair. "She shot him dead."

10

Eliot sat alone in the Norfolk Hotel's terrace restaurant sipping his coffee. Although it was too early for it to open, a modest tip to one of the kitchen workers had organized the coffee and solitude.

Jet lag and anxiety had made it impossible for him to sleep. He looked at his watch. In an hour they would meet Jack Meade for breakfast, go over the safari schedule, check out of the Norfolk, and start the eight-hour drive to their first camp in the Samburu.

A lingering anxiety had dogged him for the past few months, ever since the idea of bringing Maggie and Ken to Africa was broached. If anything, it had become even more urgent.

Nairobi had already begun its languorous morning stretch, rising slowly into the sun, which by noon would scorch the city and peel away its fragile veneer of civilization.

Eliot had learned that the best method of rating a city was by the way its people were shod. Studying feet raising dust in the broken paved street, he could spot sandals made of old tires, battered shoes with cracked tops, raised heels of dirty pumps which made a feeble effort to appear fashionable, and, only occasionally,

143

the slick shined shoe of the poseur who carried a briefcase, although he might be a waiter or clerk in some fly-blown Nairobi café or butcher shop.

He could spot one or two fairly decent shoes, but it was far too early for those. Besides, the people who ran things rarely walked.

This part of Nairobi always depressed him, although the oasis of affluence provided by the Norfolk Hotel was isolation enough from the mean streets where mismanagement, confusion, and poverty walked hand in hand. There was a good life here as well, but that was in the suburbs, where the Europeans residing there made a grand attempt at the good life. It was not the way it had been under British rule, but they could still buy servants cheaply and live the illusion of colonial grandeur.

For him, of course, this was political Africa, not the real Africa, the wild Africa where those magnificent creatures who shared the earth with man were losing their war to survive.

He mocked himself over his propensity to reflect on the big issues, the so-called universal themes. Man and his future in a world of diminishing resources. Man replicating himself at a faster rate than the technology to manage his absorption. The disappearing rain forests and the thinning ozone layer. Man's losing battle with the priorities of his survival. And his vulnerabilities. The power of greed, the joy of war, the lure of heroism, the urge for immortality. The big questions, the grand themes. He had dedicated his mind to the contemplation of these issues, to deciphering the riddles, to discovering greater and greater levels of knowledge and awareness. He had given his life to it.

He sipped his coffee. There was much to be said for Kenyan coffee. He was also a man who cultivated his palate for food, trained his ear for music, concentrated his eye for dance and art, and had nurtured his intellect. He had always revered the value of art, the exquisite aesthetic, the wonder of the mind. Thinking, contemplating, reflecting, learning, were the ways he spent his most productive waking hours.

He took a piece of folded yellow lined paper from an inside pocket, unfolded it, patted it flat, and spread it on the table. The immutable laws of numbers were indivisible from logic, he instructed himself. There was no way to maintain his present life-style on a net income of no more than thirty-five thousand dollars a year.

Granted that this was well above the statistical average of what constituted a living wage for a family of four, it was hardly enough to finance the kind of life-style he had maintained for years. He chuckled wryly. By that standard it was below the poverty level.

He had dutifully written a column of figures representing expenses abstracted by his accountant. They included his office expenses, alimony for Helen, tuition and support for the children, travel, entertainment, books, telephone, utilities, and on and on.

Twenty-five years ago, his father had left him what was once the extraordinary sum of four million dollars, a more than sufficient amount, he once supposed, to provide the kind of net income, taking tax loopholes into account, that could adequately support his life-style, the centerpiece of which was the dedicated pursuit of those burning questions that engaged his mind. A thinking man's life, was the way he put it to himself.

Before his father's death, the family business had been able to supply enough money for these pursuits as well as the raising of a family. He had married Helen, more as a way to validate to his father and mother his adherence to traditional values than for any reason that had to do with the usual emotional considerations.

That, of course, was his conclusion after the fact of their divorce. Actually, it was Helen's assessment and it was unassailable. They had two children, more attributable, according to Helen, to the potency of his sperm than the frequency of their procreative activities.

Her divorce grounds were mental cruelty and, from her point of view, she was probably right. On the surface she had been dutiful, organizing his external life, enabling him to avoid the nitty-gritty of modern living, mothering his children, keeping his house, supervising his meals, clothing him properly, and generally upholding the appearance of a contented, if not happy, marriage.

She became bored. He was sorry for that and, as befitting his position and standards and on the advice of his attorney, had offered a generous settlement for Helen to pursue a happier life free from his neglect, but one that had immediately lopped nearly two million dollars off his net worth. He hadn't then calculated the devastating effects of inflation on the remainder.

Then, too, after the settlement, he had learned on good authority that his wife had been less than faithful, taking a series of tennis pros as lovers, a fact that underlined his naïveté, made him furious, and prompted the immediate dismissal of his lawyer.

At the time of his marriage to Carol he hired another attorney who was far less sanguine and far more ruthless. Eliot was determined not to make the same mistake twice. Thus, to protect what was left of what he thought was his "fortune," his lawyer had devised an aggressive prenuptial agreement for Carol that was airtight, designed to protect him against most eventualities, from cuckcolding to desertion.

It was this overzealous prenuptial agreement with Carol that had come back to haunt him. The timing couldn't be worse.

Lifting his cup, he noted that his hand shook, causing a drop to land on a certain row of figures. He was not a superstitious man, but the placement of the drop of coffee made him pause.

The figure on which the drop had fallen was the most baffling of all. It was the inventory value of all the purchases of antiques and artwork that Carol had accumulated over the years of their marriage, her entitlement by the agreement that he had promulgated. That figure came to roughly $2.5 million. It was the "roughly," spoken by the accountant, that finally got his dander up. He had reared up like a stuck pig, finally losing his temper in the accountant's office.

Actually, it wasn't the accountant's fault. He had already fired the business manager who gave him the primary news that his so-called "fortune" was a myth, overcome by either his own financial judgment; bad investments, most of them instigated by himself since he was not one to follow other people's advice; or, the other extreme, simple neglect. Then, of course, there was his ridiculous divorce settlement.

The accountant, a large man named Bernstein, calmed him down and explained that the value of "things" like art and antiques had gone up higher than the value of money. In the eight years of his marriage the two hundred odd thousand that Carol had spent on canny purchases in her name had simply multiplied more than ten times. He had painstakingly made a list of these purchases, twenty-three items in all. Then he had surreptitiously photographed them and given the accountant the task of appraisal.

Roughly, two and a half million, Bernstein had said. A burst of blood had clanged to the top of Eliot's head. Not a fortune by today's standards, he told himself later, but she was a damned sight richer than he was. He was, in fact, verging on being broke, living on capital that would probably be depleted in a few months.

He certainly couldn't say he had been bilked by Carol, despite the fact that the bills of sale were in her name alone. This did not violate the "agreement."

What Eliot detested most, however, was the very idea of it. The subject of finances was always far down the list of his priorities. In fact, he rarely thought about it, devoting his energy to subjects that interested him far more.

He was hardly a spendthrift in the classic sense, certainly not overly indulgent or addicted to conspicuous consumption. But he did enjoy living well and all the emoluments of first-class services and custom-made clothes. The fact was, considering his upbringing and inheritance, he was accustomed to the so-called good life and, frankly, he was panicked by the possibility of its ending. For that, he was totally unprepared.

Not that Carol was profligate when it came to money. Indeed, to be fair, she could be considered frugal, although she had taken clever advantage of what he was beginning to view as a "loophole" in their prenuptial agreement.

He had married Carol primarily because she had the allure of classic good looks, artistic credentials, and the ability to organize him, taking up where Helen had left off. She had been devoted, supportive, companionable, decent, and proper in every way. He was also flattered by her willingness to marry him, a much older man. And he took pleasure in squiring her around and showing her off, enjoying the aesthetics of her graceful ballet dancer's carriage and movement.

How was he to know that suddenly his predictable world would explode and he would discover that, for all of his life, he had lived only within his mind, while his, heart, body, and soul had atrophied. One might say that his intellectual pursuits, his devotion to the big issues, had stunted him and undervalued the rest of him. Measured quantitatively, he had become merely a quarter of a man.

His life was never about money. Even now it wasn't about money, although money was at the heart of his present dilemma. Under ordinary circumstances, he might have approached Carol, explaining to her that his alleged fortune had evaporated and that their present life-style was at the end of its tether. He would have presented her with the reality of their financial plight. Because of this, she would have to increase her teaching chores. And he would have to find himself a real job. He would also have to admit that, according to their agreement, those assets in her name constituted their only hope of maintaining that life-style.

Under ordinary circumstances, he might have offered such a logical and realistic explanation. But that would be under ordinary marital circumstances. Unfortunately, ordinary marital circumstances were not applicable. These were extraordinary marital circumstances.

In fact, his life was now extraordinary.

Maggie had made it extraordinary.

He watched her coming toward him in silhouette, walking with the bright ball of rising sun to her back as she came forward. As she passed into the shadows, he saw the now familiar movement of her body, the strong fullness, now swathed in khakis that emphasized her swelling hips and wonderful breasts. She wore a wide-brimmed bush hat fastened with a string held tight to her chin.

Seeing her coming toward him in this way made his heart jump into his throat. It was truly extraordinary, the effect this woman had on his . . . he always searched his mind for some unique way to say it . . . his totality.

She looked cautiously around the deserted terrace before she sat down beside him. His hand reached for hers and their fingers applied a joint pressure. Again, she studied the deserted terrace, then brought his hand to her lips.

"I miss you so," she whispered.

"Forced to be apart like this . . ." he began. "I hate it." With his free hand he refolded the paper and slipped it into his pocket.

"You mustn't brood about that," she said, pointing with her

chin. He had discussed it with her at length for the past six months. "We're going to work it out."

"Contemplating is not brooding."

"I've left him sleeping," Maggie said, looking at her watch. "He should be getting the wake-up call now. We're packed and ready."

"So are we," Eliot said. "Soon we'll be on our way."

"God, I hope it does the trick," she said, pressing her leg against his. She bent toward him, whispering, "My darling."

"Too late for second thoughts, I'm afraid," he sighed, thinking also of the additional debt he had incurred in getting here. He must be more positive, he berated himself. It can work. It will work.

Given the right circumstances, he and Maggie had convinced themselves, it might be quite possible to create the moods, contrive the circumstances, and arrange the opportunities for Carol and Ken to discover each other in a romantic, hopefully erotic, sense. It was certainly a tantalizing possibility. And an ideal solution for their dilemma.

For Maggie it would, of course, mitigate the guilt engendered by her infidelity. For Eliot, it would provide the legal solution to his financial troubles, the trigger to activate their prenuptial agreement. This would have a further practical side in shifting the burden of total child support to Ken and, if all went as hoped, perhaps allow him and Carol, too, a reasonably comfortable future.

Pie in the sky? Perhaps. But an ingenious solution. We have to give it our best try, he and Maggie had finally agreed.

And they had started the process going by that very first get-together dinner at Pumpkins.

Their first real ploy had not been as successful as they might have wished, but it proved that they could be clever enough, subtle enough, to engineer Carol and Ken's "proximity." They had literally coerced them that summer afternoon to go to the theater together without their spouses. It was, at the very least, a beginning. So far their efforts had brought no measurable results. Indeed, there had not been the slightest signs of romantic conflagration stirring between them. That, however, did not deter them. It would take time. Patience. Ingenuity.

Both he and Maggie had perceived that Ken and Carol had a

great deal in common. They were both "artistic" and sensitive. Ken's ambition to write surely must be an attraction for Carol. And Ken, according to Maggie, appreciated creative and aesthetic types like Carol.

Naturally, Eliot and Maggie knew that you could not legislate attraction. But you certainly could coax it along. The power of persuasion was awesome. Whole nations had been brainwashed into accepting ideologies. Mind control was a notion that was scientifically based, they had learned. One merely had to focus on it, devote all one's energies to its achievement. It required, above all, effort, dedication, commitment.

It had its dark side, of course. They would have to be manipulative, a somewhat sinister idea, and dissimulating, which was equally offensive. They would have to playact and, much worse, they would have to lie. In the end, of course, it would be worth it, especially if any emotional damage was kept to a minimum.

Unfortunately, Maggie had not spent much time contemplating Ken's vulnerability to the blandishments of women, although he was, after all, an attractive healthy man in a fast-track profession where ambition and sexuality often intersected and few marriages survived. But he had given her no concrete evidence of ever straying and she had deliberately avoided any temptation to be curious. As for Carol, well, they had reasoned, she had been in show business, notorious for its open sexuality, albeit a presumption for which Carol could offer little personal evidence.

But if such a match could be engineered and, hopefully, confronted at exactly the right moment, then everything between them would, in effect, equal out. Barring that, it would be impossible to contemplate a comfortable future together for him and Maggie.

A wild dream? Maybe. But certainly, if they could pull it off, an effective solution. If it could happen anywhere, it could happen in Africa. Africa was primitive, suggestive, erotic. In Africa civilization disappeared.

"You'd think they would already have taken advantage of the opportunities we afforded them," Eliot said. He could not hide his apprehension.

"Like us," Maggie giggled, putting her arm through his and embracing him with the other.

"Like us," Eliot said, "except that now, my darling, we have to be . . ."

"Alert, disciplined, and discreet," she said, nodding. They had been over this ground before. She immediately disengaged.

"Also focused," Eliot said. "Not on us. But on them."

"We stick to the game plan," she said, showing him a smart salute. *"Mon Capitaine."*

"And above all, remember," Eliot said, pointing his finger. She took it and with her free hand put it between her teeth, biting gently. Then she sucked it. "Sounds carry in the bush."

"Lovemaking sounds?"

"Especially that."

He smiled, looked about him, then bent and kissed her, putting his tongue in her ear.

"I'm dying for you," he said. She unlocked their fingers and caressed him under the table.

"Me, too. We're not in the bush yet," she said.

He looked into her eyes, saw his own yearning in them, and stood up. He left some money on the table and, walking through the lobby, came out on the garden. They walked past a large aviary displaying a great variety of African birds, then moved, her following, to the pool area, which at that hour, seemed deserted.

To one side was a dressing pavilion and he headed for that.

"Puts you on your mettle," he said. "Makes you crafty and resourceful."

"Necessity is the mother of invention," Maggie said, taking his hand and moving toward the pavilion.

They stood against the rear wall of the pavilion, which was not in the field of vision of anyone who might be in the garden, the hotel, or the restaurant. He enfolded her in his arms and pressed his lips to hers.

"Not here," she whispered. Opening his eyes, he saw her looking up. Beyond a knoll a group of men were repairing a road. Some of them looked down at them and leered, white teeth flashing broad smiles.

To get out of their field of vision, they moved toward the side of the pavilion, ducking into a door, only to discover that they were in the ladies' dressing room. They started to embrace.

Then Eliot saw her. Carol! She had her back toward them and was pulling on tights, preparing for her unwavering exercise routine.

Eliot had forgotten. Since it was winter in New York, she had expressed the desire to go for a swim in the warm morning sunshine in Nairobi this time of year. She would then be expected to do her morning exercises by the pool.

Quickly he stepped backward, then turned and ran out the door, leaving Maggie, hoping he had disappeared before Carol had seen him. He leaned flat against the wall just outside the pavilion, his heart beating a fast tattoo in his chest. There was no way to begin the walk back to the hotel without risking being seen by Carol through the window of the dressing room.

To prevent that, he ducked into the men's dressing section. Ken was just emerging from one of the toilet stalls.

"Eliot," he said. "Thought I might take a quick swim before we leave."

"Great idea," Eliot said cautiously, inspecting Ken's face, clearing his throat. "We were just exploring the place, Maggie and I. Hell of a spot. Beautiful pool, don't you think?"

"Super," Ken said.

"Carol and Maggie are in the ladies' side," Eliot said.

"Are they?" Ken said, getting into his bathing suit.

"You didn't come down with Carol?" Eliot asked, alert now to any suggestive nuance.

"Why would I do that?"

Eliot ignored the question that answered his question as Ken started to move out through the door. Eliot looked at his watch.

"We've only got a half hour before we meet Jack Meade," he said.

"We're all packed," Ken called over his shoulder, then Eliot heard the splash as Ken dived into the pool. At that moment, Eliot saw Carol starting her routine on the pool deck.

"Close call," Maggie whispered behind him.

He turned and nodded, then waved to the others as they moved back toward the restaurant, which was now officially opened for breakfast. Guests were also filling the garden.

"Don't be late," Eliot shouted, making a bullhorn out of his hands.

"We'll be there," Carol called back.

"Nearly blew the whole thing," Eliot said.

"That was the general idea," Maggie said, winking.

Such antics would have been unthinkable nearly ten months earlier when their affair began. "Exploded" was the way they preferred to describe it to each other. They were behaving like rutting adolescents, awakened to a sensuality that neither had believed their natures capable of possessing. They had fallen in love. It was both baffling and wonderful.

Romantic love, for Eliot, had always been an intellectual notion, an artistic convention, a philosophical conundrum, a broad symbol sometimes used to illustrate a bedrock truth about the natural kinship of the genders.

It had happened to him, he had decided, on another level of consciousness. He could even pinpoint the exact moment in time when his sublimation cracked the surface of his awareness, erupting like a volcano. Often he and Maggie would amuse themselves by arguing over exactly when it had occurred, concluding finally that it had happened to them simultaneously.

Of course, it had probably been building in their subconscious for weeks before their mutual epiphany. Before that point, certainly on the surface of their intense strictly business interaction, they both had been scrupulously correct. He had, after all, hired her to organize and computerize data that he had collected over a long period of years. Not that their original purpose had ever been compromised by their affair. In fact, it had actually improved their working relationship.

There had been, of course, tiny hints, stirrings, signposts that indicated their growing mutual attraction. When he was away from her, her image intruded on his thoughts. And when he was with her he felt an ever-accelerating awareness of her presence, as if he were studying her with every nerve ending in his body.

At first he had tried to deny it to himself, berating himself for what he decided was imaginative meandering, childish fantasy, erotic foolishness. But soon he was impatient to get to the office, to see her, to immerse herself in her presence. When their eyes met, they had even begun to lock briefly, and he had the sensation that he was on the verge of disappearing into hers.

At first he had tried to steer his mind into some logical analysis of what he was convinced was some transient psychological episode. But no amount of investigation or dissection of his emotions made any sense out of it. Finally, it became evident that it, the idea of it, call it love or whatever, had a powerful stranglehold on him. Consummation became an obsession.

Perhaps it was the light, an orange twilight, that had suffused her in a radiant glow as she stood by the window that afternoon. Her face, he remembered, had turned in such a way that the shadows blocked out all other features and made her eyes appear luminous, like beacons in a foggy night.

They were talking, debating a computerized classification in what an observer might determine was a perfectly ordinary discussion. He was standing not three feet from her, sorting papers on his bookshelves. Suddenly, he had discovered that he had no understanding of what she was saying, or, for that matter, of his own words. The full concentration of his mind and body was focused in another place, on this woman, not her mind or voice but her aura.

She had turned, he remembered, a kind of twisted motion, held briefly, but enough to reveal the full outline of her breasts. The shadows changed on her face as she moved toward him as if to assist him with the papers he was sorting. His body's response was totally foreign to his experience, troubling in fact, very confusing. Words constricted in his throat. He was suddenly engulfed in a yearning to touch her, absorb her into him.

It was irrational and certainly involuntary. He hated unexplained mysteries and irrational certainties. But in this case, he felt compelled, irresistibly drawn to possess her.

Then, suddenly, she had not stopped in her advance and she was folding into his outstretched arms. The full length of their bodies embraced and his mouth spread hungrily over hers, and they kissed in a way that, if they were able, they would have swallowed each other totally.

Their sense of time seemed to go awry as they entwined themselves, conscious only of sinking to his leather office couch.

"Thank God," she had said, her first words after they had kissed. "How long was I expected to wait?"

Her words startled and confused him.

"And I thought," he remembered telling her, "that I was the only one."

She had giggled like a young girl, sitting up for a moment to look at him. Then she had stood up, watching his eyes as she began to undress. He was certain that this act was a ritual way she had chosen to exhibit herself for his pleasure. He was even then urging his mind to adapt some mystical interpretation of what was happening between them.

"God, you're beautiful," he whispered. Her movements were slow and deliberate.

"I have been wanting to do this for weeks," she said without embarrassment. "To show you myself."

"And I've wanted to see you," he whispered.

She removed her dress, her brassiere, caressing her breasts in a way that seemed as if she were giving them to him as an offering. Her breasts were large and full with big round areolas and nipples that stood straight out. He was still fully dressed when he reached out to her and touched them, kneaded them, kissed them.

Then he started to undress and she stopped him.

"No. You must let me."

She then knelt down and removed his clothes and squeezed his hard erection between her breasts, watching him as he rose and fell and her tongue flicked the tip of his penis until finally he guided her to a sitting position on his lap and she reached out to insert him into her body.

It was beyond anything he had ever experienced, the totality of it. And when their orgasms exploded, it was as if they were mutually claiming the substance of each other.

"Is this really me?" he had asked her as they cooled, but remained entwined.

"Yes," she had told him. "The real you." They kissed deeply and it began again.

"And the real me," she had said.

He knew even then that he would not be content with simply accepting the fact of his overwhelming yearning to be one with this woman. He would want his logic system to understand it since it was so foreign to his view of himself and to his experience.

*   *   *

From the beginning of his life, from the first stirrings of memory, he had followed a preordained track. There were do's and don'ts, proprieties and conventions.

The idea of superiority was inbred in his genes. While it was never fully articulated by his parents, his stockbroker father and his social doyenne mother, it was assumed that family, position, and class proscribed a certain code of conduct.

"We must always control ourselves," his mother had intoned from earliest memory. By that she meant that he must never exhibit the licentious conduct and uninhibited mores of the lower orders. He had actually come to his own first marriage bed a virgin, after suffering through an adolescence of sexual repression that even the permissive atmosphere of the sixties failed to dislodge.

Perhaps it was this repression that made him take refuge in his causes, his "thinking" endeavors. It was an idea never explored until recently, until Maggie had opened the locked door to this secret life.

From the very first moment of the consummation of their passions, both he and Maggie had searched for an explanation.

"Why you?" he had asked after they had made love for the third time that evening. Twilight had given way to darkness and they had not turned on the lights in his office. They had left the phone unanswered. Their sole concentration had been on themselves, on plumbing the mystery of this awesome attraction between them.

"Why you?" she had responded.

"I've always thought of myself as the least likely candidate for this type of thing," he had told her.

"Proves how little we really know about ourselves," she had replied. "This is not my usual conduct either. I've never been unfaithful to Ken. It was unthinkable." She held his face in her hands and kissed him deeply. "Until you."

"We're an unlikely pair," he had said.

"More likely than we think."

He admitted to himself that she might possess some superior insight into the mysteries of human behavior, just as she knew about the mysteries of computers. She certainly had brought him into emotional areas that he had never before traversed.

But, then, she had confessed that she, too, was confronting this side of her nature for the first time.

"I come from a very traditional background," she had told him. "Practical, midwestern, Norwegian. Hard-working achieving types, family, the work ethic, the whole nine yards." She had interrupted her explanation with a wry laugh. "I'm the first woman in our family that is not a housewife. Imagine that. Infidelity wouldn't have crossed my mother's mind." She was lying beside him naked on his office couch. Suddenly, she reached out and caressed his penis. "And here I am making love to a man who is not my husband and who I have yearned for ever since I laid eyes on him. Can you explain that to me?"

He had chuckled a response.

"I'm having my own problems understanding any of it, Maggie."

"Then let's just go with the flow," she had said, guiding him into her.

They had parted after that first episode in his office with a conspiratorial air, but without broaching any serious questions as to their future relationship. The immediate aftermath provided yet another sortie into strange turf, the territory of lies and deception.

"I was frantic," Carol had said when he returned to their apartment that evening. It was nearly ten. He could understand her consternation, since he was a man of regular habits, his time carefully structured.

He remembered he had felt the first tug of guilt and had deliberately remained silent, fearful that any explanation would be transparent.

"I called the office three times," she had told him. He was relieved that he had chosen the correct strategy. He might have told her that he was working late, a lie that could be disputed by her attempts to reach him. Which would trigger yet another lie. Something about the breakdown of the telephone system.

"I just walked around," he told her. "I've had to think about certain things." Perfect, he had decided. Wasn't his work "thinking"?

"I wish you would have called, Eliot," Carol had said. "I was worried."

"I will in the future," he had told her. "I promise."

It was odd, he remembered thinking, how easy it was to lie when the cause seemed justified.

He awoke early the next morning. He could barely wait to see Maggie, having discovered that she also hungered for him. Within moments, they were making love again on his office couch.

"No regrets?" she had asked after he had told her about his lies to Carol and his reactions to them. His response was a deep kiss, traveling down her body to touch every square inch of her.

"I didn't have that problem. I knew Ken was working late," she had told him. "The odd thing was that I was able to compartmentalize my guilt. Okay, I told myself. I feel guilt and remorse. No regrets, mind you. But I am a good wife and mother, so I'll just leave that in the same compartment with the other. And keep the rest of me free for this, for you."

"Does that mean we have no consciences?" Eliot had asked.

"My conclusion was that we mustn't dwell on that," she had told him, showing what he believed was the depth of her wisdom. "Let's just let it happen."

"And where do we go when they find out?" he had asked.

"We mustn't let that happen," she told him, visibly upset by the idea. For her, he had learned, the principal fear was hurting Ken and breaking up her family.

"Maybe all this will disappear," he told her. "Burn out."

"Maybe."

It showed no signs of doing so. In fact, if anything, things between them became even more intense and adventurous. Inevitably, though, anxiety began to creep into their relationship.

There was, of course, the fear of discovery, that a wrong word or action at home might give them away. They were not concerned that they would be discovered at Eliot's office, reasoning that if they were clever enough not to arouse suspicion, they would not motivate any desire for further investigation.

This led them to an exploration of the whole area of dissimulation.

"There is an actor's art to it," Eliot had told her. "Like creating a character that is the old Eliot and acting like the old Eliot would act, using the old Eliot as the role model. I do not respond to Carol without first measuring the response against how the old Eliot would have done it."

"Yes," she had agreed. "That would also explain my own actions in terms of Ken."

There was a measure of security in knowing that they had successfully managed their situations at home. It did not pressure them to discuss the future. At least they had each other for five days a week, sometimes six.

Then other concerns had surfaced. Eliot had discovered that, despite the clever dissimulation, he was never comfortable being away from Maggie. It was a yearning that defied logic.

"It's love, my darling," Maggie had explained.

"Being away from you tortures me. It's agony."

"For me as well."

Disturbing images floated through his mind. He saw Maggie with Ken, making love. It was, after all, perfectly natural between husband and wife, but it did not stem his jealousy. It opened up more painful explorations between them, becoming a repetitive litany.

"What happens between you when you make love with Ken?"

"You mustn't ask," she had responded. "Notice that I don't ask what happens between you and Carol."

"I can tell you that. I act like the old Eliot. I do it once a week, a purely mechanical process. It ends when I climax."

"Must you, Eliot?"

"I thought you would like to know."

"No, I wouldn't."

He pressed on.

"Do you climax when Ken makes love to you?"

"No, I don't. I fake it."

"Do you fake it with me?"

Of course, she was insulted. She was silent for a long time, not pouting exactly, but obviously introspective. Then she raised moist eyes to his and kissed him deeply and they made love again until she had an orgasm and he was dead certain that she was not faking.

"I can't bear knowing that you still make love to him," he told her one day. It was getting increasingly difficult to endure the pain and tension of their relationship.

"What choice have I?"

"Please don't. Avoid it."

"He's my husband."

"I can't stand it."

"If we don't, it will create all sorts of problems." She had paused and sighed. "I haven't asked you to stop with Carol. It would break the pattern, make her suspicious."

Then he began to fear that the pressure was too much for her to bear, that she would break it off, that she was too guilt-ridden and fearful that she would hurt Ken and emotionally injure the children.

"Do you want this to end?" he asked her one day. He had confessed to her that he was growing increasingly paranoid that she would have to bring things to a conclusion, say good-bye. Her response only fueled his insecurity.

"Do you?"

He hadn't expected the question, but he had considered it. A plan was already forming in his mind.

The two questions hung in the air between them as they made love. He remembered that a thunderstorm raged outside and at each bolt of lightning and roar of thunder she had clung to him. He had embraced her in the missionary position and she had begun to accelerate her response.

Suddenly he had pulled away from her.

"Now answer me. Do you want this to end?"

"Please, Eliot."

"Answer me."

She shook her head and pressed his buttocks to her.

"Never," she cried. "Never. Never. Never."

Later she told him that he had taken unfair advantage.

"Which brings up another question," he told her. "Is this lust or do you really love me?"

"What is it for you?" she had asked.

"Need," he had responded.

By then, it had become apparent to both of them that the pressure of living this lie was becoming unbearable.

"Can you leave him?" he had asked.

Apparently she, too, had given the question a great deal of thought.

"Under the right circumstances, yes I can," she told him. "I don't want a traumatic rupture, although I believe the children are at an age where they could weather this. It's Ken I worry about. I don't want him hurt."

"That's a tall order," he had told her.

"And you? Can you see yourself leaving Carol?"

"That may be easier than you think."

He had already worked it out in his mind. Since his affair with Maggie was still secret, he did not have to worry about the prenuptial agreement with Carol. He would simply confront her, tell her that he would like the marriage ended. No real reason was required. Upon his death, Carol, if she didn't remarry, would be entitled to inherit those items she had acquired in her own name during the term of the marriage, and they would divorce. He would even provide her with the small stipend that was also contained in the agreement.

"Would she be devastated?" Carol had asked after he had explained it to her.

"Hurt, yes," he had said. "Devastated? I don't think so. Carol would be resilient. She could always support herself teaching."

"I still feel awful about this," Maggie had said, then she suddenly brightened. "But relieved."

"Consider it from a purely practical viewpoint," Eliot had reasoned. "You and Ken would work out whatever is fair and practical. The point is that we would be free to enjoy a fine life together."

She had been overcome with emotion.

"Oh, God, Eliot. I'm so happy."

Unfortunately, it hadn't worked out as he'd intended. A meeting with his business manager and accountant informed him of the true nature of his financial affairs. But when he learned the actual worth of Carol's acquisitions, he was furious.

"It wasn't devious on her part, Mr. Butterfield," his accountant told him. "She simply made the right choices."

At first he thought that the best approach now would be to confront Carol with his financial circumstances, ask her to compromise the points in their agreement, perhaps even borrow against the value of her possessions. He rejected that idea, knowing that it would open himself up to a never-ending lawsuit, especially when Carol found out that he was seeking to divorce her and marry Maggie.

No, he decided. There had to be another way.

The disclosure stunned Maggie.

"But you're still paying me," she had protested. "How can you do it?"

"It's called eating into capital," he had explained. "We are very swiftly working into another financial activity, borrowing on lines of credit without sufficient backing. In short, in less than a year, I'll be broke."

"While what she owns has grown in value?"

"That's an understatement, Maggie. She's actually rich."

"That's not fair."

"No, it's not," he had agreed.

In the end, it was the reality of what was "fair" that had triggered his imagination and he had conceived this new idea, this ultimate solution.

"It sounds so . . . so wishfully naïve," Maggie said when he first explained it to her.

"But do you agree that it's an ideal solution? If we do succeed we restore a balance of fairness to the situation."

Her skepticism was not easily mollified.

"People can't be programmed like computers, Eliot."

"Why not?"

"Because they're not made up of bytes that have a predictable response."

"Science may yet dispute that."

"You can't manufacture attraction," Maggie persisted.

"You can try," Eliot said.

They did not argue about the necessity of Eliot's regaining possession of his property. It was his property. That was a given. Love was a wondrous thing, they both agreed, glorious, essential, and marvelous. But so was money. They did not live in a vacuum, or on a desert island. Money counted.

Eliot researched brainwashing techniques. Although most of them were theoretical, they were successful under the right circumstances. Get the subject into a situation outside his normal life, a controlled environment, and maybe, just maybe, a drumbeat of information manipulated into his unsuspecting head might get that person to think what the manipulator wants him to think. Or feel.

Africa! He was on the verge of canceling the safari when it occurred to him that Africa would offer an ideal opportunity, a perfect venue, for what they had in mind. At a certain level of desperation, one takes one's chances. Certainly, it was worth the investment.

If it could happen anywhere, it could happen in Africa.

11

URING THE trip south to the Samburu, images of Africa had flung themselves into Maggie's vision. Passing villages barely over the cusp of the Stone Age, living side by side with the internal combustion engine and under the ubiquitous antennae of the television age, she had the impression that modern civilization was still making up its mind about absorbing Africa into its bosom.

Fifty miles out of Nairobi, paved highways had disappeared and they had to bounce through walls of dust particles that burned their way down their throats and up their nasal passages.

Jack Meade, his W. C. Fields nose shiny and ulcerated with drink and sunburn, kept up a running commentary on the African dilemma, which according to Meade was dire, teetering on the edge of chaos and disaster.

"No self-restraint with these Africans," Meade explained. "It's all greed and corruption. Padding pockets it is. Not a black-white thing." He took pains to point this out. "There's no self-discipline anywhere. Babies, babies. They know how to make them. They do that better than anything. Where they miss is what to do with them. No jobs, you see." He pointed to rows

164

upon rows of makeshift dwellings, many of them roofless, constructed mostly of flattened cans. "Poor buggers. They also have to compete with the wildlife. Well, who's going to win that one? Not the wildlife."

He went on and on about the poaching situation.

"They come down from Somalia mostly and machine-gun the elephants for their bloody ivory. Not that the killers see any of the real lucre. They get peanuts for the killing. The rhino's been finished, all for a dagger's handle and the myth of aphrodisiacs. The leopard's seen his day as well. Game wardens are in on the take, too. At the same time the bloody powers-that-be want to increase tourism to three million people. More spectators in their friggin' Volks buses. God, I hate those things."

"It's an international disaster," Eliot said, showing his agreement with Meade's assessment. "That's why we're here." He paused and briefly glanced toward Maggie. "We've got to monitor the situation and bring the message back."

The road grew rougher as they drew farther and farther away from Nairobi. Waves of dust blew through the open windows, filling their nostrils, caking their faces.

Meade struck Maggie as one of those colorful characters who popped up in old movies, a kind of Humphrey Bogart type in *The African Queen*. She glanced toward Ken, who looked bored and uncomfortable, making skeptical facial expressions as Meade's voice droned on with its endless patter. Carol, taking the tack of all seasoned travelers, dozed sporadically, raising her head occasionally to check their location. It was apparent that she had heard all of Meade's stories before.

Their camp in the Samburu had already been set up before their arrival and the servants were lined up to greet them and attend to their immediate needs. Tents were allocated and Meade explained the schedule and procedures.

There were three fly tents, one for Ken and Maggie, one for Eliot and Carol, and one for Meade. The servants slept in less elaborate tents on the working side of the camp. A large mess tent looked out on a fire circle in which a fire burned merrily.

Each fly tent for the principals was equipped with twin cots and folding camp tables and mirrors set up under the fly at either end for washing, shaving, applying makeup, and other ablutions.

There were also two director's chairs and a writing table for sitting, reading, and writing during camp breaks.

At the rear of each tent, entered through zippered flaps, was the "outhouse" tent, equipped with a black plastic toilet seat placed over a deep hole and a shower which one entered through another flap. For showering, the men brought hot water in buckets and poured them into an overhead device. A pull on a chain released the water and gravity provided the rest.

Primitive but comfortable and effective, Maggie observed. A nineteenth-century fantasy, she decided, beginning to understand the otherworldliness that was implied by this kind of romantic Victorian adventure. She wished that she were here alone with Eliot. Already the frustration and pressure of showing indifference toward him were beginning to make her tense.

Because of the exhausting drive, Meade had abbreviated the ritual of the evening meal to just a light salad, cooked vegetables, and a cool white wine of Eliot's choice, served by the servants in white jacket and gloves. The conversation consisted of Meade and Eliot explaining how the safari was to be conducted and what was expected of the participants for its fullest enjoyment.

Meade, Maggie noted, was a big burly man, a second-generation Kenyan who had been a white hunter, one of an intrepid band of legendary British-descended big-game hunting guides that had flourished in East Africa until the government banned the practice in 1977.

Like all the white hunters of Kenya, Eliot had told them earlier, Meade longed for the good old days, tolerating the present with a cynicism that bordered on despair. Eliot had also briefed them on the man's character and habits, warning them about his affection for booze, which Eliot had strictly forbidden during the working safari day.

Meade, he had also warned, could be moody, gruff, and crude at times, but he was extremely knowledgeable and reliable when it counted. There was also, Maggie had observed, an air of tragedy about him, as if his life's experience had left him bitter and disappointed.

Eliot had debated changing guides, but in the end he had decided to stick with Meade, who had taken him out on other occasions. There's not a better man to have in a tight spot, he had told the others. The bush, after all, was fraught with many dangers.

"Our lives are in his hands," Eliot had told them.

It did not take Maggie long to determine that the toughest part of the safari would not be the absence of creature comforts, but the forced separation from Eliot and the pressure of influencing Ken to take more of an interest in Carol.

She and Eliot had agreed that casual but friendly disinterest between them was to be the accepted mode of behavior. There must be no long, lingering eye contact between them in Carol and Ken's presence. Not the slightest hint that there was this explosive intimacy between them.

"No touchee, feelee, kissee," she had whispered playfully in Eliot's ear as they stood in a quiet corner of the Norfolk lobby waiting for their bags to be loaded. It was turning out to be harder than she thought.

Thankfully, there was much to learn and absorb on this first night. It deflected her attention. That and the sudden injection of the element of fear. In the distance, they could hear the fierce rumble of African night creatures.

"Listen," Meade said. "The lion's roar. It carries long distances."

It was an eerie, yearning, anguished sound and it filled Maggie with dread.

"It's the female," Eliot said. "She is the efficient killer, the true predator."

"Like all females," Meade grumbled as he led them to their tents, lighting the way with his flashlight. It struck Maggie that failure with women might be one of the ways life had disappointed Meade.

"You'll find flashlights hanging in your tents," Meade told them as he said good night to each couple and proceeded to his own tent farther away from the others. In front of it, he had parked the van.

"You're awfully quiet," Ken said after he had put on his pajamas and slipped beneath the covers of his cot.

"I'm just absorbing the strangeness," Maggie responded.

"It's quite wonderful," he whispered. "Just what Eliot said it would be."

"Yes," she said. "They were accurate as well as eloquent in their explanation of what to expect."

"I'm really impressed by that guy," Ken said after a long pause. "He sort of grows on you. He really believes that certain things can be saved for posterity. There's something heroic and stirring about that kind of commitment."

She agreed, of course, but said nothing, waiting for the right moment to offer a telling comment.

"Don't you think Carol looks marvelous in her bush clothes?"

"I suppose," he agreed noncommittally.

"I find her so perceptive and intelligent," she offered casually. "Don't you?"

She waited for him to answer as she searched her mind for more to say, but soon his rhythmic breathing told her he was asleep.

Maggie lay on top of the covers in her nightgown, not yet ready for sleep, trying to sort out the images of the day but unable to think of much else but Eliot. She hated the idea of sharing Eliot with the others. They belonged together, working together, joining together in doing things that mattered, pursuing a lifetime of meaningful projects.

With what she believed was her innate sense of fairness, Maggie tried to resist making comparisons between Eliot and Ken. Wouldn't that be onerous and mean-spirited?

Eliot and Ken were different people with different sensibilities. Not that it mattered. Ken was a closing chapter now. She wished him nothing but the best, the best of everything. She hoped that he would one day realize his ambition to be the next Hemingway, or whatever it was he wanted.

As for her, she knew exactly what she wanted. She wanted Eliot. She needed Eliot Butterfield.

There was no point in trying to rationalize why this conflagration had occurred between them. On the surface, Eliot would have seemed to her to be the least likely candidate for a lover. She chuckled at the memory of her first impression of him. He had struck her as too prissy, too controlled, too fastidious, too spoiled by money and personal indulgence, and, yes, snobbish and superior.

Odd how people see only what they wish to see. Maggie was happy, of course, that Ken also seemed to be viewing Eliot in a new light of appreciation. She liked that. Of course, what Ken couldn't see was how she and Eliot were two halves of one whole. How could he?

The soft night air seemed to heighten her thoughts and excite her mind, which now seemed to fill with erotic images of Eliot and her together. She could not believe the heights of sexuality that they had reached. How was it possible for her, at her age and maturity, to feel so joyously mad with lust and romantic longing? It was uncanny, mysterious. And delicious.

Her flesh suddenly felt hot and her mouth etched a wry smile. This was the prim and proper mother of teenage girls who snickered to themselves, commenting openly about their parents' old-fashioned attitudes, dead certain that they were too old to experience sexual passion. If they only knew, she thought, summoning up mental pictures of herself being mounted rearwise by Eliot. My God. Was it Africa stimulating her? Or deprivation?

She spread her legs, bare under her nightgown, and let the night African air play with her moist womanness, longing for him, her man, Eliot. Come to me, she whispered, lifting her arms.

If only she had the guts to enter his tent, kick out the usurper, the sexless Carol, her boylike body tight like hard wood. Enough of all this sham and playacting and private lies.

A lioness roared again. As if in defense, Maggie closed her legs and drew her nightgown over her knees. No no no. It wasn't fair. Carol had no license to steal Eliot's right to his own life, to prevent him from pursuing his ideas and causes to make the world better for others. Still, she would not give in to pessimism or depression. She had no quarrel with the practical considerations of Eliot's dilemma. He was thinking of her as well, of their life together.

She understood his sudden anxiety about money. It had never been an issue in his life, and having it had given him the freedom to serve meaningful causes. To be plagued with money worries now was debilitating for him. Worse, it placed obstacles in the way of their future.

Maggie wished that she did not carry the baggage of motherhood and maturity. In her heart, she could abandon herself to the idea that love conquers all. But even in this Roman spring of her life, she could not escape from the reality of responsibility. It grew painful to think about and she rebuked herself for indulging this bout of depression. The solution was in hand, she told herself. They would take control of their own destiny.

Finally, on this note of optimism, she grew drowsy, crawled under the blankets, and slept.

Sometime later, a loud ground-shaking screech filled the night air, like the mad braking-tire burning sound that precedes a vehicle crash. Both she and Ken sat up, startled. The racket continued for some moments, then disappeared.

"Bloody rogue elephant somewhere," Jack Meade's voice carried to them. "No danger now. Gone to muck up elsewhere."

"I like that," Ken said, settling back.

"Like what?" Maggie asked, her heart still pounding.

"The sense of danger," he murmured, turning his back toward her. "Like Hemingway described it."

Danger came in all shapes, sounds, and sizes, she decided, thinking suddenly of another kind of danger, the danger of a life without feeling. She longed for Eliot to comfort her, thinking of him as he lay in his own cot a mere few yards away.

Oh, God, how she yearned for a life with Eliot, with Eliot as he was, with Eliot as he needed to be. Which meant Eliot pursuing his bent, his "thinking," his causes, his philosophical concerns. She admired this quality of Eliot's, so unlike Ken, who wallowed in excuses, nursing his frustration as if it were a baby's pacifier.

She could foresee a life of joyous partnership, intellectually and physically. They would mesh without seams. Eliot would continue to collect thoughts, ideas, evidence, phenomena. And she would organize them, place them in context for further contemplation.

Ken, she concluded, was a morbid man. He took his pleasure as she gave it, had always given it, as a mere marriage right. Eliot both gave and took pleasure and she reveled in his joy and her own. Their sexual awakening had been simultaneous, which had deep implications of a magnetism beyond logic. When Eliot touched her all nerve endings responded. She yearned to suck him into her, engulf him.

Even now Ken was a supernumerary in her life. He had given her children and a transitional life, of which more than half was statistically over. Had she loved him once? No, she decided firmly. That was an illusion, a construction of what was acceptable and expected of a woman in her time and place. Real love was powerful, volcanic, basic, and unfettered.

Unable to go back to sleep, she slipped out of bed and, un-zipping the tent, went outside to sit under the fly. She looked into the predawn darkness, barely able to pick out the outlines of the tall trees that stood in a semicircle around their camp.

The hot embers of the cooking fires near the servants' tent glowed pink, occasionally provoked to red by a rare breeze that whispered through the branches of the low brush. Surrounding the camp was the black void of night Africa, alive with sounds.

She heard another lioness roar. Or was it the roar of a lion, she wondered? It sounded very close. Then she heard footsteps and saw the outline of one of the servants. He was holding a flash-light as he marched around the perimeter of the camp, sweeping the darkness with beams of light.

An ill wind of an idea brushed her cheek and made her shiver. Suppose, she thought, trying to hold down the ugliness of it, then risking it. After all, it was only an idea, only a fleeting image. The big cats, probably two fierce and hungry lionesses, would enter the camp, silent, cautious, padded step after padded step. For some unknown reason, like the random selection of lovers, the lionesses would split up and home in on the sleeping Ken and Carol. Death would come swiftly, silently, painlessly, then they would drag their carcasses like fallen wildebeests back to the pride.

On that note, Maggie went back into the tent and crawled between the covers of the cot. She shivered. Goose bumps broke out on her skin. The idea was frightening, unworthy, hateful. She rebuked herself for her unfeeling callousness.

Above all, she vowed, she must not poison the well of her love for Eliot with such terrible thoughts.

12

FOR THE next three days, they were summoned by the servants at the crack of dawn with the familiar and lyrical cry of "Jambo" and presented with a tray of hot tea. Then the servants would bring warm water for the basins and they would wash, dress, breakfast, and be out on safari as the sun peeked its fiery golden ball over the horizon.

They roamed for miles over the vast plains of the Samburu, through herds of gazelles, impalas, African buffaloes, zebras, giraffes, baboons, and elephants. They came across the occasional warthog, oryx, duiker, mongoose, jackal, and dik-dik, all appropriately described by both Meade and Eliot.

Standing in the van, they poked their heads through the portals in the roof and snapped hundreds of pictures. They searched copses and underbrush and found cheetahs and leopards and lions munching on carcasses and vultures eating carrion. Above them flew eagles and plovers and buzzards, quails, pigeons, guinea fowl, herons, and egrets.

No doubt about it, Maggie thought. It was a feast to the eyes and heart. Nature's wild creatures in their natural habitat, living in harmony according to the natural order. Why not man, she

wondered? Why not her and Eliot, prime examples of natural selection?

They would head back to the camp to escape the hot midday
sun and have lunch and siesta and head out again in the late
afternoon, returning to camp after a long hard drive looking for
the new species and unique sights. After showering, they would
have drinks around the log fire as the purple sunsets faded into
night, then they would adjourn to the mess tent for dinner.

After dinner, they would return to the fire, for more drinks
and conversation. This was the routine of African safari life, exactly as Eliot had described it, stimulating, romantic, and mysterious.

There was little time for her and Eliot to discuss aspects of
their real agenda. So far, they had made little effort to fade away
and leave Ken and Carol to their own devices. The most frustrating part was not finding a spare moment for themselves. Not
being able to make love, especially against the stimulating back-
drop of this gorgeous wonderland. It was a deprivation not easily
endured.

But to Ken she did make periodic references to Carol's
beauty, charm, and grace, or whatever flattering attribution
sprung to mind.

"She looks wonderful, doesn't she?" Maggie would say to
Ken as Carol emerged from the tent she and Eliot shared. With
her exquisitely tailored khaki slacks and khaki jacket with
epaulets and pockets, and her wide-brimmed hunter's hat,
rakishly angled on her head and held steady with leather thongs
around her chin, Carol, indeed, looked like an African queen. Although Maggie wore a similar hat, she could never quite get it as
angled and dashing as Carol's.

Though one might say they all looked dashing and wonderful in their safari outfits and leather boots. Even the cameras and
binoculars they carried slung around their necks and shoulders
added to the illusion that they were, somehow, superior beings;
royalty come to observe their subjects, the animals, who stared
laconically at them as they passed in the van, their royal carriage.

There were two rows of leather benches in the van. Eliot
normally sat up front with the driver and Maggie maneuvered
herself to stand in the rear, her head in the portal, leaving Ken

and Carol to share the back bench and its portal for viewing and taking pictures. Proximity had its virtues in their scheme. Ken and Carol had to squeeze together in their shared portal if they were to take simultaneous pictures. Yet so far, in three days, nothing in the relationship between Ken and Carol had changed perceptibly.

Maggie waited for Eliot's signals.

"Be late for lunch," Eliot had whispered as they left the van after the morning run.

Obedient to his wishes, she lingered under the fly of her tent, slowly applying her makeup. The others had gone into the mess tent. Then Eliot had emerged from his tent, directing her with a movement of his head. Instantly, Maggie moved back into the tent, zipping up the back flap and emerging from the rear. They met in a stand of trees that shielded them from the mess tent.

Maggie rushed into his arms. They kissed deeply, then Eliot gently moved her away.

"You mustn't," he said.

"I can't stand it."

"Neither can I."

"Maybe we can get away, take a walk," she whispered, looking for emphasis at the endless plain beyond the trees.

"Not yet," Eliot whispered. "But tonight I'm going to turn in early. I'll say I don't feel well or that I need to rest. I'll go in the middle of dinner."

"What should I do?"

"The point is to get them to be alone around the campfire."

"And Meade?"

"He'll be tinkering with the van as usual."

"And tomorrow?" Maggie asked.

"You'll have a stomach upset," Eliot said. "And I'll beg off on other grounds. My work." He had brought some books and journals and was making notes.

He started to leave, but they embraced again.

"What about us?" Maggie asked.

"If they go off alone, we've got our chance."

"Your tent or mine," Maggie said, caressing his ear with her tongue.

But that evening, after they had showered, Ken said to Maggie:

"You go on without me. I'm a bit tired. I might join you later."

"You've got to eat, Ken."

"I just need a short nap," Ken said. "You go ahead."

"Really, Ken. Isn't that a little rude?"

"I told you. I'm tired. No sweat. You go on ahead. I'll join you."

"Please do," Maggie said angrily, storming out of the tent.

She took her seat at the mess table and exchanged glances with Eliot. Carol seemed unconcerned.

"Ken will be along soon," Maggie said.

"He's not under the weather, is he?" Eliot asked.

"He did look kind of piqued," Carol said, concentrating on carefully covering a sliver of toast with the pâté appetizer.

"He seemed fine to me," Maggie said, exchanging urgent glances with Eliot. "Just needed a little rest."

Meade, sitting at the head of the table, led the conversation, previewing what they could expect tomorrow.

"We'll be looking for leopard on the morning run. Might not see any, though. They're tough to find. But there'll be other species. Come afternoon we'll go for elephant. We'll time it so we hit the river when they all come for tea and crumpets."

"It's a sight," Eliot said. "If we hit it right we might get to see more than a hundred at one time. One of the wonders of the world."

"Is it dangerous?" Maggie asked.

"Only if we get Auntie mad," Meade said, laughing at what seemed like a private joke, which he quickly explained. "It's a matriarchal society, you see. Usually some overbearing auntie is in charge of things. The bulls make lots of noise but spend their time mostly on their own. The ladies drive them from the herd. Sometimes a bull goes bonkers, like that rogue last night."

"He did sound quite angry," Carol said.

"Madder than hell."

"Why?" Maggie asked.

"Lonely. Frustrated. Unhappy," Meade said. "Happens to people, too."

There seemed no point in commenting and they ate in silence until Meade spoke again.

"Not coming, is he," Meade said when it was apparent that Ken was going to miss his dinner. The others had already finished theirs. "Too bad. Our chef takes great pains." Meade was proud of the meals served on his safari, which were wholesome and tasty and as "gourmet" as one could get cooking on a charcoal ground fire. "Shall I have one of the boys bring him a tray?"

Maggie felt anger bubble in her chest. Damn Ken. "I'll go see," she said, getting up.

She returned to the tent. Ken was lying on the cot with his eyes closed. She shook him.

"Come on now, get up," she said testily.

He opened his eyes slowly. "I told you. I'd rather sleep. Go ahead and eat without me. It's no big deal."

"It is a big deal. It's not polite."

"I'm tired," Ken said, turning to face the sides of the tent.

"You're spoiling everything," Maggie said.

He turned again and faced her, opening one eye, studying her face.

"Join them, for crissakes. I'm fine."

"Considering what this is costing Eliot, I think you're being a shit."

"It's jet lag," Ken said.

"It's rudeness," Maggie persisted, feeling a rising sense of frustration. She wanted to reach out and shake him, but she repressed the urge and stood for a moment in the tent, watching him and collecting herself.

"I'll have a tray sent in," she said.

He shrugged and grunted noncommittally.

She went out of the tent and stood for a moment gulping deep breaths of the clear night air. Mustn't get discouraged, she told herself. Gears had to be shifted, strategies recalibrated. Hiding her irritation, she came back to the mess tent. A pudding and chocolate cake were being served. Carol, unconcerned, sipped her coffee. As Maggie sat down she looked at Eliot.

"He's tired," she said.

"It's not unusual the first few days," Eliot shrugged, calming her with his eyes.

"I guess we should send him a tray," Maggie said to Meade, who gave orders in Swahili to one of the waiters.

They finished the dessert and Meade said:

"Coffee and brandy round the fire?"

The routine was to linger around the campfire until they got sleepy. Meade, after presiding politely for a while, would go off to check the van for the next day's excursion.

Carol was the first to rise. "Eliot, I'm bushed, too. Would you mind if I turned in?"

"So early?" Eliot asked, exchanging glances with Maggie. What did it matter? The original idea was aborted anyway.

"Early to bed, early to rise," Carol said. She blew a kiss to Maggie and pecked Eliot on the cheek. Then she left the mess tent and they heard her making her way back to her tent.

Later, Eliot and Maggie sat on director's chairs, sipping brandy and watching the play of living shadows created by the firelight on the leaves of the trees. Above the trees, Maggie could see an astounding display of stars, a canopy of the universe.

As expected, Meade had gone to his tent and they could see him fiddling with the exposed inner works of the van under a bright light.

Eliot threw more wood on the fire, which crackled into flames.

"Too bad," Eliot said. "It's a lovely night."

"Spectacular," Maggie said, her eyes staring upward at the stars.

"Maybe tomorrow," Eliot said. He sipped the brandy and seemed lost in thought.

"It's maddening," Maggie said. "They're the ones that are supposed to be sitting here making goo-goo eyes. Not us."

She smiled and looked at Eliot, who lifted his head and smiled.

"Can you see my goo-goo eyes?" she teased. The brandy had heated her insides and made her lightheaded.

"Barely," he said. Then he lapsed into silence again.

"Maybe we can both have upset stomachs tomorrow. Let them go see the elephants." She paused. "Give us the time to get reacquainted." But he seemed lost in thought.

"I'll come up with something," Eliot muttered at last. He turned his face toward her and she could see the outline of his features but not his complete expression.

"I wish we were teenagers meeting for the first time, without these complications."

"Yes," Eliot agreed. She heard him sigh. "But with any luck we could have twenty-five, maybe more, good years."

"I'm counting on it."

But it troubled Maggie to know he was thinking in those terms. Twenty-five years looked good, but only when she looked backward.

"If I was younger I don't think I would be worried about things like money. I would go for love alone."

"Isn't that what we're going for now?" Maggie asked, although she knew what he meant. He had acted calmly at the sudden change of plans, but she could tell that he was not calm inside, that the factor of time was beginning to lean heavily on his mind and he was turning gloomy.

She looked around her. The fire was settling down, the flames licking lazily along the length of the last piece of wood put on the pile of glowing embers, shrinking the circle of light. She looked into the darkness, seeing the outline of their tents.

"We should be finishing our drinks now," she said. "Getting up and going to our tent together to cuddle in one of those uncomfortable single cots."

"No matter what the hardship to our bodies," Eliot laughed. Maggie was happy to see him throw off his sadness.

"We would fit ourselves together."

"Like a pretzel."

She wanted to reach out and touch him, but she desisted, fearing that someone might see. Then suddenly she heard a sound coming from the direction of their tents.

"You hear that?" she asked, looking toward the tent. He followed her line of sight.

"Maybe a lost baboon scavenging," he replied. "Lots of things here that go plunk in the night."

They were distracted by the sounds of the boys puttering nearby. Meade continued to work on the van. Then they turned back to each other.

"Tell me you love me," Maggie whispered.

"I love you."

"It is very unfair that we should find each other and be faced with such obstacles."

"I'm sorry," Eliot said. "I wish it were otherwise."

They did not talk for a long time, watching each other as the fire went down.

"Like more wood?" one of the African boys came over and asked.

"No," Eliot said, speaking again after the boy had gone. "You see how they watch us."

"Funny. I feel as though I was being watched," Maggie said. Then they both sank into silence, looking into the burning embers.

"I really don't want to see them hurt," Maggie said suddenly. She was the first to break the silence.

Eliot did not respond. She could barely see his face for the darkness.

"Hurt?" he said finally. "No. Something painless, quick and final."

Maggie felt a sudden chill and was strangely grateful that it was impossible to see his expression.

13

THROUGH THE mesh window of the tent nearest to the fire, they watched Maggie and Eliot sitting in the circle of light. The couple was talking in low tones and it was impossible to hear their words. In another, smaller circle, this one of artificial light, they could see Meade working on the van.

Carol and Ken were kneeling on the cot that afforded the best view of the couple by the fire. They were in Carol's tent, on Eliot's cot.

"They are certainly congenial," Carol whispered.

"They are always that," Ken replied, also in a whisper. When they spoke they talked into each other's ears, kissing lightly as they switched from ear to ear.

Suddenly the couple around the fire looked toward the tent, then turned away.

"Do you think they can hear us?" Carol whispered.

"Not when we talk like this."

Ken kneeled behind her, legs spread so that his knees were on either side of hers. He held her with his arms clasped in front of her body.

The couple continued to talk and made no move to leave the fire.

"They are obviously enjoying each other's company," Carol said.

"They always do."

"What do you suppose they're talking about?"

"Something that pertains to their work," Ken said. "Maybe wildlife."

Ken unclasped his arms and began to massage Carol's breasts.

"Maggie seemed very put out by your not coming to dinner," Carol said.

"How else were we to get them to spend time together alone? The more scarce we make ourselves, the better it will be for the idea."

"Do you really think it can work?" Carol asked. He accepted her doubts as a regular refrain. They also reflected his own, but did not deter his optimism. Seeing Eliot and Maggie together near the fire, sipping their brandy and talking in hushed whispers, was a good sign.

"It's getting harder and harder to show my indifference, Ken. Even when we're in the van sitting together, I want to sneak a pet."

"Me, too."

He kissed her on the neck and earlobes and she reached behind him and stroked his penis, hardening under his trousers.

It was risky. He'd have to leave the tent through the back flap, which she had unzipped, but that would expose him for a minisecond as he moved back into his own tent through the opened back flap. If Eliot and Maggie decided to leave the fire and moved too quickly, he might be spotted. There was also the possibility that Meade might look up from his work and see him scurry back to his own tent. That, of course, wouldn't be fatal, except that Meade did not seem like the best candidate in the world to keep a secret.

"What about tomorrow?" Carol asked. "Do we go with the others in the van?"

"Maybe in the morning. In the afternoon we can make excuses," Ken said. He hadn't quite worked it out in his mind.

Meade, of course, was an obstacle to solitude, but it was a stroke
of luck that he chose to attend to the van after dinner.

Carol turned suddenly and guided Ken off the bed, embracing him, undoing his pants, hugging him.

"Can you see them clearly?" she asked.

He bent from the shoulder and could still get a clear view
from where he stood.

"Good," she said, guiding his erect penis to her mouth, starting to make love to him that way. "You keep watch."

He obeyed, watching the couple, but his mind was elsewhere
and he had all he could do to keep his breath coming in hard
gasps. After a while, she stopped and started to remove her
slacks.

"I want you in me," she whispered.

At that moment, Ken saw the couple around the fire move
and stand up.

"My God, no," he said in a whispered shout. "They're coming." He lifted his pants and moved quickly out of the tent
through the opened back flap. Before he could button his pants,
he tripped over one of the tent ropes and fell to the ground with a
thud. Carol rushed out to see what had happened, but he had
gotten up and run across the space between their tents just ahead
of the oncoming couple's flashlight beams. Then he jumped into
his cot and pulled the blanket over his body, feigning sleep.

In the morning, all Ken could think of was the absurdity of
it. It was farce, all farce. But it did not in any way diminish his
resolve.

"Are you feeling better?" Maggie asked as they sat on the
edges of their cots drinking the morning tea.

"Yes. Much better," he answered cheerfully, searching her
face for any sign that she had seen anything the night before.

"That's good," she said.

He paused for a moment, then said casually, "How was it by
the fire last night?"

"Oh, lovely."

"I got up to go to the loo and saw you and Eliot sitting there
deep in conversation. It looked nice. You both seemed contented."

"We were."

"Wonderful of him to have this kind of an interest, to dedicate himself to such a cause. He was right about Africa. He's quite a guy."

He watched her as he spoke.

"Yes, he is," she said, her eyes touching his then drifting away.

"We're lucky. Don't you feel safe in his hands?"

"Yes, I do."

"Man knows his Africa."

"Yes, he does."

"You looked good together out there by the fire. Very . . ." He searched for a word. "Belonging."

She appeared somewhat puzzled, then put her cup down.

"Today we'll see elephants," Maggie said, standing up.

"Sounds great."

Had he detected something in Maggie that he hadn't seen before? He wasn't sure. Yet there was a definite difference. She seemed less intimate, as if she were withdrawing from him. He was surprised at being disturbed by this observation since it was exactly the result he wanted their relationship to have. Withdraw from him. Be drawn to Eliot.

Meade left breakfast early to get the van ready, and Maggie asked Eliot if he couldn't load up her camera, leaving Carol and Ken alone in the mess tent sipping their coffee. Maggie wasn't very good with mechanical things and Eliot had a knack.

"I think we're making headway," Ken said.

"Based upon what?" Carol asked.

He had expected her question, but wasn't quite certain how to answer it.

"A feeling," Ken said. From where he sat in the mess tent, he could see Eliot working on Maggie's camera in the entrance to his and Maggie's tent. Eliot spoke as he concentrated on loading the film into her camera. But his words could not be heard from that distance. Ken saw Maggie smile, then look toward the mess tent. She turned away and her smile disappeared. "It's an attitude that seems to be developing," he continued. "Especially when they're together. Don't you see it?"

"I'm afraid I don't," Carol said. "And I find it curious the way Eliot prods me on the subject of you."

"Me?" It puzzled him.

She lowered her voice. "He wants me to show more friendship toward you."

"He's still on that, is he?"

Ken was certain he knew what that was all about. Eliot was
as infatuated as Maggie on the idea of their being the happy foursome, "couple friends." That, Ken and Carol both felt, would be a
detriment to the plan. The idea was to make them two twosomes,
not a congenial foursome.

"Maybe we should show more outward affection," Carol
said. "Show them the way."

"Like role models."

"Yes," she agreed. "Sort of monkey see, monkey do."

She looked into his eyes and started to laugh, which esca-
lated, and for some time she couldn't stop laughing.

"Must be some joke," Maggie said, coming into the tent and
pouring another cup of coffee. Eliot followed her. "How about
letting us in on it, Carol?"

"I'll save it for the right moment," she said, calming herself.

"Anyway, I'm glad to see you two enjoying yourselves,"
Maggie said.

There it was again, that urge to make them one big happy
family.

They loaded up with binoculars and cameras and got into
the van and began the long drive over the wide plains. They followed the well-rutted road, skirting the rocks and dry river bed.
From time to time Meade stopped the van to peer into the hard
dirt of the road, looking for animal signs.

At one such stop, Meade looked at the ground and muttered,
"Leopard. Toughest bugger to find out here." He peered into the
surrounding plain and headed for a low hollow, moving the van
slowly as he squinted ahead then into the road looking for signs,
then faster as was appropriate to the hunt.

The four of them poked their heads out of the roof portals as
the van moved forward across the rolling plain in search of the
elusive animal. They held on tight to the handles on the van's
roof, cameras bouncing on their neck straps, as Meade hit the gas
and the tires gripped the dry grass to make its own track.

The motion of the van and the tight quarters of the middle
portal pressed Ken's body toward Carol at every sway and there

were times when one side of the van was higher than the other and they were pressed together like glued parts.

Suddenly Eliot banged his knuckles in a tattoo on the rooftop and Meade stopped the Rover.

"We stop now we'll lose him," Meade said.

"Never mind," Eliot said. "Look at that."

A strange large bird was standing in the middle of the plain no more than twenty yards from them. He seemed disfigured, his neck puffed to immense proportions over his beaked head, which twitched and croaked out a strange squawking sound.

"It's a kori bustard," Eliot said.

"What's he doing?" Maggie asked from where she stood behind them.

Carol turned to her. "Sending out the signal," she said.

"What signal?" Maggie asked.

"The one that's as old as time. Come and get fucked," Carol said.

Such talk worried Ken. He caught her eye and tossed out a brief glance of rebuke. Meade grunted out a cracked laugh.

"Where's the lady?" Maggie asked, scouring the plain.

They all concentrated on scanning the horizon looking for the lady bird. This kori bustard wasn't expending all that effort to puff himself up for nothing. Then Eliot pointed.

"Thar she blows."

A female bustard, he supposed, made her way cautiously over the plain, stopping, listening, moving again as the male beat out his tune, his carriage stiff and bloated with inflated desire.

"Way of the world," Carol said. "His call is making her sexy."

"Seems to be the pervasive activity of Africa," Ken said, chuckling. "All so natural and without inhibitions. Wonder if it has its effect on people, too."

Carol and Ken exchanged glances but made no comment.

They watched as the female moved forward, responding to the squawk, the male's show-off appearance, and the instinct of her sex.

"Obviously turned her on," Carol said, her leg caressing Ken's unseen from anyone else's vantage above the roof of the van. Meade, who might have seen if he had turned, was seated in the driver's seat also concentrating on watching the show through the windshield.

Ken, despite knowing what Carol was trying to do, found himself physically responding to the suggestive power in both the sight of the courting birds and Carol's touch. He felt the tingle in his crotch and the beginning of an erection. But it was not without a sense of personal embarrassment. They're only birds for crissakes, he thought.

Cameras were unleashed, lenses at the ready, as the female moved slowly toward her lecherous bird-man. Soon she was closing the gap.

"Sock it to her," Carol whispered through clenched teeth, her camera poised.

Ken pretended to be taking a picture, but mostly he was watching Eliot from the corner of his eye, observing what he assumed was consternation. Was Carol going too far, exhibiting a side of her that Eliot might never have seen, that private wild side of her that she had apparently revealed to Ken alone? He would hate to have to confront a backlash, just when things seemed to be moving along. Or so he assumed.

Finally the female bird reached the bloated bustard, turning her bottom to him. She was quickly taken. It was all over in seconds. Finished, she moved away from the male, who continued to stay where he was, still puffed and squawking.

"Damned fine show," Ken said.

"Different," Maggie acknowledged.

"Not much," Carol said. "Just in style and configuration."

"He's still out there," Maggie observed. "Still puffed up."

"For some there's never enough," Carol said.

Eliot tapped the roof of the van and Meade started up again across the plains. But he seemed to have lost all his enthusiasm for tracking the leopard.

"Worked for me," Ken said as he walked with Carol from the van back to their respective tents. Maggie and Eliot took their time about leaving the van, gathering up their film.

"Me, too," Carol acknowledged. "But, then, we don't need that kind of stimulation."

"You really pushed it," Ken murmured. She turned to search his face.

"We have to move this forward," she said.

She was right, of course. There was an element of time to be considered. When he had first conceived this idea he hadn't thought much about time. Only the doing of what had to be done. The process of using the very potent power of suggestion. But, of course, the goal all along was time.

"You think it had any effect?" Carol asked.

"On them or us?" Ken asked, smiling shyly, before each disappeared into their tents.

They had covered lots of miles that morning, had seen some elephants and two cheetahs. They had waited for the cheetahs to make a kill, but the two cats didn't oblige, preferring instead to play around the van, jumping on its roof and pawing its tires like curious and harmless kittens.

On their return, Ken had ordered a shower. When the boy came to tell him it was ready, Ken undressed and went through the backflap of the main tent into the john tent, through to the makeshift shower stall above which the tank had been loaded with hot water.

Soaping himself, he pulled the chain and slicked away the suds. Then he shampooed and came out again, a towel wrapped around his middle.

"That was quite a spectacle," Maggie said. She had stripped to her bra and panties and was awaiting her shower. It occurred to him suddenly, seeing her in her underwear, that she might be aroused and he would be forced to perform an act that he wasn't up to, not with her. Nor did he feel at all like the kori bustard. No way.

"Nature's way," he said, turning his back to her and pulling on his undershorts.

"Carol has always impressed me as quite the little lady," Maggie said. "But I bet there's more to that girl than one might think. Lusty, isn't she?"

"I'd say Eliot was a lucky guy."

"I don't think Eliot's into that," she said.

"Into what?"

"You know. Sexiness. But I'll bet Carol is. I always sensed that. A woman senses things like that. The way she walks. The way she carries herself."

Ken heard the boy preparing the shower.

"Shower ready," the boy called.

Maggie put on a toweled robe and started toward the shower.

"Come and get fucked," she said, laughing, repeating Carol's remark. "I like that."

14

"**M**IND IF I borrow Maggie here while you fellows take the afternoon hop?" Eliot said pleasantly, hoping he was being businesslike in a casual way. Maggie looked up, searching his face. Last night he had mentioned the possibility of arranging something but he hadn't given her any advance notice.

They had come out of the tents after siesta, all four of them ready for the afternoon ride, when he had made his announcement.

"I had this idea," he explained, "about how we could improve the wildlife data-base program." He turned to Maggie. "Hope it's not an imposition." He had been making notes during the siesta while everyone else napped. He had, indeed, spent the siesta time working at the table under the fly of the tent.

"Of course not, Eliot," Maggie said. "I'd be delighted."

"There'll be lots more elephants, especially in the Masai Mara," Meade said.

Soon they would be heading to the country of the Masai. It was even more spectacular than the Samburu, which was drier, less green, at this time of year. Eliot had decided that the Masai Mara was more seductive.

The episode of the kori bustard had affected Eliot in an odd way. He felt a sense of deprivation. Worse, of desolation. His woman, his one true love, was standing there just a few feet from him and here he was trapped in a manmade maze of his own absurd design. He envied the silly old bird, free to follow the dictates of his instincts.

He looked at Carol and Ken, wondering if they were buying his excuse. Above all, he wanted it to seem natural, certainly not a ploy to give Carol and Ken more time together. Of course, with Meade ever present and inhibiting his maneuverings, the plan would have less impact than if they were truly alone. But it did have its virtues as a means to promote some emotional bonding.

"Okay with me," Carol said, moving forward, Ken following. He turned as he prepared to get in the van.

"Hope you won't miss anything spectacular," he called back to them. They waved. Meade started the motor and they headed out of the camp into the plain.

"Smart ass," Maggie said when they had gone. She made no move to be affectionate. The servants were busy clearing the table.

"Of course, I'd rather that they were really alone," Eliot said, rising from the table. They moved out of the mess tent to Eliot's tent, where they sat side by side in director's chairs under the fly.

"Well, we bought us a delicious afternoon. That's something."

"I'm trying to buy us a life," Eliot said. He looked over to where the servants were busy washing the dishes and clothes. One was using a hot iron on a flat rock, pressing a pair of slacks.

Maggie reached out and put her hand in his. He took it and squeezed.

"Dammit," she said. "It's not fair."

"I've stopped considering fair. I'm paying more attention to what's doable."

"We're doable now," Maggie said, lifting his hand to her lips.

"Not with them around," Eliot said, pointing to the servants as they performed their chores.

"They barely speak English."

"But they have eyes—and ears. And Meade understands Swahili."

"You're not worried about Meade?"

"Everybody is a potential troublemaker," Eliot said. "This is Africa and news travels fast in Africa. Too fast."

"So what?" Maggie asked.

He knew it was difficult for her to understand, not coming as he had from an environment of privilege. One always had to be careful about the servants. They were always observing their employers, looking for gossip. The objective was never to give them anything to wag their tongues about. Many an employer has been done in by a servant who knew too much.

"Are you saying that we're going to spend the rest of the day together and not take advantage of this opportunity?"

Her words had a half-sarcastic tone. Eliot smiled.

"Actually, we're going to take a walk."

"Isn't it dangerous?" Maggie asked.

"Not really. Especially at this time of the day. Most of the predators have full bellies, having made their kills during the night. Besides, for most of them we're not on the menu."

He led her around the backs of the tents, pausing to make certain that none of the men had noticed, then took a route through the tree-studded campsite that came out on the plain. By hugging the tree line they would not be seen, even by the occasional vehicle that might be crisscrossing the plain.

Eliot moved fast, having mapped out the route carefully. From previous trips, he knew the various natural landmarks, the highest ridgeline to the north, the river bend to the south, the west being where the sun was going.

"You weren't fooling," Maggie said from behind him.

He took her on a route alongside the trees that afforded shade, avoiding any strenuous uphill areas, to keep down their level of exertion. They saw animals along the way, a herd of zebras intermixed with a group of giraffes, who moved gracefully through patches of trees, stopping to munch leaves from the branches.

In the distance, they could see the silhouettes of the occasional groups of elephants moving deliberately over the plain. He knew where the real dangers lurked and his eye searched for lionesses on the move, cubs in tow, a rare sight for this time of the day, but nevertheless a real danger. Any cat with cubs was dangerous. The mother instinct to protect one's young could be a genuine killer in this part of the world.

"Isn't it lovely, seeing it this way?" Eliot asked. They walked in single file, although there was no specific trail, he leading, she following.

"Beyond words," Maggie said.

"Are you tired?" he asked.

"Exhilarated," she said. "I can walk forever."

He turned back to look at her and smiled.

He could not help indulging in the philosophical significance of their being in this vastness, a species vastly different from those creatures with whom they shared this place. Although he thought of these animals reverently, he rejoiced in the idea that man, because of his more complex brain and its resultant powers of reason, logic, and ability to absorb knowledge, was the superior being, and therefore the most powerful.

And in this environment, he was sensing this superior power in himself. To achieve his present goal he needed every ounce of cleverness, every morsel of resourcefulness. And guile. Mostly guile. He was not going to be deprived.

They moved through grassy terrain to a gentle rise overlooking the river, which moved in a sparkling ribbon below them. A family of baboons played along its edge, and they squatted for a while watching them gambol among the trees along the river before they scampered away deep into the thicket. A lone oryx stood on an anthill not far away, his body outlined against the sun, now arced to throw longer shadows as it began the process of slowly falling from the western sky.

"Beguiling, isn't it?" Eliot said, his glance surveying the various dips in the contour of the land. He knew exactly where they were, and in the distance he could spot the tops of the trees of their campsite.

Then he heard Maggie's voice.

"Eliot," she cried.

When he turned she was naked, her clothes strewn in a pile beside her, her arms outstretched toward him. The sun seemed to spangle her skin as she stood there, and he looked at her for a long moment, feeling the goading force of his own arousal.

"I feel free, so free," she cried. "Oh, Eliot, I need you so badly."

He tore off his clothes and ran toward her, feeling the same sense of abandonment, the joyous kinship with all those other creatures that inhabited this vast plain.

But when he reached her she inexplicably turned and ran toward the river, looking back at him, as if she too needed to perform her own mating ritual. He followed after her, enjoying the sensation of the sun on his naked flesh and the cooling breeze created by his own movement as he followed her to the embankment.

But she did not stop at the river's edge, wading into it. The tribe of gamboling baboons turned to look at her for a moment, then continued their movement in the trees. Eliot noted, too, that the lone oryx on the anthill remained unconcerned as he kept his solitary vigil.

He felt a thrilling sensation of danger as he moved in her wake into the river. It was shallow, the water barely reaching his knees, but it felt cool on his flesh and it was clean. Looking down, he could clearly see his toes. As he followed, she looked back at him and waved, and he pressed on. She headed for a wide flat rock that formed a dry island in the dead center of the narrow river.

Reaching it, she turned toward him, awaiting his arrival, and when he got closer, she sat down on the rock, tucking her legs under her, smiling as she watched him. When he was finally close enough she reached out and grasped his hand and helped him up.

There on this rock, with Maggie in his embrace, feeling the fullness of his desire, he was conscious of assuming a totally different persona, shedding every vestige of the civilized world, as if he were suddenly reborn a primitive in a wild, untrammeled world.

When she touched him, caressing his manhood as she kissed him deeply, he truly felt time disappear and the full sense of what it meant to be part of the primal force of mankind. He entered her body, with both his own will and the power of her womanhood, as if she were the great Earth Mother drawing one of her sons back into herself.

Then came the mystical sensation that this was the true first time for both of them, the consummation of some holy quest, the culmination of which was only to be found on the crest of their mutual ecstasy.

Nor was he disappointed as their bodies hungrily accelerated toward the climactic moment and they both screamed out their pleasure as each reached a shuddering orgasm.

After that, they were quiet for a long time, watching the

river's flow as it eddied around the rock. Occasionally birds dived into the water and glided upward again in a wide arc. They watched the tree shadows elongate as the sun's angle dipped westward.

As they lay there, Eliot felt his conscious body float upward as if to observe the conduct of his other self below, this self connected to the woman by his side. The floating consciousness believed these two people to be the beginning of mankind, dropped into this rich cornucopia of Africa to begin the world all over again.

With her fingers Maggie traced his body as they lay there, her head lying on his chest.

"Must we go back?" she asked. "Can't we just fade into the bush, become part of the creatures on the plain, flee all the responsibilities and cares we carry with us?" She looked into the trees, where the tribe of baboons were temporarily resting. "Escape with them."

"We're too late," he said. "We've beat them in the evolutionary race."

"Beat them?" she laughed. "And here we are suffering all the agonies and pain of being civilized and responsible, when we know in our hearts we belong just as we are."

"That's exactly why nothing can stop us, Maggie," he said, feeling a resurgence of optimism and confidence. "Nothing. We belong together."

They kissed deeply again and stretched out on the rock like sea lions sunning themselves.

A shadow passed across Eliot's mind as the thought of civilization and all its portents rushed back at him. Their dilemma, he decided, was unjust and the unfairness of it was skewering his most cherished values. Carol had become not only the usurper of his material goods but also the usurper of his happiness. He saw her now as having used him badly, of cheating him.

Suddenly the shriek of a baboon startled them and they stood up. The baboon who had shrieked had apparently spied another male who was attempting to copulate with a female baboon who belonged to him. The shrieking baboon chased the other male into the river. They watched the chase until both baboons were out of sight.

"No prenuptial agreements for them," Eliot said archly. The thought brought him to a new level of determination.

"Lucky them," Maggie sighed.

Then they waded back to the embankment and reached the spot where they had thrown their clothes. They got dressed and started back to camp.

15

Meade was telling them how they had followed this huge imaginary semicircle where herds of elephants coming from different parts of the plain were moving toward the same objective, which was this certain spot in the river.

"I feel awful about missing it," Maggie said.

"It was fabulous," Carol said. "Wasn't it, Ken?"

"Super," Ken said.

Firelight flickered in Meade's eyes as he talked, pausing only to drink, then refilling his glass from the whiskey bottle sitting on the ground near the legs of his director's chair. Up to then he had been on his best behavior, holding the intake down to two or three at the most, including before and after dinner. He was above the limit now, his bulbous nose showing the signs of his inebriation like litmus paper.

Carol knew, of course, that he liked his whiskey, and over the years he had repressed his temptations on safari, as if it were a tacit understanding with Eliot, who admired his expertise and devotion but detested his weakness.

Every time he had started to excuse himself, Maggie had

held him back by wanting to know more about their afternoon with the elephants. Encouraging Meade to spin his yarns, especially at this hour, was for him, Carol knew, a prescription for inebriation. He was a man who loved this life, loved the wilderness and the animals, and greatly enjoyed rehashing the oral record of his exploits.

Carol also understood that as an old hunter he lived with deep regrets that hunting had been abolished. Often, he had explained the idea of the hunt, the poetry of its mission, the mysterious natural kinship between the killer and the victim, the need to assert man's status as the king of all the predators. The ritual of killing, he explained, was merely the symbol of mankind's necessary domination of all species on this earth. Man is the real king of the jungle, he would proclaim.

He provided practical reasons for the old ways as well. The herds had to be trimmed. There was too much competition for space and food. A hunting death was an honorable death, much preferred to the indignity and agony of a death without grace, from starvation or poaching or an unclean killing.

And, like all true hunters, Meade abhorred the visitors' predilection for killing for trophies and, always, if somewhat symbolically, ate the kill.

Meade's explanations and opinions invariably struck Carol as pretentious or self-righteous, but fascinating. She would be prompted to ask him baiting questions such as: How do you choose who shall live and who shall die? Instinct, he would explain without hesitation. The hunter knows who must die. It was an idea that always troubled her, but he was unshaken in his belief.

Meade's supply of talk was inexhaustible and, if properly stoked with booze, a belt or two beyond the limit, he could easily go on all night. Indeed, until his tongue thickened beyond articulation, he could actually be incisive and entertaining. Eliot had turned in early.

"We parked the van," Meade said, "off to the side of the river bank and they came down this flat incline. It was a bloody parade, it was. How many did we count?" He turned to Ken, who was sitting in the director's chair beside Meade.

"Oh, God, nearly two hundred," Ken said.

"Two hundred bloody elephants. The whole community

come to gossip and meander and play in the river, the babies under the watchful eyes of the aunties, mums, and nannies while the teenage boys banged heads. It was lovely. Lovely."

He upended his glass and poured another.

"Was it scary?" Maggie asked.

Meade shrugged with macho disdain.

"I was scared," Carol said.

"Sometimes these aunties get this idea in their head that you want to hurt the calves. That's the prime no-no. Show them evil intent and they'll swing a trunk and knock you all to pieces. Biggest killer, the elephant. Just look at the zoo statistics. More keepers killed by elephants. They get to not liking you, then *bam*. I've seen it. I can tell you."

Miraculously, he spoke as if he were dead sober without the slightest slurring.

"But how can they tell the difference between benign and evil intent?" Maggie pressed.

"Paranoia, you see," Meade said.

"Paranoia in elephants?" Maggie asked.

"They're scared. Poachers will come with automatic weapons and mow down a whole herd for their ivory. So their fear is real and somehow they communicate it to the others. Damndest thing."

"Poachers," Ken said, shaking his head. "Dirty bastards."

"Worse than slime," Meade continued, helping himself to another drink. "It's the ivory, the bloody ivory. Hell, they're also poaching me and my buddies out of business. First the rhino, then the elephant. We humans are a bastardly bunch of coconuts."

He would soon be past the point, Carol knew. But there was no stopping him and Maggie was not running out of questions.

"Do you think we'll see it again?" Maggie persisted.

"Question of numbers," Meade said. "You'll see them, but how many I cannot tell you. Today was one of a kind."

"Just my luck," Maggie said, throwing another piece of wood on the fire. In a moment it caught and flared, casting a bright circle of light beyond which they could make out nothing but blackness.

"You must be really tired, Meade," Carol said.

"Surely something must be done about the poachers," Mag-

gie interjected, opening up still another subject, which Meade bit
on, proceeding to trace all the reasons for poaching and what
must be done about it.

"Money, money, money. The elephant's ivory, the rhino's
horn. And the sheer competition for grazing domesticated animals. Bloody wogs haven't got a clue about land management.
Bloody awful to sacrifice these magnificent beasts to that kind of
bloody ignorance. Shoot the bloody bastards on sight." He barely
took a breath, stopping only to refill his glass, but passion and
booze were making him repetitive and surly.

"Do you think those measures will work?" Maggie asked.

Was she blind to his condition? Carol wondered.

"Fuck, no," Meade answered. He was showing it now. Soon
he would grow belligerent.

"I think we'd better turn in," Carol said, standing up, glancing toward Maggie, who averted her eyes.

"I can listen to his stories all night," Maggie said.

"Seems like we have," Ken said, standing and stretching.
"Shouldn't you be doing the same, Meade."

"You my nanny?" Meade shot back.

"Hell, no," Ken said.

Perhaps recognizing his condition, Meade got up and immediately began to sway. He was very drunk, having difficulty taking a step forward, holding his arms in front of him in self-
protection against a misstep that would fling him to the ground.

"Let's go, fella," Maggie said, lifting his arm and putting it
on her shoulder. Meade mumbled a brief protest, but gave her
little fight.

"You'll need help," Ken said.

"Please, no," Maggie said, waving him away. "It's no problem. Besides, I feel responsible for keeping him going. You guys
stay. I'll deposit the great white hunter and turn in."

Then she moved off with him into the darkness. When they
were gone, Carol and Ken sat down again. They had been trying,
unsuccessfully, to be alone all evening.

"She's right about one thing. She did keep him going," Carol
said. "Surefire way to prime the pump."

"When she gets curious, there's no stopping her," Ken
sighed.

"You'd think she'd have some insight into the man's weakness. He was gone an hour ago," Carol said testily.

"Never mind her," Ken said. "More importantly, did you spot anything promising between them when we got back?"

"Hard to tell," she whispered.

"Eliot seemed exhausted. He yawned a lot at dinner," Ken said.

"I'm not sure that means anything," Carol said.

At dinner, Eliot had told them that he and Maggie had walked for a bit on the plain. "I think we both needed a stretch," Eliot had explained.

"You think anything might have happened between them?" Carol asked.

She had entertained this fantasy idea all day that she and Ken would persuade Meade to head back to camp early on some ruse or other and they would discover Eliot and Maggie making love. But the elephants had intervened and pushed that idea from her mind. Besides, it was good being alone with Ken, despite Meade's presence.

"Be great if it was just us on this trip," Ken said.

"Wouldn't that be wonderful?"

"When we're free at last we'll do just that," Ken whispered. He had tippled a few himself and was beginning to feel optimistic about their future together. "Maybe we'll go up to Tanzania and shoot the big stuff."

Hunting was still legal in Tanzania.

"Old Meade really got to you," Carol laughed.

"Not just Meade," Ken acknowledged. "Hemingway saw it as well, the mystique about this place, as if somehow we were closer to the truth of it out here. It was Hemingway who may have posed the eternal question of Africa."

"What was that?" Carol asked.

Ken paused, his eyes growing vague as if he were looking inward. "Why the leopard climbed Kilimanjaro, beyond the altitude that could support his life. It's in the introduction to his short story 'The Snows of Kilimanjaro.'"

"And why do you think the leopard did that?" Carol asked.

Ken shrugged, then his face brightened.

"Maybe because here, in this fantastic place, one gets to believe that anything is possible."

"Did the leopard discover that?" Carol asked.

"No. His frozen carcass was found on the western summit," Ken muttered, peering into the fire. "He apparently tried to reach for the stars, which may be the point of the question."

Carol shivered and looked around her, surveying the perimeter of the circle of light thrown by the fire's flames. She wanted to reach out and touch Ken. Instead she contrived to touch him in another way.

"Someday our story and this place will find its way into a book. A Kramer. People will say he got his inspiration in Africa. Like Hemingway," Carol said, suddenly remembering her own lost dream.

Yes, she thought, when they were free, they would put everything they had into that. Finally, unable to resist, she reached for his hand.

"Hey," Ken said, pulling his hand away in mock surprise and looking toward the darkness and the tents beyond. By then, Maggie must have deposited Meade and gone off to their tent. "That's taking a big chance."

"I'm tired of all this restraint," Carol said.

"You mustn't lose heart, baby," Ken said.

"Frankly, I see no change."

"I beg to differ. There's a subtle difference in the way they look at each other."

"I fail to see that."

He tapped his forehead.

"The writer's eye."

"Maybe so. But I see no change and it's beginning to frustrate me."

She felt herself becoming mean-minded and impatient, a dangerous combination. Her resentment, which she had held in check since arriving in Africa, burst once again into her awareness. She had let love endanger her security. Perhaps their initial success in arranging this trip was merely a tease, a come-on to raise false hopes. Perhaps all these convoluted strategies would come to nothing. Africa would be a bust. And then?

She hated the dilemma, hated finding herself the victim of this injustice, this ridiculous legality. It was inhuman, against nature. Why must she be punished for her feelings? But to pursue any other course, to confront Eliot, offering compromise, frightened her.

Perhaps Ken had been right back in the States. Perhaps there was a chance of compromise. Again she pulled back on that point. Eliot was too rigid and controlled to comprehend the demands of love and passion.

On the other hand, he was man whose causes displayed empathy for humanity as a whole. Surely he could particularize this feeling to the point of view of a single individual. Yet, that, too, was worrisome. Eliot might completely comprehend her motives, but her insistence on keeping her valuable collections could be interpreted by him as a venal display of greed and grasping acquisitiveness. He might also claim that she had deliberately defrauded him, siphoned off his funds for her own secret purposes. A case could be made on that point. She had, indeed, bought things in her own name with a selfish eye to appreciation. How else was she to circumvent that terrible prenuptial agreement?

Yet Eliot had plenty of money. Surely he could show some compassion, release her out of the contract with her possessions intact. Perhaps she should simply put it on the table: Let me take what is mine as compensation for years of faithful service. In that context it sounded so logical. Would she take less? she wondered, suddenly upset by the idea of negotiating for what was rightfully hers. But love, too, had its value, value without measure. After all, a life without love was barren and lonely. And a life without money, without security? She had seen both and they were equally awful.

It angered her to feel so helpless, so dependent on Eliot's decision. Had she a choice? She looked at Ken. Yes, she decided, she would confront Eliot. Now.

She stood up. They had both been lost in their thoughts and hadn't fed the fire, which was dying.

"Tonight," Ken whispered. "Make love to me in your dreams."

"Yes. Yes, I will," she said.

But the other matter absorbed her now. Despite her trepidation, she felt hopeful. Hadn't Eliot always been fair? Hadn't she performed her role with gracious submission and understanding, waiting patiently in the wings until needed? When a cue for a wife was signaled, there she was onstage, hostess and helpmate, ornament and intimate. In its way, being a wife to Eliot could be considered a job that required compensation, along with a pension-and-profit-sharing plan. We struck a deal to marry, she told herself. Why not strike a deal to unmarry? This last thought spurred her courage. Have it out. Now!

They started toward the tents. A lantern's light shone in Maggie and Ken's tent. Obviously, she was still up, waiting for her man. Not hers, mine, Carol thought bitterly. In the distance they heard a lion's roar. Then, as they reached their tents, the clarion of the rogue elephant rang out again, a chilling plaint of loneliness and frustration.

"Poor bastard," Ken mumbled.

"Like us," Carol whispered.

She heard Ken's greeting to Maggie as he entered their tent. Taking the lantern from its outside hook, she lit it and let herself into the tent she shared with Eliot. In the dim, vaguely orange light, she could see Eliot, eyes closed, on his back, his chest rising in the steady rhythm of sleep.

Standing above him, she stirred him gently, then more forcefully. It had to be now, she had decided. No postponements.

"You up?" she asked.

His eyes flickered open.

"Oh, Carol," he said, swallowing, rubbing his eyes. "Is it morning?"

"Not yet," Carol said, sitting on her cot, looking at his face watching her in the dim light. She felt her courage falter suddenly, and she had to buck it up before the words froze in her mouth. "Just how important am I to you?" she asked him.

He looked at her calmly, his eyes narrowing as he focused on her.

"What do you mean?" he asked, and she could immediately sense his caution.

She repeated her question.

"Just how important am I to you?"

"Why do you ask?"

"I need to know."

He studied her carefully. She knew the expression. His mind had entered its analytical mode.

"Have I done something?" he asked tentatively.

"Have you?" she asked, sensing a note of hope.

"Is something troubling you, Carol?"

Damned straight, she thought. With effort, she did not take her eyes off his face. Set me free, she cried within herself. Let me take what is mine and go.

"What I'm asking is . . ." She paused. "Can you do without me?"

He grew thoughtful.

"Do you want to go home? Is that it? Leave Africa?"

"No."

"Are you having a good time?"

"Very much so."

"But something is disturbing you."

She paused, her courage really waning now. He had this manner that could always intimidate her.

"In a way, yes," she mumbled.

She had turned her eyes away but felt him continue to study her intensely.

"Something Maggie might have said?" The question puzzled her.

"Of course not Maggie," she replied testily. He seemed oddly relieved.

"Something about Ken, then?"

"Jesus."

The question came at her like a thrown spear aimed in her direction. Did he suspect? My God. Were they seen? Paranoia began to attack her now as she went over every risk in her mind. Did he know? Had someone told him anything? Was he biding his time, ready to strike? Spring a trap?

"What the hell does Ken have to do with anything?"

The lie bit at her insides as she searched his face for some clue.

"I don't know. You spent the day with him. And you've just come in. I thought perhaps you've had some argument."

"An argument?"

"He's really a grand fellow, you know."

Testing me, are you? She felt her anger rise.

"It's not Ken," she said.

"Then what's the trouble?" he asked. Yes, she decided, he is suspicious. She had better retreat.

"I just wish you would show some feeling." Under the cir-

cumstances, it was a bold strategy. But she had to deflect his suspicion, hadn't she?

He reached out and touched her knee. She had all she could
do to keep from recoiling.

"The fact is," he said pleasantly, "these cots are too damned
uncomfortable for that."

Christ, she thought. Did he have that all wrong. Then he
turned toward the tent wall, hitched the covers up to his chin,
and said nothing further while she undressed and went to bed
herself, emptied of all courage.

16

MEADE, BLEARY-eyed, strung
out, and smelling of booze, headed the van out of camp. All four
of them were inside, configured as before, Eliot beside Meade,
Maggie in the rear, and Ken and Carol hip to hip in the middle
seat.

Meade hadn't shown up for breakfast. Eliot had seen one of
the boys bring a pot of coffee to his tent.

"Expect a rough ride," Eliot said, observing the boy balanc-
ing the tray on his palm. "He gets pretty rocky when he's
boozed up."

"I think I set him off," Maggie confessed. "I kept him round
the fire spinning war stories, telling about the elephants."

"It was something to tell," Ken said.

"You mustn't blame yourself, Maggie," Carol said. "When he
falls off, he falls off." She turned to Eliot. "That hasn't happened
for years, has it, Eliot?"

Eliot shook his head. No point in feeding this fire, he told
himself. He stole a glance at Maggie, blinking to show his support.

It had all been staged. Maggie had done her job zealously,

which was to keep Meade round the fire spinning his yarns. When he entertained like that he needed oiling, lots of it.

"I'll try," Maggie had told Eliot when he had asked her to do this as they had walked back to camp. He explained Meade's propensity for drink and foreclosed on any questions before she could ask. The idea had come to him in the river.

"Just trust me on this, Maggie."

"You know I do," she had told him.

"It's for us," he had reassured her. "To hurry things along."

To spare her the pressure, he wanted her conspiring, but not totally knowledgeable.

"We mustn't hurt them," Maggie had said. "Above all, that."

"Never."

From his tent, he had watched the activity around the fire, observing Meade's growing inebriation and loquaciousness, waiting for the moment when he judged it safe to act. It was, of course, cruel work to take advantage of a man's weakness. Under the right circumstances, Meade could be plied with whiskey and the outcome was predictable.

When Eliot sensed the opportunity was at hand, he crouched low, plunged into the darkness, and, cutting a wide swath through the forest, came up behind Meade's tent. There he paused, peered out to observe the group around the fire, then crept up to the far side of the van.

There was a charged moment of danger when he unlatched the hood, making a clicking sound. He waited, and noted no reaction from the people around the fire or the boys in their area at the other end of the camp.

With a hand shielding the beam from his smallest-caliber flashlight, he surveyed the complicated inner works of the motor. Quietly, he unlatched the toolbox and chose the wrenches he would need. Having helped Meade on other occasions, he knew just enough about his vehicle to loosen various key nuts to the end of their thread line. Eyeballed, they would still appear tightly threaded.

He had chosen this method rather than disabling the van so that it couldn't leave the camp. That would smack of sabotage. The canny Meade would surely blame one of the boys and that would sour the trip. The idea was to cause the breakdown along the road, hopefully sooner than later.

The job done, Eliot crept back to his tent and lay on his cot until the acrobatics of cold logic and reason could justify to himself this desperate act.

Such methods, of course, were new to him. He had never seen himself as a man of action, or, for that matter, as an intriguing conspirator in a scenario like this. But he had never seen himself as a lover either; had never, until now, felt a lover's compulsion. The fact was that he had been transformed, had passed through an emotional Rubicon and received an epiphany. His life was now governed by this new equation.

Yes, he could envision himself with Maggie on some idyllic island far from the madding crowd, nurturing their love in the splendor of isolation. Hadn't he felt something of that during that time in the river? It was glorious, unfettered joy. It baffled him that it had come so late in his life. Unfortunately, for him, such a fantasy could not survive the cold light of reality, or the pitfalls of his own ingrained habit of logic. Most of all he feared that economic hardship, in the end, might overpower love. No, he decided, he must never let that happen. Never.

He had fallen into a troubled half-sleep when he heard Carol come into the tent with her odd and disturbing complaint. But it was only when he suspected that these complaints might be rooted in the soil of his and Maggie's objective that he became instantly exhilarated and alert. Were the gods smiling? Was this devoutly wished for thing happening?

Or, and it was this "or" that chilled him, had she read some sign that made her suspect that he and Maggie were emotionally involved. His mind seethed with possible motives as he analyzed every psychological nuance of Carol's words. What he needed to know was if something was happening between her and Ken. Or the "or": Had she discovered what had happened between him and Maggie?

By morning, the matter had resolved itself. The glowing morning sun made the moist dew speckling the surrounding scrubs, grass, and leaves seem silvery and sparkling. It put him in a hopeful mood. His act of last night, he was certain, would swing the pendulum farther in his direction. This was no morning to contemplate disaster.

At breakfast Carol showed no signs of upset. In fact, a neutral observer would see a happy foursome, envied couple friends, preparing for this outing in glorious Africa.

Only Meade looked the worse for wear. His foot was heavy as he gunned the motor, sending the van forward onto the pitted road of the plain, jostling them over the predictable rough spots, which seemed to add a green tint to Meade's complexion.

Eliot concentrated on the welcome severity of the bumps as the others held on and watched the now-familiar passing parade of gazelles, impalas, and zebras, which seemed to claim the plains at that hour.

"That's an impala harem," Eliot explained, pointing to a group of female impalas being herded by an alert male. "That fellow controls a bevy of females, sometimes up to a hundred."

Meade, who would have provided the commentary, was not up to speech.

"Poor fellow," Maggie said. "All those wives to service and keep in line."

"He's just a caretaker," Eliot corrected.

"The eunuch of the harem," Ken commented.

"The assumption is that another male is guarding this fellow's group of ladies," Eliot said.

"Not that they're above tearing off a bit or two of the other's harem," Meade croaked.

About a mile out, by Eliot's calculation, the van began to buck and clank. Then, after a final jolting metallic roar, the van stopped completely.

"Bloody hell," Meade said, stepping out and unlatching the hood.

Eliot and Carol exchanged glances as Meade poked around in the motor works. He came up red-faced and angry, in no condition to put a kind face on the dilemma.

"How the bloody fuck did these damned things come apart? Where the devil are the nuts? Motor block's off her moorings." He poked into the motor works with his hands. "Parts gone. Never happened before. Bloody hell." In a fit of temper he kicked at the nearest front tire. "Have to walk back to camp and pick up spare parts." He squinted back in the direction of camp. "Hour or so might do it."

"We'll hang out, then," Ken said.

"Maybe take a stroll," Eliot said. "Take some pictures."

"You do that, but be bloody careful," Meade said, angrily muttering to himself as he set off toward camp.

"Little problem at this hour," Eliot said, looking at Carol who nodded.

"I felt perfectly safe during our walk yesterday," Maggie said, picking up the cue for reassurance.

"Might be fun," Ken said, surveying the horizon. "It's a gorgeous day."

"We'll head for the river," Eliot said, striking out, the others following. He moved leisurely at first, aiming for the tree line as they moved through the herds of gazelles and impalas who looked at them curiously, then darted away.

Occasionally they stopped to take pictures of the landscape and the animals. This early-morning time on the plain was lovely, peaceful, serene, with no sign of the violence of the night. Eliot scouted the terrain for signs of buffalo or elephant, which could pose difficulties if confronted head-on.

Crossing through the brush near the tree line, he followed an animal track to where it led to another part of the plain, then moved through a stand of trees and up a gentle rise. He knew exactly where he was. He also knew that to a stranger it would be disorienting. So many African vistas had the same basic look. The landmarks were subtle and often confusing.

"It's beautiful country, all right," Ken said. "Be nice if they had street signs."

"If we get lost, we'll call for a cab," Maggie said.

"What better way to see Africa," Eliot said. He had subtly slowed his pace. The sun was rising, but it was still cool as Eliot led them through loops and turnings sketched in his mind.

"You think we should start back?" Carol asked when they had walked for nearly an hour.

"Meade will be wrong by half," Eliot said. "Why lose the day?"

"It is so lovely out here," Maggie said, again taking her cue from Eliot.

"We could use the exercise," Ken said. "Just as long as you know where you are."

Eliot led them down an incline, then through more loops and arcs until another half hour passed.

"He's probably back by now," Ken said, looking at his watch.

"Really, Eliot," Carol said. "I think we should head back."

"This is the way to really see Africa," Maggie said. "Don't you think?" It was a question posed generally.

"An adventurous way, that's for sure," Ken said.

Eliot stood on a high knoll, shielding his eyes from the sun. He brought his binoculars to his eyes and scanned the horizon.

"Buffalo herd," he said, pointing. All along he had been hoping to spot a potential danger that could be validated, giving him a logical excuse to widen the arc of their walk. "Take a peek." He handed the binoculars to Ken and rotated him in the direction of the herd.

"Funny-looking bunch," Ken said with forced cheerfulness. "I've been told they're not overly friendly critters." He returned the binoculars to Eliot.

"They're not," Carol agreed.

"They're far off," Eliot said, "but heading in the direction where we have to cross the plain."

"What does that mean?" Ken asked.

"A bit more leg power," Eliot said, deliberately smiling, as he headed off in yet another loop.

When they had walked for almost another hour, Ken asked: "I suppose you call this the long way, Eliot."

"More or less," he replied, hoping he sounded somewhat tentative.

Eliot knew where he was, of course. He looked at his watch. It was time to act. He glanced toward Maggie, who looked somewhat puzzled by his actions, then he moved resolutely forward, putting distance between himself and the others. Coming to a rise, he stopped abruptly and waited for the others to catch up.

"Bit of a problem here," he said, surveying the landscape with his binoculars. "We are dealing here with alternatives."

"Alternatives to what?" Ken asked.

"In Africa the shortest way defies geometry. It is not a straight line," Eliot replied.

"Meaning we're lost?"

"Not really. Merely temporarily disoriented. I should have taken the compass," Eliot said. Meade had a compass attached above the driver's seat of the van. "Bloody Africa, as Meade would say. Never seems to stay put."

"You're really joshing, aren't you, Eliot?" Maggie asked innocently.

"It's not like you to get lost, Eliot," Carol said.

But there was no panic in the air.

"No real problem, folks," Eliot said as he continued to scan the horizon. In the distance he could see the stand of trees where their camp was pitched. Not much danger here, he decided.

"I can tell two things from the position of the sun," Ken joked. "East is there." He pointed to where he assumed the sun had risen. "And west is there."

Maggie chuckled.

Eliot appeared to contemplate a course of action. Suddenly, he lifted his arm and pointed.

"Thataway," he said, striding forward, bringing them up an incline in the plain and heading toward a kind of large copse. Tire tracks crisscrossed the plain but there was no clear road. He had deliberately led them away from the more traveled track. Just a little privacy, he told himself, whispering the tune "Getting to Know You."

As they walked, a pair of spotted hyenas in search of carrion crossed within fifty yards of them.

"Take comfort in knowing that you're not on the menu," Eliot reassured them. Above all, he must not frighten them. He led them through a path into the copse, stopping in a grassy clearing surrounded by thickets of brush and trees.

"Things are beginning to look familiar again. I know this place," he said. "But I think I'll have to hit a rise to get a good look-see. There's a hillock about a half mile to the east. My suggestion would be that you all stay here and conserve your energy while I stake out the way."

"Suits me," Ken said, sitting on a boulder and untying his shoes. "Might as well get this gravel out of my sock."

"We're not lost?" Carol asked.

"Not at all," Eliot replied. "But with the sun heating up, I'd like to find the expressway back to the van."

"That makes sense," Maggie said.

They were standing near a tree that had fallen, its trunk parallel to the ground. Carol swung one leg onto it to stretch out her hamstrings.

"No sweat," Eliot said. "Chalk it up to a very slight loss of bearings. We've just overshot our position a bit and Meade's van should be just beyond the rise. If it's close enough, I'll hail Meade

and we'll come and get you in the van, which might be fixed
shortly. Not to worry. Just make yourselves comfortable."

Was he being overly cheerful, he wondered? He was certain
Maggie would get the message. Actually, they were no more than
a forty-five-minute walk from the van, but only if you knew
the way.

He felt, he admitted to himself, some very slight trepidation
about safety, but the odds of danger, at least from animals,
seemed small, considering that they were approaching midday,
siesta time for man and beast. Also, Carol was well versed in
safety procedures.

Briefly, an errant thought flew into his mind. And if there
was danger, real danger? He would not allow such an idea to take
root as he started on the trail through the copse back to the plain.

"May I go?" Maggie asked, as if on perfect cue. He stopped
and turned.

"Good idea, Maggie," Ken chirped, good-naturedly. "Keep
him from getting lost."

"Of course you're welcome," Eliot said. "But it's not necessary."

"Really, I'd love to."

"I'll sit this dance out," Ken said. "You go on."

"And I can use the time to stretch out," Carol said as she
swung the other leg over the fallen trunk and bent down low.
"Then do my daily dozen."

"Just don't stray," Eliot called over his shoulder, chuckling
at his double entendre. Indeed stray, Eliot thought. Stray with all
your might. He increased the speed of his stride.

"Wait for me," Maggie said, catching up to Eliot, walking
behind him until they broke into the clear. "I see the method in
your madness."

"I thought you would," Eliot said.

"And there's no danger?"

"Minimum," Eliot said. "Carol understands all the do's and
don'ts."

"You are one foxy fellow," Maggie said cheerfully.

"We'll sort of meander back to the van. Meade probably has
the truck fixed by now and is waiting for us. We'll take him on a
merry chase until we find them. Give them a few glorious hours
alone together."

"One might say you've certainly led the horse to water."

"Best I could do," he said, laughing, feeling good. "We may just get lucky."

They continued their walk, reaching a rise that afforded a view of a vast perimeter. To the west, he could see herds of zebras and gazelles. To the east, impalas and the occasional oryx. And above them, small puffs of cottony white clouds floating in a cerulean sky.

"Can they see us?" Maggie asked.

"Through binoculars, yes."

"Can I kiss you?"

"Not until we clear the rise."

"Spoilsport."

They continued to climb, expanding the perimeter of their vision.

"Can't say we haven't given them every opportunity," Eliot said. So far the day's conspiracy had worked as he had planned it. A miracle in its way. After a while, when he didn't return for them, Ken and Carol would confront some level of anxiety. This could bond them, establish a commonality, a point of reference between them. Naturally, he hoped it would spark something more.

"Now?" Maggie asked, interrupting his thoughts.

They were over the rise and he recognized the landmarks as they continued to move.

"Soon," he said, taking her hand and heading in the direction of an acacia tree on a low rise ahead of them. The sun was rising steadily, but a strong breeze kept the heat at bay.

When they reached the tree, he embraced her, kissing her deeply.

"I love you," he said.

"With all your soul? With all your heart? With all your body?"

"With everything," he said.

They made love hard and quick against the acacia tree.

"Will it work, Eliot? Will we be together always?" she asked when they had finished and straightened their clothing.

"Absolutely."

"No matter what?"

"I'll find a way. You must trust me."

"Maybe . . ."

"No, we mustn't even think that."

"How do you know what I'm thinking?"

"I know. I've thought the same thing."

"It's horrible, I know."

"Yes, quite horrible."

He put his finger on her lips to stop her from saying more and they prepared themselves to walk again.

Holding hands, they moved silently over the plain. On the next rise they could see the van and Meade and one of his men working on the motor. They released their hands and moved toward it.

As they came closer, Meade lifted his head and squinted as he focused on them. The back of his khaki shirt was soaked with perspiration and great droplets hung from his chin. He observed them with scowling bloodshot eyes and a snarl.

"Bloody hell. I swear, if I wasn't a trusting man, I'd say we were sabotaged. I could see one loose, maybe two, even three, but this is bloody hell."

His man, black skin glistening with sweat, stood to one side, ignoring them. It was obvious that he had worked hard.

"Damn thing bent the block and got it off alignment. We've been hammering it back to true, but it's not exactly easy pickings out here."

"Can I help?" Eliot asked, cutting a glance at Maggie. He hadn't expected the damage to be that extensive.

"Can't get more than two working on this at once," Meade said, poking his head under the hood. After a few moments of grunting and clanking, Meade with a hammer and his man with a huge wrench, he straightened up and wiped his brow with a sweat-soaked handkerchief. Then he looked at them in mid-wipe.

"Where are the others?"

"Back there," Eliot said, making a vague gesture with his hand.

Meade seemed puzzled.

"You left them out there?" he asked, frowning, inspecting Maggie's face as if to say: Why is this one here?

"We thought you'd be ready by now," Eliot said. "We're no more than minutes away."

Miracles multiplied, he thought. His plan was to take Meade

in circles in order to give Ken and Carol a few more hours together before they would be "found."

"You should have brought them back with you," Meade
muttered.

"We could go back now and get them," Eliot said.

Meade looked at his watch and shrugged. Then he talked to
his man in Swahili and turned back to Eliot.

"Six of one," Meade said. "We think we can get it fixed before too long. An hour at most."

He poked his head under the hood again and started clanking, his man beside him. A moment later he poked his head up
again.

"Mrs. Butterfield know her location?" he asked.

"She's okay on lore. Bad on direction," Eliot answered cautiously. In general, it was the truth.

Meade surveyed the horizon, studying the animals. He could
read any danger by their mood. After he finished his hard look, he
turned to the man again and they exchanged words in Swahili.

"Says he heard that damned rogue elephant before dawn.
But not since." Meade shrugged. "It's a long shot. But these bulls
can cover lots of ground. Nasty temper, they have, especially if
you make any move to approach them. Then they'll sooner charge
as look at you."

"Carol would know how to handle it," Eliot said, his words
belying his true feelings. The fact was that a rogue elephant could
not be handled, although he was less likely to charge someone
who remained still and ignored his carryings on.

"It's a needless risk," Meade said. "Ultimately I'm responsible."

"You did say long shot," Eliot reminded him.

"Let's get this bugger on the road," Meade growled, ducking
his head into the motor works again. The clanking sounded like
an endless discordant symphony. Meade and his man appeared to
be accelerating their pace.

Maggie and Eliot moved a few yards away to get into the
shade of an acacia tree and squatted down, their backs leaning
against the trunk.

"I hope one of us is not worried," Maggie said.

"Then it must be you, because I am." Eliot paused and
squinted into the distance. "Carol isn't as knowledgeable as I
made her out to be."

"I think we should go back and be with them," Maggie said.

Eliot wavered for a moment. No, he decided. He had gone through too much trouble to create this situation.

"He's exaggerated the risk," he said.

They squatted silently, watching Meade and his man bang the block into shape, pushing and sweating, resting briefly, wiping their faces. In the distance clouds were gathering.

"I'm having dark thoughts again, Eliot," Maggie said suddenly.

"I know," Eliot said. His own thoughts had also taken a dark turn. Hadn't he, after all, willed them away in his mind, fantasized their demise? He searched himself for any feelings of guilt and found none, for which he was thankful. "Considering the circumstances, Maggie," Eliot continued, "it's perfectly natural."

"Natural?"

"What I'm saying is that we don't mean it to really happen. It's not even an option since it's totally out of our control. Isn't it?"

She did not answer him, but her eyes met his. He looked into them deeply.

"Yes," she said. "Completely out of our control."

But she did not turn away.

17

KEN WOKE with a start and looked at his watch.

"Mother of God," he cried, shaking Carol awake.

She was nestled in his arms. They had made love just inside the perimeter of the copse but a good ten minutes' walk from where Eliot and Maggie had left them.

The idea was to move to a place from where they could view the egress to that spot in the copse marked by the fallen tree and yet to be hidden while they waited.

They had found this perfect spot where they had made love, and then, despite their pledge to the contrary, had fallen asleep.

"They could have been and gone," Carol suggested, although Ken thought that unlikely.

"Surely we would have heard them," Ken said. "No way they would approach silently. Then they would have called out."

Carol looked at her watch. More than five hours had passed since Eliot and Maggie had gone.

"Maybe the van hasn't been fixed yet," Ken speculated.

"Or they're really lost."

"That's two not-so-good possibilities," Ken said. He had

meant to keep his real and growing worries to himself, then had silently reneged. No lies between us. No disguises and dissimulation. The fact was that he was anxious.

"Maybe they did come and . . . well, saw us making love," Carol said.

"That's a third not-so-good possibility."

"And highly unlikely unless they sneaked up on us, which is doubtful."

They stood up, adjusted and brushed off their clothes, and backtracked to where they had been originally. There was no problem finding the fallen tree. The sun had arced toward the west by then, throwing the area into shadows.

"You think we should strike out for ourselves?" Ken asked.

"I've been warned about that," Carol said. "Experts suggest staying put. A great deal of this country looks alike."

"But if Eliot and Maggie are lost, then we're lost as well. And if Meade's van is still out, we're up shit's creek without a paddle."

"Above all, we must not panic," Carol warned. "In such a situation panic is just as dangerous."

"All right, then, let's put it in a good-news-bad-news context," Ken said. Talking about it was making him feel better. "Quite by accident, we've thrown them together. That, after all, was the intention. Maybe they've found true love or got turned on or . . ." He paused. "Whatever."

"Don't be ominous," Carol snapped.

"Nervous banter," Ken said. The idea had thrown a strange sense of elation into his thoughts, which he tried, half successfully, to shoo away. But it did bring up the matter of danger, despite Eliot's earlier assurances. After all, this was a primitive wilderness. There were lots of predatory animals out there who did not conform to any schedules but the rhythm of their appetites. "Fact is, I'd feel a lot better if I knew exactly where we were in relation to our camp."

He concentrated on that thought, trying to summon up a picture of the landscape surrounding the camp, the direction of any landmarks that lingered in memory, and the position of the sun as it rose and set. He conveyed the idea to Carol, who thought about it, closing her eyes to concentrate the picture in her mind. She was the first to make an observation.

She stood near the fallen log and spread her arms.

"The mess tent was open to the north. The sun rose on my right hand and set on my left hand."

"There you go."

"Which means that the camp is in that direction." She pointed with her right arm. "More or less."

They did the same exercise to determine the position of the van, recalling how they had ridden a short distance into the orange sunrise. It was, Ken knew, a primitive calculation, but a good starting point.

"Chances are, then, that the van would come from that direction," Ken said, pointing vaguely in an easterly direction. Looking up, he noted that the arc of the sun was dropping toward what had to be the west. "We should at least move into the plain and keep this spot in our sights."

He had paid little attention to where they were going when Eliot was leading them.

"As long as we don't stray too far," Carol said. "At least he knows where he last saw us. It's really not like Eliot to get lost. He knows this land."

Again the unthinkable crossed Ken's thoughts and again he tried to push it away.

"How would Meade react if his van stayed broken and Eliot didn't show?" Ken asked.

"Sounds like panic," Carol said, studying him.

"It's not."

Her eyes opened like saucers and he detected a slight tremor of her lips.

"Why lie to ourselves? The possibility exists."

She seemed to reflect for a moment and the tremors stopped abruptly.

"In that case, he'd send the boys out on foot. They know the Samburu well. They're Meade's boys from his hunting days and are superb trackers."

"Well, then, we should get out into the open and give them tracks."

"Eliot went in the direction of a rise so that he could see the surrounding area," Carol said.

"That wouldn't qualify as straying if we kept this place in view."

He started back over the animal trail they had followed into the copse, and in a half hour they were once again into the vast plain. For a moment, Ken studied the topography, looking for the nearest high point. They were actually in a saucer and he found himself having difficulty choosing which high ground to head for.

"There first," he said finally, pointing. He struck out strongly and Carol followed without objection. It took them another half hour to arrive at the spot he had chosen.

Reaching it, they looked out over the plain. Through his binoculars, he could see the various herds, predominantly zebras, gazelles, and impalas, but there was no sign of Meade's van. Behind him, he could still see the tree-studded thicket that marked where they had just come from.

"Nothing," he said, letting his binoculars hang from the leather ribbon around his neck. Ken studied the sky and the position of the sun, estimating that the sun would begin its descent in a couple of hours. "Now there." He pointed to another high spot across the plain and started downhill, the stand of trees still in their sights.

As they crossed the plain they passed within yards of a pair of hyenas tearing apart what was left of a zebra's carcass.

"With their bellies full, they won't bother us," Carol said. The hyenas, their mouths bloody and their bellies distended, looked up for a moment to watch them before going back to their feast.

"I'd feel a lot safer with a gun," Ken muttered, although he had never shot a gun in his life. "In Hemingway's time, they would have guns at the ready, both for the hunt and for protection."

They reached the other rise and once again Ken surveyed the surrounding landscape with his binoculars.

"*Nada*," he said, looking back to their landmark.

He noted, too, the blanket of silence that hung over everything. The animals seemed especially silent. He also noted that the clouds had formed a large thunderhead to the east.

"Looks like a storm is brewing," Carol said.

"A big one?" Ken asked.

"It will make a racket and get us soaked," Carol said. "If Meade doesn't find us by then, he'll have a fit."

"He's probably already having one."

"As long as he doesn't have a drink," Carol said. "Maggie was a fool to encourage him like that last night. It almost seemed as if she was encouraging him deliberately."

That hadn't occurred to him before. Maggie, like the rest of them, had been warned of Meade's problems with alcohol. Surely she had seen that she was encouraging him toward greater drunkenness.

"Maybe she didn't realize what was happening," Ken said.

"She'd have to be blind."

He noted that there was another rise across the plain with yet another vantage, which would be their last observation point from which they could still see the stand of trees where they had been.

"Game?" he asked her.

"Why not?" she said, smiling. "We've gone this far together."

Ken reached out and gathered her in, kissing her deeply on the lips. When they parted, he looked up at the sky.

"I'm not afraid," he said.

"Nor am I," Carol said. "Not with you."

He surveyed the surrounding area and the storm clouds approaching.

"I think daylight is our top priority," Ken said.

"I agree," she said.

They started down the rise into the saucer, then crossed the flat. The herds of animals seemed to be thickening and there was also the sense of movement, as if the animals had become suddenly alerted.

"Something is happening," he told her.

"I'm afraid so."

"What?"

"Some lioness looking for the pride's supper, I suppose," Carol said.

"Hope it won't be us," he said, offering a chuckle.

"We'd be their last desperate choice," Carol said.

By the time they reached the high point at the other end, the light had changed and the sun was descending rapidly. To the east the clouds were building. They would definitely have rain.

Ken surveyed the surrounding area with his binoculars. Nothing familiar. An untracked land. Like life, he thought suddenly, feeling the exhilaration of facing the unknown, perhaps death. From this perspective, he could understand the haunting beauty of this massive land, the hypnotic spell it cast on visitors. Above all, he could feel the high that came from the sense of unpredictability and danger that lurked here.

"Fantastic," he whispered, turning to face Carol, this woman whom he loved, truly loved. What is all this business of money and ease and security against the grandeur of this? And their love, in which there was nobility and danger as well.

He looked up at the threatening sky and gripped her hand, pointing with the other.

"That's the way," he said, sensing a renewal of his strength and decisiveness as a man, as if he had found some lost part of himself here, the essence of his manhood.

"Are you sure?" Carol asked.

"Nothing's sure," Ken said, turning to look at her. He gathered her in his arms and kissed her long and deeply. "Except us," he whispered when they parted.

Then he took her hand and led her forward.

18

"FUCKING BLOODY hell," Meade shouted, kicking the tires. He had taken off his shirt and his body glistened with sweat.

Be ready in an hour he had told them. That was three hours ago.

"You think we should go after them on foot?" Maggie asked Eliot. She had asked that same question at least twice before.

"Won't be long," Eliot replied, watching the men struggle with the motor block.

"I'm really getting anxious, Eliot," she responded.

"How long, Meade?" Eliot asked.

"Soon, maybe, if you stop your bloody distractions," Meade cried, looking up from his work in frustration. "You shouldn't have left them there." He grunted as he and his man grappled with the engine. At this point they seemed close to finishing, but Meade's level of tolerance was strained to the breaking point and his constant nipping away on a silver flask was not improving his disposition.

"Let's hope the whiskey in that flask is finite," Eliot whispered. Ordinarily he would have insisted on Meade's sobriety during the day. Nor would he have stood for the man's surly behavior. Obviously, he feared upsetting the man further.

Meade was getting progressively nasty as his frustration and drunkenness increased. Maggie analyzed her concern. Of course, she assured herself, she didn't want anything serious to happen to Ken and Carol, nothing life-threatening. Eliot, too, appeared concerned. Surely, he hadn't expected his little rearranging of the inner works of Meade's van to have such time-consuming consequences. It was Meade's fault, she decided. It was he, because of his drunkenness, who was not fulfilling his part of the silent bargain.

"Looks like he's nearly got it fixed," Eliot said.

"I hope so," Maggie said. She scanned the horizon. The sun was setting rapidly.

"They'll be fine," Eliot said.

"It will be getting dark," she said.

"My God, Maggie, you are a worrywart," Eliot said with some testiness.

"I don't know how I'd handle it if anything happened to them," Maggie said, biting her lip.

"Nothing will. Trust me."

"You know I do."

"We agreed," Eliot said gently. "The more time for them to be together the better."

"Yes," she replied. "We agreed."

By now the idea of going back by foot was becoming a moot point since it was apparent that Meade could have the van operating long before they reached the spot where Ken and Carol were.

"A little anxiety is a small price to pay," Eliot said suddenly. The idea surprised Maggie. She looked at him and he averted his eyes. But he had injected a measurement which frightened her. What price was he prepared to pay for their freedom? And she? Any price? She felt a cold stab of guilt shoot through her. What if . . . she began to ask herself, then tried to push the inchoate question from her mind. It was unthinkable. Then why was she thinking it?

Whose fault would it be? Accidents happen. No one could

plumb the mind of a predator searching for the means of survival. All life out here was risk and hazard.

With this dash of logic, she absolved Eliot, who had meant well in this endeavor with Meade's van. Hadn't he? Yes, she decided, she could be comfortable with such a conclusion.

She watched Eliot's eyes roam the sky. He pointed to the east.

"Storm clouds," he said. "It will be quick and hard."

"Won't that complicate things?" Maggie asked.

"Depends when it hits," Eliot responded. Somehow she expected him to show more concern.

The clouds on the horizon grew darker and were now moving in their direction. In the west the sky was turning purple as the sun's descent accelerated.

"Got the bloody fucker now," Meade exclaimed. He seemed in better humor, toasting them as he upended his flask and wiped his lips with the back of his hand. Then, still shirtless, he hopped into the driver's seat and started the motor, driving the van forward over bumps, then backward, to test its tightness. "Got the bugger." He waved them in. "Better hop it. There's a storm coming up and we've got no more than a half hour of daylight."

The black man climbed into the rear of the van and poked his head out the top of it. Eliot sat beside Meade and Maggie stood up in the center portal.

"Hang on," Meade said, gunning the motor, flicking on the van's brights as he sped over the terrain. Following Eliot's directions they were at the place where they had left Ken and Carol in twenty minutes.

"In there," Eliot instructed, pointing to the copse that they had all entered earlier.

Darkness was descending quickly now. The purple in the west was blackening and the storm clouds were coming closer. The breeze had quickened, chilling the air. Maggie got into her woolen pullover and Meade put on a bush jacket over his bare torso.

Meade moved the van as close to the copse as possible, shining his brights into the point where the trail began.

"Give the horn a few long blows at intervals," Eliot said as he jumped out of the van and headed for the trail into the copse.

Meade pressed the horn as directed, which croaked an angry clarion into the silence. Turning in the portal, Maggie could see shadows of animal herds in the fading light, their tranquillity disturbed, moving away from the sound.

"If they're in there, they'll hear us," Meade said, peering into the area, the definition of which was fading into the blackness. "Bloody stupid," he mumbled.

Then suddenly from the storm clouds came a flash of lightning and the rumble of crashing thunder.

"Coming fast," Meade said, shouting up to Maggie. "Better duck under and close the port." He talked to his man in Swahili, presumably offering the same advice.

Both of them did as he advised, keeping the side windows of the van open. Again and again Meade hit the horn in the quiet intervals between the rolling thunder. Heavy raindrops suddenly began to crash against the metal roof of the van and they quickly rolled up the side windows.

Between the thunder, the horn, and the pounding rain, the cacophony was awesome. Then, behind Maggie, the black man reopened his window and broke out into an avalanche of Swahili.

"What is it?" Maggie asked, genuinely frightened.

"Bloody hell, shut up," Meade cried, peering into the beams of light thrown by his headlights.

Again the black man shouted something in Swahili.

"Please tell me," Maggie begged.

"I said shut the bloody hell up," Meade shouted over the din.

Then she heard it, a cry of rage, more compelling than the other sounds. Then the recent memory of the sound struck her and she quickly determined what was happening. Her heart pounded with fear and a layer of perspiration oozed out of the skin of her back. She started to open the door, but Meade moved quickly, grabbing an arm, pulling her back.

"Eliot," she screamed. "Eliot."

She started to resist and soon Meade was asking the black man for help, each taking one arm.

"Eliot," she screamed again, fighting to free herself with all her strength. Suddenly Meade slapped her face, which shocked her out of her hysterics. He pounded his fist on the horn.

"Please, God, save him, save my love," she cried. "Oh, please, God, save my love."

"Well, you won't save him by going out there," Meade said.

"We can't just do nothing."

The awesome elephant sound seemed to be coming closer. She felt her body shudder and her entreaty became a litany.

"Oh, God, save him, save my love, God, save him."

"Well, you're talking to the right bloke." Meade shouted, peering into the darkness beyond the headlights. Suddenly the black man shouted in Swahili and pointed.

"What is it?" Maggie cried.

Meade ignored her, listening to the black man's excited remarks.

"Where?" Meade asked, following the man's finger.

"Eliot. Is it Eliot?" She rolled down her window and they made no effort to stop her. "Eliot, my dear, sweet love. Come to me. Come." Her words seemed drowned by the avalanche of other sounds.

"He's coming, for crissakes," Meade cried, and at that moment she saw him, rushing madly toward them. Behind him she could see the outline of the elephant, ears flapping wildly, pounding forward, as the bloodcurdling screeching sound rang in the air, dominating all the others.

Meade opened the door.

The massive elephant, his eyes caught in the glare of the headlights' beam, suddenly slowed, reared up on his hind legs, his forelegs poised and bent, ears flapping wildly, his thick wet skin shining like ebony, shouting his blind rage into the stormy night.

Coming toward them was the vulnerable figure of Eliot, on the verge of exhaustion from fright and effort. The elephant hit the ground with his forelegs again and resumed his charge, moving with unbelievable speed for such a massive creature.

Eliot faltered, tripped, fell to one knee, and rose, coming forward toward the van again.

"Eliot, move, move. My love. Here," Maggie screamed, opening the door to the van on her side, starting to step out to meet him.

"Bloody bitch," Meade cried, grabbing her shirt and wrenching her back inside just as Eliot came crashing through the front door of the van, fighting for breath, his legs hanging over the side. With the door to the front still open, holding Eliot fast with the grip of one hand, Meade gunned the motor and the car shot backward inches from the swinging trunk of the charging elephant.

With his free hand Meade turned the wheel a hard right and the van angled out of the behemoth's path. Again the elephant reared, ears flapping, his two front legs sparring with the black rain.

In that split second of relief, Meade snapped the van into forward and pulled a U-turn, stalled suddenly in the soft earth, then shot forward with the elephant resuming his charge directly behind him. As he drove, the elephant fast on the heels of the van, Meade worked his free hand to support Eliot's attempt to pull himself fully into the van.

Maggie reached over the seat to help him, and finally he was in and she managed to grab the handle and shut the door while the black man scrambled to the door of the backseat and slammed it shut as well.

"Good show," Meade screamed, shooting the van across the plain pursued by the elephant. Occasionally, the van's tires slipped, churned, broke loose, then moved forward. He squinted into the darkness, looking for ground not yet softened by the pelting rain.

Eliot, awash with perspiration, panted for breath in the front seat. Ahead was a stand of trees with a narrow wheel track moving through it. Meade maneuvered the van toward it, then plunged onto the track, as the elephant followed hard on its heels, inhibited finally by the narrowness of the passage through the trees.

In fits and starts, the van made its way through the trees, then came out on the other side of the plain, heading up a rise to the top of it, then down again and across another plain. They heard the elephant's cry grow dimmer as they drove, and it was soon apparent that they were out of danger.

Maggie ripped off the tail of her shirt and mopped Eliot's brow.

"Thank God," she said, kissing his face. "I thought I lost you."

"Bloody nearly did," Meade muttered.

Eliot nodded, smiling thinly, as he sucked in deep breaths.

"Thought you might be in the bloody food chain," Meade said, chuckling. "Could use a bloody drink." He looked at Eliot. "You could use one yourself."

They rode for a while in silence. Maggie continued to caress Eliot's face and smooth his hair.

"Better get our bearings. Not a good night to be lost," Meade said, bringing the van to a stop. Around them was nothing but pitch black and the pounding rain. Meade took a flashlight from the glove compartment and looked at his compass.

"Keeps up like this, we'll be riding around in mud soup," he said. He looked toward Eliot, his head resting on Maggie's lap, her hands gently massaging his face and forehead. She knew she was being bold and indiscreet, but, in her mind, she had very nearly lost him. In that moment of terror, the rest of her life had seemed to hang in the balance. She was relieved, grateful. She bent over and kissed his lips again.

"Quite chummy, you two," Meade said.

It triggered a response in Eliot, who found the strength to sit up immediately and push Maggie away.

"None of my bloody business," Meade muttered.

Maggie saw the men exchange glances.

"They weren't there," Eliot said, his voice nearly up to its normal timbre. "Not where I left them."

"Could be that big bastard chased them out," Meade said. "There'll be hell to pay if we find them all mashed up. Bad publicity kills our business."

"Now, there's an attitude for you," Maggie snapped.

"Don't listen to him, Maggie," Eliot said. "He's jumping to conclusions."

"Maybe so," Meade growled, looking at Maggie. "He should have brought them back with you." Meade scowled at her, jabbing a thumb in Eliot's direction. She felt the intensity of his stare as she waited through the long silence, hearing only the rain smashing against the roof and windows of the van. The thunder and lightning seemed to be moving away, but the rain was relentless.

"I won't argue the point, Meade," Eliot said. "In retrospect it was a damned fool thing to do."

"Yes. And I'm responsible for you people," Meade said. "It's my bloody ass."

"And my wife," Eliot said. "And her husband."

Meade looked at them and shook his head, blowing air through his lips in obvious ridicule.

"For one thing, there'll have to be a hearing," Meade said in a tone redolent with implication. "Someone always around to fix blame. And I don't intend to get my balls caught in some bloody government wringer."

"You're making wild assumptions, Meade," Eliot said. Maggie sensed his double meaning, but was too frightened and upset to intrude. Did Meade suspect that it was Eliot who sabotaged his van? Or worse? She felt a tightening in her gut.

"Am I?" Meade muttered. "There's more here than meets the eye." He shot Eliot a hostile glance.

"More fantasy than truth, I suspect," Eliot said gamely. "You mustn't panic, Meade. Things are not always as they seem."

Eliot, she noted, seemed determined to remain calm and rational. She decided to follow his lead and not let dark portents dominate her thoughts.

"As you know, Meade, Mrs. Butterfield has considerable experience with the ways of Africa," Eliot said.

"And my husband is a very bright and resourceful man," Maggie said defensively, taking her cue from Eliot.

"Who doesn't know a damned thing about Africa," Meade countered.

Both she and Eliot, she observed, had assumed a posture of injured dignity. Meade scratched his head and sucked in a deep breath.

"Bloody good, then," Meade sneered, but their attitude seemed to have done its work. "Then we'll not think the worst." He peered through the windshield into the relentless rain. "I suppose we could cruise for a while. If they're still out there, they could see our lights."

Meade gunned the motor and started across the plain, which had softened even more, creating tire slippage and zigzagging. The rain had slowed considerably and the thunder and lightning grew fainter. They no longer heard the agonizing cry of the elephant.

They drove through the darkness for what seemed like hours. Occasionally Meade would exchange words in Swahili with the black man, who stood in the rear, his head poking out the portal. At intervals Meade would stop the van, flash his brights, and honk the horn. Then they would wait. After getting no response, they would move on.

"We had better get back to camp. Start again at first light," Meade said. "Mustn't get the men edgy."

"I'd prefer that we keep going," Maggie protested.

"Afraid we can't oblige your preference, Mrs. Kramer," Meade said with disgust.

"He's right, Maggie," Eliot said. "And we'll need rest."

"That we will," Meade muttered between clenched teeth. "Rest and hope for a miracle."

He beamed his flashlight at the compass again, set a course, and headed back to camp.

Maggie felt queasy from hunger and fright. She reached out, grasped Eliot's hand, and felt him return the pressure.

"I'd prefer to be optimistic," Eliot said.

Meade shrugged.

"No point in contacting the authorities until we've had another go at it," Meade said in a tone that sounded ominously conspiratorial. Maggie imagined herself and Eliot on trial for murder, both of them in prison garb and short haircuts. The image terrified her. Not guilty, she protested in her mind. We are innocent. Aren't we? Remorse began to attack her. She looked toward Eliot and their eyes locked. He seemed to want to tell her something. She imagined the message. Not our fault? She nodded in agreement. Poor Ken, she sobbed inside of her. Forgive me.

It took more than an hour to get back to the camp. The rain had diminished to a light drizzle. A group of the men stood waiting for them, smiling incongruously as they came into the rim of light from the van. There was even a welcoming orange lantern glow in their tents.

When the van came to a stop, Maggie jumped to the ground and felt her knees buckle. Eliot caught her before she fell. She leaned against him as they made their way toward their tents. Meade got out of the van and strode over to where the men were waiting under a canopy that kept the rain from dousing the cooking fire.

"He knows about us," Maggie said. She had begun to shake.

"We won't think about that," Eliot said.

"And he suspects about the van," Maggie said.

Eliot didn't respond and they moved toward their tents. Suddenly Maggie heard Ken's voice.

"You sure had us worried," he called from inside the tent. She could see his form through the mesh window of the undone flap.

Carol came out of her tent, catching them in the beam of her flashlight.

"We thought you were lost," Eliot said. "Or had tangled with that mad elephant."

"Eliot was nearly trampled," Maggie said with some resentment, as if it had been Ken's fault. "He went in to look for you."

At that point, Meade came up behind them.

"He's bloody lucky," he said, glancing at Eliot with a knowing, insidious smile.

"Thank God," Carol said.

"Jesus, I'm sorry, Eliot," Ken mumbled.

"I know we should have stayed put. But Ken got this fool notion," Carol said.

"Once you pick up the rhythm of Africa," Ken said with theatrical modesty, "the rest is easy. If you concentrate hard enough, you can see the signposts along the way. So we struck out, followed our noses, and blundered through." He shrugged. "Actually, you weren't far wrong, Eliot. We were a lot closer than we realized."

"Yes," Eliot said, with a telling glance toward Meade. "The trick is not to panic."

"We didn't," Carol said. "Anyway, we're all here and that's what counts."

When Maggie came out of the shower, Ken was lying on his cot, a book open on his belly.

"You know, I could really get into this African shit."

She felt her anger rise but with effort she repressed it. "We practically went crazy looking for you both," she said, falling exhausted on her cot.

"Well, now you've found us," Ken said.

Fuck you, she told him silently, crying inside herself with rage.

"We thought you both were killed, trampled by that elephant." She grew suddenly silent. The point was that everything had ended happily.

Hadn't it?

She turned away from him, fearful that he might see her disappointment.

19

SOMETHING WAS different. It was as if the calibration that governed their environment had gone awry, like a subtle change of musical pace in the middle of a ballet.

At first Carol attributed it to her own concentration. She was too watchful, too focused, too concerned with every nuance—a raised eyebrow, a stolen glance, an uncommon retort. She found herself growing edgy, looking forward to leaving the Samburu for their next camp in the Masai Mara.

Eliot seemed more reflective, less talkative. For the past two nights he had muttered words in his sleep, had tossed and turned in his cot. On the second night she had been awakened by a lion's roar and discovered that he was gone. It was still dark, jet black with a thick cloud cover that hid the moon and the stars. Unzipping the front flap of the tent, she had peered out and saw him sitting alone near the fire's dying embers wrapped in a blanket. Just before dawn he had come back into the tent. She pretended to be asleep. But the experience reinforced the notion that something very profound was going on inside him, something she had never seen in him before.

235

She worried that their original plan had somehow gone terribly wrong, had taken them into strange and uncharted territory. She chose not to share this fear with Ken. Not yet. For some reason, too, it was increasingly difficult to find a moment to be alone with him physically. Or perhaps it was her own heightened sense of caution.

Nor were Eliot and Maggie as outwardly friendly to each other as they had been before. In fact, Maggie also seemed withdrawn, different. She did not hang on Eliot's every word as before and they appeared to have less to say to each other. Perhaps she was simply reacting to the aftermath of what had happened with the elephant. Meade had recounted the experience the next day at breakfast.

"It was a bloody close shave," he told them. "Bugger came this close." He showed his hand, indicating a small space between thumb and forefinger.

"It was frightening. I can't remember coming this close to my maker," Eliot admitted, looking toward Maggie.

"We were all a bit shaky. He was a bloody big bastard," Meade emphasized. "Wasn't he?" he said, turning to Maggie as if cuing her reaction.

"I wish . . ." Maggie said tentatively with an odd glance at Meade. "I wish I had shown less hysteria."

"Only natural," Meade said. "I thought she was going out the door to pull him in." Maggie flushed, as if the memory embarrassed her.

Carol also detected a discordant note of ridicule and disrespect in Meade's tone that seemed inappropriate to the explanation. She noted, too, that his face was unusually mottled and that there was a distinct odor of whiskey fluming out of his mouth as he spoke. It was obvious that he had spiked his coffee.

"Maybe we should have stayed put," Ken said.

"That elephant would have made you both into a pudding. Might have provided a tasty breakfast for the hyenas," Meade said, again turning to Carol. "Or a snack for the vultures."

"Getting back to camp was dumb luck on our part," Ken said, taking a deep sip on his coffee.

"Dumb it was," Meade muttered as if it were a rebuke. He seemed strangely out of synch with his previous attitude, which was one of authority tempered with deference. They were, after all, his clients, which implied certain rules of respectful behavior.

Eliot's attitude toward Meade also seemed odd, Carol noted. On other trips Eliot wouldn't have stood for either sarcasm or surliness.

"What would you have done, Meade?" Ken asked, cutting a glance at Eliot, who turned away as if in retreat.

"I'd have gone back with Butterfield. You don't know this country." He turned toward Carol. "Nor is Mrs. Butterfield, despite some experience, an expert. It was damned stupid of you both to stay in the first place."

Carol prepared an argument, then demurred. Meade's anger seemed to be building. No point in exacerbating things. She recycled the experience in her memory. Eliot was going to check his bearings, come back with the man. Maggie opted to tag along, which meant she was to be alone with Eliot, which, of course, was what she and Ken wanted. And, certainly, she had reveled in being alone with her lover.

Perhaps it had gotten slightly out of hand. Ken had seemed determined to lead the way back to the camp. All right, it was against all previous safety instructions, but he had been right. And it turned out that they weren't really that far from camp at all.

Ken had shown resourcefulness and courage. When they had seen the smoke from the cooking fire, they had stopped and embraced, celebrating their good fortune with a long furtive kiss. It had turned out to be a wonderful adventure.

"Meade's right," Eliot said. "I should never have left you and Carol there. It would have saved us all lots of anxiety."

But Meade hadn't said that at all, Carol remembered. He had called Ken and her fools for not going with Eliot. Another item out of sync, she thought, her concern growing.

"Bloody van is still a puzzle to me," Meade said, directing his remark to Eliot.

"I vote we put all this behind us," Maggie interjected suddenly. "Chalk it up to good grist for the memory mill and we leave it at that." She offered a smile that seemed forced.

"I second that," Eliot said.

"Do something like that again," Meade grumbled, "and I pack you all in. Leave you here to play Tarzans and Janes. I could have lost my license."

"And what are our lives compared to that?" Ken said with cheerful sarcasm.

A flash of tension crossed Meade's face and he turned angry eyes to Ken. For a brief moment, Carol thought a confrontation might be in the making, then Meade said:

"Bus leaves in ten minutes." He got up and headed toward the van.

"Bit on the moody side this morning," Ken said.

"I'm afraid he had a rough time of it yesterday," Eliot said, as if he were offering an apology for Meade's conduct.

"He's also boozing," Ken pointed out.

"He'll be fine," Eliot said, but he sounded tentative.

It was Eliot's docility and acceptance that surprised Carol most of all. Somehow it was this attitude that lay at the heart of the puzzle.

They roamed the plains for two days, snapping pictures, following herds of different animal species, tracking the elusive leopard, finding none. Each afternoon, clouds gathered and angry storms soaked the plains, turning the ground to mud and making it too soupy to take the afternoon trips.

"Hope it's drier in the Masai," Meade remarked, his surliness proportional to the booze he was taking in. He had at least the partial good sense to limit himself to one flask when they traveled in the van.

It was too wet to sit by the open fire during their two remaining evenings in the Samburu and more time was spent in the mess tent, which contributed to Carol's sense of constriction. She hadn't been able to find a way to be safely alone with Ken for two days. Both couples seemed always together now and she began to have confused feelings of insecurity, as if she were under observation.

During dinner on their last evening in the Samburu, Carol's sense of unease seemed to reach a breaking point and, sending Ken a determined message with her eyes, she moved out of the mess tent in the middle of the main course.

"Bit of a stomach upset," she said.

"Better turn in, then," Meade said. "We've got a long haul ahead of us over bad roads to the Masai country."

Considering Meade's accelerating drinking problem it was a bleak prospect. The road leading to the Masai, Carol knew from experience, was a mess.

Carol waited for Ken on the far side of her tent, out of view of the others. She felt depressed, despairing. It was becoming more and more difficult to suppress her fears. She needed to be with Ken alone.

He came up behind her and she turned and looked beyond him, making sure they could not be seen.

"What did you tell them?" she whispered.

"This is a visit to the loo," Ken replied. "Anyway, I seemed to have been out of the conversation."

He put his arms around her. When they spoke, they kept their voices low, speaking directly into each other's ears.

"I'm frightened, Ken," she said. "Something isn't right."

"You sensed that, too."

"Do they seem to be watching us more closely?" she asked. "I think they suspect. Maybe they know something."

"How could they?" Ken said, but the question seemed purely rhetorical. "We've been careful as hell."

"No, we haven't," Carol protested. "We've taken chances."

"Not in front of them. We've been proper and indifferent." He looked around them suddenly. "Unless they've got us under surveillance." He chuckled lightly.

"They could have seen us," Carol replied. "That day on the plain. Meade, too. He's part of it. He would be their witness. Haven't you seen the difference in him as well? They're conspiring. I feel it. They know and they're playing with us now like cat and mouse." She felt the cutting edge of hysteria beginning. "Eliot is going to take everything away from me. I feel it, Ken. He's just biding his time."

"Well, then," Ken said. "Let him. We'll still have each other."

She stiffened and moved out of his embrace. Not that again, she told herself, her mind groping for logic.

"I know," Ken whispered, holding up his hands. "Forgive me."

She was not going to give up what was rightfully hers. It wasn't fair for Eliot to do this to her. It was unjust, mean-spirited.

"We've got to do something," she whispered. He reached out and she came into his arms again.

"You've got to calm down, think things out."

Then it occurred to her that maybe she was investing Eliot with evil motives that might be totally unjustified. She had been a good wife to him, caring and efficient. He had not been harsh or cruel to her. Cautious, yes, but not ungenerous. The fact was that she was the unfaithful one, the betrayer, and Eliot was the injured party. This was a very worrisome condition. From her African experiences, she knew that an injured animal was the most dangerous of all.

"You're only assuming, Carol. You can't know this for sure."

"Then why do things seem changed?" Carol asked. "You told me you sensed it, too."

"Sensing isn't knowing."

"The feeling is strong," Carol said. "Very."

"Could be the weather," Ken replied calmly. "Weather has a profound effect on the mind."

"I don't think so," she said after a moment's reflection. "It's just not working out the way we hoped."

"I don't think all the votes are in yet, Carol."

"Eliot and Maggie barely looked at each other the last few days. That's hardly a sign of growing affection. For some reason, they seem to be drawing apart."

"Or they're faking," Ken replied. "Like us. Playing their own game."

His observation surprised her, set off a new path in her mind. Perhaps panic was making her paranoid, making her lose sight of their true purpose, encouraging Eliot's and Maggie's attraction, creating the conditions for a divorce on her terms. Recalling that, she felt somewhat calmer.

"You really think that?" Carol asked, grasping at the idea. "The part about playing their own game."

"Well, we are playing ours," Ken said. "I don't think we should ever underestimate the opposition."

She thought about that for a moment. Opposition? It implied confrontation. War!

"I suppose that is the reality of it," Carol sighed.

"The fact is, Carol, Eliot is the enemy. We are trying to outfox him, aren't we?"

"The reverse of that is troubling me. He could be trying to outfox us. Especially if he knows what's happening between us." She looked up at him. "And Maggie as well."

"That is not a very comforting thought," Ken said. "Maggie is not one to be scorned. She is also capable of extracting a healthy pound of flesh."

"Maggie?"

She could not keep the surprise out of her voice. Maggie, whom Ken had characterized as the nurturer, the great Earth Mother, had seemed the most vulnerable to their persuasion. She had always appeared to both of them to be halfway there already, Eliot's admirer and sycophant and, therefore, more open to suggestion. Up to that moment, Ken had assured her of that. They had both calculated that Maggie, with her big, amply endowed body and good mind, had the physical and intellectual allure to entice Eliot, and, given their persuasive manipulations, the seductive power to force Eliot into returning the affection.

Perhaps, she thought, their initial victory had made them too optimistic. Or, contrary to their original intention, maybe they had been too indiscreet themselves, giving themselves away. The fact was that they had never calculated that Eliot and Maggie would discover their affair.

"She certainly wouldn't be approving," Ken said. "She would consider her options."

"Take what she can?"

"Of course. She's a businesswoman. And there are the girls. I was talking of a pound of emotional flesh."

"Eliot would be ruthless. Leaving us with nothing."

He shrugged and they were silent for a long time.

"You think I'm overreacting," she said, "reading too much into things?"

"Maybe. After all, they haven't really shown their hand."

"Just in case, then," she replied, "we had better be more discreet."

"In the future, you mean," he said, reaching out to her. She pressed her body against him as he embraced her. "I love you I love you I love you," he whispered, his lips finding hers.

She felt him tug at her pants, unbutton them, push them down. She did the same to him and soon they were feeling each other's bare flesh.

Through her closed eyes, she saw the flash of brightness, the sudden beam of light that washed over her for a brief moment, then disappeared. When she opened her eyes it was gone.

"What is it?" Ken asked. Facing the opposite direction, he hadn't seen it.

A cough rent the air, unmistakably Meade's. She took the sound of it as confirmation. The man had seen them in his flashlight's beam. A chill swept through her. It was out now, definitely, no longer a private secret between them. She forced herself out of his embrace and they quickly refastened their clothes.

"It was Meade. He flashed his light on us." Again, paranoia charged back at her. "He could be watching us for them. Spying on us. I feel it, Ken. They know."

"Not Meade," Ken said. "He would never do anyone else's dirty work."

Carol felt hostility stir deep inside her. It was, indeed, war. Something had to be done, some new action mounted. She wasn't certain what, but she knew she would think of something. This was one war she must not lose.

Then she heard Ken's low chuckle. It was out of context to her own thoughts.

"What's so funny?" She forced down an edge of anger.

"At least I mooned the bastard," he said.

She started to protest, but held back. There was humor in it, she supposed. But she didn't laugh and it didn't chase her fear.

20

"**T**HEY ARE not what they seem," Meade said, throwing Eliot a sharp meaningful look. The message was quite clear. They were standing on a knoll in the Masai Mara, watching a herd of cattle straggle out of a Masai village.

A gentle breeze brought the stinging effluvial vapors up from the village. Walking beside their cattle, the tall, graceful Masai in their colorful orange robes prodded the herd into the plain.

"They look so beautiful," Maggie said.

"A bloody filthy lot. Don't be taken in. They're greedy and they stink of dung. Everything they do is dung. They build their houses with dung. That center there"—Meade pointed to a kind of courtyard surrounded by huts made of dung and branches—"is literally a cattle-shit dump."

"Meade is offended by them," Eliot interjected, wishing to explain the man's hostility rather than rebuke him for his now nonstop drinking. Meade had become exceedingly vocal and abusive and his drinking had accelerated since they had made their camp in the Masai Mara two days before.

Meade's drinking was very worrisome to Eliot. Uninhibited

243

by his alcoholic euphoria, a chance remark could set him off, cause him to blurt out information that would be better left unsaid.

"The women and kids do the work. The men hang out all day on their bums passing the time drinking and screwing."

"Not all bad," Ken said.

"Their cattle also muck up the plain and the so-called brave Masai warriors kill any wildlife that gets in their way."

"I've read that a Masai man gains his manhood when he kills a lion with a spear," Maggie said.

"Bloody bullshit myth," Meade said. "They carry those spears for show. Oh, they kill lions all right. Come across one sleeping on a full belly and they'll stick a spear in his gut. Real brave, they are."

Eliot had never approved of Meade's intense dislike of the Masai. But hating Masai was a kind of tradition among the safari guides. The Masai made them pay to traverse their land, made them pay for any pictures taken by tourists, and hustled and stole from safari clients.

But this was Masai land, and Eliot believed that they were entitled to some respect. He had visited them in their villages on a number of occasions. It was true that they stank and drank an offensive concoction of milk and cattle blood, but they were a cultural phenomenon with different values, worthy of preservation and toleration.

Ordinarily he would have rebuked Meade for his criticism. But this was not an ordinary time, and Meade was obviously using his knowledge to get back at Eliot for sabotaging his van. Eliot had no illusions on this point. The man suspected him and rightly so. It was, in retrospect, a stupid act. He would have to be more clever in the future.

He had no intentions of giving up, surrendering what rightly belonged to him. Life had opened up to him in a way he had never imagined. He would have to be more resourceful, more resolute. It was growing increasingly obvious that there was little hope that Ken and Carol might ever be attracted to each other. He needed to find another way, stronger means.

"Bloody bastards," Meade said as they all clambered back into the van to resume their afternoon safari.

Gone was the easygoing, albeit surface camaraderie of their

first days in the Samburu. Now the tension was palpable, inescapable. Everyone was touched by it.

On the way to the Masai Mara they had stopped at Narok, a fly-blown dust-ridden township, to freshen up and buy carvings, magazines, and postcards. Maggie signaled Eliot with her eyes to follow, then drifted down the main thoroughfare into the post office where she took her place in the queue for buying stamps. Eliot followed.

"Meade's torturing us," Maggie whispered.

"He thinks what he knows gives him the right," Eliot said.

"I'm so sorry, Eliot. But I was so afraid, then so grateful. I couldn't control myself."

"It's not your fault. I'm sure he suspects that I sabotaged the van."

"Has he confronted you?" Maggie asked anxiously.

"Not yet. So far he's just toying with us."

"Do you think he'll say anything to Carol or Ken?"

"Who can say? When he's drunk he might do anything."

"It's my fault. All my fault."

"We'll tough it out, Maggie. He's got no proof on either score, only his word, and in his present state that's not too good."

"But if he does say anything it will plant ideas in their minds. Alert them."

"Well, so far he hasn't," Eliot said. It seemed a hollow reassurance.

The line in front stalled. A woman was arguing with one of the clerks in Swahili. Eliot waited through a long silence. Then Maggie whispered: "It's not happening the way we wanted, is it, Eliot?"

"No, it isn't," he admitted.

"Why don't we just tell them? Get it over with."

"We've been through that," Eliot sighed.

The line had begun to move again. Maggie opened her pocketbook and got money out to give the clerk.

"What are we going to do?"

"I'll think of something, Maggie, something foolproof. We mustn't lose heart. It means too much to both of us."

"Of course it does. It's that terrible man, Meade. He's making me nervous."

"We'll handle him," Eliot whispered.

Maggie reached the window and bought stamps. As Eliot waited, he inadvertently turned his gaze. Meade had attached himself to the line. How long had he been there watching them? Eliot wondered.

Maggie turned away from the counter, began to speak to Eliot again, then saw Meade and her features grew rigid with fear. She said nothing and moved toward the exit.

Eliot detested the man for making them both self-conscious and fearful. Yes, he thought, he'd find a foolproof way to accomplish what they had set out to do. Despite Meade, that drunken sinister bastard. He moved up to the counter and bought stamps.

Meade no longer joined them at the campfire either before or after dinner. He sat on the director's chair on his tent porch sipping from his flask and, it seemed to Eliot, guarding his van. He had also placed the tents closer together than at the Samburu, which troubled Eliot. It was as if he wanted to keep them as close as possible, within his vision.

The four of them did not stay long at the campfire, and the conversation between them was confined to platitudes and African lore. Even the way they seated themselves had changed. Normally Eliot and Maggie would be seated together. It seemed expected that, as business colleagues first, there would be much in common for them to share.

Somehow that had changed. Eliot and Ken found themselves side by side and Maggie and Carol now sat on the other side of their spouses. Eliot was not sure how that had happened. It crossed his mind that perhaps Meade had somehow conveyed his suspicions to Carol and she was orchestrating this new design. He decided to explore the idea cautiously.

"They seem to be more aloof," Eliot said to Carol when they were back at their tent to prepare for bed. He kept his voice modulated to a whisper.

"I've noticed that," Carol replied.

"You think it's something we've done, something gone wrong?"

"Maybe it's Meade, his drinking, putting a pall on everything."

"Maybe."

He allowed himself a period of silence before he spoke again.

"We seem to be pulling apart." He paused. "As couple friends."

"I thought you and Maggie were buddies," Carol said. She had slipped into her cot and he had put out the lantern. He turned his head, waiting for his eyes to grow accustomed to the darkness. Then he saw her clearly. Her eyes were open and she was looking at the ceiling of the tent. He offered no comment, remaining alert and cautious.

"As a matter of fact, Eliot, I thought she had a crush on you."

Her statement confused him. What was she saying? Was she testing him, baiting him? Did she suspect? Had Meade said anything?

"That's ridiculous," he said.

"I don't think so," Carol said. "I think you and she complement each other."

"I won't have that," Eliot said, his stomach in knots.

"Why not? She's bright, sexy. And she seems to dote on you." There was a certain relentlessness in the way she pursued the subject. "Frankly, I think you'd make a great pair."

He ripped away the blanket and stood up.

"What are you telling me, Carol?" he asked. "Has Ken been saying this?"

"He's not blind."

"What has he said?"

"That you two go together. A better match than you and I. And them."

"Have you actually discussed this with Ken?" Her remarks were beyond his wildest expectations. His uncertainty was acute. He had no idea what to make of her sudden outburst. Did she know? Was this her way of telling him? "Well, did you?" Eliot prodded.

"Yes. I have," she said hesitantly.

And had Ken discussed this with Maggie? Had they been that obvious? He was certain Carol was precipitating something, setting him up. He would stop it right there. It would go no further.

"Well, then. There it is. That's the problem. That's why they're so aloof now. You've stirred a pot of trouble, Carol. Frankly, I'm ashamed of you."

"Ashamed of me?"

Had he gone too far? He saw it quite plainly now. Meade had told her, had agreed to be a witness. They were conspiring against him. He had better retreat, he told himself, think things out. Hasty action now could be disastrous.

Eliot remade the cot and slipped back between the sheets.

"I don't think this is worthy of you, Carol," he muttered. "Your connotation is filthy-minded. The woman is my employee, a colleague, more like a sister to me."

He closed his eyes, his mind spinning, hoping that this outburst might quickly checkmate her accusations. But one thing was certain. He must not underestimate her.

It was growing more and more apparent that he would have to take some drastic action.

21

"**B**LOODY GOOP," Meade cursed as the wheels of the van slipped in the mud. He rocked it backward and forward until the tires gripped, found rock, and started their forward motion again.

It had rained all night, soaking the plain, swelling the rivers and streams that rolled down from the foothills.

"I thought this wasn't the rainy season," Ken said, addressing Eliot, who did not seem amused.

"Freak weather," he replied evenly. "It happens."

Meade was too busy fighting the van's wheel to respond. The inside of the van stank of stale alcohol. He hadn't shown up for breakfast, which was becoming increasingly common, and when he did appear his eyes were two maps of red tributaries and his nose was swollen and pitted with red lumps.

"We're going for lion today," he had announced, his words slurry. He had given Ken no more than a cursory glance. Could it be that Carol had been wrong in her observation that Meade had caught their lovemaking in the beam of his flashlight? Ken had accepted her observation as gospel. It could be that the light had merely washed over them, that Meade had detected nothing.

Ken was getting worried about Carol. Her imagination seemed to be overheating. All right, he told himself, suppose Meade had seen them. As an experienced safari guide, Meade must have witnessed all kinds of odd liaisons. It would be counterproductive to his business to gossip.

But Carol's paranoia had pushed her to contemplate a truly bizarre idea, that Meade was conspiring with Eliot, spying on them. Such a wild scenario had a terrible logic. There was certainly a lot of money at stake here. He understood clearly what it meant to Carol, and, therefore, to himself.

What worried him most was that that kind of suspicion could feed on itself. It implied that Eliot knew what was going on between them, that Maggie knew, that Meade knew. Was it making Carol lose confidence in their original plan? No, he cautioned himself. He mustn't let this happen, mustn't give it up. His future, their future, was at stake.

Ken noted that Meade was carrying something in a leather bag which he had put beside him on the floor. When it rolled, a clanking sound revealed that it was unmistakably a bottle. Yet no one challenged him, which seemed strange to Ken. Certainly Eliot should have admonished him. Eliot had arranged the safari. Eliot was in charge. But he seemed not to notice.

Ken and Carol had exchanged glances but not words, although the communication between them was quite clear. Considering what Meade had observed, neither Ken nor Carol was prepared to make waves. No way.

Despite the muddy terrain, the plain was studded with wildlife. Thompson's and Grant's gazelles pranced in the wake of zebras, giraffes, wildebeests, and impalas. They saw topi and duiker and herds of African buffalos adorned with their perpetual tick birds. Even the birds were out in force—buzzards, eagles, plovers, hawks, bustards, and hoards of quail.

If only he could eliminate this fear that had gripped Carol, Ken thought as he and Carol stood in the portal observing the spectacular display of wild creatures that studded the plains, thickets, and riverines. To avoid any suspicion that things had changed radically, Ken and Carol still shared the middle portal seats. Maggie, sitting as always in the rear of the van, seemed to have, inexplicably, lost interest in the sights, and Eliot actually looked dull and forlorn in his seat beside Meade. What was happening here?

The sun had risen, but it would be hours before the plain would dry out.

"We should be crossing that bloody river," Meade pointed. The Mara River was swollen and moving at high speed. "Maybe tomorrow."

Meade took a hard right and crossed high ground, which was drier, headed up a hill, then down again, watching the ground as he drove. Occasionally, he stopped suddenly and studied the animal tracks.

"A pride," he muttered, heading the van in the direction of the tracks.

The van jostled along. At times the sudden movement would throw their bodies together and Ken would feel Carol's warmth. Why the fear? he wondered. Why all this angst and anxiety? Why care who knew? Meade, Eliot, Maggie. What did it matter?

Out here, in the freedom and beauty of the African plain, pessimism evaporated. Financial cares were trivial. So-called civilization back somewhere in that other world seemed stultifying and corrupt. Here, possibilities were infinite.

There was something revitalizing in that idea, as if he were getting back to that place of his youth where anything was possible, where dreams had power and he was suffused with boundless hope. He looked toward Carol. Their eyes met and she smiled. Despite her present fears, hadn't her life, too, been renewed by their love?

Another jostling turn forced Carol's body against him.

No more of this, he decided. Their love was all, was everything. Under no circumstances, he vowed, would he lose this opportunity. He seemed to swell with the full force of his conviction. No, he would not throw away their chance for happiness.

Of course, he would have to rein in temptation, be less compulsive and more discreet. If things could be worked out as they had originally contemplated, well and good. But if not, they would have to find a new path. Carol must be mine one way or another, Ken assured himself, using the heroic cliché as if he were the star of some medieval romance.

To avoid the van's wheels slipping onto a muddy track, Meade zigzagged to cut across the driest spots. At the top of a rise, he stopped the van and, standing up in the portal, surveyed the plain with his binoculars.

"Got a pair," he snickered, sinking back down into the driver's seat and moving the van forward in the direction he had been studying.

"What does he mean?" Ken asked Carol.

"You'll see."

For the first time that day he saw her smile.

They pulled up beside a lion and a lioness stretched beside each other. They looked up indifferently as the van approached, then turned away, the male lion resting on his great paws while the female, legs up, warmed her belly in the sun.

"Zip it up," Meade whispered, inching the van as close to the pair as possible. Then he braked the van and withdrew his flask for another deep swallow.

The four of them stood up to observe the animals from the portals. They were beautiful, free, utterly unfazed by their human observers. The lioness, her coat gleaming, looked as if she had been groomed for the occasion.

Cameras clicked as they took their pictures.

"Save some for the show, folks," Meade said, taking another sip from his flask. Eliot said nothing. Ken noted that he cut Meade sidelong glances of disgust.

"What show?" Ken asked.

"Find out soon enough," Meade snapped, offering a cackling laugh.

Suddenly the lion stood up, shook his mane, and ambled over to the lioness, who, as if on cue, rolled over onto her belly. The lion moved behind her, reared over her with his two front paws, and, his penis erect, mounted her. His muscled haunches pumped, then suddenly he let out a loud roar, his jaws closing on the back of the lioness's neck.

"There's a fucker for you," Meade said, laughing, upending his flask.

"I wish you wouldn't," Eliot said. His attitude, Ken noted, seemed to be one of pleading.

Meade looked up at him malevolently.

"Surely, Butterfield, you know all about a good fuck," Meade said. When he looked up he caught Ken's eye and winked. Ken turned away embarrassed.

Eliot's docility puzzled Ken. In his drunken state, there was no telling what Meade might say. Carol, standing beside him, poked him in the thigh.

"He's being goddamned offensive," Ken whispered.

"Leave him alone, Ken."

It was Maggie's voice behind him, which further confused him. The man was terrorizing them and they were taking it.

At that point, the male lion moved away from the female and the lioness rolled over on her back again.

"They'll do this repeatedly," Eliot said. "Twenty times at least. It's the constant stimulation that gets her eggs to react and be fertilized. They rarely miss conception."

"That's why they call the bloody bugger king of the jungle," Meade cackled, gurgling the remains of his flask. "Fucks and fucks and fucks, he does." Reaching beside him, he found the bottle of whiskey and took a deep swallow from it.

"Come on, Meade. Easy there," Eliot said, but his rebuke lacked conviction.

"I think you're being a jerk," Ken said.

He felt all their eyes engulf him at once.

"Do you, now, Kramer, old sod?" Meade said. "I wouldn't be so quick to pass judgment if I were you." His air of menace was inescapable.

"He doesn't mean anything," Maggie said quickly.

"Good show, lady. Playing the loyal wife, are ya?"

Maggie seemed struck dumb by his remark.

"Are you all right?" Ken asked his wife.

"No fuss, please. I'm fine."

"You look pale as a ghost," Ken said.

"She said she's fine, Ken," Carol said.

Eliot observed them, but said nothing. Nobody spoke for a long time. They all watched the lions. In a few minutes, the male lion got up and mounted the lioness again.

"Small doodle for a big bugger like that," Meade said, watching the performance. The lion roared. "Feels good, eh, laddie," Meade croaked. "Earth move for ya, laddie?"

"Ignore him," Carol said, watching her husband, whose level of infuriation was visible and rising.

"Listen to the lady, Butterfield. Another good and faithful wife is heard from."

"Must you?" Ken blurted.

"Well. Well. Well. Pot calls the kettle," Meade cackled drunkenly.

"I think we should head back to camp," Eliot said. "We've got plenty of pictures."

"Bad luck, mate," Meade said. "You must never leave until after the third fuck."

"Jesus," Ken blurted. The man was insulting, crude, and contemptible.

"He's beyond the pale when he's drunk," Carol whispered, hoping Meade might not hear her. "Might say anything that comes into his head. Pay no attention."

"I'm not feeling well. I really think I'd like to get back to camp," Maggie said, addressing Meade.

"Show us a little decency, Meade," Eliot urged.

At that moment, the lion rose again, mounted the lioness, and roared. Then he moved away, stretched out, lay on his paws, and closed his eyes.

"Now can we go?" Eliot asked.

"Had enough, have you?" Meade said. "That's a surprise, considering."

Considering what, Ken wondered. That he and Carol were yielding to this disgusting form of blackmail, letting this man abuse them? What had he seen? He rolled that over in his mind. Plenty, I suppose. But why this cruelty? And why had Eliot reacted so tepidly?

Meade gunned the motor and the van shot forward as the four of them pitched backward, jolted by the fast start.

"Sorry, folks, for the fast getaway," Meade muttered, squinting through the windshield. "It's all right. I'm concentrating."

He nosed the van into the plain, moving cautiously with the exaggerated care of the drunkard who knows his condition. He did not take the same route over which they had come, easing the van down the rise and heading between two extended thickets, realizing too late that there was only the muddy track between them. Meade brought the van chugging and wheezing into the track. It was rough going. The ground churned beneath them. At one point, the wheels sank into the mud and no amount of rocking could dislodge them.

"Bloody slop," Meade grumbled as the van sank deeper.

"I'm afraid you'll have to winch it," Eliot said.

"My show," Meade cried. "I'll bloody well decide."

Ken looked at Eliot, whom he could see in profile through

the front portal. His face had flushed, but he provided no response to Meade's insolence.

"Surly bastard," Maggie whispered. She was standing in the portal behind Ken.

Pressing full force on the accelerator did little good. The wheels spun as if they were hanging in midair, forcing all four wheels down to the fender line.

"This is crazy," Ken said, catching Carol's glance. She shook her head quickly, a signal for him to desist.

"Fuck," Meade said. He took the bottle from beside the seat and took a long swig. The bumps on his nose reddened. "Everybody, the fuck out," he shouted.

The four of them jumped out in turn, trying to clear the muddy track. Ken's left foot sunk to mid ankle and he pulled it out with a plopping sound.

Meade unrolled the cable attached to the winch which was mounted on the front of the van.

"Need help?" Eliot asked.

"You'll be the first to know," Meade barked.

"Drunken asshole," Ken whispered to Carol, who put a finger up to her lips.

"He'll hear," she whispered.

"So what," he mumbled, resenting being held hostage by this abusive drunk.

Meade looked about for a solid tree that would accommodate the cable's length.

"There," he said, pointing to a tree in a nearby thicket. "That will have to do." He pulled at the cable, which unwound from the mounted winch, calling back to them as he entered the thicket. "And don't touch a fucking thing."

They watched as he entered the thicket, heading for the sturdy tree he had spotted.

"We can't let this go on," Ken said.

"He gets this way when he drinks," Eliot said for what seemed like the umpteenth time.

"The man is dangerous," Ken said.

"If we push him, he'll get worse," Carol said.

"Let's just ride it out," Maggie muttered.

At that moment, they heard a screeching roar and a human scream. Two lion cubs appeared at the edge of the thicket.

"It's the pride, dammit," Eliot shouted. "He's stumbled into the pride."

They rushed into the van and slammed the doors shut. The screeching of the big cats continued.

"The winch," Meade screamed above the din. "Help me."

"What do you suppose he means?" Eliot said suddenly, surprisingly calm.

It seemed pretty clear to Ken.

"For the love of God," Meade screamed, his voice desperate and pleading. "The winch."

"He wants us to activate the winch," Ken said, understanding the logic of the plea. The winch would pull the van out of the muddy track and bring it close to the tree to give Meade a chance to escape, if he wasn't yet torn to shreds by the lionesses who hovered just below him, snarling their anger at his intrusion.

"What good would that do?" Eliot asked.

Ken eased the portal cover up and stood, peering into the thicket. From that vantage he could see a partial view of Meade, who had apparently managed to ascend to one of the limbs of the tree. The lionesses were still kicking up a racket.

"The winch," Meade pleaded.

Eliot eased himself into the driver's seat and studied the dashboard.

"I've never done this," he said.

Ken observed Carol's face beside him. She seemed too petrified to speak. He turned to Maggie, who also appeared fear-stricken and immobilized.

"I need help," Meade screamed. "Can't you hear me?"

"We hear you," Ken yelled, cupping his hands and shouting above the roar of the lionesses. The lion cubs, he noted, had disappeared into the thicket.

"Winch. Use the winch."

His entreaty was pitiful, agonizing.

Ken ducked down and, grabbing at Eliot's shoulder, pushed him aside and leaned into the driver's area. He surveyed the instruments on the dashboard. One of them clearly said "Winch."

"No sweat," Ken said, cutting a glance of disapproval at Eliot.

"Their bellies are full," Eliot said. "They won't attack him for a while, if he makes no move toward the cubs. Could sober him up."

"The man is obviously in trouble," Ken said.

"Serves him right," Eliot muttered.

"The winch," Meade screamed out. "Start the winch, for crying out loud. Start the winch."

Ken pulled at the lever marked "Winch" and the van shuddered and wheezed as the cable stretched taut. The van rose with effort from its muddy trap as the cable started to wind around its mounting.

Slowly the van angled out of the track and was pulled toward the thicket. As it drew closer, Ken could see Meade standing on a limb of the tree, one arm wrapped around the trunk, the other holding a long branch, obviously a weapon to ward off the lionesses. Below him three lionesses scowled and roared. Beside them was the carcass of a wildebeest and a number of cubs chomping on it.

Meade was sweating profusely, but the redness in his complexion had evaporated. He was pale and drawn. His shirt was ripped and there were scratches on his arm. Beyond that he seemed intact.

The winch brought the van closer to the tree, then its front wheels jammed against a big rock and refused to go farther. Ken stopped the winch, then started it up again. It huffed and creaked, but the rock held the wheels fast, a good ten feet from the tree. This meant that Meade would have to drop down from the tree and run a hazardous gauntlet of unhappy lionesses to get to the safety of the van.

"Now what?" Ken said.

Three mature lionesses stood at the base of the tree watching Meade, who observed the van's predicament with discouragement.

"The cable has to be removed from the tree to free the van," Eliot said. "Then we've got to back up and pull up around the other side just under Meade."

"That's obvious," Ken agreed.

"Are you prepared to get out and try it?" Eliot asked. He turned toward the two women behind him. "Anyone game for that fool's errand?" His tone was strangely sardonic.

As Ken contemplated the dilemma, Meade reached down with the branch he had been using to ward off the lionesses and tried to undo the clamp that held the cable to the tree. It was obvious that this method was of little avail.

Finally Meade shouted down to them.

"Under the bench of the rear seat. There's an ax."

"A what?" Ken called back.

Meade repeated what he had said and Ken called to the women, who had been sitting on the bench, to climb to the rear. They obeyed instantly.

Ken lifted the bench, saw the ax, and quickly removed it, holding it so that Meade could get a better view of it. He saw it and nodded.

"Now chop the cable," he shouted.

"Is he crazy?" Eliot said. "Nobody in their right mind is going out there."

"I wouldn't, Ken," Maggie said. He turned and looked at Carol, who shook her head.

"Then what are we supposed to do?" Ken asked.

"Not that," Eliot said.

"What, then?"

"Wait, I suppose," Eliot murmured.

"I'd listen to Eliot, Ken," Maggie said. "It's too much of a risk."

"You've got to help me, people, please," Meade shouted. "This bloody limb can't hold me forever."

"One false move and they'll tear you to pieces, Kramer," Eliot said. Did Ken detect satisfaction in Eliot's tone?

"What is it with you, Eliot?" Ken shouted. At the same time, he considered the danger. Eliot could be right. He stood up and opened the portal above him. The three lionesses looked at him with what he was certain was sinister intent.

Slowly, Ken extended himself through the portal, drawing out the ax by the handle.

"Just give it a quick chop," Meade said frantically.

"What about them?" Ken asked, looking at the three lionesses.

"Move slowly. Nothing sudden."

"I'm not sure," Ken said. He would have to climb onto the hood of the vehicle, brace himself, then swing, an act that seemed certain to disturb the animals. As if to confirm this assessment, they growled angrily.

"Ken, stop this," Maggie shouted. "Throw him the ax. Let him swing it from where he is."

Meade's eyes blazed with contempt.

"No way to brace myself," he said.

"I really wouldn't, Ken," Eliot said, almost casually.

"Listen to Eliot, Ken," Maggie said.

"Please," Meade pleaded, his arm hugging the trunk. Ken could see the fissure at the joint where the limb met the trunk. "One step further out and this bloody limb will break."

"Jesus," Ken said, looking back into the van. "He's right. He can't."

"I'd suggest we just wait them out," Eliot said. "They'll take off by nightfall as soon as they get hungry."

"Bloody hell, they will. I'm for supper," Meade shouted. "And this branch won't hold me that long."

"Looks okay to me," Eliot mumbled.

Ken contemplated the distance. If he removed the ax fully from the van and leveraged himself carefully, he might start his swing as he stepped out onto the hood.

"Ken . . ." Maggie cried, then stopped as he lifted himself out of the portal and sat on its rim, watching the lionesses.

"They get it into their heads that you're up to something, they'll be at you as fast as you can blink," Eliot said. His clinical calm was baffling.

"This man is in mortal danger," Ken said.

"It's your life, Ken."

"Listen to him," Maggie shouted. "Stop this."

At that moment Meade stirred and Ken heard the branch creak.

"A couple of hard bloody chops at it. That's all it needs," Meade said. His shirt was soaked with perspiration. Ken hesitated, took a deep breath, then lifted one foot over the windshield onto the hood. The three animals watched him, feral eyes alert.

"It's all right," Meade said. "Take it slow. No sudden moves."

Ken started moving along the hood on his knees, dragging the ax. His heart pounded in his chest and perspiration ran out of him like water.

"Damned fool," he heard Eliot mumble behind him.

He felt himself committed, moving deliberately now, trying to gauge his point of maximum leverage. He hefted the ax and started to rise.

"Christ, not you too, Carol," Eliot hissed. Ken turned to see Carol rising in the portal. She reached out.

"Stay back," Ken warned. But she kept moving, her hand gripping his belt. Then suddenly he understood the logic of her act. She was bracing him, her legs anchored to the portal.

Ken straightened now, not looking at the three lionesses no more than a few feet from him. Gripping the ax handle firmly, he swung and came down hard on the cable. The lionesses stood up on all fours and glared at him. But the cable hadn't been cut through. He swung again and again, feeling Carol's bracing pressure, knowing he could not have been able to do this without her help.

"One more, mate. Just one more," Meade cried.

Ken felt all his strength going into the final blow, which very nearly toppled him. But it was enough to break the last strands of the cable. He let go of the ax and quickly clambered back into the van, falling back onto Carol and slapping shut the portal cover. Just in time. One of the lionesses had jumped onto the hood and stood there glaring at the occupants inside the van.

Eliot, who had moved back into the driver's seat, backed up the van, then skirted the rock and headed to a spot directly under the branch of the tree on which Meade stood.

Carol climbed over into the backseat beside Maggie to make room for Meade if he was able to get back into the van. He would come through the center portal.

Interpreting the movement of the van as an attack attempt, all three lionesses moved in on it, mounting the hood and snarling through the windshield.

With the heel of his hand, Ken banged the horn and the three predators, momentarily stunned by the sound, jumped off the hood. Then Ken opened the portal. Meade's hand was outstretched and he had lowered his body from its precarious perch on the tree's limb. Ken reached out and grabbed Meade's waiting hand.

"Jump," Ken ordered. Meade who had put the branch he had used as a weapon in the crook of the tree, reached for it with his free hand, threw it at the three lionesses, and jumped down into the open portal. Ken quickly pulled him fully into the van and closed the hatch while Eliot backed the van out of the thicket.

Meade stank of sweat and booze as he lay lengthwise along the middle bench, breathing heavily. He closed his eyes. "I sure as hell could use a quaff," he said.

Eliot reached beside him with his left hand and held up the bottle, which was about half full.

"Bloody good," Meade said, reaching for it.

Suddenly, Eliot pulled hard on the wheel with his right hand, causing the van to swerve and the bottle to slip from Meade's hand to the floor of the van, where it broke.

"Sorry, Meade," Eliot said. "Not used to driving this baby."

Meade opened bloodshot eyes, looked at him, and smiled malevolently.

"Well, we did see the lions," Ken said, hoping this try at humor might take the heaviness out of the situation. It didn't.

22

MAGGIE STOOD in the shower stall toweling her skin dry. She was certain that one bucket of water hadn't done the job and was tempted to call out for another. She didn't. Nor was she satisfied that the toweling was truly drying her. Clamminess clung to her skin. Like a shroud, she thought, the idea of death surfacing in her mind. Whose death? Hadn't she shown true wifely concern about the danger to Ken in climbing out on the hood of the van? What more could she have done to dissuade him? Her response troubled her deeply. Had it been truly sincere? She began to shiver and goose bumps erupted like a moonscape on her skin.

And yet no willful act on her part could deny the illicit thrill of elation that shot through her when Ken climbed up on that hood and exposed himself to that terrible danger. But when she saw Carol lift herself out of the portal, her heart seemed to jump into her throat. There it was. The answer.

Only then did she realize that this was actually the second time that she had conspired to abet the unthinkable, that her previous collusion with Eliot in leaving them in the bush was also inspired by this desire to create a final solution to their problem, an ending.

How awful. How sinister. How arrogantly selfish. She tried to disregard the reflection, but it persisted. She remembered that there had been a moment during the crisis in the van when her eyes had met Eliot's and she saw in them the mirror of her own ugly unthinkable wish.

Neither she nor Eliot, aside from lip service, had made any move to assist in helping to rescue Meade. Each knew, she was certain, that their inaction was willful and deliberate, that the single issue that dominated their thoughts was their freedom, their future together.

Still, she could not wipe away the idea. She was not, after all, a hateful person. She could not hate Ken. This offered her a glimmer of rationalization. After all, how could she hate the father of her children? When she compared him with Eliot, of course, he became a pallid, ineffective figure, but hardly an object of such dark thoughts. He had been a good husband and father.

But when it came to Carol she was less forgiving. It was Carol, after all, who stood in her way. It was she who was at the heart of Maggie's secret wish. By her desperate act to assist Ken, she had deliberately exposed herself to danger, had deliberately created the possibility in Maggie's mind of this final solution to the dilemma. It was only natural for such dark thoughts to surface in her mind. Wasn't it? Maggie tried desperately to press this convoluted logic on herself.

Even now, as she made a massive internal effort to rub away the awfulness of her and Eliot's inaction, she could understand the power of the wish and how it could give rise to such thoughts. Hadn't she tried other rationalizations while she sat there in the van? After all, humans had invaded the lions' turf, their pride. The creatures had an absolute right to eliminate the intruders. They were trespassing. But Maggie knew that her rooting was highly selective. What she wished for was the elimination of Carol, Ken, and Meade. They were the true intruders, the enemy.

Yet, for a brief moment, Carol's action had also struck a hopeful, less lethal, note. It had, indeed, crossed her mind that perhaps Carol had acted out of love for Ken. Hadn't Maggie been equally as spontaneous when she tried to rescue Eliot from the mad elephant? Except that she had publicly and indiscreetly expressed her love for Eliot, thereby putting herself and her lover at Meade's mercy. Carol, on the other hand, had not been vocal at all. Which led Maggie to the conclusion that Carol had probably acted out of simple humanity, as Ken had, to save a human life.

Sadly, it was becoming increasingly obvious that nothing was working out as she and Eliot had planned. The original idea, the wish itself, certainly the process of persuasion, had become frustrated by events. She was running out of hope. All doors seemed to be closing at once on their dream of a life together.

So here she was, like Lady Macbeth, trying to rub away the sludge of ugly memory, acting out the only defense she could think of, knowing that it was transparently futile. What she needed was a more direct act of expiation, a confrontation with the truth.

But all this dread and self-disgust did open a tiny window of vindication in her mind. She was simply exhausted by all the lies, internal and external, the role playing, the dissimulation, the fear of discovery, the tension of danger. Enough, she told herself. Enough.

Finally, her skin rubbed to irritation, Maggie was assailed by this compelling need to be cleansed from the inside, wrung dry of cant and hypocrisy. Surely, there was goodness, honesty, sincerity, and honor left inside her. Wasn't there? She could no longer bear the claustrophobic smallness of the tented shower stall and she slid between the flaps back into the tent.

Ken was lying on his cot, hands behind his head, staring up at the tent ceiling. Through a sliver of mesh she could see the men preparing the evening meal. She started to dress, searching her mind for a beginning, a way to start the journey to catharsis and atonement.

"That was very brave of you, Ken," she said. Throughout the trip back to camp, they had remained silent, each one, Maggie supposed, evaluating the experience according to his or her own interpretation. She hadn't had a chance to discuss it with Eliot, although they had continued to exchange conspiratorial glances.

"Not really," he reflected. "Impulsive or foolhardy might describe it better."

"No," Maggie insisted. "Brave is absolutely correct." She sucked in a deep breath. "I should have been the one to assist you."

She watched his face. His eyes blinked, but he did not turn to face her.

"I guess Carol just got there first."

"It wasn't cowardice," Maggie said cautiously. Expiation demanded truth, she knew. Truth within reason, she told herself. Was there such a thing? "I . . ." She hesitated, summoning courage. She had lived with this man for nearly two decades. Whatever happened, their life together was over and she was obligated to tell him that, at least that. "I've been analyzing why I didn't."

"It doesn't matter," Ken mumbled. It was then that he turned to face her. "Forget it. It's no big deal."

"No," she said. "It's important to me."

"Well, not to me. In situations like that, some people, I suppose, react faster than others."

He sat up abruptly, obviously trying to divert her remarks.

"Maybe," she began, feeling her heartbeat flutter. "But I've come to a different conclusion."

"Leave it alone, Maggie," Ken said, obviously uncomfortable.

"I don't think I cared enough." There, she thought. It's said.

She waited for herself to feel better for it. Not that it was a full-scale confession. But partially clean was better than completely dirty.

Ken's eyes narrowed, as if he were having trouble focusing on her. Was he thinking, For Meade? No. She was certain that the arrow had found its mark.

"Now, there's an act of courage," Ken said. She had expected his reaction to be more crestfallen and it confused her.

"Surely, I owe you that much," she whispered. A lump had formed in her throat.

"Are you telling me that you wanted me"—he paused— "done in?" He chuckled. "Lionized?"

"Of course not," she replied, not responding to his misplaced wisecrack, hoping that he might not have noted the hesitation in her voice.

"What is it, then?" Ken asked. He seemed to be looking at her suspiciously.

"What I'm trying to convey," she said, struggling to find the right words, "is that I'm seeing a different perspective on our lives out here. You and I." It was awful, trying to find the right balance. "No." She shook her head. "I didn't want you done in. I just didn't seem to care enough to want to prevent it."

"Jesus." He stood up. "It must have been really important to get that out." He turned away and looked toward the mess tent. "All right. With that said, can we now go and get some dinner?"

"It doesn't bother you?"

"I'm not sure I know what you're saying."

Was he being deliberately obtuse? she wondered. Had he really received her message?

"It means . . ." Maggie began. She was discovering that telling the partial truth was even harder than telling the whole lie. Nevertheless, she forced herself to press forward. It must be said, she decided. "It means that I want us to separate."

Ken cocked his head and studied her. Closely observed like this, she felt uncomfortable, naked. She wanted to scream out the full truth. I love another man. She wanted to shout it out at the top of her lungs.

"That's a bit of a bolt from the blue."

"It was necessary for me to tell you that, Ken." She sucked in a deep breath. "I'm sorry."

"And this has just come upon you today?"

"No. I've been thinking about it for some time."

He looked at her for a long moment, then shook his head and shrugged.

"Somehow it doesn't seem like the appropriate moment to discuss this."

He seemed remarkably calm and cerebral. In a perverse way, she would have been more comfortable with emotion, perhaps tears, although she had never seen him cry.

"I know. But it's been nagging at me and I needed to say it. Maybe what happened today was a catalyst." She spoke slowly, nodding with emphasis. Yes, she was beginning to feel better. That burden had been lifted.

"You don't think we should put this on hold, until we get back home?"

She felt another burst of guilt.

"There's never a good time for this. Maybe our getting used to the idea might make it better later, when the children are confronted, although they're certainly old enough to accept it. And I know you'll be fair."

"You seem to have thought things out rather carefully," Ken said, looking at her archly.

She detected an element of sarcasm in his remark. Did he suspect Eliot? Had she gone too far? It suddenly troubled her also that he did not ask for more specific reasons. It was important now to bring this matter to a close. She had gone as far as she could go.

"I'm glad that you're taking this so well," she said.

He reached over to his where his bush jacket hung and began to put it on.

"I assume that we're to keep this little matter top secret until we get home," he said, pulling up the zipper of the jacket.

She pondered the idea for a moment. She would tell Eliot, of course. He would be delighted. Wouldn't he? At least one of them would be free. That was something anyway. She had shown him her true love, her total commitment to him, body and soul. Then another thought superimposed itself, making her hesitate. She had done this on her own, without consulting him. Perhaps he would be furious, reasoning that she might have triggered Ken's suspicions about their affair. Had she? Oh, God, she thought, have I botched things up?

"No need for the others to get worked up about it," Ken continued.

"That seems like the best course," Maggie agreed, her mind groping for a way to allay any suspicions she might have raised in Ken's mind. "Yes. I think you're right. Carol and Eliot would be very upset with us if we told them. They might think that they were somehow to blame."

"Maybe so," Ken said after some thought. "Anyway, there's no need to spoil the trip for them."

His remark relieved her considerably.

"The four of us could still be friends, of course," Maggie said, conjuring up the possibility. She had not yet reckoned with that complicated matter. It was enough that she had taken the first step to attain her own freedom.

"I guess we'll just have to accept things as they come," Ken said, as if he were directing the thought generally, to both of them.

"That's what I thought."

"May I ask a question?" Ken asked. He had taken the flashlight from a hook next to his cot.

"Of course."

Unburdened, she felt magnanimous. She had mustered courage, spoken truth, secured her freedom.

"Is there someone else?"

She felt his eyes boring in on her. Despite its not having occurred to her that he would ask, it was a perfectly logical question, actually a clichéd question in these circumstances. She swallowed and felt a quivering in her chest. There was, indeed, an answer waiting to be voiced. Could she dare it?

But the nagging practicality of her midwestern background held her back. Perhaps she had acted too hastily. Ken's remarks had made one thing seem obvious, that the hoped-for relationship between Ken and Carol was as remote as ever.

She speculated suddenly on what effect her admission of infidelity would have on Ken. Surely, despite his essential fairness, he might use it as a case for custody of the children or some other legal or emotional form of vengeance.

Indeed, a new Pandora's box blew open. She supposed there would be another inside that, and another. And so on.

Without a negation of that damned prenuptial agreement, she might have to face the possibility of a future as Eliot's clandestine mistress, a distasteful prospect, especially for a single woman with two teenage children. She shivered at the thought, telescoping in her mind long lonely stretches without the comforting presence of her lover.

Still another possibility opened in her mind. More boxes within boxes. Eliot, fearing the consequences of economic deprivation, might opt for scuttling his new emotional epiphany in favor of the more tranquil intellectual life, continue his bloodless marriage with Carol, and dedicate himself wholly to his causes.

That would mean an end to their relationship. She would be devastated, of course. But her only choice would be to start over again, somehow keep going.

Still she hesitated providing an answer to Ken's question, continuing to turn over potential consequences in her mind. She could, as they say, go the full nine yards. Admit the truth. Tell him of her affair with Eliot. In a way there was a commonality of interest between Ken and her. Ken would assume that since she was involved with an allegedly wealthy man he might be relieved of some of his future financial obligations.

Eventually that would require still another explanation.

Would she reveal the truth about Eliot's precarious financial condition, his agreement with Carol? Questions would continue to pile upon questions. Boxes in boxes.

Yet, despite all these considerations, the one that dominated all others was that if she were to name Eliot, she would be betraying her lover's confidence, her absolute commitment to him.

"I have a right to know the answer to that, Maggie," Ken pressed. "Under the circumstances, it seems like a very appropriate question."

Had she hesitated too long to make a credible denial? She wondered suddenly about what lies he might have told her during their long years together. The innocent, self-protective lies that underlay any marriage. Someday, perhaps, they would exchange honest confidences, reveal to each other their ugly little secrets and private deceptions. The thought triggered a revelation.

She drew in a deep breath. She had already learned to live with partial lies. Why not one more?

"The answer to your question is no," she said, jutting out her chin pugnaciously, as if she were daring him to probe deeper. He studied her, then nodded.

"I never thought otherwise," he said, but he had turned away too quickly to confirm the statement with his eyes.

He unzipped the front flap of the tent and started to move into the darkness. Suddenly he turned and looked at her.

"Hemingway also discovered his truth in Africa," he said.

He did not rezip the flap, leaving her to watch him follow the beam of his flashlight toward the mess tent.

Had she really discovered hers? she wondered. She wasn't quite certain.

23

Eliot sat by the fire, watching the flames lick at the wood. He looked toward the tents, waiting for Maggie to emerge.

"Later," she had whispered to him after dinner, which had been tense and strained for her, but mercifully short. Thankfully, Meade had not come out of his tent.

Of course he and Maggie had to talk. This African adventure was taking on strange aspects.

All his life, Eliot had put his faith in his inner voice of reason. Always he had eschewed emotion as being untrustworthy, the foe of reason.

The discovery of passion, of love, of the revitalizing effects of this experience had, of course, enriched his life, had taught him that emotion could actually dominate logic. Maggie, if reason was all that dictated, would not have made a natural match for him, certainly not socially or aesthetically. His innate snobbery would have prevented that.

But emotion, the mystery of love, had mesmerized him, made him a literal slave to its conventions. It had awakened him from a long, deep sleep. His body reveled in the pleasure and joy of it. He was captivated, seduced beyond logic, and he had surrendered himself to its power and its commitment.

It certainly had reordered his priorities, although he had not calculated that it might require profound changes in his style of life, changes he was not certain he was prepared to make.

He supposed that if he mustered every bit of his concentration, he might be able to, if not eliminate it, tame it. But wouldn't that be thwarting nature? Like caging those species that roamed these African plains in perfect harmony.

Instead, his only course was to draw upon the superhuman strength of his inner self, to reharness the power of reason, to create his personal wildlife preserve. That was his new metaphor. Reason would set the boundaries of his future life with Maggie, assure its inevitability and its comfortable environment. Their love demanded it.

First, he would have to eliminate the dangers. Meade, goaded by drunkenness and the knowledge that he and Maggie were being unfaithful to their spouses, no longer felt subject to his authority. Eliot supposed it was a natural resentment of any free spirit forced to make compromises that betrayed that freedom. White hunters like Meade who were reduced to the level of mere tour guides were an embittered breed to begin with. He was certain that Meade had always resented him, as he resented all rich dilettantes who arrived in Africa to see the wildlife.

Perhaps, too, Meade the true hunter disliked Eliot the true thinker, a perfectly natural hostility between opposites. Mixed with alcohol, such resentment could be lethal. And secret knowledge, such as that which Meade believed he possessed, could easily be personalized.

As it was, the danger Meade presented to him notwithstanding, this African experience had turned out so far to be a mistake. Any hope that Carol and Ken might be nudged into infidelity seemed as unlikely as ever, although, for a moment, Eliot had been encouraged by Carol's protective act toward Ken in the pride. But then, on the way home and thereafter through dinner, they had reverted to their usual behavior of indifference and disinterest in each other.

Good sense dictated that he abort the safari immediately. But another idea was emerging in his mind, a very powerful and conclusive idea.

Reason, after all, demanded honesty. He had deliberately sat on his hands during Meade's struggle in the pride. It was a tricky moment, demanding discipline. Ken's macho grandstanding had complicated matters considerably, but it was Carol's act that had offered the greatest embellishment of the idea, had set off an explosion of "what ifs" in his mind.

The incident had been especially useful in testing the parameters of his own remorse. He had exchanged glances with Maggie. Had he seen wishfulness in her eyes? Or abject fear? He wasn't certain. She had, however, taken no action to save her husband's life. Was that paralysis? Or, like his, a deliberate act? He suspected the latter.

He was now quite certain of his own reaction. If an accident or a natural disaster somehow intervened to take Carol's life, he would be able to handle it. Reason would absolve him of any complicity. There would be emotional consequences, of course, perhaps some residual guilt. But that would fade with time. In fact, he had already gone through the process as Carol held fast to Ken's legs.

"In retrospect," Carol told Ken at dinner, "what I did was blind dumb stupidity."

"I'll agree with that," Ken replied. "Second only to mine." He offered a mock salute. "But I thank you just the same."

"The situation made the choice I suppose," Carol went on. "Eliot had the wheel and Maggie was in the wrong position to act quickly."

"I should have done something," Maggie said.

"All because of that idiot drunk," Eliot interjected, pumping up into a flash of anger. He had been concerned that his lack of action had been noted. Now he felt relieved.

"I'm surprised you let him get away with it," Carol said. She looked toward Ken. "I would have expected one of you to chew him out."

"It would only have inflamed him further," Eliot said, turning to Ken. "Don't you agree?"

"You have a point," Ken said.

"He very nearly caused a massacre," Carol said. "I felt sure those cats would attack."

"Blind luck," Eliot said.

"No less than a miracle," Maggie pointed out.

"It would be unthinkable for us to go back out with him again," Carol said. "The man's a menace."

"I plan to talk to him first thing in the morning. He's in no condition to communicate. The boys had to carry him to his tent."

"We should quit now," Carol said. "He's gone off the deep end."

"I'm afraid I agree with her," Ken said.

"I don't disagree," Eliot said, thinking of this other agenda that had suddenly intruded. "But he's a good man when sober. Safari guides like Meade, what with the poaching and corrupt wildlife management in this country, are very worried about their livelihood. I suspect he's just overwrought."

"And out of control," Ken said. "Our lives are his first responsibility. It's not the other way around. So we'll lose a few days."

"Better lose days than our lives," Carol said.

Eliot looked at her, his eyes narrowing, but said nothing. He did not want it settled. Not just yet.

They had run out of conversation after that and soon Maggie, Carol, and Ken went off to their tents.

Eliot was not tired. In fact, as he sat alone now before the dying campfire, he was exhilarated. This new idea was taking hold and his mind was groping for the correct strategy, the foolproof strategy that would, once and for all, resolve the dilemma.

He debated telling Maggie what was churning in his head, remembering how she had reacted during the incident with the lions. Like him, she had held back. Nor had he seen any sign of either terror or remorse in her eyes. If the actual deed of what he was now contemplating offended her, could she, nevertheless, cope with the idea of it?

He smiled when he heard the lion's roar, the only sound to rise above that of the crackling fire.

"I did it, Eliot," Maggie said. She had come up silently, a robe thrown over her nightgown. She sat down in a chair beside him. Her voice had startled him. Then its content had communicated itself and his stomach knotted.

"Did what?"

"I hope you won't be angry," she said, a tremor in her voice.

He had turned toward her, noting her nervousness. Her eyes glowed like agates from the fire's reflection.

"After today, I felt I had to," she said, stopping suddenly as if she were out of breath. He feared for the worst.

"You told him about us?" he asked with a sense of rising panic.

"God, no, Eliot," she said, letting out a burst of air. "It's just that I had to stop living part of the lie. Eliot, dear dear Eliot. Today I felt myself rejoicing at the idea of Ken's and Carol's deaths. It wasn't the first time and it shook me up. It was, after all, close to happening and there I was wishing it."

He knew, of course, what she meant.

"You mustn't flagellate yourself over it," he said cautiously. "It wouldn't have been your fault."

"But I was wishing it, you see."

"Under the circumstances, it would seem like a natural reaction."

"You thought it, too?"

He nodded, knowing there was more to be said. But her reaction seemed to indicate a validation of her own suspicion.

"I wish I felt more remorse about it," she said. "But I don't."

"People murder people in their thoughts all the time," he said. "As for remorse." He shrugged. "We can't be remorseful just for thinking things."

"But suppose something had happened, something had gone wrong?"

"It was out of our hands," Eliot said.

"Except that if we wanted to we could have done something. Like Carol."

"Pure reflex," he told her. "She had access. She was available and she was athletic. Nothing more. It would be dangerous to read more than that into her action."

"I understand that part. It's just that I needed to cleanse myself, to tell him at least part of the truth."

"What did you tell him?" Eliot asked harshly.

"I . . ." She started to speak, then stopped. He looked toward the tents where the others slept. "I told him I wanted my freedom."

He felt her studying him, waiting for his response. Was there harm in it? he wondered.

Maggie looked around her. Her voice became a whisper. "My darling. There was no point to it being otherwise. I detest these lies and subterfuges. Besides, it's you I love. It can't continue like this."

"And what was his reaction?" Eliot asked.

"Acceptance. He didn't protest. He didn't argue. I think he must have sensed my feelings." She paused to reflect for a moment, then continued. "He asked me if there was another man." She paused. "I told him no. Also, we both agreed to keep it from you and Carol. I couldn't, of course. I couldn't bear keeping secrets from you, Eliot."

"We're going to resolve this," Eliot said. "One way or another."

"But how?"

It was clear to him now that he could never tell her of his plan. She was too caring, too sensitive, too prone to guilt and fear. He understood that in her. It was, he supposed, part of why he loved her.

"You've talked to her?" Maggie asked expectantly.

"I intend to," he said.

"It's the best way, my darling," Maggie said, showing her elation. "I feel so relieved." She grew silent and stared into the fire. "I'm so glad you made that decision." She paused, reflected for a time, then asked, "Will you talk to her before we leave? Or when we get home?"

"As soon as possible."

"Good. We should resolve it before we get home."

"Exactly my sentiments, Maggie."

"What do you think she'll do?" she asked abruptly, adding quickly, "You might be quite surprised at her generosity."

"I'm not sure," he whispered. Not that he would dare risk such a conversation with Carol. He realized suddenly that his plan already had been put into play.

"Either way, Eliot. It won't matter. You'll see. The important thing is that we'll be together, together always. Between us we'll be able to earn enough to have the kind of life you want. My business . . . I'll work. Oh, God, Eliot, I promise you . . ." A sob escaped her. He turned toward her, saw tears roll onto her cheeks. She sniffled and smiled at him. "It's happiness," she whispered.

The fire had died down completely, shedding little light. But at that distance they were able to exchange glances for a long moment, then she kneeled before him and rested her head on his lap. Except for the normal sounds of the African night, nothing stirred. Perhaps because of what he had told her, she no longer saw a risk in it. He did not protest.

Just how long they stayed like that he could not guess, but the night's stillness was a rhapsody of their mutual contentment. She looked up at him and smiled, then mimed: "I love you."

He was prevented by responding in kind by a sudden whiff of a wretched effluvia. It filled the warm night air and, looking past her, he saw the beast, a spotted hyena, breathing in short gasps, each exhale a stream of the foulest stink.

Following his glance, Maggie turned slowly but did not rise. They remained motionless, rooted to where they were, she kneeling on the ground, he sitting in his chair.

He could see the hyena's face, the heavy jaw, the alert greedy dark saucers of eyes, and the misshapen nonsymmetrical body. Ugly bastard, he told himself, staring it down, his eyes boring into the hyena's. For a long moment, there was a standoff between them.

Then, as quickly and silently as he came, the animal melted away. Eliot stood up and lifted Maggie, who was shivering.

"It's all right now," he whispered.

She waited until she stopped shivering to speak.

"What do you suppose it means?" she asked, speaking directly into his ear.

The question surprised him.

"Nothing," he said, and for a brief moment he felt the tension of uncertainty.

24

$\mathbf{F}$ULLY DRESSED, Eliot dozed fitfully. Most of the night he had spent arranging and rearranging the matrix in his mind. No other outside stimuli intruded, until he sensed the stirring for which he had waited. Sitting up abruptly, he peered through the exposed corner of the mesh window and saw the faint glow in Meade's tent. He looked at his watch. It was nearly four. In an hour dawn would begin to lift the darkness.

Carefully, with long pauses, he unzipped the entry flap of the tent and slipped out into the soft African night.

Meade, his hair ruffled, his face bearded and mottled, sat on the edge of his cot rubbing the shiny barrel of a big Armsport rifle with oiled cheesecloth. He acknowledged Eliot with a lugubrious nod. On the floor beside him was an almost empty whiskey bottle.

"You could turn me in for this, too," Meade croaked hoarsely as he lifted the rifle.

Carrying arms on photo safaris was against the licensing regulations for safari operators. For Meade it would be evidence of one of any number of gross infractions if Eliot was inclined to press charges against him with the governing authorities.

"I could, you know," Eliot said. "And you'd be finished."

Meade observed him with bloodshot eyes.

"I was a goddamned fool," he acknowledged. He looked at the bottle but made no move to reach for it. "Fucking booze."

"The others want out," Eliot said. Only then did he sit down beside Meade on the cot.

"Who could bloody blame them?" Meade said, putting the rifle aside. He jabbed one of his hands into the air, palm down. It shook uncontrollably. "Hands of the great white hunter," he mocked. "I'll tell the boys to pack it up first thing. Just give me a bit of time to pull it together, Butterfield, and we'll head back to Nairobi, say late morning."

He was the picture of contrition and shame, a man who had shattered his own pride by weakness. Having known and worked with Meade in happier days, Eliot had hoped for such a reaction.

"I think another day would do just fine," Eliot said. He did not look at Meade's face as he spoke. "That is, if you can handle it."

"What about the others?"

"If I vouch for you, they'll go along."

"I don't know," Meade said.

"Yes, you do," Eliot pressed. "The fact is that I can cause you lots of grief, maybe shut you down for good."

"I won't deny it," Meade sighed. "Especially the part about the grief. Not many alternatives for a one-use bloke like me."

"You're too good a man to waste," Eliot said, offering a tight smile. "Give us one good day more." Yes, one good day more, he thought. That should do it. "And we'll call it, as we Yanks say, square."

"And I'm home free?"

Eliot nodded. "But no booze," he said. "Absolutely no booze."

At that point Eliot turned to study him. Meade was having trouble with that one.

"I won't bullshit you, Butterfield. I'd need one or two for the road. I'll promise nothing on board. My word always holds. You know that."

"If you say so," Eliot said. A drunk's word, he knew, was always dubious.

The man's eyes met his glance for a moment before turning away.

"You're worried about the other, too?" Meade asked. It was a soft question, without malice.

"What other?"

Both of them knew that that, too, needed to be addressed.

"People come to Africa to discover something," Meade said. "They tear off the outer skin of so-called civilization. Seen it a thousand times."

"You're going to give me philosophy now, Meade?" Eliot asked wryly.

"Just truth. I know you're a searching man."

"If you say so," Eliot responded, his relief palpable. The quid pro quo had been agreed to.

"You were afraid the booze would talk, weren't you?"

"You're pressing it now, Meade," Eliot cautioned. He had expected the contrition to be deeper. "I can ruin you, you know."

"This isn't business," he said, shaking his head. "I won't fuck up on that. It's been bugging me, though."

"What has?" Eliot was genuinely curious now.

"You just sat there. I saw you making no move. You wanted me out of it, didn't you? Because of what I knew."

"That's paranoia talking. Ken Kramer was in a better spot," Eliot said calmly. "Somebody had to stay at the wheel."

"I'm grateful to them both," Meade said, his bloodshot eyes studying Eliot's face. He seemed to have an urge to say something more. Then he shook his head as if he had rejected the idea and cleared his throat. "Mrs. Butterfield showed a lot of guts."

"Yes, she did," Eliot said. "They got you out of a tight spot. That's all that matters."

"One good turn deserves another," Meade muttered. It seemed too esoteric to challenge and Eliot offered no response.

Meade shrugged, picked up the rifle, and resumed polishing it. "I'll be damned if I go out without one of these again."

"They catch you, it's suspension," Eliot warned. "And it wouldn't be my fault."

"If I ever use it, it'll be a choice between my career and my life." He blew out a mouthful of nauseating whiskey stink. "Probably neither worth much these days. Anyway, it's a stupid regulation. How the bloody hell do they expect us to protect our clients?"

Eliot slapped his thighs and stood up. He had no desire to hear Meade rant about the world's injustices.

"It's settled, then." Eliot put out his hand. Meade took it. The man's hand was hot. He imagined he could feel his gratitude.

"We'll make it a great day," Meade said, raising his hand. "There's my pledge. Except for just a swallow to steady the hands."

"That's a given, Meade," Eliot said, smiling. He started to move out of the tent, then paused at the entrance. "And let's try to avoid the cats."

"We've seen enough of those bloody bastards."

"I was thinking, maybe crocs and hippos."

Meade nodded. "Crocs and hippos, it is."

25

CAROL AWOKE, surprised to see Eliot's cot empty. Through the mesh window she noted that the eastern sky had not yet begun to lighten. A faint orange glow and murmuring voices emanated from Meade's tent.

Eliot, as promised, was having his little talk with Meade. Why now, at this hour? Why clandestine? She debated with herself about sneaking behind Meade's tent to listen in. It troubled her to note that their voices were low, barely audible. One would think that loud arguments were in order.

She had awakened in a burst of optimism, certain now that yesterday's act in helping Ken was her epiphany. It wasn't blind stupidity at all. Snug in her cot last night, she was able to look deep inside herself and see the truth of it.

Nothing could be worth the loss of Ken, of their love. Nothing. She had been at war with her instincts. She had been given this second chance, and since time was finite she must snatch it, nourish it. Failure, rejection, and hardship had skewered her value system, distorted her priorities.

The fact was that she had been lucky. She must not try to tinker with the inevitability of fate. In the face of love, greed was supposed to pale. Their prenuptial agreement had been created at a time when Eliot was suffering the terrible after effects of betrayal. Surely, time had softened the painfulness of that experience.

Hadn't she been a good wife? If not loving, certainly dutiful? Trusting and loyal, at least, up until the point that Ken had reentered her life? She had made assumptions, based on a rationalization of her own betrayal, that Eliot must punish her for what she had done. It followed that he would then invoke the hated agreement, strip her of her possessions, banish her with nothing.

But was Eliot really that cruel and dispassionate? Above all, wasn't he a man who valued truth? She pondered this question, allowing that she might, if she left out any reference to Ken, effect a compromise with Eliot. He was, after all, quite comfortable financially. If necessary, she could even do well with half the value of her possessions. Well, maybe that was too generous. Certainly some reasonable percentage might be arranged. She checked herself from negotiating in her mind, but the idea of approaching Eliot exhilarated her.

Nevertheless, the old paranoia was difficult to eradicate. She needed to tell Eliot in her own way and as soon as possible. Immediately, if possible. She wanted it out of the way before they got to Nairobi. A speech surfaced in her mind. She would cite the need for space, for separation, for a different life, asking only fairness, equity. Her confidence soared. Eliot, after all, was a fair man. Wasn't he?

There was no sense in postponement. Besides, she wanted relief from this pressure and she needed to remove the strain. Above all, she did not want Eliot to receive any inflammatory information from others, especially Meade, who might be spiteful and vitriolic in the telling. Please don't do it, she begged Meade in her heart.

In truth, she knew that Eliot, tempered by the experience of his marriage and his acute sense of loyalty, could not abide betrayal. This was the caveat that underlined the prenuptial agreement in the first place. To Eliot, she had come to believe, infidelity and betrayal were mortal sins. She could understand that trait in him. How was one to protect oneself against that?

Whatever happened, win, lose, or draw, even if Eliot stuck to the letter of the agreement and she left the marriage with nothing, she and Ken would be together, together without lies and secrets. The nobility of the idea stirred her, although she granted that she could never go that far.

It occurred to her that maybe the way to Eliot's sense of fairness was to admit all. She tested the idea in her mind. Yes, she might throw herself on his mercy, confess her love for Ken, and try to make him understand that loving someone else poisons a marriage. She would deny any infidelity, however. Would he believe her?

"Jambo!"

She was startled. It was one of the boys bringing her the tray of morning coffee. He put it on the table between the cots. She was sipping it when Eliot came in.

"One more day," he said. "I've been talking to Meade. He's promised to behave."

"Do you think that's wise?"

She was genuinely disappointed. As far as she was concerned, the safari was over.

"Actually, I wanted him to vindicate himself and, thereby, avoid turning him in."

"You would have done that, wouldn't you?"

"Absolutely. He put us in jeopardy. But we were lucky. If he doesn't knock off the boozing, he could be a killer. We'll leave tomorrow. Maybe use the extra days in Europe." He looked at her and smiled. "Time for a second honeymoon."

Europe? She remembered what she had told Ken. They would go to Europe. He would find inspiration in Europe.

Eliot's sudden injection of sentiment confused her. Does he know? she wondered. Was this a deliberate attempt to motivate guilt? She made no comment, hoping that she could chase the idea away. She would tell him today, she decided, summoning the words, sculpting in her mind the form it would take.

Meade came to breakfast smelling of wintergreen mouthwash. The whites of his eyes were covered with a network of red rivulets, but he was, otherwise, chipper. He offered no apologies.

"We've got hippos and crocs on the agenda today," he said.

"And tomorrow we break camp," Eliot said cheerfully. There was no point in recriminations at this stage. Carol looked toward Ken. Go with the flow, her eyes told him. He seemed to understand.

After breakfast, she called to him, loud enough for the others to hear.

"My camera is stuck, Ken. Think you can get it right?"

He came over to her, just out of earshot of the others. She handed him her camera.

"I'm going to tell him, darling," she whispered.

He looked up at her, startled. She felt a flush beginning beneath her tan.

"Thank God," he said, his voice low. "I love you."

"Today," she said. "I want it all finished."

"And the agreement."

She shrugged. "It's Ken Kramer I need most of all."

He looked at the camera, fiddled with it, looked through the lens. She could see Maggie and Eliot heading toward the van, watching them, but still too far away to hear them.

"May I kiss you now? Right here? In front of them?"

She flashed a radiant smile instead and stepped back from him.

"I must make love to you," he said, moving forward. "I am choking with desire. At this moment."

"When we're free, will it be like this?"

"Yes. Always."

"I am very happy, Ken."

"And so am I."

She sensed that he wanted to say more. His face seemed alight with playfulness.

"The gods are smiling, Carol," he said.

"Yes, they are."

"Maggie wants out of our marriage." He said it slowly, his eyes beaming.

She felt a sudden thump of blood in her chest.

"She knows about us?"

He shook his head and laughed.

"She has her own agenda. Apparently she wants to make a new life for herself."

She thought about that for a moment. Doubt flashed through her mind. Was it possible?

"You're sure it's not someone else? Not Eliot?"

"She says no."

She watched his eyes. Did he see her doubt?

"Do you believe her?"

Suddenly she saw the picture in compressed time. The hours Maggie and Eliot had spent together in his office. Couple friends, Maggie had called them. Couple friends, indeed. Maybe she and Ken had accomplished their goal, after all. Images of Maggie and Eliot together unreeled in her mind. Realization grew concrete. Intuition seeped into her. No woman would suddenly rearrange her life if there wasn't someone else in the picture. Not in today's world.

Of course, she thought, feeling the jolt of joyous revelation. Who else but Eliot? Maybe we've won, after all. A sunrise of hope filled her. Just in time, she thought. She would confront Eliot with that, before her own truncated confession. Her conclusion was pure instinct, but the possibility of certainty was compelling.

"She's lying, Ken."

He started to say something, but it was too late. The others had come too close. Ken handed her the camera and they started to move toward the van. Then an odd thing happened. Eliot opened the door for Carol and got in beside her. Not once during the entire safari had he done that.

"Why don't you ride shotgun today," Eliot said to Ken with a smile. Maggie took her usual position in back of the van.

Meade gunned the motor and they headed out of camp into the plains.

Carol was confused now, getting mixed signals. Why was Eliot suddenly being so solicitous? And Maggie? If Eliot was not the other man, then why choose Africa in which to confess? Why not wait until they got home? Why not, indeed? She had just gone through that argument herself and came out on the side of action. Maybe she was being premature with her own confession. Maybe the best course was to wait, to see how things unfolded.

They passed the usual herds of gazelles, zebras, impalas, giraffes, buffaloes, and the canopy of exotic birds. It was a glorious morning under a cerulean sky without a puff of cloud. The ground had drained and hardened and the van moved swiftly and smoothly.

But Carol could not muster any interest in the sights. Her mind buzzed with imagined possibilities. She looked toward

Eliot, who, catching her gaze, smiled benignly and patted her hand.

What was going on here?

"It's a gorgeous day," Eliot said. "All creatures love the aftermath of a rain. The earth is clean, sweet." His nostrils flared as he sucked in gulps of the fresh African air.

"The green hills of Africa," Ken said, looking into the distance. Carol knew where his thoughts lay and she longed to share them. But this new wrinkle absorbed her attention. She was searching her memory for signs. She recalled bits and pieces of conversations. Eliot singing Ken's praises. Ken telling her how hard Maggie worked to contrive to make her and Ken friends.

And all those attempts to throw them together. That first summer day when Maggie and Eliot begged off going to the theater. The Wildlife convention. It was Eliot, after all, who had brought up Africa in the first place. It was they, Carol and Ken, who had been manipulated, the real victims of the ploy. But why?

She wanted to laugh. They were fools. All along it had been Eliot and Maggie calling the shots. She was sure of that. But why? She would have gone like a docile lamb, banished with her possessions, avoiding all this angst and deception.

Anger replaced elation. She turned to look at Eliot. He smiled broadly, his face serene and attentive, while her heart was filled with hate. Then why didn't he offer compromise? What was behind his sinister actions?

As they rode, Meade pointed out the sights. A huge herd of buffaloes, a black bovine mass, moved beside the track carting their army of tick birds. Ahead a trio of warthogs ran for cover. They passed a white bearded wildebeest, or, better described, a gnu, his face like a wise man stoically observing their folly. Above, a flock of vultures glided in the distance.

"Table set for the last sitting," Meade said, pointing.

"That's Africa for you. All about death," Ken said.

"On the contrary," Eliot said. "It's about life. Death is transitory. It's the life force that is immortal."

"It's a morning for philosophy, is it?" Meade asked cheerfully.

The van climbed then moved downward, where the hills flattened toward the river. The track led through groves of acacia trees and a riverine forest that paralleled the river. Meade drove the van until it dead-ended at a promontory about twenty feet above the water. As he set the brake, they could see foot trails running along the bank following the river's sharp, curving flow.

"Be alert and concentrate here," Meade said. "A misstep could mean breakfast for the crocs."

They got out of the van and moved along the trail, stopping occasionally to observe the hippos gamboling in the river, looking like giant rubber bath dolls emerging and submerging with noisy inhalations, their gaping mouths exhibiting enormous teeth and huge pinkish tongues.

Meade moved out ahead, Ken and Maggie following, while Eliot and Carol brought up the rear. Carol was deliberately lagging behind, and since Eliot was attentive, which continued to baffle her, he kept at her pace. Perhaps her attitude had signaled its message to him. She needed to talk, needed to explore her speculations further.

The others moved around a bend, intent on their observations. Carol heard Meade offering them a running commentary. Letting them move on, she stopped to observe the creatures in the river through her binoculars. Eliot, standing beside her, did the same.

She panned the river and its banks, noting the crocs, their hides looking like long rock formations.

"They'd never win a beauty contest," Eliot muttered next to her. Just beyond the bend, she could hear the buzz of Meade's nonstop explanations.

She kept the binoculars held to her eyes, watching the creatures in the river. Eliot had moved closer to her. She felt the words erupting inside her, the thing that had to be said. If it was imagined, fancied wishfully, she would know that, too.

"I know about you and Maggie," she whispered.

He looked back at her quickly, eyes narrowing, lips pressed tightly together.

"You are much too close to the edge, Carol," he said, his voice sounding harsh as it rose. "You are too close."

She let the binoculars drop to her chest, looking downward watching his approaching shadow. But she did not turn, confident of her dancer's balance, holding her ground. Then she felt his hand touch her upper arm, grasping it. She shifted her stance,

trying to pry loose his fingers. He was losing his footing, unable
to anchor himself, beginning to fall forward. She moved with
him, alert to the danger.

As she toppled, one leg reached out and she was able to hook
one foot in an outcrop of root that hung just over the edge of the
bank. It stopped her fall briefly, but gave her leverage to reach
out to his retreating body. Her head jerked upward and she was
able to see his eyes and note the terror in them as she tried without success once again to loosen his hold on her forearm. It was
only when he fell forward, taking her with him, that his grip
loosened.

She heard his long, frightened, whining scream as they tum-
bled into the river. It wasn't a high fall, but she had no illusions
about its danger. She hadn't heard his splash, but when she surfaced, she could see him floundering a few yards away, slapping
the water with his arms, as he tried to maneuver his body into a
swimming mode.

For a moment, she bobbed on the surface, looking upward at
the three figures running along the trail above. She saw Ken grab
Maggie and wrestle her to the ground, her screams echoing over
the river.

Then she was aware of other sounds, the shushing sound of
the great beasts rising and submerging in the water around her,
and on the shore at the far bank she saw the crocodiles stirring,
their heads rising in curiosity.

She did not panic, as if instinct told her that it would cloud
her judgment. Under the promontory from which they had fallen,
she saw a sliver of bank and a narrow foot trail winding upward.
Reaching that place became the goal of her survival and she
headed toward it, crowding out all other thoughts.

She continued to hear the gasps of the hippos around her
and Maggie's screams, less audible now, as she cut through the
water's surface, her heart pumping, using every energy resource
in her body. I'm coming, Ken, she cried inside as she struggled
with the current, hoping it would not cause her to overshoot her
goal.

Unfortunately, she was no match for the current and she began to drift downstream within inches of the diving hippos.
Thankfully, they paid her little attention, although she expected
at any moment to be chomped or swallowed by the crocodiles.

Still, she did not panic, trying to force her body into a pattern with the current that would bring her to the shore.

Suddenly a shot rang out. A few yards away, she saw the thrashing of a crocodile's tail and a growing overlay of red blood on the green surface of the water. She continued to fight the current, getting closer, reaching out as she swam for some outcropping that might hold her against the river's current.

Another shot rang out. She heard more thrashing beside her, then blood spreading like molasses on the river surface around her. The events and concerns of her life crowded out of memory, her focus on pure survival as she struggled with the current, striking out with her arms as she reached for any root, stone, or outcrop on the bank that might hold her.

She heard another shot. And another. Then, suddenly, her hand gripped something. She reached out with the other hand, holding fast now, no longer a slave to the current.

She swung her legs upward toward a flat rock and heaved forward, finding herself completely out of the water. She lay on the rock fighting for breath, her heart pounding in her chest. It was then that she saw the crocodile heading toward her, emerging from the water, moving swiftly.

Leading with his massive jaws, she could see his eyes blink in their wrinkled sockets as he slithered forward, lifting his scaly armored body out of the water, intent on his prey. She watched, unable to move, paralyzed by either fear or exhaustion, certain that this was the end of Carol Stein Butterfield, the end of striving and dreams. The end of life and love.

Then the crocodile exploded in front of her, blood pluming out of its shattered eye as it rolled over on its back, its white moist belly shooting glints of sunlight. Only then did her energy return and she struggled up the rocks to Ken's waiting arms.

"Thank God. Thank God," he cried, smoothing her hair, kissing her face. Above her she could see Meade holding his rifle, her nostrils filling with the acrid smell of gunpowder.

Ken's arms enveloped Carol as he helped her find a sitting position against the trunk of a tree. Then he rose beside her, watched her for a moment, then moved away. She saw him talk briefly with Meade, who looked downward, kicking the ground with his foot and shaking his head. Then they both disappeared out of sight along the trail beside the river.

Carol felt herself settling, her heartbeat subsiding, her mind just beginning to respond to events beyond her survival. Only then was she conscious of Maggie's eyes watching her. She was leaning against the side of the tree against which Carol was sitting. Maggie's face was stark white, her eyes seemed to be floating in their sockets.

"Eliot?" Maggie asked, her voice a whisper.

Carol struggled up from the ground, felt a brief faintness, then rested for a moment against the tree until it subsided. She was no more than a foot from Maggie and their eyes locked for a long moment.

"Eliot?" Maggie asked again. Then Maggie fell into Carol's arms, her body shuddering with hysterical sobs. There was no point in explanations, Carol decided. We were all lousy detectives, missed the clues and the murderer got away. Besides, loving was the only truth here and who could possibly explain that.

For some reason Carol's eyes drifted upward. A wide winged bird glided against the clear sky. It flew closer and she recognized its white ugly head. A vulture, she thought, surprised at the graceful way it swooped and dived.

26

KEN SAT in a corner of the Nor-
folk lounge nursing a golden brandy in a snifter. The mostly
white pub crowd at the far end of the veranda had dwindled
while the dinner groups in the main restaurant lingered over des-
cort and coffee.

He looked at his watch. By ten in the evening at the latest,
Meade had said, estimating that it would take him seven or eight
hard hours to bring back the van loaded with their luggage over
two hundred miles of bad roads from the Masai Mara. A light
plane chartered out of Nairobi had picked up the three of them at
a landing strip in the Mara and flown them back to the city in
less than an hour. Thankfully, the noise of the plane's motor had
made communication between them impossible.

Ken expected Meade's estimate to be accurate. Time was the
only certainty in this place. It was the measure of everything, the
one true thing.

He had been searching for something to anchor the endlessly
spinning reel of images that had assailed him since yesterday
morning. Only time could be that anchor. Everything else seemed
subject to inaccuracies: observations, speculations, thoughts, in-

tuition, words, especially words. Only time was precise. *Rashomon*, he remembered suddenly. Everyone sees everything from their own perspective. Truth shifts like a grasshopper, from mind to mind.

Hopefully tomorrow, if they could maneuver themselves through the various official authorities, a jet plane would lift them back to New York, backward in time, but forward in chronology, another irony. Like memory. The images of what had occurred in those few moments of compressed time had changed him forever.

He would always hear Carol's scream, the piercing terror of it. Slowed down in his mind, he would see Eliot and Carol struggling at the edge of the cliff. An odd pas de deux, it had seemed at the time, totally out of context. A danse macabre at death's door. Why was it happening? he remembered wondering. Who had initiated it? Had one lost his balance, then the other? Had one tried to save the other from falling? Nagging questions, he supposed, would plague him forever.

He had seen in their eyes glimpses of intense concentration, like two arm-wrestlers probing each other, locked at the point of maximum resistance. A duel of hatred, he remembered thinking. But it had all happened so fast. Later he had distrusted the observation.

But, despite the mystery of how it had begun, he did remember the pure physicality of the event. He had seen Carol's foot wrapped around an exposed knuckle of root and Eliot leaning over her, losing balance. Finally, their weight could not defy the laws of physics and they had slipped over the edge, like falling trees. As they fell, they continued to hold together, separating only as they reached the river's surface.

Behind him, Maggie had screamed. It was a cry of pain from deep inside her, a clear clarion.

"Eliot!"

It echoed and reechoed, slammed hard against his eardrum, as Maggie moved forward beyond him to the very edge of the high bank. If he had not reached out, he was certain she would have gone over. He had had to put her in a hammerlock to stop her. Then she had collapsed like a puppet whose strings had been cut and they peered down into the green water at the hippos emerging and submerging and, along the opposite shore, saw the crocodiles begin to move.

He had seen both Carol and Eliot at that moment, floundering in the current, tiny shapes among the giant hippos.

"Eliot. Eliot. Oh, my God," he had heard Maggie shout. But by then the truth had hatched full-grown in his mind, the shell of secrecy soundly cracked by the birth of revelation. It confronted him suddenly with the limitations of his own insight. His imagination, too, he realized, was a faulty piece of work.

He did not cry out Carol's name. Perhaps he was too paralyzed by fear and too stunned to act, except to save Maggie from flinging herself into the river. The slithering movement of those creatures at the opposite bank and those dark swimming monsters in the river carried the message of inevitability. Death was arriving for those two in the river. The choice was to join them or not. Death or life.

Maggie, he was still convinced, would have, at that moment, chosen death. He would never be certain of his own choice, except that he had not acted. From now to forever, he would always have the excuse of saving Maggie, leaving open the question of which was the more powerful drive, love or death.

Again Hemingway's story "The Short Happy Life of Francis Macomber" surfaced in his mind, reminding him of those ambiguous wells of hidden choices, invoking, too, the power of the writer's art to embed an idea in one's mind, like finding one's truth in Africa. Death and love. He hadn't fully realized how closely they were related.

Of course, he had not debated the question during those confused moments. He could see the crocs advancing on the two swimmers. Behind him he could hear the uncommon but unmistakable metallic click of a rifle, then the ear-shattering blast. The croc nearest Carol flumed out of the water, his white belly gleaming in the sun, his tail flailing the green water now overlaid with a glaze of blood.

There had been another blast, a numbing explosion near him, and another croc leaped in agony, his narrow brow blown open, brains spilling into the water, just short of Eliot. Another click, a pause. He had turned to see the sweating Meade loading, aiming, the barrel hesitating. The crocs were moving against their prey. The new shot stopped the croc inches from Carol; another hit one running parallel to her, his white belly, as it turned, stained red by his companion's blood.

Another pause, loading, more shots.

"No. No," Maggie was screaming, twisting to catch a better view of the embattled swimmer as he passed around the river's bend. But Ken was watching Carol, struggling to make the shore. Obviously, they were each watching the one who meant most to them.

Another shot rang out. Then another. Meade was concentrating his fire now on the crocs heading for Carol, stopping them abruptly with what must have been deadly accuracy. The water surrounding Carol had turned blood-red.

Then she had reached the other side. Another shot caught a croc through one eye, out of which spurted a fountain of blood. By then, Maggie had collapsed in Ken's arms and he had put her gently on the ground and scrambled down the rocks to reach Carol. He reached her just as she touched dry ground, then literally dragged her up to the footpath. Embracing her with gratitude, and without shame, he settled her against a tree a few paces from Maggie and ran off with Meade to search for Eliot along the river trail.

They found no trace of him. Even the signs of the early carnage had disappeared. The hippos, oblivious, still gamboled in the now green water, and the remaining crocodiles, also oblivious to recent events, slept still and lifeless on the opposite shore. Africa, Ken realized, takes care of its own refuse collection.

The truth was out there now, fully revealed, the skin of private lies peeled clean. Their incredible blind stupidity as well. Fools, he berated them all. Himself included. Only it was too late for Eliot.

Finally Meade had turned toward him, his face drawn and pale, his shirt sweat-stained and foul-smelling.

"Not a clue," he said, shaking his head.

The aftermath would always be jumbled in his head. Authorities had appeared, including a doctor, who gave Maggie a mild sedative, which Carol had refused, and stayed with them at the camp while he and Meade and various officials searched the river's banks for any sign of Eliot.

"We'll never find anything," Meade had said with an air of finality. It had become a chorus of agreement.

"A tragic accident," Ken remembered telling them at some point, stealing a quick glance at Meade's now impassive face.

A black policeman had interrogated all of them, writing

down their various statements. "Yes, I saw them fall," Ken had said. "They were walking behind us and one of them, I can't tell which, lost his balance."

"Who tried to save who?" the policeman asked Carol.

"My husband lost his balance," Carol told him. "He grabbed me as a reflex. I tried to keep my footing, but it was impossible."

Ken remembered having looked at Maggie, who had been listening. The vague look in her eyes had disappeared for a moment and she had been suddenly alert glancing toward Ken. Then, quickly, she had turned away. He would never mistake the message of this glance. The wrong man was dead.

There was an awkwardness in the Norfolk when they had arrived, having said nothing to each other on the short flight.

"Three rooms," he had told the clerk, who had looked at him incredulously as he filled out the registration for all of them. Sometime during the night he had tried Carol's door. It was locked. He had then tried Maggie's. It, too, was locked.

Wise of them, he decided. Words would have been forced and meaningless. He had things to work out as well. What troubled him most was the realization that four reasonably intelligent people had been victimized by such blunted and stigmatized perceptions.

Where, he wondered, was the vaunted writer's insight, that sustained vision that would allow him to enter the world of true sentences, Hemingway's magic kingdom? No wonder he had failed. How was it possible that he could be so sideswiped by his own psychic wish list? Had blind love shattered his five senses of observation and corrupted his insight as well?

Looking back over the last few months, he was amazed at the clues that lay strewn across the landscape like an Easter egg hunt, so completely obvious, so patently transparent.

He tossed all night, leaving his hotel room at first light. Passing Carol's room, he paused, then inexplicably pressed his ear to her door. He heard nothing, of course. Nor did he attempt to turn the doorknob. What was the point? Besides, he reasoned, she would need all her strength and composure for their scheduled meeting with the authorities.

He also stopped briefly in front of the door to Maggie's room. For a long moment, he looked at the door blankly, imagining Maggie, her pillow wet with tears, shoulders shaking with sobs of frustration and grief. A flash of anger passed through him and he turned away. Could she be forgiven? he wondered. Of all the people on this earth, was it possible that Maggie, the open, honest, caring Maggie, could have played this role so flawlessly, fooled them so completely?

He had a light breakfast in the restaurant, attempted to read the papers, and tried valiantly to rid himself of his gloom and the certain knowledge of his failed insight.

A United States Embassy official picked them up in front of the Norfolk at mid-morning. Both Carol and Maggie were composed. Neither had put on any makeup, although he could tell from Maggie's mottled skin and puffy eyes that his earlier assessment of how she had spent the night was correct.

Carol wore black slacks and a black short-sleeved blouse over which she wore a single strand of costume pearls. With her black hair parted in the middle and a carefully composed expression of stoicism, she looked severe, more bitter than grief-stricken. It struck Ken as the perfect pose.

Occasionally, their eyes drifted toward each other and they exchanged glances of understanding. He did not try to look at Maggie and it was obvious that Maggie deliberately kept her face hidden from his.

"I know it must be awful for you," the man from the embassy said as he drove. He was a bright-eyed youngish man who wore a light gray suit and snappy polka-dot bow tie and a suitably sympathetic expression. "The Kenyans would like to get this over with as quickly as possible. Bad for business, you see. They're paranoid about any accidents in the bush that might keep the tourists away. They have your statements given to the game-park authorities and the police in the Masai Mara. Poor Mr. Butterfield." He had already given Carol appropriately elaborate condolences, noting that the embassy was busy getting their plane bookings arranged for the early-morning flight to Europe and home.

"These freak accidents are the worst," the man from the embassy said. "And I'm so sorry about their not finding . . ." He checked himself and grew silent.

Meade had instructed them on how they must handle themselves with the authorities. Apparently he had been through it all before.

"Above all," he had cautioned them, "stick to the letter of what we've already told them. And please, you must not mention the rifle. It's illegal and could get my license revoked, but that's not the issue here. If they hear that guns were involved they'll hold you in Kenya. There'll be hearings and red tape. Believe me, you wouldn't want that. Besides, we all saw what happened. It was an accident. At least we were lucky enough to save Mrs. Butterfield."

They had, of course, agreed. Even Maggie, who had acknowledged it through her genuine grief.

By then, all evidence had disappeared. The crocodile carcasses had drifted downstream.

"All flesh disappears in the African bush," Meade had explained to him privately. "Including poor old Butterfield."

They met in a small room of a government office with the man from the embassy present. As both Ken and Meade had predicted, the representative of the government, a pleasant smiling black man with a clipped British accent, made quick work of the conference. Carol was appropriately somber. Maggie, Ken noted, was viewed merely as a grieving friend, and he was hardly noticed.

"I am so terribly sorry for this situation, Mrs. Butterfield," the Kenyan said. "It is very rare for us. But there is danger out there in the park."

He went on to explain that Kenya was an emerging country that needed its tourist industry. He provided broad hints that any publicity on this matter would be harmful and Carol nodded agreement.

Then the official provided them with neatly typed versions of their previous statements. A clerk came in to notarize the papers and other affidavits put in front of Carol to sign.

When she had finished, the Kenyan official stood up and put out his hand.

"We hope very much," the man said, "that you will not hold our government liable for this situation."

Carol took the man's hand.

"No," she whispered in a tremulous voice. "I can't blame the government. It was simply a very, very unfortunate accident."

They were driven back to their hotel by the embassy official, who, apparently relieved that everything had gone smoothly, did not feel the need to be overly loquacious. It seemed to fit into their present need for silence, and when he dropped them off at the hotel, both women, without exchanging a word, went back to their respective rooms. Ken avoided them for the rest of the day.

Ken finished his brandy and ordered another. Then Meade was coming toward him, looking unshaven and exhausted, but surprisingly sober. He slumped into a chair opposite him.

"Bitch of a drive," he said.

"Drink?"

"I think I'll pass," he said, grinning. "Lost the taste."

"Tough luck," Ken said, sipping his drink.

"Lost another once. Stupid accidents. I understand things went smoothly." He rubbed his chin. "I appreciate your coopera- tion in the matter of the rifle."

"If it wasn't for the gun, Carol would have died."

"Catch-22," Meade said gloomily, then brightened. "Saved her for you, I suppose." He shrugged, as if to say: What did it matter now?

Ken nodded. There was no longer any point in hiding it.

"Didn't have much time," Meade said. "Had to make a quick choice." He started to speak, then waved the words away with a gesture.

"A tough call," Ken acknowledged.

"Not so tough," Meade said.

Ken remembered. The hunter knows who has to die, Meade had told them.

Meade took an envelope out of his bush jacket and gave it to Ken.

"Final damage," he said. "Just drop the check in the mail." He stood up and smiled. "Mrs. Butterfield should have plenty of shekels to cover it. Besides, I gave you all a healthy discount."

Money again, Ken thought as he watched Meade's lined sun- ruddy face crack into a crooked smile. But wait, Ken told himself. One more thing.

"What's your view of it, Meade?" Ken asked in a deliber- ately casual way. "I mean, was it really a freak accident?"

Meade looked at him for a long time, then shook his head.

"No way," he croaked.

"He or she?" Ken asked.

"Therein lies the riddle, old boy," Meade said, turning on his heel. Ken watched his broad back retreat into the night.

So there would always be this question between them, he mused. Someday he would ask her. He wasn't sure when, wasn't sure of anything. Live by the lie. Die by the lie.

She had told the authorities it had been an accident. And if she was lying? Did he try to murder you? He wanted to ask that. Did you try to murder him? He wanted to ask that as well.

Better leave sleeping dogs lie. Eliot, like Francis Macomber, had had his short happy life.

Ken lifted his glass in a silent toast, then swallowed it down in one gulp.

It was still dark when the wake-up call blasted Ken out of a dead, dreamless sleep. The airport transportation would arrive in an hour. He shaved, showered, and dressed, then moved quickly down the corridor to Maggie's room. There were still mundane details to be arranged—their joint luggage, passports—the problems associated with travel.

It had occurred to him that many unpleasant chores still lay ahead for all of them. In his and Maggie's case, the children had to be told of their plans for separation, a divorce settlement had to be reached, details of their separate lives arranged. For Carol there would be the terrible pressures of notifying the members of Eliot's family, his children, the preparation for a memorial service, doubly unpleasant because of the absence of Eliot's body. Then would come the grueling legalities connected with her possessions, the details of inheritance.

Unavoidable problems, he sighed, then he smiled to himself, feeling the tension leak out of him. He decided that he was quickly approaching the moment when he would give himself permission to rejoice.

Maggie's room had a DO NOT DISTURB sign on the door. Disregarding it he knocked, surprised when it was quickly opened by Maggie, who was fully dressed. Carol, also dressed, was sitting in a chair. She looked up at him and gave him a thin smile. Room service had brought up breakfast.

"We were talking," Maggie said. Her face was pale, her eyes sad and puffy. Obviously she had been crying, but she seemed to have regained her composure.

"Eliot was going to tell me about him and Maggie," Carol said.

"He had promised," Maggie said. "Enough lies. We had both agreed."

Ken leaned against the wall, watching them, his eyes darting from one woman's face to the other. It was hard to fathom, this sudden outpouring of revelation.

"Yes," Carol agreed, looking at Ken, as if she were speaking for both of them. "The lies were wearing us down as well." She turned toward Maggie. "The fact is that, however hard you tried to bring us together, we were already there." She paused, again turning to Ken. "I told her, Ken, how long ago it had started for us."

Ken glanced at Maggie with some trepidation. So Carol had told Maggie their entire history. Perhaps that was what had brought on this new surge of tears. He could tell from watching her that the anger from Carol's confession still lingered.

"So our marriage had a rotten foundation from the beginning," Maggie said bitterly.

"Maggie, you know that can't be true," Ken said. He felt his eyes mist. "We had a life together, children." Then it occurred to him that he wasn't the only villain, that she, too, had been an unfaithful spouse. But he held back his rebuke. After all, she had lost her lover. "The thing is," he said, haltingly, "we didn't want anyone to get hurt. That was the point."

Maggie stood up and walked over to the window, which overlooked the hotel's manicured lawn. Suddenly she turned.

"Does anybody really know anybody?" she asked.

"That's the wrong question for this group," Ken said.

"We shouldn't have come here," Carol said. "It wasn't necessary."

But it was, he protested to himself. There was a long awkward silence.

"Eliot was broke, you know," Maggie said with a shrug. "That's why we couldn't . . ." Her voice broke and her lips began to tremble. It took a moment to get herself under control.

Carol started to stand, then hesitated and sat back in the chair, a deep frown wrinkling her smooth forehead.

"It was that damned agreement," Maggie said, her voice now firm with anger. "Yes, he loved me. But he couldn't give up his way of life. Not for me. Not for anybody. Dammit, he died for it."

Her lips began to quiver and she turned away and faced the garden again.

"My God," Carol said. "He could have . . ." But she looked at Ken and said nothing more. No, Ken thought, he couldn't have come to her. No more than Carol could go to him.

Ken moved across the room and stood behind Maggie. He reached out his hand, then pulled back.

"It will be all right, Maggie," Ken whispered. "You'll have the apartment and, of course, there'll be no custody problems." He paused, remembering her words to him a few nights ago when she had asked for her separation. "You'll find somebody. I know you will."

She turned suddenly and glared at him.

"Don't you understand? I loved him. I loved Eliot. There will never ever be anyone for me but Eliot."

He stood silently watching her. What could he say? He looked toward Carol.

"We'd better get going," he said, picking up the suitcases from the luggage rack. But before he could leave the room, Maggie's voice held him for a moment.

"Odd, isn't it, that none of us were what we seemed?" she said.

Ken stopped, nodded slowly, then continued to carry the suitcases into the corridor.

27

"A CALVADOS," Ken said to the waiter.

"Yes, that would be nice," Carol agreed.

"It's a lovely view," Ken said, looking out across the speeding traffic on the Rue de Rivoli to the gardens beyond. From where he sat at the sidewalk café he could also see the flowers blooming in the gardens across the street and the reflection of the late-afternoon sun on the Seine.

"Coming to Paris in August was a fabulous idea, Carol," Ken said.

"I thought it was your idea."

"No. Both of our ideas, remember?"

They had been staying at Saint-John-Cap-Ferrat, where they had taken a wonderful little flat overlooking the port. He had set up his computer at a table in front of a window that afforded a beautiful view of the Mediterranean and he had plunged ahead on this new idea that had been rattling around in his mind since Marbella.

The plot of his novel, the one he had begun in Marbella, had revolved around a newspaperman in New York who had fallen in love with an aspiring opera singer.

Carol would come into his room of the villa they had rented on the cliffs above the sea after he had been working all morning and she would look over his shoulder to see what he had written. That was when he would shut off the computer.

"Only when it's finished," he would tell her firmly. "Call it rule one of the novelist at work."

She didn't protest. She was happy, he knew, to be near him, and afternoons were dedicated to each other. Hadn't they earned it?

They would head down for lunch at an open café overlooking the sea, walk along the quay or visit the shops in the center of town. Often, they would poke around the galleries and antique shops and Carol would bargain for various pieces that she felt would appreciate in value, sometimes making a purchase, sometimes not.

Then they would go back to the villa and take a long, very long siesta, mostly making love. Without the need to be furtive and with the absence of guilt, their lovemaking was less frenetic, calmer, more lingering, comfortable.

"It's like we've died and gone to paradise," she would remind him often.

The idea of death would sometimes rekindle memories of Africa. At first, he had been troubled by the circumstances of Eliot's death and had gone over it in his mind many times. He would see them walking along the high ground over the river. Each of them wore hiking boots with deep cleats that were designed to give them a good walking grip on the ground. Then he would try to recall the specific image of Eliot and Carol's struggle on the path overlooking the river. Finally, the event began slowly to disappear into memory. Details faded. Recollection became more difficult and less pressing. Maybe someday, when he was ready, he would write about Africa and it would all resurface again.

The resolution of Eliot's estate had gone well, and even Carol had been surprised by the value of her art and antiques. On expert advice she had liquidated several pieces that had brought her more than a million and a half dollars after taxes, and still there were three-quarters of her pieces unsold.

Ken had been more than generous to Maggie and the girls. She got to keep the Brooklyn apartment and he had given her most of his company pension-and-profit-sharing money, which came to a tidy sum. And Maggie had quickly acquired a number of new clients. The girls, the eldest of whom would be going off to college in September, had been shocked and resentful at first, but finally had accepted the situation. Maggie, he knew, would survive. Their uncontested divorce was consummated swiftly.

His colleagues at the advertising agency envied his decision to resign.

"A man has got to follow his dream," he had told them at the farewell party they gave him at the office. They had all stood up and applauded.

He and Carol were married in New York's City Hall the week before the Memorial Day holiday and went off to Spain. He to write. She to be the loving wife.

It was, they both agreed, how it was meant to be from the beginning. They had, after all, twenty-odd years to make up.

"You'll write and I'll be there beside you, loving you always," she had assured him.

"Is that a solemn, irrevocable promise?"

She raised her right hand and crossed her heart.

They had no set itinerary, no plans other than to take each day as it came. They had Carol's inheritance. They had each other. That was everything.

It was his idea to leave Marbella. They had been there less than a month.

"Somehow I like the idea of keeping on the move," he had told her. At first she had protested.

"But it's so lovely here."

"It's lovely everywhere we're together. And we're free to go where we please."

"Yes, free as birds," she agreed.

"I also think it would help my work," he explained. "A writer needs a constant supply of new images."

"Yes," she agreed. "A writer must have inspiration. I understand, my darling. That has got to be a priority."

"Second only to loving you."

"Absolutely. Second to that."

Actually, he had abandoned the novel about the young journalist and the opera singer after the first chapter. It didn't panic him. He was rusty. He would need more time to get in the groove, he told himself. Anyway, he was toying with a new idea set in the advertising world and already he felt that the characters were coming alive in his mind. He was certain it would spill out of him when he started work at this new place.

Saint-John-Cap-Ferrat was perfect at first. Afternoons they would drive into Antibes for lunch, then take a ride along the sea and wind up at Cannes or Mougins or some other quaint French village, and they would visit the galleries and antique shops and stop at a sidewalk café for an aperitif before going back to their place for a late siesta. Evenings they would head into Monte Carlo for dinner and some very light gambling at the casinos.

He had managed to get through fifty pages of his new novel when a certain restlessness began to afflict him and he got the idea of going to Paris. Perhaps, he reasoned, the resort life was too routine, too laid back. Also, he sensed that this new novel was aground. He was losing interest in the characters; the plot was dead-ending.

Of course, he hadn't told her that the writing wasn't going well. He couldn't do that. It would greatly upset her own vision of how their marriage must be conducted. Mornings were still devoted to sitting in front of his computer, although he found that he was spending more time in the morning reading the *International Herald* or a book. Research, he called it when she arrived in his room just before lunch.

By late July, the tourists were beginning to pour into Cap-Ferrat. Traffic became impossible. The streets and restaurants were much too crowded. It became a welcome excuse to leave.

"Paris might be fun in August. No crowds. We'd have it all to ourselves," he told her. And Paris, of course, was a legendary Mecca for writers. Especially those of the so-called lost generation. Hemingway wrote his first novels in Paris, which was lure enough.

"Yes, Ken," Carol said, offering no resistance at all. "Paris has always inspired writers. Sounds like a great idea."

"Ken Kramer!"

He turned quickly. The voice sounded familiar.

"Jill Harrison," the woman said, smiling broadly, holding out her hand. "Remember me?" She was dark-haired and attractive. Beyond her, at a table at the other end of the café, a man, presumably her companion, sat watching them.

"Jill," Ken said, rising to greet her with a friendly kiss on her cheek. He introduced her to Carol, who looked up and touched the woman's outstretched hand. "Jill and I worked on Slender Benders," Ken explained.

"And how, we did," Jill said. Ken felt the woman searching for his glance, which he quickly avoided.

"It was a great campaign," Ken said.

"So this is where you've decided to camp," she said. "Lucky you. Paris in August. A fabulous time to be here, don't you think?"

"And we don't intend to spread it around," Ken said, looking at Carol, who was emptying her glass of Calvados. It struck him that her expression had suddenly changed, her lips tightly pressed together, her eyes narrowed. She had stood up and picked up her purse. It was obvious that she wished to leave. He was puzzled by her oddly hostile attitude.

"Maybe we could get together while we're in town," Jill suggested.

"Yes, of course," Ken said vaguely. "As soon as we're settled."

"We're at George Cinq," the woman volunteered as they shook hands. She headed back to her table.

"What is it?" Ken asked when they had left the café and were walking on the Rue de Rivoli. Carol had put her arm through his, but said little.

"I'm not sure," Carol said. "That woman . . ." Her voice trailed off.

"Jill? We were colleagues at the agency."

They walked on, then Carol stopped and turned to face him.

"Did you ever sleep with her?"

"Are you serious?"

"Yes, I'm serious, Ken."

"Why would you want to know that?" Ken asked, confused by her question.

"Curiosity." Carol shrugged. Studying her, Ken was certain she meant business.

"We worked together," he said.

They had resumed their walk. Cars sped by. Across the street were the gardens.

"I know that," Carol said. "I asked if you ever slept with her."

"You are a tiger, Carol," Ken said, laughing.

"Well, did you?"

"It was so long ago," Ken replied.

"So you did?"

"Hey," Ken said. "It wasn't important. A quickie now and then. No big deal."

Carol nodded, then stopped abruptly at an intersection, waiting for the light to change.

He felt strange justifying himself over this. "I was locked in a loveless marriage. You know that."

At that moment, he felt himself being propelled forward into the path of an oncoming car. He could see the driver's panicked face and he felt helpless and totally vulnerable as the car bore down on him.

Then, barely before the terror could register in his mind, he felt himself jerk backward. A nick of breeze from the speeding car soundlessly brushed past his chest. Only then did he turn toward Carol. His eyes met hers, and in their deep, deadly calm he caught the flash of revelation. As he turned away in confusion, his hand reached back and his flesh touched the rumpled linen of his jacket.

He had been pushed by Carol. As she had pushed Eliot to his death.

My God, he screamed inside himself. He tripped briefly over the curb and she helped steady him.

"Ken, you've got to be more careful," Carol admonished. He turned again to look at her, his heart banging in his chest. Their eyes locked for a split second. He had no doubts. She had pushed him, then saved him. He saw the truth as clearly as the summer sky.

The lights changed and they crossed the street arm in arm. His legs felt unsteady as they walked over the garden path, but he fought it and managed to keep the meandering pace. He looked at her in profile, the perfect Dresden doll face, the swanlike neck, the graceful way she held herself.

Despite what he now knew, he loved this woman. He would always be trapped in the net of his love for her. And he was certain that she loved him, and by this gesture she had warned him of the ferocity of this love.

Nor was he puzzled by her motive. He had told her that he

had been faithful to Maggie. He had lied and she had caught him in this lie.

She was telling him that the time had come to put an end to all lies. All lies. And he knew he had to put to rest the great lie of his talent. He would never become the great writer of his dreams. He didn't have what Hemingway had. No way. Not the stuff that could burn in the truth like "The Short Happy Life of Francis Macomber," like the leopard on Mount Kilimanjaro.

Yes, he decided. She had made her point and the truth had ignited inside him. She would kill for love as she had killed for wealth. Without guilt or remorse. He felt goose bumps rise on his skin.

He knew he would never confront her. Never. Like the phases of the moon, everything in life had its dark side. Take love and be done with it, he told himself. Love was true. Love was clean. Love was the moon's bright side. It was as good as anything there was. Wasn't it?

Nor would he tell her that his dream was dead. They were free, weren't they? Free to wonder. Free to search for inspiration. Free to love. Why spoil anything?

Not saying meant not lying.

Didn't it?